Aylaen coul[illegible]
tl[illegible]

. . . as she touched it with the tips of her fingers. Closing her eyes she saw, not for the first time, the bodies in the river, the corpses littering the street, mothers wailing over dead children, husbands weeping over dead wives; families lying dead in the rubble of their homes: an entire city destroyed.

She opened her eyes to look at the boy shifting restlessly from one bare foot to the other.

Aylaen felt the muscles in her face stiffen, her mouth dry. Down below, she could hear the men swearing and shuffling about. She didn't have much time. She held out the spiritbone to the boy.

"You must hide this away. Put it in the same place as before."

"You mean in the—"

"Stop!" Aylaen said harshly. "Don't tell me. Hide it away now. Hide it quickly before the fog lifts."

Wulfe eyed the necklace and put his hands behind his back. "I can't. It will burn me. Maybe kill me."

"It's not going to kill you. Look, I'll wrap it up in part of my shirt—"

Wulfe was shaking his head. "It doesn't like me. I can tell . . ."

"Wulfe, I need you to hide this!" Aylaen said desperately. "We might be captured and . . . and . . ."

Wulfe slipped his hand into hers. "We'll hide it together. I'll show you where. You put it inside and I'll use my magic to keep it safe. And the dragon will help us."

Wulfe started running, tugging her along. She stumbled after him and tried not to think about tumbling overboard.

Tor Books by Margaret Weis
and Tracy Hickman

Bones of the Dragon

Secret of the Dragon

Rage of the Dragon

By Margaret Weis

DRAGONVARLD

Mistress of Dragons

The Dragon's Son

Master of Dragons

RAGE
OF THE
DRAGON

MARGARET WEIS

AND

TRACY HICKMAN

A TOM DOHERTY ASSOCIATES BOOK
NEW YORK

RAGE OF THE DRAGON

Edited by James Frenkel

A Tor Book
Published by Tom Doherty Associates, LLC
175 Fifth Avenue
New York, NY 10010

www.tor-forge.com

ISBN 978-0-7653-5926-1

First Edition: April 2012
First Mass Market Edition: April 2013

Printed in the United States of America

0 9 8 7 6 5 4 3 2 1

RAGE
OF THE
DRAGON

KINGDOM

NURN STRAIGHT

DRAGONHOLM

DIVOLK BAY

KARAJIS

KAIRNHOLM MOUNTAIN

THE STEPPE

OCEAN AYLITHIA

THE COMMONWEALTH

THE DJAN'SEIO WESTREACH

URD

FAE TRIBES (UNCHARTED)

THE FORGED KINGDOMS OF THUR

THE ORAN: EMPIRE OF LIGHT

THE STORMLORDS

Miles

100 300 500 700 900

DRAGONSHIPS

HART OF THE KHRAKIS

OCEAN ESTARTHIA
ISLAND HESVIA
VOLM SEA
STERN XPANSE
SEA OF TEARS
30000 ft
27000 ft
24000 ft
21000 ft
18000 ft
15000 ft
12000 ft
9000 ft
6000 ft
3000 ft
-0 ft
-3000 ft
-6000 ft
-9000 ft
-12000 ft
-15000 ft
-18000 ft
-21000 ft
-24000 ft
-27000 ft
-30000 ft
A T C R

RAGE
OF THE
DRAGON

PROLOGUE

"I am Farinn the Talgogroth, the Voice of Gogroth, God of the World Tree. Attend me! For now I will tell the tale of Skylan Ivorson, Chief of Chiefs of the Vindrasi, the greatest of the Chiefs of the mighty Dragonships." The old man paused and then said, with a sigh, "The greatest and the last."

He paused, both for dramatic effect and to soothe his throat with a honey posset.

The time was winter, the time for the telling of tales. Outside the great hall made of stout beams and hewn logs, the land was white with snow. The night was still and bitter cold. Inside the hall an enormous fire burned. Men and women sat at their ease on benches at long tables, holding small, sleepy children in their laps. The young woman and her friends sat on the floor in front of the old man, as close as she could manage, for his voice, like him, was frail and liable to break. The young woman did not want to miss a word of this part of the tale, for it was her favorite part.

Sitting between two young warriors of the Torgun, she surreptitiously glanced over her shoulder to see if her mother was watching, for fear her mother would find her and seize her and drag her away. Her mother was always scolding her for acting in an unmaidenly manner, running off to play at war with the young men instead of tending to her household chores.

The young woman was sixteen and her mother was talking of finding a husband for her wayward daughter, of grandbabies. The young woman wanted none of that. Not yet. Maybe not ever. She thirsted for adventure, like the heroes of the Voyage of the *Venjekar*. She hungered to visit those wondrous far-off lands, see them with her eyes, not just in her mind. She longed to do battle with ogres and fight a fury in the Para Dix and dance with the fae in their faerie kingdom. Her dream was an impossible dream, perhaps, but only the gods knew where her wyrd led. The gods, and this young woman, for she had made plans, secret plans.

Her mother was, thankfully, gossiping with a friend and paying no heed to her daughter. Her father had his eyes on her. She smiled at him and he smiled back. She was her father's favorite. Many (her mother among them) said he spoiled her. He indulged her odd whims to learn to use a sword and shield. He lied for her when she was practicing wielding her sword; he'd tell her mother she was in the fields tending the sheep. Her mother claimed he treated her like a boy because he had no sons.

The young woman knew better and so did her father. Both of them rarely listened to her mother.

Her father, at least, was not in a hurry for her to marry. When he had refused an offer of marriage (to an old man of thirty!), it had sent her mother into a rage that lasted for weeks.

The young woman glanced at each of the young men seated on either side of her. They exchanged conspiratorial grins. They often called themselves "Skylan" and "Garn," and she was "Aylaen" after the three heroes of the epic tale. Like the heroes in the story, the three had been friends from childhood. And because they were young and filled with hope, they had resolved that unlike Skylan Ivorson and his friends no tragedies would befall them on their grand adventure. They would never quarrel. There would be no misunderstandings or heartbreak. Nothing would ever come between them. No one would ever die.

The three had made plans to travel to those far distant lands. There they would fight rousing battles and maybe suffer a bloody wound or two, nothing fatal, of course, just severe enough to leave an interesting scar. And most important of all, the three would remain true to each other. In the ruins of the Hall of the Old Gods, the three swore a solemn oath of friendship, making their vows to Torval and to Vindrash. The three swore this oath in the dead of night, for if the Torgun priestess of the new gods found out, they would be in no end of trouble.

Her two friends were both chuckling over some jest and started to whisper it to her, but she hushed them. The old man, Farinn, was starting to speak.

"When I left the telling of the tale of our heroes last night, Skylan Ivorson had built the funeral pyre and mourned the death of his dearest friend, Garn. Aylaen, the woman Skylan loved, had denounced him, blaming him for Garn's death. Skylan was alone and desolate, and he thought he could sink no lower. But the gods were angry at Skylan, angry at his lies that shielded a murderer, angry at his lies regarding the cruel fate of his warriors at the hands of the Druids. The gods were themselves dishonored by the dishonor Skylan had brought upon the Vindrasi and the gods were determined to continue their punishment of him. Skylan and his people were ambushed and taken into slavery by Raegar Gustafson, Skylan's cousin, who had betrayed his people and his gods."

The Torgun hissed, the young woman loudest among them. Raegar was the villain of the tale.

Farinn was accustomed to the interruption and allowed time for them to settle down again before he resumed.

"Raegar was now a priest of the new god, Aelon, and served on board the ship of Legate Acronis, who was pleased with his new slaves. He planned to train them to fight in the game known as the Para Dix.

"Skylan and his men were shackled and made prisoners aboard their own ship, the *Venjekar*, which Legate Acronis was towing back to the city of Sinaria, to put it on display. The *Venjekar*'s dragon, Kahg, had not been there to save them, for he had been wounded in battle and fled back to his own realm to heal. His spiritbone, which the priestess used to summon him, had vanished.

"Skylan and Aylaen and the other Vindrasi warriors, of which I myself was one," the old man added with pardonable pride, "entered the once great city of Sinaria as slaves of the Legate Acronis. Skylan believed that he had been enslaved as punishment for his sins, but he soon came to think that Vindrash, the dragon goddess, had brought the Torgun here for a purpose—to recover one of the sacred Five Vektia spiritbones."

The old man went on to relate the various adventures and mishaps that had befallen Skylan and Aylaen and their comrades. The young woman knew them by heart, could repeat them word for word and fill in the gaps of the story the old man inadvertently left out. He had seen eighty-five summers; his memory was not what it had been.

When the story reached its dreadful climax, the three friends drew nearer to one another, listening with grim disapproval to hear how Aylaen's treacherous sister, Treia, using the Vektia spiritbone, disobeyed the command of Vindrash, the dragon goddess, and summoned one of the Five dragons in order to defend Sinaria against the invading ogres.

In a fatal paradox, the misuse of the power that was meant to create brought about death and destruction.

"Skylan and his comrades escaped the terror of the Vektia dragon and the ogres, only to find themselves and their ship, the *Venjekar,* alone in the sea, surrounded by their enemies with no hope or chance of escape."

The old man paused. His dimming eyes looked back in time and they brightened. These days, he could see the past far more clearly than the present. The three friends hardly dared to breathe. They knew what was coming and the three clasped hands, held fast to one another.

"I remember well that moment of despair," said the old man softly. "We all of us looked to Skylan and we asked him what we were going to do. And he said . . ."

"We stand together," said the young woman.

The old man paused to look at her fondly. The young woman had not meant to speak and she felt her cheeks burn. Her mother, clucking in dismay over her hoyden of a daughter, shook herself loose from her husband's attempts to restrain her and began to make her way through the tables and people to scold her daughter and send her to bed.

The young woman and the two young men scrambled to their feet and dashed outside into the biting cold of the winter night.

The young woman heard her mother's voice rising in shrill anger, calling her name and ordering her to come back. Shaking her head, the young woman gathered up her skirts and continued to run over the hard, frost-rimed ground. Her two friends laughed and called out for her to slow down. She taunted them as she outpaced them, for though the men were stronger, she was the swiftest of the three and always won their races. She ran until she came to the boundless sea, inky black except for the frothy white waves that broke upon the shore at her feet and the gleaming stars above her head.

Her two friends soon caught up with her. The three stood on the beach in silence, for the heart needs no voice. The threads of their destinies unrolled before them, leading to distant horizons, star-bright and sparkling with promise.

For they were young and knew they would live forever.

As had the tale of Skylan Ivorson . . .

BOOK 1

CHAPTER

1

"Where's Keeper?" Sigurd asked, peering down into the hold.

"Dead," said Skylan.

His comrades stared at him in shocked silence. Then some of the men glanced grimly at the ogre ships with their triangular sails that were approaching them cautiously, wary, no doubt, of the reputation of the Vindrasi dragonships.

Other men watched Raegar sailing after them in his new dragonship, *Aelon's Triumph*, that he had ordered built along the same lines as the fabled dragonships of his cousins. Raegar's ship was dedicated to the God of the New Dawn, Aelon. His dragon, Fala, was dedicated to the new god, as well. Both of them were traitors to the Vindrasi and the Old Gods, the true gods.

"So what do we do now?" Sigurd demanded, breaking the silence.

"We stand together," said Skylan.

Sigurd snorted. "You mean we die together."

"Better than dying alone," said Skylan. "Like Keeper."

"How did our Keeper die?" asked Legate

Acronis, frowning. He had known the ogre god-lord a long time and although they were nominally slave and master, the two had long been friends. "He had a cracked head, nothing for an ogre with their thick skulls."

Skylan's gaze flicked to Aylaen. Worn out after her battle with the Vektia dragon, she was sitting on the deck, slumped back against the bulkhead. He and Aylaen had fled Sinaria disguised as the military escort for Legate Acronis and they were both wearing the segmented armor worn by the Sinarian soldiers, as well as the breastplate and the leather skirt that was too big for her slender waist. Aylaen had removed the helm, claiming that she couldn't see properly. Her legs were bare from her thighs to her tightly laced boots. Skylan was surprised her stepfather, Sigurd, hadn't berated her for exposing her body in such an unseemly manner. Perhaps Sigurd had given up the fight to salvage his wayward daughter's honor. She had, after all, just saved his life. Skylan hoped Aylaen was asleep.

She wasn't. Hearing the news of Keeper's death, she opened her eyes wide and pushed herself to her feet.

"Keeper's dead?" she said in dismay. "How did he die? What happened?"

"How he died doesn't matter," Skylan said in flat, dry tones. "What matters is how *we* die. If Raegar captures us, he will take us back to Sinaria and slavery."

Skylan held out his arm, still bloody from where

the blessed sword of Vindrash had slashed through the tattoo that had branded him a slave. "For myself, I choose the ogres."

"The brutes will board our ship to find one of their godlords dead," Erdmun pointed out. "They'll think we killed him. They'll butcher us."

Skylan sighed. Erdmun could always be counted on to take a negative view of the situation. Though Skylan had to admit, in this instance there wasn't much positive.

"So we're going to just sit here and wait for death," Sigurd said, scowling.

"We will not sit here. We will pray," Aylaen said. "We will turn to our gods."

"Our gods have been such a big help to us up to now," Erdmun sneered.

Aylaen angrily rounded on Erdmun.

"We're still alive," she said, her green eyes flashing. She pointed back to the city, to the smoke that blacked the sky and the orange flames that burned so fiercely not even the torrential rains could douse them. "The people in that city cannot say as much. We are alive and we are free. We have our ship and we have our dragon and we have each other."

The men were listening to her. She was wet and bedraggled, her face smeared with grime and soot, her red curls plastered to her head. She was a mess, but to Skylan she was beautiful. He had never loved her more than he loved her now, and he had loved Aylaen all his life.

"Our gods fight for their survival even as we fight for ours," Aylaen continued. "They have given us what help they can. The rest we must do for ourselves."

The men were impressed. Aylaen turned to face the carved figurehead of the dragon that proudly graced the prow of the *Venjekar*. Kahg's eyes glittered red. The dragon had refused to fight Raegar's dragon, Fala, saying he would not fight one of his own kind, no matter that she served a treacherous god. Kahg had not abandoned them, however. The dragon was with them, sailing the dragonship, imbuing the ship with his spirit.

Aylaen began praying to Vindrash, the dragon goddess, thanking her for her blessings, for her help in saving them from a Vektia dragon. Skylan was proud of her, proud of her courage, her strength. She had become a Bone Priestess reluctantly, led to the decision by a lie that held more truth for her than she wanted to admit.

"Vindrash," Aylaen said in conclusion, gazing up at the heavens tinged with smoke. "We need a miracle."

Skylan said his own prayer. He did not pray to Vindrash. Now that the Dragon Goddess had given him the secret to the Five Vektia dragons, Skylan hoped she was done with him, that she had punished him enough and there would be no more horror-ridden dragonbone games played night after dreadful night with the draugr of his dead wife, Draya. Skylan had worked hard to make amends for his past misdeeds. Aylaen was a Bone Priestess now. She and Vindrash could commune and leave Skylan out of it. He clasped his hand over his amulet, the silver hammer he wore around his neck.

"I don't need a miracle, Torval. I need a favor. I need time," Skylan said beneath his breath. "Anything that will gain me more time. Do that, and we can handle the rest."

His prayer dispatched, Skylan looked with concern at his warriors. They had escaped Sinaria aboard the *Venjekar,* hauling the ship overland until they reached the river and then launching it. They were wearing the traditional armor of the Torgun, "barbaric armor," the Sinarians termed it—leather tunics, padded leather vests, and chain mail, newly made for the Para Dix games. Some wore swords, others carried axes, depending on their preference. Skylan, as a Sinarian soldier, carried a standard-issue sword; a weapon neither good nor bad.

Sigurd's head was bowed in prayer, but Skylan thought he was only pretending. Sigurd cast darting glances at the ogre ship from out of the corner of his eye. Grimuir, his friend and ally (allied in their dislike of Skylan), was watching Raegar's ship. Acronis, former Legate of the doomed city of Sinaria, did not bow his head. Skylan knew he did not believe in gods, in any gods. His only beloved daughter had died yesterday. His beautiful home had been burned to the ground. His city was still in flames; the smoke from the burning buildings crept over the water, stinging the throat and eyes. He had lost everything except his life and he must hold that life very cheap right now, for he had tried to kill himself. Small wonder he turned his back on the gods, who had turned their backs on him. He was dressed in his ceremonial Sinarian armor, his finely made sword at his side. He gazed out across the restless sea and scratched his grizzled chin.

Bjorn seemed to pray in earnest; Erdmun prayed, Skylan was sure, because he was hedging his bets. Farinn, the youngest of them all, looked as if he prayed fervently through lips that trembled.

Farinn is afraid of death, Skylan realized. And he imagines he is alone in his fear. I must remember to give him some task to keep him occupied.

The ship was quiet, the only sounds the waves slapping against the hull and the murmurs of men praying. Wulfe, the fae child, son (so he claimed) of the daughter of the Faerie Queen, sidled up to Skylan and announced in a loud voice, "Treia murdered Keeper."

"Shut up!" Skylan clapped his hand over Wulfe's mouth, but he was too late. Aylaen turned to stare at the boy in shock.

"What do you mean?" She looked at Skylan. "What does he mean?"

"He's just talking. He doesn't know anything," Skylan said, gripping Wulfe by the arm.

"I do, too," said Wulfe defiantly. "Treia poisoned him. I'll tell you how. She gave him a potion and told him it would help—Ouch!"

Wulfe glared at Skylan indignantly and rubbed his head. "You hit me."

"Because you tell tales," Skylan said. "Don't

pay any attention to him, Aylaen. He's crazy. He thinks he talks to dryads—"

"Does he also think he can turn himself into a man-beast?" Aylaen retorted. "Because he can."

Skylan opened his mouth and closed it. There was no denying that. They had both been witness to the startling transformation. One moment a scrawny boy of about eleven years had been standing before them and the next moment he was a yellow-eyed, sharp-fanged wolf.

"Tell me the truth about Keeper, Skylan," said Aylaen.

"He died," said Skylan. "He just died."

Aylaen shook her head and then she vanished. Wulfe vanished. The mast behind Skylan vanished. The dragonhead prow above him vanished. Fog, thick, gray, greasy smoke-tinged fog rolled down from the heavens and engulfed them in a blinding cloud.

Skylan could see nothing for the thick mist that floated before his eyes. He knew he was standing on the deck of his ship only because he could feel it solid beneath his feet. He couldn't see the deck, he couldn't see his feet. He had to hold his hand close to his face to see it. He was reminded of the terrifying journey he had made on the ghost ship, haunted by the draugr of his dead wife, Draya. He wondered if he was the only person on board the *Venjekar*; he had to swallow twice before he could force his voice to work.

"Aylaen!" he called.

"Here!" she gasped, somewhere to his right.

"The rest of you shout out," Skylan ordered.

One by one they all replied—from Sigurd's deep bass to Wulfe's shrill, excited yelp.

"Aylaen, ask the Dragon Kahg if he can see." She was a Bone Priestess, the only person on board who could commune with the dragon.

"Kahg is as blind as the rest of us," Aylaen reported. She paused a moment, then said wryly, "The dragon tells me you did not pray for a miracle. You asked Torval for a favor. The Dragon Kahg says you have it. The fog blankets the ocean, blinds our enemies. Make the best of it."

Skylan almost laughed. A thick, blinding, soul-smothering fog wasn't exactly the favor he'd had in mind, but he'd take it. The Dragon Kahg slowed the ship's progress through the sullenly stirring waves to a halt. Every ship's captain must be doing the same, for Skylan could hear muted horn calls, while voices, muffled by the fog, shouted orders. The last he had seen of the ogres' ships, they had been clustered together and were likely to smash into each other. Raegar's ship was too far away for Skylan to hear anything, but he had no doubt Raegar would also be forced to stop lest he inadvertently sail into what remained of the ogre fleet.

"I'm standing near the hold," Skylan called out to the crew. "I'm going to keep talking. Follow the sound of my voice and come to me."

The men made their way to him. He could mark their progress by their swearing as they stumbled over the oars, barked their shins on the sea chests, or bumped into each other.

"A strange phenomenon, this fog," Acronis observed.

"Nothing strange. Torval sent it," said Skylan.

Acronis regarded him with good-natured amusement. "On the contrary, my friend, the fog was caused by the smoke from the fires combined with the humidity."

The two stood practically toe-to-toe and yet they could barely see each other. The air was heavy and difficult to breathe. Skylan could feel the fog catch in his throat.

"You and I will argue about the gods when we are safely back in my homeland," said Skylan impatiently. "Now I need your learning for more important matters, Legate—"

Acronis shook his head. "I am no longer Legate, Skylan. I am no longer your master." He gave a wry chuckle. "You would say I never was . . ."

Skylan had once hated Legate Acronis as the man who had enslaved him. He had since come to honor and respect the older man as an able military commander and because they had ended up on the same side in this war, fighting the same foe. Having lost everything, Acronis had elected to bind his wyrd to Skylan and his Torgun warriors.

"You are not my master," Skylan agreed, smiling in turn. "But you are a learned man, worthy of respect. You have made a study of ogres, sir, so Keeper told me. What do you know of their rituals for the dead?"

"I know quite a bit," said Acronis, puzzled. "Why?"

"Because Torval sent you to me, as well," said Skylan.

"Skylan, over here," Aylaen called.

He made his way to her and found her clutching Wulfe by the arm. "He almost fell."

"I was trying to talk to the oceanaids," Wulfe said.

"Keep hold of him," Skylan said to Aylaen. "Stay by the mast. Both of you."

"What are you going to do?" she asked.

"What I have to," he said.

Aylaen silently nodded. Her face was the gray of the fog. Her green eyes and red hair seemed the only color in a gray world. She feared Wulfe was telling the truth, that Treia had poisoned Keeper. Skylan wished he could stay with her, talk to her, tell her some comforting lie. But there wasn't time. Torval's favor would not last forever and when the fog lifted, they had to be ready.

Led by Skylan, the Torgun warriors stumbled down the ladder that led into the hold. They had to feel their way, for the hold was dark, the mists were thick, and they couldn't see a thing. Skylan heard a terrified gasp and a rustling and he remembered that Treia was down there somewhere.

She must be afraid we are coming after her.

He said nothing to disabuse her. Let her spend a few moments in terror. None of the others spoke to her. They had all heard Wulfe's accusation and most probably believed it. Still, murdering the ogre was not the worst of her crimes. He had kept from his comrades the fact that Treia had summoned the Vektia dragon who had leveled a city and nearly killed them all. Skylan had kept silent not because he gave a damn about Treia. He cared about Aylaen, who cared about Treia.

The men gathered around Keeper's body lying on the deck of the hold, shrouded in the gloom and the darkness.

"All right, we're down here," said Sigurd. "What do we do now?"

"We are going to honor the dead," said Skylan. "We are going to return Keeper to his people."

CHAPTER 2

Aylaen listened to the heavy footfalls, muffled in the thick fog, clumping down the stairs into the hold. She heard the men fumbling about, bumping into each other and then, when they were quiet, Skylan stating that they were going to honor the dead. Of course, Sigurd immediately launched into an angry tirade about how Skylan was wasting time honoring a dead ogre when they should be arming for battle against live ones. Skylan patiently explained his plan. Aylaen smiled. She remembered a time when the hotheaded Skylan would have used his fists to explain. As it was, the men listened and Sigurd grumbled that it might work. Skylan asked Acronis to tell them about ogre funeral rites. Aylaen could hear the creaking of the *Venjekar*'s timbers, the waves rolling beneath the keel, water dripping. In the distance, an eerie-sounding horn called from one ship to another.

She was still keeping fast hold of Wulfe, who was growing bored and starting to squirm. Aylaen bent down and whispered into his ear. "I need you to do something for me."

Wulfe looked up suspiciously. "I'm not going to take a bath."

Aylaen removed the necklace she had been wearing. Golden bands twined around the spiritbone forming the tail of a dragon. Golden wings spread from the bone with a golden chain attached to the tips of each of the wings. The head of the dragon reared up from the bone. Emeralds adorned the spiritbone, set above the head. Two smaller emeralds were embedded in the wings.

"What's that?" Wulfe asked, eying it curiously.

"The spiritbone of one of the five Vektia dragons," Aylaen replied.

"What's a Vektia dragon?" Wulfe asked.

"You've heard Skylan and me talk about the Vektia dragons," said Aylaen.

"You Uglies are always talking," said Wulfe, shrugging. "Mostly your talk is boring and I don't listen. Is it like our dragon?"

"You have to listen now," said Aylaen sternly. "I'm going to depend on you and I need you to understand that this is important."

Wulfe heaved a deep sigh. "I'm listening."

Aylaen told him how Torval was roaming the universe and how he came upon this world, ruled by the great dragon, Ilyrion. How Torval wanted this world and he and the great dragon fought over it.

"The world didn't belong to either of them," Wulfe interrupted, scowling. "It belonged to the faeries. My mother told me so."

"Just listen!" Aylaen said, exasperated. "We don't have much time."

Then, as concisely as she could, she told him the rest. How Torval killed the dragon, Ilyrion, but had come to admire his foe and honored her by placing the power of creation in five of her bones. Fearing that other roving gods might come to try to take the world, Torval gave the five bones to his consort, Vindrash, the dragon goddess, to hide away. She gave one each to four of the gods who had come to join them in ruling over the world. The fifth she gave to the Vindrasi, her chosen people.

For many thousands of years, the gods remained undisturbed, and then came the Gods of Raj and of Aelon, God of the New Dawn, to challenge them. They fought a great battle in heaven. The Old Gods were defeated and forced to retreat. One of their own, Desiria, the daughter of Sund, God of Farseeing, and Aylis, Goddess of the Sun, was slain in that battle.

"Sund grieved the loss of his child," said Aylaen. "He looked into the future and saw only death and despair and to try to prevent that, he gave the spiritbone of the Vektia that was in his care to Aelon. When the ogres attacked, Aelon's Warrior-Priests tried to use this spiritbone to stop them. Treia was a Bone Priestess and she summoned the Vektia dragon and ended up destroying a city."

Aylaen gazed at the spiritbone, admiring its delicate beauty even as she trembled at its terrible power. Someone who knew the secret of the Five could tame the dragon's destructive power: the only way to control the Vektia was to obtain all five spiritbones, summon all five dragons. If that could be achieved, the Old Gods would be able to use the power to drive out the interloper gods and retain rulership of the world.

How? Aylaen wondered, turning the spiritbone in her hand. What will happen when the Five come together?

She had no answer. All she had was one spiritbone, one given by the traitor god, Sund, to his enemy. The Vindrasi had lost their spiritbone, through fear, when the cowardly Chief of Chiefs, Horg, gave the spiritbone set in the Vektan Torque to the ogres in an effort to save his own skin.

Aylaen had one. They needed to find all five. They had been planning to sail to the ogre kingdom to take back their spiritbone. But that plan had gone sadly awry. Now they were drifting on a fog-bound sea, surrounded by their enemies, and the fate of her people and her gods was going to be in the hands of a fae child.

Wulfe was eleven years old or somewhere thereabouts. His hair was shaggy and uncombed; he wore whatever came to hand, which by now had mostly been reduced to rags and was unrecognizable. He was a fae child, if one believed his tale about being the grandson of the Faerie Queen. And he was a savage killer. In his man-beast form, he had murdered and dismembered two men. According to his story, he had been certain those men were going to kill him and he had decided to kill them first. Aylaen had watched him turn into a wolf. She had watched the fur sprout from his body, his teeth lengthen into fangs, his yellow eyes gleam.

"I listened to the story. Why are you staring at me like that?" Wulfe asked. "What do you want me to do?"

"You and I are going to hide this away," said Aylaen. "But first I must ask you a question and you must tell me the truth. Did my sister kill Keeper?"

Wulfe flung up his arm. "You're going to hit me!"

"I'm not going to hit you. Is it true?" Aylaen asked, giving him a little shake.

"Yes," he said sullenly.

"How do you know?"

"I saw her do it. I was watching her," said Wulfe. His eyes narrowed. "I always watch her."

"Why?" Aylaen asked, startled.

"Because she hates me. She wants me dead. My daemons keep telling me to kill her, but I don't listen to them. I know if I hurt her you would be mad at me."

"Telling me my sister is a murderer makes me mad at you," said Aylaen. "So you better not be lying."

Wulfe wriggled in her grasp. She tightened her grip. "Tell me what you saw."

"Treia was being nice to Keeper, asking him how he felt and if he was in pain and if there was anything she could do for him. She was nice to me once like that and she ended up hurting me."

Wulfe shrugged. "He should have known better, for he didn't trust her, either, but I guess he must have been groggy from being hit on the head. He told her the injury was nothing. He'd suffered a cracked skull more than once in the Para Dix. Treia went to that chest of hers where she keeps her stuff and mixed something in a cup and gave it to him and told him to drink it. She said it would ease the pain. He drank it and then he slumped over and I thought he was asleep. But then Skylan came down and said something to him and shook him and Keeper toppled over and Skylan said he was dead."

"And how do you know my sister killed him?"

Wulfe shrugged his thin shoulders. "Because Keeper wasn't dead until he drank whatever Treia gave him. Skylan knows what she did," the boy added defensively. "Ask him."

Aylaen touched the spiritbone with the tips of her fingers. She could feel the terrible power, a tingling vibration. Closing her eyes, she saw, not for the first time, the bodies in the river, the corpses littering the street, mothers wailing over dead children, husbands weeping over dead wives; families lying dead in the rubble of their homes: an entire city destroyed.

She opened her eyes to look at the boy shifting restlessly from one bare foot to the other.

Aylaen felt the muscles in her face stiffen, her mouth dry. Down below, she could hear the men swearing and shuffling about. They were trying to lift Keeper's body. Skylan knew the truth about

Treia. That's why he hadn't answered her. She didn't have much time. She held out the spiritbone to the boy.

"You must hide this away. Put this in the same place where you hid the spiritbone for the Dragon Kahg."

"You mean in the—"

"Stop!" Aylaen said harshly. "Don't tell me. Hide it away now. Hide it quickly before the fog lifts."

Wulfe eyed the necklace and put his hands behind his back. "I can't. It will burn me. Maybe kill me."

Aylaen had forgotten that the fey child could not—or would not—touch metal of any kind.

"It's not going to kill you. Look, I'll wrap it up in part of my shirt—"

Wulfe was shaking his head. "It doesn't like me. I can tell . . ."

"Wulfe, I need you to hide this!" Aylaen said desperately. "We might be captured and . . . and . . ."

"You don't want Treia to find it," said Wulfe.

Aylaen was quiet a moment and then she said softly, "Yes."

Wulfe slipped his hand into hers. "We'll hide it together. I'll show you where. You put it inside and I'll use my magic to keep it safe. And the dragon will help us."

Wulfe started running, tugging her along. The moment Aylaen let go of the mast and stepped into the gray world she became disoriented and confused. She could not see anything; the mist swam before her eyes. Wulfe appeared to have some sense of where he was going, for he dragged her along confidently. She stumbled after him and tried not to think about tumbling overboard.

"We're here," Wulfe said. "There's my hiding hole."

Aylaen put her hand on the carved wooden neck of the dragonhead prow. Above her was the nail from which hung the spiritbone of the Dragon Kahg. Aylaen knelt down on the deck and stared intently where Wulfe was pointing at the bulkhead.

"Where? I don't see anything."

"Of course you don't," said Wulfe. "It's hidden." He added something beneath his breath about "stupid Uglies."

"How do you get into it?" Aylaen asked. The wooden planks looked as though they hadn't been touched in years, since the carpenter nailed them in place.

Wulfe began to sing.

Open to my waiting hand.
Open to my knowing eye.
Open to my little song.
Open it and don't take long.

To Aylaen's vast astonishment, a piece of the plank disappeared, revealing a snug cubbyhole that had been carved out of the bulkhead. The hole was lined with sail cloth and filled with objects too varied and numerous to count. Aylaen caught a quick glimpse of what looked like a lock of her hair, a piece of charred bone, and a silver thimble. Then Wulfe clapped his grubby hands over her eyes.

"Don't look!" Wulfe ordered. "I have important things in here that you mustn't see."

"I'll keep my eyes closed," Aylaen offered, mystified by what she had seen.

"You better," said Wulfe, and he slowly drew away his hand.

He put his hand on her hand that was holding the spiritbone and guided her to the cubbyhole. She wondered if there would be room inside for the necklace, for it was large, and the cubbyhole had seemed very small and almost stuffed to capacity. It must have been larger than she imagined, for she had no trouble sliding the necklace inside.

"Don't open your eyes yet," Wulfe cautioned.

Aylaen obeyed and sat back on her heels, her eyes squinched tightly shut. She heard him rooting about in the cubbyhole and then, when he apparently had arranged everything to his liking, he told her she could open her eyes. Aylaen saw that everything, presumably including the spiritbone, was now covered with the sail cloth.

Aylaen hesitated. "Will I be able to the find the hiding hole again? Will the magic work for me?"

Wulfe snorted in derision. "You're an Ugly! No, it won't work!"

He cast a glance in the direction of the dragon's head that was somewhere above them and whispered, "But I think if you wanted the necklace and the dragon wanted you to have it, the dragon would help."

Aylaen couldn't see the dragon's head, obscured by the thick mist, but she could see a flicker of red gleam from Kahg's eye.

"You can close the hole now," said Aylaen.

Wulfe replaced the plank and began to sing another song.

Keep safe from thieving hands.
Keep safe from spying eyes.
Let them meet a swift demise.

Aylaen blinked. The cubbyhole was gone. The bulkhead looked as though it had never been disturbed. She could even discern rust on the nail heads. She reached out her hand to touch it and felt the wood, rough and solid and wet beneath her fingers.

"What does 'demise' mean?" Wulfe asked.

"'Dying,'" Aylaen answered. She wrapped her arms around herself. The fog was chill and damp. "In this instance, 'death.' 'Let them meet a swift death.' If you didn't know what the word meant, why did you use it?"

"My mother taught me the song. She taught me lots of songs and all of them are magic like this one. Only some of them are a lot more powerful."

"Like turning yourself into a wolf?" Aylaen asked, shivering. The chill was creeping into her bones.

"My mother didn't do that to me!" Wulfe cried, bouncing up angrily. "My mother loves me. She came to me every night and she held me and sang to me and told me to remember the songs because they would protect me from you Uglies who hate us and fear us."

"I don't hate you," said Aylaen gently.

"But you're afraid of me," Wulfe mumbled. His eyes brimmed with tears that spilled over and ran down his cheeks, leaving tracks in the dirt. He dragged his hand across his nose. "Because I can change into a wolf."

Aylaen leaned back against the bulkhead.

"I am afraid of you. Like you're afraid of Skylan."

"I'm not!" Wulfe said indignantly.

"Even though you know Skylan loves you and would never hurt you, you run away when he draws his sword."

"I don't like swords," said Wulfe.

He sat down beside her. He was silent a long while, considering her words, then he lifted his eyes to meet hers. "I think I understand. And I want you to know that even if I am a wolf sometimes I would never hurt you or Skylan."

Aylaen smoothed back the shaggy hair from his forehead. "I'm not afraid that you would hurt me. I'm afraid because I don't understand why this happens to you."

"My grandmother," said Wulfe. "She put a curse on me because I am part human. My mother tried to lift the curse, but she couldn't."

Wulfe sighed. "I miss my mother."

"I miss my mother, too," said Aylaen.

She put her arm around him and felt his tense body relax against hers.

"I might hurt Treia, though," Wulfe said, and before Aylaen could say anything, he jumped to his feet and ran off, disappearing into the fog. Aylaen could hear his bare feet pattering across the deck.

Hurt Treia . . . Back in Sinaria, Treia had looked straight at Aylaen and cried in fury, *This is your fault. You should be dead! Why aren't you dead?*

"My fault," Aylaen repeated softly. "I am the one who should be dead."

Aylaen was supposed to have died in Sinaria. But she had survived and her survival had somehow ruined Treia's plans. Aylaen had tried for so long to love her sister. She had defended Treia. She had forced Skylan to rescue Treia from the dragon Treia had brought into being. Keeper had planned to take them to the ogres, speak for them. Treia had poisoned Keeper. Skylan had tried to warn Aylaen about her sister, but she had refused to listen. Now if the ogres captured them, they would die and it would be her fault.

Aylaen heard Skylan calling softly to her. She stood up and groped her way across the deck, following the sound of his voice.

"Where's Wulfe?" he asked, and then his gaze went to her neck. His eyes widened in alarm. "Where's the spiritbone?"

"I hid it," she said. "Wulfe helped me."

Aylaen was afraid he would be angry and was relieved when Skylan smiled. "He showed you his cubbyhole."

"You know about that?"

"I know he has one. I don't know where it is and I don't want to know. Are you confident it is safe?"

"I don't even know how to find it," said Aylaen. "It is hidden in the bones of the ship. If something happens to us, the Dragon Kahg will protect it."

"Nothing is going to happen," said Skylan.

Aylaen shook her head. She felt a heaviness settle over her soul, as though the fog had crept inside her. She was so tired. The battle was so hopeless. She looked bleakly at Skylan, expecting to see him grim, preparing for death. She was surprised to see he was smiling, his blue eyes bright in the mist. He was soaked to the skin, like all of them. He had removed the segmented plate armor of a Sinarian soldier and put on the familiar leather armor of a Torgun warrior. He must have been as exhausted as she was. Yet he was smiling.

Aylaen was annoyed. "We're going to die. You know that. What do you have to smile about?"

Skylan shrugged. "I *don't* know we're going to die. Our wyrd is in the hands of the gods and I am smiling because I am not a slave anymore. I smile because the bravest warriors in the history of the Vindrasi are on this ship. They will fight at my side."

He held out to her the sword of Vindrash, the sword she had found in the temple.

"I am not a warrior," Aylaen said. "True, I cut my hair and dressed in men's clothes and pretended to be a man-woman, dedicating myself to Vindrash, but that was all a lie."

"Vindrash does not think so," said Skylan. "The goddess saw what was in your heart. She saw the truth. She gave you her blessed sword. I look at you and I see a warrior who is as brave and bold as any man on this ship. And who smells much better."

She laughed. He was pleased to see her laugh. She looked into Skylan's blue eyes and her breath caught in her throat, her heartbeat quickened. His breath was coming a little faster. The fog closed around them. They were the only two people in the world. They drew near, their lips touched . . .

Wulfe appeared out of nowhere, wriggling his way between them. He looked at them with wide, solemn eyes.

"The oceanaids say we should leave. We're not safe here."

At the dumbfounded look on Skylan's face, Aylaen laughed again, laughed until she cried.

CHAPTER 3

Hauling the ogre's heavy body up out of the hold proved to be a daunting task. Sigurd and Grimuir gripped Keeper by his massive shoulders, dragging the corpse up the ladder, while Bjorn and Erdmun and Farinn pushed from below. Sigurd called on Skylan to come help. Skylan didn't hear. He stood in a daze, his hand tingling from Aylaen's touch. She had kissed him. Well, she had almost kissed him, before Wulfe with his stupid oceanaids had interrupted. Skylan had tried to detain her, but she had hurried away and he lost her in the mist.

What exactly did an almost-kiss mean? Was she falling in love with him?

"Skylan! This was your idea!" Sigurd grumbled. "Stop daydreaming and come over and help us before we drop the bastard and he slides back down and we have to do this all over again!"

Skylan went to help and, grunting and sweating and swearing, they hauled Keeper's body up out of the hold and dumped it thankfully down onto the deck. Skylan wiped sweat and mist from his face and gazed down at the dead ogre with true grief and sorrow. Keeper had been Skylan's trainer in the Para Dix game and although their friendship had started with a blow to the jaw that had knocked Skylan flat, the two had ended up friends. Skylan asked the ogre's spirit to forgive him for the rough treatment.

"When we meet in Torval's Hall, I will explain and we will laugh over this together," Skylan promised.

He had no doubt that Torval would admit Keeper into the Hall of Heroes. Enemies of the Vindrasi who fought valiantly and died bravely were honored by both men and gods. Keeper had not died in battle with his sword in his hand. He had been basely murdered.

Skylan, as a true friend, should promise to avenge the ogre's murder, bring his killer to account. Treia had, of course, denied that she had harmed Keeper and Skylan had no way to prove she had. He had seen the truth on her stone-hard, cold face, the faint curl of her lips as she had watched the men carry the ogre's body out of the hold. All Skylan could do was to leave her to the gods.

The *Venjekar* was still wrapped in fog, though it seemed to Skylan that the mist was growing thinner. He could hear ogre voices and the flapping of their odd-looking triangular sails, but all sound was distorted by the fog and he could not tell if the ogres were near or a mile distant. He posted young Farinn, who had the keenest eyesight, and Wulfe to keep watch for ogre ships.

"We're going to carry Keeper to the prow," Skylan said, keeping his voice low and warning the others to be as quiet as possible. "Arrange the body as Acronis told you."

Bjorn carried Keeper's heavy sword.

"Damn thing weighs more than young Farinn," Bjorn complained.

"You've just grown weak," said Skylan. "The lazy life you've been leading."

Bjorn grinned at him and Skylan grinned back. The shadow of Skylan's misdeeds had once been dark between them. That was gone, their friendship restored. The same was true of the other men, even Sigurd, who would never like him, but at least had come to regard him with grudging respect. Skylan had worked hard to regain their trust and their confidence. They had forgiven him for the terrible things he had done. He could dare to hope now that Aylaen had forgiven him. Skylan would never forgive himself, but that was between him and the gods.

Acronis directed the men to place Keeper's hands on his chest and rest his sword in his hands. The rain had washed off most of his white and black face paint.

"We have to put his paint back on," said Acronis.

The men stared at him.

"Those designs marked Keeper as a godlord," Acronis explained. "His people won't believe us if we claim he is a godlord without them."

Skylan scratched his stubbly growth of beard. "A good idea, sir, except we don't have any paint."

"We have flour we could use for the white paint," said Aylaen. "I could make a paste and we could smear it on. I don't know about the black paint . . ."

"I have ink," said a voice from the fog.

For a moment no one could tell who had spoken. Then Grimuir grabbed hold of Farinn, who had been standing by the rail, watching for ogres, and shoved him forward.

"Ink!" Skylan repeated, staring at the young man in amazement. "What are you doing with ink?"

"I have been teaching myself to read and write," said Farinn, ducking his head, as though confessing a shameful sin.

"You are a warrior," said Skylan. "A warrior needs to know how to wield a sword, not how to wield a pen."

Farinn flushed red and spoke in a nearly inaudible murmur. "I am making a song of our journey."

The men regarded Farinn in frowning disapproval. None of the Vindrasi could read or write. There was no need. Their laws and history were kept by the Talgogroth, who committed the laws and every major event and many minor ones to memory and, once a year, recited them to the people. Heroic battles should be told aloud in words that stirred the heart, not reduced to squiggly lines scrawled on animal skin.

Skylan was as shocked as the rest of the Torgun, though he had to secretly admit that being able to read the squiggly lines on what Raegar termed a "map" might be of some benefit. Still, that was why he had brought along Acronis. The Sinarian was a scholar, as well as an able commander and an experienced seaman.

"Fetch your ink," Skylan said gruffly to Farinn. "We'll put it to *good* use."

Farinn disappeared thankfully into the fog and could be heard tripping over the oars as he searched for his sea chest. Aylaen went down into the hold after the flour.

A song of their journey. Skylan had never before considered such a thing. He tried to imagine years hence the Torgun people sitting around a Talgogroth to hear the *Song of* . . . what? What would be the title of this tale? The *Song of Skylan Ivorson*? Skylan smiled ruefully. Not long ago, he would have been arrogant enough to consider that title appropriate. A better title would be the *Song of the Venjekar,* he thought. He would have to remember to tell young Farinn.

Not that the title would matter if neither Skylan nor Farinn nor any of the rest of his people were alive to sing it.

Aylaen descended into the hold. She lit a lamp, made of cloth soaked in olive oil, to help her search. The ship was well stocked for their journey. They had flour, olives and olive oil, salted pork, beef in brine. When Sigurd and the others, herself included, had believed Treia's lie that she was going to help them escape, they had packed the hold of the *Venjekar* with supplies enough to last for a long sea voyage.

Aylaen was glad to escape the sight of the others. She needed some time to herself, to try to sort out her new feelings for Skylan. She stood at the bottom of the ladder, in the fog-bound darkness, and realized that these feelings weren't new. That was the problem. She had always loved Skylan. She had loved Garn more, or so she had told Skylan—and Garn.

Aylaen closed her eyes and turned her gaze inward. In that moment, she was forced to see the truth. Her grief over Garn's death was not because she had loved him well. She grieved because she had not loved Garn well enough. She had loved him because she was afraid Sigurd was going to arrange a marriage to some stranger. She had loved Garn to escape her home and her stepfather's abuse. She had loved Garn because she had wanted a baby. She had loved Garn because—and this shamed her—she could control Garn. He would do anything she asked for love of her. And ever since she had been a little girl and knocked him flat on his ass for teasing her, she had loved Skylan.

Skylan—brash, handsome, bold. Skylan, who had a string of women hanging from his line like fresh-caught fish. Skylan, who had claimed to love her, but who had really been in love with war and honor and being a hero and rising to power among the Vindrasi. Looking into his blue eyes then she had seen a boy's arrogance, confidence, the idea that he could do anything he wanted, have anything he wanted.

Now when she looked into his blue eyes, she saw the shadow of grief and loss and the bitter knowledge of his own failure. She saw a man trying to make up for his misdeeds, trying to earn the right to call himself a leader instead of claiming it, trying to regain his lost honor. She saw his love for her, a man's love for a woman . . .

He has changed and I have changed, Aylaen thought. We were children then. We are children no longer. We have waded through blood and ridden through fire. We fought the Vektia dragon side by side. He owes his life to me. I owe my life to him. We are bound together by our love for Garn and by grief at his death.

What truly saddened Aylaen and filled her with guilt was that Garn had understood all of this. He knew that she was using him and he had gone on loving her because he also knew that she needed him. He had come back from the dead to make her understand, to make her let go.

She was standing in the hold, lost in her thoughts, when a hand snaked out of the mists and grabbed her wrist. A shrill voice made her heart lurch.

"Is Skylan going to kill me?"

"Treia!" Aylaen gasped. "You scared me half to death!"

Aylaen had forgotten her sister was down here. Treia gripped her, hard.

"Is he going to kill me?"

Treia's face was livid. Her hair was wet and tangled. The thin robes of a priestess of Aelon clung to her body, revealing her breasts and the bones of her thin, spare frame. Her eyes were large and burned with a frightening luster.

Aylaen shivered in the chill, dank closeness of the hold. The armor she wore was cold and it pinched. She tried to pull away.

"No, of course he's not going to kill you," Aylaen said sharply. She tried to behave normally around her sister. All she could think of was Keeper's body lying on the deck, Treia handing him something to drink.

"Then Skylan's a weak fool." Treia let go of her sister's arm and sank back down onto the sea chest. She smiled an unpleasant smile. "But I've always thought that. I overheard the two of you talking and now I know the secret that Vindrash kept from all the world. I know the secret of the Five Vektia dragons. I know that to control one of the Five, you must have all of the Five. And if Skylan does not kill me, I will find all five."

"And give them to Aelon?" Aylaen asked.

"I won't 'give' the Five to anyone," said Treia. "The god will have to come to me."

"You poisoned the guards. You poisoned Keeper," said Aylaen shakily. "I've tried to love you, Treia. I've defended you, even knowing you tried to kill me along with our comrades. You sent us into the catacombs knowing that Raegar was plotting our deaths. I am your sister, Treia! These men are your friends!"

Treia gave a bitter laugh. "Friends who mock me, call me 'spinster,' term me 'frigid.' My own stepfather deemed me too ugly to try to arrange a marriage for me." She cast Aylaen a scathing glance. "As for you, I never asked you to love me."

Treia looked away. She sat on the sea chest, her arms clasped tight around her. She was tense, rigid, her jaw clenched. For all her talk, she was afraid.

"Skylan won't kill you," Aylaen said. "He won't kill you because he is Skylan and you are defenseless and alone, just as Keeper was defenseless and alone when you poisoned him."

"What else could I do?" Treia cried angrily. "You were going to surrender to the ogres. And Raegar was coming to save me. He loves me! No one else. Only him."

Aylaen understood. Treia was right. With Keeper, one of their godlords, on board the *Venjekar* to vouch for the Torgun, the ogres would have welcomed them as friends and allies. Keeper and Skylan planned to rally the ogres, urge them to attack Raegar's new dragonship. Treia couldn't allow that to happen and she had murdered Keeper.

"I pity you," said Aylaen softly.

Treia stared into the darkness of the hold. "You should have died. If you had, all would be well now . . ."

Aylaen turned away, a sick feeling in the pit of her stomach, and went to search for the flour.

"Aylaen," Skylan called tensely down into the hold. "Are you all right?"

"He must think Treia's going to murder me," Aylaen muttered. Remembering Treia's burning eyes, Aylaen was suddenly glad she was wearing armor.

She called back that she was fine as she made her way to the stern where the jars containing the supplies were stored. The jars were well secured. Only one had broken in the tumultuous trip downriver and that jar had not, thank the gods, contained the flour. Aylaen groped about until she found a piece of the broken jar to use as a crude bowl. She mixed some of the flour with the water to form a whitish paste.

"Give me the spiritbone of the Vektia," said Treia. "If you don't give it to me, Skylan will die."

Aylaen tried to shove past. Treia blocked her way.

"I've seen the way you look at Skylan," Treia sneered. "You little whore. First you jump into Garn's bed, and now that he's dead you leap into Skylan's."

Aylaen gasped as though Treia had punched her. "I'm not—"

"Be quiet and listen to me. If you keep that spiritbone, Skylan is marked for death. The god, Sund, looked into the future and saw Skylan with the Five bones and the Old Gods defeated. That's why the gods want Skylan dead."

"That makes no sense! I don't believe you,"

said Aylaen scornfully. "And I won't give you the spiritbone."

Treia shrugged. "Then Skylan is doomed."

Aylaen swept past her sister and, carrying the paste, she doused the light and climbed the ladder and went up on deck.

CHAPTER 4

The Torgun gathered around Keeper in solemn reverence. Death comes to all, ogre and human, and must be respected. Each of them said something to honor the dead, sharing a story that spoke to Keeper's bravery and courage. Aylaen spoke a prayer to speed his soul.

"His gods are not our gods," she said. "I do not know their names, except that they are called the Gods of Raj. If they are listening, let them hear that Keeper was a good man, a brave warrior, and that I counted him as my friend."

"If Keeper had died at home, his family would paint his face to honor him," Acronis explained. "If he had died on the field of battle, his friends and comrades-in-arms would honor him in this way."

"I do this as his friend and comrade," said Skylan.

"And I do this as Keeper's family," said Acronis. "For he *was* part of my family. Chloe loved him."

The two dabbed the flour on the skin that was now cold. Acronis smeared the white paste over the bald skull. Skylan drew a black stripe from

Keeper's neck to the chin and another black stripe across his nose and cheekbones.

"You must help me one last time, my friend. In return, I will take you back to your people," said Skylan. He kissed the silver amulet around his neck. "Torval be my witness."

Bjorn placed the giant two-handed sword in the ogre's hands, then they covered his body with one of the spare sails to keep the dampness from smearing the paint. And then they stood staring at each other.

"Now what do we do?" Sigurd asked, subdued.

Erdmun's stomach growled loudly and the men all laughed.

"I think we had better eat something," said Skylan. "Before Erdmun's belly brings the ogres down on us."

Aylaen and Farinn carried up food—dried meat, bread, and olives, a Sinarian fruit for which the Vindrasi had developed a taste. The men sat on their sea chests, eating ravenously. Wulfe, who had been quietly munching on some soggy bread, shoved the last bit under the sail near Keeper's cold hand.

"He might be hungry," said Wulfe, and he gave the body a little pat.

And then there was nothing more they could do. Darkness was falling. The night was thick around them, muffling sound. Erdmun's head fell forward, resting on his chest, and he began to snore. His brother, Bjorn, started to wake him.

"Let him sleep," said Skylan, who felt as if he

would drop from fatigue himself. He tried to remember back to when he had last slept, but too much had happened, events were blurred. Yesterday was distant, today was shrouded in mist. Tomorrow might not exist.

"We should all get some sleep while we can," Skylan added. "I will take first watch."

"I'll stand with you," said Sigurd.

No one argued. They slumped down on the deck.

Skylan leaned over the rail near the dragonhead prow, staring into the fog. When he found himself dozing off, he shook his head and went back to talk to Sigurd, who had been pacing the deck, to keep himself awake.

He found Sigurd leaning against the mast. His eyes were closed. He had fallen asleep standing up. Skylan shook him.

"I'm awake!" Sigurd protested.

"Lie down," said Skylan. "Before you fall and break something. The Dragon Kahg and I will keep watch."

Sigurd continued to swear that he wasn't the least bit tired, even as his eyes closed and his head lolled.

Skylan walked about, checking on his people. Aylaen had taken off her armor, complaining that it was too heavy. Dressed in the leather tunic worn by the Sinarian soldiers underneath their armor, she had wrapped herself in a relatively dry blanket she'd found in the hold. Wulfe was curled up at her side, pressing against her for warmth. The rest lay sprawled on the deck. Grimuir had his hand on his sword. Farinn was mumbling in his sleep, perhaps the words to his song. Erdmun snored. Acronis, an old campaigner, had made his cloak into a pillow. Not far from the rest, Keeper lay beneath the sail in eternal slumber.

Skylan walked forward, stationed himself beside the dragonhead prow, and stood gazing out on a dark and silent world. He felt a deep love for these people. They had been through so much. They were all dear to him, even Sigurd.

Skylan's eyes burned. He was so tired. He would sit for just a moment. He blinked and closed his eyes, to ease the burning . . .

Night. Black and cold. The stars small with sharp, bright edges. The moon pale and wan. Skylan walked across the frost-hard ground. He had been walking a long time. He was tired and cold and yet he kept walking, a sense of purpose driving him. He did not recognize his surroundings, and yet he knew he was in his homeland, in Vindraholm. He wore chain mail and a helm and carried his sword and shield.

He crested a hill and looked down. Spread out before him was a battlefield. Grass was trampled, churned, wet with blood. The pale moonlight gleamed on the armor of the dead. Skylan stared, sick with dread and dismay. The armor was Vindrasi; the dead were his people.

An ugly red-orange glow flared on the horizon.

A city in flames. Homes, temples, halls—like black skeletons, writhing in the fire. Skylan listened for cries or screams. He realized suddenly that there was no one left alive to scream.

He ran down the hill and onto the battlefield, stumbling over bodies, slipping in the blood, coughing in the smoke, hoping to find someone still alive. He ran for a long time until, on the verge of collapse, he came to his village. He stopped running. Nothing was left. Here and there flame flickered amid the wreckage, but that was all.

Bodies of women lay in the street. Their men dead, they had fought to defend their homes with axes or scythes or even, pitifully, brooms. Their children had died, too; the older ones fighting, the little ones speared as they sat wailing in the blood of their dead mothers.

The thought came to him that some of his people might have been able to escape and were now hiding in the caves in the hills. He hurried into the woods, calling out names, but no one answered. He froze when he saw fire in the night until he realized that the glow was small—a hearth fire. He hurried toward the warming glow and he recognized the house.

It belonged to Owl Mother.

Skylan stopped in his tracks. He had always been afraid of Owl Mother.

The door to the house swung open and a woman emerged. But it was not Owl Mother. The woman was dressed in armor that had once shone with a radiant light. Now it was dented and bloody and grimed with ash and soot. She was still beautiful, though her face was aged with sorrow; she stood tall, unbowed, undefeated.

Skylan recognized Vindrash, the dragon goddess.

"You can stop searching," she told him. "The Torgun are all dead."

Skylan looked behind her and saw the body of the old woman, Owl Mother, lying on the floor. Her white hair was matted with blood. Her wolf lay dead at her side, his throat slashed. He had died defending her.

"Vindrash, what happened?" Skylan asked.

"The enemy came upon them in the night." The words of the goddess floated out of her mouth and hung, ghostly white, in the frigid air. "Your people woke to a sea filled with strange-looking ships. They heard the blare of trumpets and the beating of drums. They saw bright, shining armor and cruel swords. The sky was black with winged serpents."

"Aelon's serpents," Skylan said. "Soldiers from the land of Oran. Are all . . ." His throat closed, he coughed and continued raggedly, "Are all the Vindrasi dead?"

"Some still live," said Vindrash. She gave a sad smile. "I know because we gods live."

Skylan was confused. "Has this battle already happened? Will it happen in the future? Can I prevent it from happening?"

Vindrash shook her head. "I cannot tell you.

We gods are as blind as mortals now. Perhaps this is the future. Perhaps not."

"Then why bring me here? Why show me this terrible sight?" Skylan demanded angrily.

"Ask yourself that question, Skylan Ivorson," said Vindrash. "This is *your* dream . . ."

CHAPTER
5

A hand touched Skylan's forehead. The touch was icy cold and he shivered in remembrance and woke with a start.

"Vindrash, answer me!" he cried, sitting bolt upright.

He saw mists swirling in gray light and felt a drop of cold water hitting him on the head. He looked up to see the Dragon Kahg glaring down, red eyes shimmering in the fog. Another drop hit Skylan, this time on the nose.

Night's darkness was gone. The sun had risen, seemingly, though the Sun Goddess, Aylis, remained hidden beneath a blanket of fog. Angry at himself for having fallen asleep on watch, Skylan was about to push himself to his feet when he felt something hit the *Venjekar* and saw the prow of an ogre ship loom out of the fog and bump gently into the *Venjekar*'s hull.

Skylan froze. His first impulse was to shout the alarm. He hesitated, waiting to see what happened.

Nothing happened. No ogre watchman shouted a warning. No ogre godlord came running to see what was going on. The ogre ship rubbed up against the *Venjekar* like an affectionate cat.

Thinking that perhaps the ogres had all fallen asleep, just as he and his men had fallen asleep, Skylan slowly stood up, trying to move as silently as possible. The segmented, metal Sinarian armor rattled and clashed. Gritting his teeth at the noise that was as loud as a thunder strike in his ears, he tried to steal quietly across the deck to wake his men one by one.

Sigurd and Grimuir and Bjorn woke instantly, needing only a few words to understand the situation. Erdmun shrugged him off and tried to go back to sleep. His brother kicked him. Farinn jumped and stared at him in confusion. Acronis had awakened at the sound of Skylan moving about and had already drawn his sword. Wulfe, panic-stricken at the sight of the weapons, was shaking Aylaen. She rubbed her eyes and gazed blearily at him.

Skylan put his lips to her ear to whisper, "Ogre ship. Off the bow."

Aylaen could see for herself. She tried to stand. Skylan took hold of her hands to help her. Her fingers were cold and he clasped her hands fast, trying to warm them. Their eyes met and held for a moment until she lowered her eyes in confusion and drew back.

"You should go into the hold," said Skylan softly without thinking. He couldn't think, not when he could still feel her touch. "Take Wulfe with you."

"And get us murdered!" the boy cried shrilly. "Treia's down there!"

The men rounded angrily, glaring at Wulfe for talking so loudly. Aylaen swiftly muzzled him, clapping her hand over his mouth.

"I won't hide in the hold!" Aylaen whispered stiffly, not looking at Skylan. "You said I was a warrior, like the others."

He hesitated, trying to think of something to say to make up for his blunder.

"Skylan!" Sigurd hissed. "Get your butt over here!"

"You better go," said Aylaen in hushed frozen tones.

Skylan left, cursing his clumsy tongue, wondering why he always managed to say the wrong thing when he spoke to her.

"Any sign of ogres?" he asked.

Sigurd shook his head. "Damn strange, if you ask me. And take a look at this ship."

The ogre ship was larger than the *Venjekar*, more massive. Vindrasi dragonships were sleek, lightweight, designed for speed. Ogres ships were designed to carry ogres, a single one of whom weighed as much as two or three full grown human men. Ogres were not known for their seamanship, nor for their shipbuilding. Looking at the hull of the huge ship wallowing sluggishly in the water, Skylan wondered how it had managed to survive the long voyage from the ogre kingdom to Sinaria. The hull was covered with what looked like runes that had been burned into the wood. Perhaps the Gods of Raj had used their magic to keep it afloat.

The ship was much taller than the *Venjekar,* which sat low in the water. Skylan could not see the deck from this vantage point. He caught a glimpse of the tip of the boom in the swirling fog and then it vanished.

"I don't think anyone's on board," said Bjorn.

"Anyone *alive,*" Wulfe said ominously.

The Torgun were nervous. Given a choice, they would be much happier fighting for their lives against an army of ogres. None of them wanted anything to do with a ship sailing the seas without a crew.

Skylan didn't like this any better than his men. He could still feel the touch of the goddess, hear her voice. He remembered walking across that cold battlefield, the smell of smoke in his nose, the bodies of the little children . . .

"Shove the accursed thing off!" said Sigurd, picking up an oar.

"No, don't," said Skylan. "I'm going on board. Who's coming with me?"

Sigurd muttered something unintelligible and spit in the water.

"The bastards could be hiding, ready to ambush us," Grimuir pointed out.

"We'd smell their stench," said Skylan.

"I can't smell myself in this damn fog," said Erdmun.

"*I* can smell you," said Skylan, grinning.

Some of the men chuckled nervously at this. Sigurd grunted and shook his head, unamused.

"I'll come with you," Acronis offered. He added with a smile, "I have never been aboard a ghost ship."

If he meant that as a jest, no one laughed.

Thick lengths of rope hanging from the ship's bow trailed in the water. Skylan took hold of one of the ropes and pulled himself up, hand-over-hand, until he reached the upper deck.

Hidden in the eerie fog, he peeped over the rail before boarding the ship. The deck was empty, at least as far as he could see in the mist. Cautiously, he swung himself up and over the rail and landed on the deck, sword in hand. He roamed the ship, went down into the hold, and came back up on deck.

He was the only living being on board.

The fact did not bring him much comfort. If no one was alive, who had been sailing the ship?

He went back to the rail to hail the *Venjekar* and realized with a start the fog was lifting. He could see his ship. He was almost eye-to-eye with the Dragon Kahg. Below him he could see everyone gathered on the deck. Aylis, the sun goddess, was burning away Torval's miracle. They didn't have much time.

Skylan reached out a hand to assist Acronis, only to find Acronis did not need help. He climbed up the rope almost as nimbly as had Skylan.

"Not bad for an old man, eh?" Acronis said,

guessing what Skylan was thinking. "Zahakis insisted that I keep in training. He used to say, 'I will not serve a man who cannot see his feet past his belly.'"

"There is no one aboard, Legate. No bodies, no blood. What do you think happened to the ogres?"

Acronis walked the deck, gazed around. "They weighed the anchor and sailed off in haste. The lines we climbed had been tied to the pier. The ogres cut them and fled, leaving the ropes to drag in the water."

"Ogres are bad sailors," said Skylan.

"Not that bad," said Acronis dryly. "Look here. And here. And here." He pointed to parts of the bulkhead that were charred black. "I think this ship was attacked by that dragon. What did you call it?"

"Vektia dragon, sir," said Skylan grimly.

"The ogres were terrified and jumped overboard."

"Then they jumped to their deaths," Skylan said. "Ogres sink like rocks."

"True," said Acronis, adding quietly, "Given a choice between the dragon and drowning, they chose drowning."

"But then who was sailing this ship?" Skylan asked.

Acronis smiled, amused. "Ghost ships are a myth."

"You are a wise man, but I know better, sir," said Skylan. "I once sailed on a ghost ship."

"You must tell me that tale sometime," said Acronis with interest. "As to how the ship came to be here, that is no great mystery. The wind and the waves carried the ship farther out to sea."

Skylan thought this over, then realized he already knew who was sailing this ship. The same god who had sailed the ghost ship on which he had sailed. He stood for a moment, saying a silent prayer, then climbed back down the rope to the *Venjekar* to explain his plan to his people.

Before he had even finished, Sigurd had decided it wouldn't work.

"We won't fool anyone, Skylan." Sigurd snorted. "We can't make ourselves look like ogres."

"You don't have to look like ogres," said Skylan patiently. "With the help of the gods, by the time this fog lifts, you will be far enough away from their fleet that no one will be able to see you."

"We'll be sailing in a different direction from the rest of the ogre fleet," Grimuir argued, siding with his friend as usual. "The ogres will be suspicious and come after us."

Skylan sucked in a seething breath and clenched his fists, ready to give up trying to reason and start banging heads. Before he could say the words that would probably start a fight, Aylaen came forward. Up until now, she had remained silent.

"The ogres have suffered a great defeat in Sinaria. They have paid dearly for their attack on the city," she said. "The Vektia dragon killed many of them and now they are like us—weary and wounded. They want only to go back to their homes."

"She speaks wisely," said Acronis. "It is every

man for himself as far as they are concerned. No ogre godlord would risk his ship to help another or chase after some foe."

"This is a god-given opportunity," said Skylan. "Vindrash has sent this ship to us so that you can carry the warning to our people."

"About a dream," Sigurd said, shaking his head.

"I saw the body of your wife, Sigurd," said Skylan. "I saw your sons lying dead, your woman with her head cleaved open. I saw your house, Grimuir, a mass of charred rubble. I saw the Chief's Hall ablaze. I saw it as I see all of you. Aelon's ships took the Torgun by surprise. Our people must be warned that war is coming."

Sigurd eyed him. "You keep saying 'you,' not 'we.' What do you plan to do?"

"I am staying with the *Venjekar,*" said Skylan. "When we embarked on this voyage, before we were captured by Raegar, our plan was to sail to Grafdongar, to take back the Vektan Torque. I will continue our voyage. Acronis has offered to sail with me. He will be my guide."

Sigurd snorted. "The ogres will kill you both and seize our ship."

"The Dragon Kahg will sail the ship and keep it from falling into the wrong hands." Skylan shrugged. "If we are killed, the dragon will sail the ship back to our people."

"And what do I tell your father?" Sigurd asked gruffly. "What do I say to Norgaard when he wants to know why I sailed safely home and left his son behind to die?"

Skylan smiled. "You will tell my father that my wyrd is bound up in the *Venjekar*. My destiny lies with my ship. He will understand."

Skylan rested his hand on the older man's shoulders. "Go back to your boys, Sigurd. Take the other men home to their families. Send swift riders to the Chiefs, warning them to gather the clans for war."

Sigurd smiled briefly at the mention of his sons. He had once, in a rare moment of camaraderie, confided to Skylan how much he missed them. But he seemed still inclined to argue.

"Sigurd, we don't have much time—" Skylan began.

"We stand together," said Sigurd abruptly. "That is what you said and you were right, Skylan. We've come this far because we stayed together."

"We always will be together," said Skylan. "Even when we are apart."

He looked around at all the Torgun, at Grimuir and Sigurd, young Farinn, Bjorn and Erdmun, and Aylaen.

"We are bound by the secret of the Five Vektia dragons. All of you know this secret. Take this knowledge back to our people. If the Dragon Kahg returns home without me, you and the rest of the Vindrasi must continue the quest, find the Five, and bring them together."

"If you are certain . . . ," said Sigurd.

"Vindrash sent us this ship," said Skylan. "It is a sign."

"So be it," said Sigurd. Then he asked the question that had been on everyone's mind, though no one had mentioned it. "What do we do with Treia?"

"Throw her to the sharks," Wulfe muttered.

"They would be better off throwing you to the sharks, acursed foe," Treia hissed. The others had been so intent on their plans, they had not heard Treia emerge from the hold. She now walked slowly across the deck. With her weak eyes, she found it difficult to see where she was going. She was shivering in her wet priestess robes—robes that reminded everyone she was a traitor, a priestess for an enemy god. She had pulled her hair back and tied it behind her head. Her face was a pinched, rigid white mask with dark holes for eyes. Skylan decided that Keeper looked more alive.

Skylan was inclined to agree with Wulfe as to what to do with her, but he couldn't. Aylaen would never forgive him. He glanced at Aylaen, assuming she would do what she had always done in the past: support her sister. He was surprised when Aylaen did not stir. She remained standing with her hand protectively on Wulfe's shoulder. The men were looking at Treia and shifting uncomfortably. No one knew what to say.

"You are all fools if you think Vindrash sent you a ship!" Treia gave a contemptuous snort. She pointed her bony finger. "I will tell you who sent this ship. Death sent it and that is where this ship will take you! Raegar will find you. He is out there. He will find you."

She folded her arms across her chest and stood defiantly, gazing into the thinning mist.

Sigurd walked over to Skylan, jerked a thumb at Treia. "Well, what about her?"

"Treia stays with us," Skylan said, knowing even as he uttered the words, he would regret it.

"Good." Sigurd grunted. "I'd sooner set sail with a hold full of vipers." He hesitated, then said uneasily, "You don't believe her, do you? What she said about the ship?"

"She speaks for a god who enslaved us," said Skylan dismissively. He grinned at Sigurd. "Are you afraid of Raegar?"

Sigurd grinned back and replied with a fairly detailed account of what Raegar could do to himself, then began shouting orders.

The Torgun set to work. Some hauled supplies from the *Venjekar*'s hold to the ogre ship, which Sigurd had named *Torval's Fist,* for the god's hand had swept away the ogres. Others boarded the ogre ship to try, as Sigurd said, to figure out how the damn thing worked. The Vindrasi were accustomed to their sleek, swift dragonship, with its single mast and sail and banks of oars. The ogre ship was far larger, bulky and poorly built, with an odd-looking triangular sail and a rat's nest of rigging. The ogres had not had time to put the oars into the water before they were attacked, apparently, for the oars had not been fitted into the oarlocks. The Vindrasi stared in dismay at the gigantic oars that would take two humans to wield even one, and prayed to Torval that the wind would hold.

Skylan was about to go onto the ogre ship to help.

Aylaen blocked his way.

"You think you're going to send me with Sigurd," she said with a defiant toss of her head. "Well, you're not."

"Aylaen—" Skylan began.

"I won't leave, Skylan," Aylaen said. "My wyrd is also bound to the *Venjekar*. I'm Bone Priestess now. You need me to summon the Dragon Kahg."

Skylan led her off to the dragonhead prow where they could speak in private.

"You must take the spiritbone of the Vektia with you, Aylaen. No, wait, listen to me," he said, seeing her eyes flash. "You will take the spiritbone and sail with Sigurd. I will draw off Raegar. He will come after me."

"And he will kill you!" Aylaen said. "You said yourself he has fifty warriors on his ship!"

"He has to catch me first," said Skylan, grinning. "I travel light. His fifty warriors make for a heavy load."

"Be serious!" Aylaen said angrily.

"I am serious, Aylaen," said Skylan. He took hold of her hands, looked into her eyes. "Vindrash sent the ship so that you could take the spiritbone to a place of safety."

Aylaen let him keep hold of her hands, which astonished him. "The spiritbone is safe where it is.

And so am I. I already told you, my wyrd is bound with the *Venjekar*."

She walked off, leaving Skylan to stare after her, his wits so much sea foam.

"She routed you, my friend—foot, horse, and chariot," said Acronis, coming up to stand beside him. "I never saw a man lose a battle faster."

"I should *make* her go," Skylan said, frowning, though he had no idea how, short of knocking her unconscious.

Acronis clapped him on the shoulder. "Give up, Skylan. Make what terms for surrender you can and leave the field to her."

In the end, five chose to stay with Skylan and the *Venjekar*.

Wulfe was one, of course. He would never leave Skylan, despite the fact that the oceanaids were adamant that something bad was going to happen. Acronis was another. He would be needed to navigate. Skylan had been hoping the others would try to persuade Aylaen to go with them, but when she told the men she would be staying with the *Venjekar*, they accepted her decision. She was the Bone Priestess and her place was with the Dragon Kahg. Treia was staying, because no one knew what to do with her. Farinn's decision to stay with Skylan caused an uproar. He was the youngest. The men urged him to come.

"I order you to go," said Skylan.

Farinn shook his head. "I can't obey, sir. I won't leave in the middle of my song!"

"Your song is liable to be very short and have a very bad ending," said Skylan grimly.

Farinn flushed and shrugged. He didn't have the courage to look at Skylan, but he wouldn't budge either. He just kept shaking his head and at last Skylan gave up.

Within a short time, *Torval's Fist* was loaded with supplies and ready to sail. The time came for farewells.

The differences, the arguments, Sigurd's dislike of Skylan and his attempt to take over as Chief of Chiefs, Bjorn's loyalty to Skylan in defiance of Sigurd, the fights, the rivalries and animosity that had once loomed so large seemed very small and petty now. The good-byes were brief, especially as the wind was starting to freshen, coming out of the south like a breath from the god. The breeze would carry the ship northward, toward home.

A few awkward embraces, several attempts at jests, messages to carry to loved ones, and then Sigurd and his men boarded *Torval's Fist*. They spent a few tense moments trying to figure out how to steer the clumsy ogre vessel, then the triangular sail caught the wind and carried them over the gray and misty sea, into the fog, and they were gone.

Skylan stood watching until he could no longer see them. He was assailed by doubts.

In the shield wall, all the warriors stand together, shoulder to shoulder, their shields overlapping. Here he was surrounded by enemies, and he had shattered his shield wall, split his forces, sent his warriors away.

Because of a dream.

Wulfe wandered over to announce cheerfully that if the ogres killed Skylan, he, Wulfe, would change into a man-beast and rip out their throats.

"I'd rather they didn't kill you, though," Wulfe added after some thought.

"Me, too," said Skylan.

CHAPTER 6

The *Venjekar* drifted on the water, rolling on the uneasy waves. Torval's fog was now only scarf-like patches of mist hanging above the sea. The sun rose. It was morning. But what morning? Skylan had lost track of time. Today might be today or it might be yesterday or maybe tomorrow. He didn't suppose it mattered. He went to take the tiller. The Dragon Kahg had kept them from drifting in the fog. Now that the sun was up, Skylan would have to set a course.

As the wind whisked away the last vestige of mist, Farinn, who had been posted as lookout from the stern, gave a cry and Acronis, standing at the prow, gave a shout. Skylan did not know where to look first. He turned one direction to see an ogre ship with ogres clustered at the rail, gabbling in amazement at the sight of the sleek, dragon-prowed *Venjekar*. He turned the other way to see Raegar's war galley raising its anchor.

The ogre ship was closest, so close that Skylan could hear an ogre, presumably a godlord, roaring orders. Skylan could not see the activity on the deck, but he could judge by the sounds of clashing steel and thudding feet that the ogres were arming themselves.

Raegar's war galley was still some distance away. Lost in the fog, fearful of blundering unwittingly into the ogre fleet, Raegar would have given orders to drop anchor and lower the sails. Now that the fog was gone, he could resume his attempt to capture the *Venjekar*.

Acronis had his spyglass—what Wulfe called his "magic seeing glass"—to his eye.

"He's sighted us," Acronis reported to Skylan. "The war galley is sailing, though I'm not sure how. They don't have their sail raised and there are no rowers."

"Look at the dragonhead prow," said Skylan. "What do you see?"

Acronis shifted his spyglass. He gasped in astonishment. "I see a dragon! The dragon's head appears to be alive! I see gleaming scales. The mouth is wide open, the eyes flash . . ."

"Raegar has summoned his dragon," said Skylan. "The Dragon Fala is sailing the ship."

"I'll be!" Acronis let out a soft sigh. "Will we summon our dragon?"

That, thought Skylan grimly, was a damn good question.

Raegar's war galley—named *Aelon's Triumph*—sped toward them, white foam flying as the dragon imbued the ship with her power. It was yet some distance away. Skylan had first to deal with the ogres. He walked back to the stern. The ogres had raised their singular triangle-shaped sail, but the ship wasn't moving. Several ogres were now leaning over the rail, staring into the water, trying to figure out what was wrong.

"Their anchor's fouled," said Farinn.

"Thank you, Torval," Skylan said, and he looked back over his shoulder at Raegar's ship.

Aelon's Triumph slowed. Raegar must have spotted the ogre ship. Raegar was proceeding cautiously, not wanting to bite off more than he could chew.

Skylan had one more ship to worry about. He shifted his gaze to a lone ogre ship that was sailing entirely the wrong direction, heading east and north instead of toward the ogre realm to the west. The rest of the ogre ships apparently had risked sailing through the fog, for they were little more than specks on the sun-spangled sea. As Acronis had predicted, none of the other ogre ships were paying the least attention to their wayward brother. Nor would they be returning to assist the unfortunate ogre ship with the fouled anchor.

The godlord was bellowing curses at his men and keeping a wary eye on the *Venjekar*. Ogres knew and respected the dragonships of the Vindrasi nation. The godlord could see that Skylan had only a handful of crew, but he might well have warriors stashed in the hold. And now, judging by yells from the ogres, they had just spotted Raegar in his dragonship.

An interesting situation. The ogres feared Skylan would ally with Raegar, while Raegar feared Skylan would ally himself with the ogres.

And as if Skylan didn't have enough trouble,

Treia came up to talk to him. She had, of course, seen *Aelon's Triumph*. Treia's pale cheeks were tinged with a faint blush. She must believe her lover was coming to save her. She circled around the body of Keeper, catching hold of the hem of her bedraggled robes, holding them up so as not to brush against the corpse of the man she had murdered.

She glanced at Aylaen, but found no help there. Aylaen turned her face away, looked out over the restless sea. Undeterred, Treia came to join Skylan. He kept his hand on the rudder, his attention fixed on the ogres.

"I wanted to thank you, Chief of Chiefs, for saving my life in Sinaria," said Treia. She thought to flatter him by using the title that she herself had said he had no right to use. She even tried to insinuate some warmth into her tone.

She could have spared herself the trouble. Skylan didn't respond. He saw, out of the corner of his eye, Treia's glance slide to Raegar's dragonship and come back to Skylan, who smiled inwardly at her dilemma. Treia frowned, drummed her fingers on her arms.

"The ogre ship is helpless!" she said abruptly. "Why don't you flee while you have the chance? Your cousin Raegar's ship is filled with troops. He would gladly protect us."

"He would gladly make us slaves again," said Skylan grimly. "I would join my friend Keeper in Torval's Hall before I let that happen."

"That is because you are a warrior and live for

death," said Treia. "If you have no care for yourself, Skylan Ivorson, think of Aylaen. Will you sacrifice her to your pride?"

Skylan cast an uncertain glance at Aylaen and said nothing. Treia saw the look and, like a skilled swordsman, moved in for the kill.

"Raegar is your kinsman, Skylan. He never wanted to enslave you. Raegar was following the orders of that man—Legate Acronis. And yet you trust him more than your own kin. Raegar will let you go free, Skylan. You and Aylaen can sail back to your homeland. You will be welcomed as a hero."

"My cousin would do all this for me," said Skylan dryly. "Raegar is truly magnanimous. What does he expect in return?"

Treia missed the sarcasm.

"Give up the Vektia spiritbone," said Treia eagerly. "It doesn't belong to you anyway."

"It damn well doesn't belong to Raegar," said Skylan.

Treia lost her temper. "You will never win, Skylan. Your own gods are against you! If you continue with this quest, it will end in tragedy."

Skylan didn't trust Treia, but he was forced to acknowledge that she had once been a Bone Priestess, close to gods who must have granted her the power to use the Vektia spiritbone, though not the power to control it. Her words had the ring of truth. Skylan remembered the fury who had been sent to kill him, the druid's enigmatic warning about powerful enemies.

Treia saw by his furrowed brow and shadowed

eyes that she had struck a telling blow. She pursued her advantage.

"Give up this ill-fated journey, Skylan. Too many have died already."

"I will—" said Skylan.

Treia's face brightened.

"—after I send Raegar to his grave."

Skylan leaned on the rudder and steered the *Venjekar* straight toward the ogre ship.

"You fool!" Treia cried. "You will get us all killed!"

"Go crawl back in your hole," Skylan told her.

Treia swore at him and, grabbing up her skirts, ran to Aylaen and seized hold of her by the arm.

"Make him listen to reason, Sister! He will pay attention to you!"

Aylaen rounded on Treia.

"Do not call me 'Sister'!" Aylaen hissed the word. She grabbed Treia's hand and flung her back. "I have no sister."

"You will be sorry," said Treia vehemently.

She did not return to the hold, but stalked over to the stern and stood there by herself, her smoldering gaze fixed on Raegar's ship.

Wulfe had been hiding behind Aylaen until Treia left. Once she was gone, he hurried over to Skylan.

"I've been talking to the oceanaids," Wulfe reported. "They are worried. Something is wrong."

"Like that ogre ship bearing down us?" Skylan asked.

"This doesn't have anything to do with ogres," Wulfe said.

Skylan was concentrating on steering the ship so as to bring it alongside the ogre vessel.

Wulfe didn't like being ignored. "Do you remember the time the Sea Goddess sent that storm that nearly drowned us? The oceanaids warned me about that and I told you and you didn't listen."

"Is there a storm coming?" Skylan asked.

"I told you it was *like* that time," said Wulfe crossly. "I didn't say it *was* that time."

Skylan shook his head in exasperation. "I'll deal with your oceanaids later. Go tell Aylaen I need to talk to her."

Wulfe scowled, then did what he was told. Skylan kept his gaze on the ogre ship. The ogres had seen the *Venjekar* heading straight for them. Ogre warriors lined the ship's rails.

Skylan could imagine what the ogres must be thinking. The Vindrasi nation was far away and yet here was a Vindrasi dragonship, where no dragonship should be. The *Venjekar* had come out of the mists, stolen upon them as silently as a ghost. The ogres massed at the rail, their combined weight causing the ship to rock dangerously. The godlord yelled at them in a rage and the ogre heads disappeared as quickly as if they had all been lopped off. Skylan had counted at least twenty ogres.

Skylan looked up at the dragon. Kahg's eyes were bright. His spirit flowed through the ship, carrying the *Venjekar* over the water. Aylaen had returned.

"If you summon Kahg, will he fight?" Skylan asked.

"He will protect us. He might fight the ogres," Aylaen said. "But he won't fight Raegar's dragon, Fala. He is upset and angry. He feels he's been betrayed."

"Not by me!" Skylan said testily. "You know damn well Raegar's going to summon his dragon, send her to attack us. I'm surprised he hasn't already."

"Raegar needs us alive," said Aylaen. "To tell him where to find the spiritbone." She cast a glance at her sister. Treia stood by herself, her arms folded across her chest. She did not take her eyes off Raegar's ship.

Skylan muttered something under his breath. The Dragon Kahg had sharp ears, apparently, for his red eyes swiveled around to glare at him.

"You should take your sister and go down into the hold," said Skylan.

"You should go jump in the ocean," said Aylaen. She walked back to the prow. She was wearing the sword of Vindrash and with one hand on the hilt, placed the other trustingly on the dragon's neck.

Wulfe was back. "The oceanaids—"

"Go tell Aylaen," Skylan said. "Stay with her."

"But—"

Skylan glowered. "Do as I say or I swear by Torval I will throw you over the side and you can swim with your damn oceanaids."

Wulfe muttered something and walked off, his bare feet stomping angrily in the puddles on the deck.

Skylan sailed near enough to be within shouting distance of the ogres, then he deftly brought the ship alongside the ogre vessel. Keeping his hands where the ogre godlord could see them, Skylan reached down, drew his sword from its sheath, and slowly and deliberately placed it on the deck at his feet. Acronis did the same with his own sword. Farinn had managed to lose his axe along the way; no great loss, since he had never been particularly skilled with it. He had been posted beside Keeper's body that was still covered by the sail cloth. Not knowing what else to do, Farinn raised his hands in the air.

Aylaen unbuckled the sheath of the sword of Vindrash and laid sword and sheath on the deck. Wulfe was at her side, hopping from one foot to the other and apparently trying to tell *her* about his oceanaids, for Skylan heard Aylaen tensely order him to hold his tongue.

Skylan cast a swift glance at Treia, hoping she would not interfere. She was still watching Raegar's ship, which was still sailing toward them, though its speed had slowed now that they were near the ogres. Treia was not pleased. Her hands clenched to fists. Her lips moved.

"Here they come!" Acronis called in warning tones.

Thick lengths of rope snaked down over the side of the ogre ship, landing on the *Venjekar*'s deck. The ogres were going to climb down the ropes, board his ship, and kill them all.

Skylan filled his lungs with air and let out a shout that echoed across the sea. "I am called

Skylan Ivorson. I am Chief of Chiefs of my people. I am not here to fight! I am here to bring my brother home."

He gestured to Farinn, who lifted the sailcloth and drew it back to reveal the body. Keeper lay in state, his face and head painted, his hands holding his sword.

The ogres were taken completely by surprise. The godlord leaned over the rail for a better view. He was an imposing sight. Most ogres towered over Skylan. This ogre godlord towered over the other ogres. He must have stood eight feet tall.

His body was hulking and massive. He wore a heavy bearskin cloak. The paws wrapped around his neck, making him appear bigger. The godlord barked a command and another ogre joined him. At the sight of this second ogre, Skylan's jaw sagged. He stared in disbelief.

The feathers in the ogre's headdress were soaked and drooping; the ogre's blue and green feather cape was in sad shape, making him look as though he were molting. The black kohl the ogre wore around his eyes had smeared over most of his face. Yet Skylan had no trouble recognizing the ogre shaman who had used his base and cowardly magicks to snatch the sacred Vektan Torque of the Vindrasi out of Skylan's hand and carry it back to his ship and, presumably, back to the ogre realm.

Aylaen and Farinn also recognized the shaman; Skylan could tell by their amazed expressions. And so did Treia; *that* he could tell by her smile of bitter triumph.

"What do we do?" Farinn asked.

"Stick to the plan," said Skylan.

It was all he had.

The shaman also recognized Skylan, it seemed, for he was talking excitedly to the godlord.

"I am Bear Walker, Godlord of the Fleet," the ogre said proudly. "My shaman tells me that you have the blood of a godlord on your hands."

Skylan couldn't very well deny this, not without lying, and he'd had a bellyful of lies.

"My friend's name is Keeper of the Flame," Skylan called back. "He saved my life and I vowed I would honor him by bringing his body to his people."

Skylan jabbed a finger behind him, pointing to the burning city. "Like Keeper, I was a slave in that evil place. He helped me and my friends escape. When the fog came, I could have dumped his body and sailed safely to my homeland. I could have ordered my dragon to attack you. Instead, I come in peace, as you see. I risk my life to fulfill my vow to my friend."

In pointing to Sinaria, Skylan had also unfortunately drawn attention to Raegar's ship, moving slowly, but closing the distance between them. The godlord eyed the war galley that had been refitted with a dragonhead prow.

"This is a trick," said the godlord angrily. "You and your human friends plan to attack us."

"Those humans are *not* my friends!" Skylan shouted. "Their evil god, Aelon, seeks to enslave the Vindrasi people, as well as yours. I come to you *and* to the Gods of Raj in friendship. I will prove it if your ship will join my ship. We will fight them together."

The godlord conferred with the shaman. The shaman was opposed, but the godlord was clearly tempted. Skylan put himself in the godlord's place. The ogres had been close to defeating the Sinarians, so close they must have been able to taste the sweetness of victory. Then the Vektia dragon had appeared, attacking friend and foe alike, raining down flood and fire, terror and destruction, and forcing the victorious ogres to flee for their lives.

The ogres had lost the battle they had assured their people they would win. Their homecoming would be dismal, if not disastrous. This godlord, commander of the fleet, would be forced to confess that he and his troops had been routed—provided he lived long enough to confess anything. Ogres gained promotion through assassination and this godlord's standing among the other ogres must be extremely low. A few of those underlings must be thinking this was now their chance. Skylan was giving him a chance to strike a parting blow, salvage at least some of his honor.

Of course Raegar had his dragon, the young Dragon Fala. Raegar was now dependent on the power of the dragon to sail his ship. If he ordered her to attack Skylan, he would have to rely on the wind or the muscle in the arms of his rowers to sail his vessel. His galley's speed would be reduced to a crawl.

The godlord made a peremptory gesture, cutting off the shaman's argument, and ordered his warriors to draw up the boarding ropes. He was going to agree to the attack. Before Skylan could say a word, a piercing shriek caused his hair to stand on end.

Screaming Raegar's name, Treia began waving her arms and jumping up and down and pointing at something.

"She's gone mad!" Skylan said to himself.

Raegar was still some distance away, too far to hear or see her. Skylan looked to see what she was pointing at so wildly and saw another ogre ship. Treia was pointing at Sigurd, trying to draw Raegar's attention.

Skylan snorted. Let her yell herself hoarse. Raegar couldn't hear her from this distance.

"Raegar's ship is changing course, Skylan!" Acronis reported.

"What? That's not possible. How—" He looked at Acronis, who had his spyglass to his eye, and he knew how. Raegar must have a spyglass of his own. He could see Treia, if he could not hear her. He could see the deck of the *Venjekar*. What he would *not* see were Sigurd and the other Torgun warriors on board the ogre ship.

"Shut her up!" Skylan bellowed. "Take her below!"

But he was too late. The harm was done.

"Raegar's changed course," Acronis repeated, adding, "He's chasing after Sigurd. And as slowly as that ogre ship your goddess gave us is moving, Raegar's new dragonship has a fair chance of catching him."

Skylan was cursing his luck and wondering if Aylaen would care very much if he lopped off her sister's head when Farinn gave a warning shout. Skylan whipped around to see the ogre godlord flanked by ten ogres, all carrying massive spears.

All the spear points were aimed at Skylan.

"It was a trap!" the godlord roared.

"No, I swear by Torval—"

"I saw your female signaling to your friends! Surrender your ship to me or die!"

Skylan barely heard. He was instead focused on a strange sight. He could suddenly see the thread of his own wyrd stretching across the sea, running from the base of the World Tree, where the three Norn sat spinning, to where he stood on the *Venjekar*. As he watched, the thread split. One strand continued on unbroken toward the far horizon. The other stopped only a short distance ahead, slashed, cut short.

Skylan clasped the amulet of Torval around his neck and spoke a prayer. The threads remained and he knew the vision was real, sent to him by the god, and that it had to do with the decision he was about to make. The question: which wyrd was which? And should that even matter?

A spear thudded to the deck at his feet.

CHAPTER 7

"Be with me, Torval!" Skylan breathed, touching the amulet. He yanked the spear out of the deck and brandished it, holding it aloft, not threatening, but as a call to battle.

"I will prove that I am a friend!" Skylan shouted. He turned to Aylaen and said loudly, for all to hear, "Command the Dragon Kahg! We are going to attack Raegar's ship."

Aylaen stared at him, open-mouthed. She could command the dragon all she liked, but would he listen? Aylaen glanced at the spear-wielding ogres, gulped a little, and then clasped the spiritbone of the Dragon Kahg in her hand. Her lips moved. She reached down, dipped the spiritbone in one of the puddles.

"What is she doing?" Acronis asked, lowering his spyglass.

"Summoning the dragon," said Skylan. He added beneath his breath, "I hope . . ."

He waited tensely, keeping an eye on the ogres.

"They've freed their anchor," Farinn reported.

Aylaen cast the spiritbone in the air. The bone hung there for a moment. Skylan watched it, praying to every god in the pantheon that the Dragon Kahg would materialize.

The bone fell to the deck.

Aylaen cast Skylan a despairing glance. He sighed deeply and wondered what he was going to do next. The ogre godlord was arguing with the shaman, who was insisting that the dragonship was cursed and they should set it on fire and destroy it. The godlord—perhaps picturing himself returning home in triumph aboard the captured *Venjekar*—wanted to seize the ship. The godlord had no objection to killing Skylan and his people, but he wanted their ship.

Skylan picked up his sword and buckled it on.

"Skylan, look!" Aylaen cried.

The wooden dragon's head had changed into a living, breathing head. Carved scales, their paint worn and faded, glittered and sparkled brilliant green-blue in the sunshine. The mouth—open in a perpetual fang-revealing snarl—roared defiance. The dragon and the *Venjekar* were one.

"Brace yourselves!" Skylan shouted, grabbing hold of the mast. The *Venjekar* swung around and surged ahead, leaping over the ocean, the white foam churning beneath the keel, the white-tipped waves breaking over the bow.

The ogres were astounded by the ship's transformation from boat to dragon. A few flung their spears, but they fell harmlessly into the water. Then one ogre cried out and soon the others were roaring. They had spotted Sigurd in the ogre vessel. Having no way of knowing that this ogre ship wasn't being manned by ogres, the godlord must be thinking his odds had improved. He began issuing orders. His ship veered round to catch the wind, the sail billowed. The godlord was determined to gain himself a dragonship.

Skylan would have to deal with the ogres eventually. But now, one foe at a time.

With the *Venjekar* sailing under the dragon's control, Skylan hoisted up the useless rudder and stowed it on the deck, then went over to Acronis, who had resumed watching Raegar's ship. Acronis offered Skylan the spyglass. Skylan shook his head. He had tried looking into that glass and had been shocked when people who were far away suddenly leaped right in front him. He considered it unnatural.

"What's Raegar doing?" Skylan asked.

"Watching us," Acronis reported. "And chasing after Sigurd."

"And Sigurd?"

Acronis shifted the spyglass. He shook his head. "He's doing his best, but ogre ships were not built for speed."

"Do we have enough speed to stop Raegar before he reaches Sigurd's ship?"

Acronis smiled. "I've never sailed with a dragon before. I find the experience exhilarating, but it's throwing off my calculations."

He squinted, gazing out over the shimmering waves, measuring the distance with his eyes. "Yes, I think we will be able to reach Raegar before he reaches your friends." Acronis lowered the glass and chuckled. "Sailing with a dragon. I cannot wait to tell Chloe."

Reassured as to their chances of catching Raegar, Skylan looked back at the ogre ship. The ogres were falling behind, but they were still coming. That godlord was persistent. The shaman shook his fist and yelled something. Skylan, remembering the magic spell the shaman had cast on him, felt his skin crawl. He hoped they were too far for the magic to have any effect.

He watched the race, dragon against dragon. The two ships bounded over the waves. He could see for himself now that the *Venjekar* was gaining. For the moment, there was nothing to do except trust in Kahg. Aylaen cast a glance at him that seemed to invite him to come join her where she stood at the bow. The wind blew her hair back from her face. Her lips were parted, her eyes shining. Wulfe was beside her, leaning over the rail, shouting at the waves.

Skylan walked over to Aylaen. She moved closer to him. More nervous than he'd ever been standing in the shield wall, facing death, he held her hand. In the past she would have been offended, drawn away, made some caustic remark. Her cheeks flushed. She gave his hand a brief squeeze.

"If I died this moment," Skylan said, "I would go to Torval's Hall happy."

Aylaen's eyes darkened, changing in an instant from warm green to frozen gray. She stalked off, moving to the other side of the dragon.

Skylan stared after her, blinking in bewilderment.

"Why is she mad at me?" Skylan asked.

"Because you have cow turds for brains," said Wulfe. "And you never listen."

"I'm listening now," said Skylan with a sigh. "What do your fish friends have to say?"

"That it's too late."

The boy went back to pouting down at the creamy froth of the waves. Skylan cast a hopeful glance at Aylaen, but she was very pointedly not interested in him. She stood tall, her back rigid, her jaw set.

Skylan walked over to Acronis. "Did you hear what I said? Why is she angry? It was a compliment!"

"Ah, son," said Acronis with a shake of his head. "You may be a mighty warrior, but you are a mewling babe when it comes to love. The man whose spirit you freed in the Temple. His name was Garn, I think. Aylaen loved him and he died in battle. And now she is learning to love you and now *you* talk about dying. She is not angry. She is afraid."

Skylan could have kicked himself. "I never thought about it that way. Why is it that every word I say to her comes out wrong?"

"Because those words come from your heart, not your head," said Acronis. He kindly changed the subject. "We're definitely gaining on Raegar."

Skylan could see that for himself. The gap between the two ships was rapidly closing. He was glad to be able to turn his thoughts from love to such uncomplicated subjects as war and death.

"Raegar's dragon is growing tired. She has traveled a far distance, all the way from Sinaria."

Acronis regarded Skylan with interest. "How is that possible? Will our dragon tire?"

"Dragons are strong, but they lack stamina and endurance," Skylan explained. "They can fly only short distances before they must stop to rest, which is why they sail the seas with us in search of the gemstones that are Ilyrion's blood. Kahg is rested."

Sounds of beating drums echoed over the water.

"That's interesting," said Acronis. "Raegar is ordering the rowers to take their positions. See, they are fitting the oars into the oarlocks."

The rowers thrust their oars in the water. The drummer pounded, beating out the time. The oars moved rhythmically, blades flashing in the sunlight, water sparkling and splashing as the oars plunged into the waves. The rowers aboard the war galley were not slaves. They were men of the city, proud of their job and skilled at their work. The rowers propelled the galley through the water, though the pace was slower than when the Dragon Fala had been sailing the ship.

Sigurd was now starting to pull away. The Dragon Kahg kept the *Venjekar* on course, aiming at Raegar's ship. Behind them, the ogre ship was trying gamely to overtake the *Venjekar*. They could not hope to keep up with the speed of the dragon through the water. The ogre godlord and the shaman stood at the prow of their ship that was falling behind, but still in the chase.

"Raegar has removed something from the dragon's carved neck," Acronis reported, staring intently through the spyglass. "I can't make out what—"

"His dragon's spiritbone," Skylan guessed, glancing at the spiritbone of the Dragon Kahg that again hung on a leather thong suspended from the carved dragonhead. "Of course, that's why he's using the rowers. He's going to summon his dragon."

Aylaen had reached the same conclusion, apparently, for she left her position near the dragon's head to hurry over to talk to them.

"Aylaen, I'm sorry," Skylan said as she drew near. "I wasn't thinking."

"That's because you have turds for brains," she told him. She turned to Acronis. "Raegar has his spiritbone. I need to know what he is doing."

"He's lighting an oil lamp," said Acronis, sounding amazed. "Broad daylight and he's lighting a lamp . . ."

Aylaen hesitated, then she reached out.

"Let me have the magic glass," she said. "I need to see for myself."

Acronis handed over the spyglass. Aylaen put it to her eye, looked where Acronis pointed. Raegar seemed to leap in front of her and she gave a start, just as Skylan had done when he first used it. Aylaen lowered the glass, regarded it with frowning suspicion.

"I don't like this magic."

"It is science, my dear, not magic," said Acronis mildly. "Someday I will explain how it works. Look again. You will get used to it."

Aylaen raised the glass reluctantly and forced herself to look through it.

"He's holding the spiritbone over the flame of the oil lamp. He's going to summon a fire dragon."

"I take it this is magic," said Acronis. "Not science. If you could explain . . ."

"Dragons have the ability to take their shape and form from the elements," said Aylaen. "The Bone Priestess dips the spiritbone in the element she believes is best-suited to her needs. You saw me splash water on the spiritbone of the Dragon Kahg. He is a water dragon now."

"Raegar has decided he's going to summon a fire dragon," said Skylan grimly. "He's likely going to order his dragon to set fire to our ship. Once Fala has destroyed us, she will go after Sigurd, set fire to his ship."

"The Dragon Kahg would never allow that," said Aylaen firmly.

"Raegar's dragon will be hard to stop if *our* dragon won't fight!" Skylan said, speaking loudly.

Kahg's red eye swiveled in his direction, a spark gleamed, the eyelid flickered. The dragon did not slow his speed through the water. The *Venjekar* flew at *Aelon's Triumph,* slicing through the waves. Acronis took the glass. He watched a moment, his expression thoughtful, then he handed the glass back to Aylaen.

"You are saying that Raegar plans to summon the fire dragon, cause it to come blazing to life." Acronis shook his head. "Your cousin Raegar is a fool. He will have a mutiny on his hands."

"Because of the dragon?" Skylan was puzzled. "His soldiers should be pleased to know that a dragon is going to fight with them."

"That is how a Vindrasi warrior would think," said Acronis. "You've been around dragons all your life. The first dragon those men saw just destroyed their city, slaughtered thousands. How do you think they're going to react when a dragon bursts into life over their heads?"

"An uprising against Raegar won't matter to us if his dragon sets the *Venjekar* on fire," Skylan pointed out.

Aylaen was keeping watch on Raegar through the magical glass. Skylan marveled at how quickly she had taken to using it. Science . . . magic . . . one and the same to him. He didn't take to either.

"Raegar is chanting," Aylaen reported. "I can see his lips moving."

"How would he know the ritual to summon a dragon?" Skylan asked. "He's not a Bone Priestess."

"The Dragon Fala must have told him," said Aylaen. "The rituals we use for our dragons are ancient, but they originated with the dragons."

A ball of fire burst in the air above the war galley and the Dragon Fala came into being. Her scales were bright burnished-orange, her crest reddish-gold, and her eyes blazed red. She was long and slender and graceful. The sunlight shone through her diaphanous wings. She opened her mouth and fire flared from her jaws. Her talons trailed flame. Raegar gazed up at her in pride. But in a moment, he was engulfed in chaos.

Raegar—thinking like a Vindrasi—had not bothered to prepare his crew and, as Acronis had predicted, the sight of a dragon blazing to life right above them sent the crew of *Aelon's Triumph* into panic. The drummer beating out the time stared up at the dragon, let out a horrified shriek, and flung himself to the deck, knocking over the drum. The rowers were stationed belowdecks and they could not see what was happening. They heard the scream, however, and the sudden silence when the drumming ceased in mid-count.

Some stopped rowing, while others continued. The blades crashed into each other. Heavy oar shafts rebounded back on the rowers, striking them in the head or chest, knocking them from the benches. On the deck above, sailors were crying out in terror; the soldiers were grabbing up their spears, ready to hurl them at the dragon. The archers were taking aim with their bows and Raegar was running across the deck, bellowing that the dragon was on their side. Two spears arced toward the dragon. Fala snorted a puff of flame at them and they went up in smoke. She cast an annoyed glance at Raegar, who was knocking the weapons out of the hands of his men.

Skylan grinned. He almost felt sorry for his cousin.

Almost, but not quite.

The Dragon Fala flew toward the *Venjekar*, her wings trailing fire.

CHAPTER
8

Fala was a young dragon, proud and vain and arrogant. The Dragon Kahg had known many such dragons down through the years and he might have dismissed her as a heedless, reckless youngster. But the Dragon Fala was different, unlike any other dragon Kahg had ever known. She was an apostate. She had abandoned her faith in the Dragon Goddess, Vindrash, to give her loyalty and service to one of the new, upstart gods. The Dragon Kahg was more curious than afraid. He wanted to know why.

Most dragons believed that their goddess, Vindrash, was lost or dead. Some were starting to think she and the Old Gods had fled. There would be many more like Fala soon, for as yet Vindrash did not dare reveal herself. The servants of their enemies had seen the power of the Vektia spiritbones and they had learned the secret to wielding that power.

The Dragon Kahg was angry at Vindrash, angry for lying to him and their people about the Vektia spiritbones, angry for telling him they were mighty dragons, the mightiest of their kind, godlike and wonderful. But when the Vektia dragon appeared, Kahg saw that it was no dragon. It was death made in the image of a dragon. Death made in the mockery of dragons.

Kahg remembered what the fey child, Wulfe, had said about it. *It's old. Really, really old. It used to run wild, but then the gods of the Uglies captured it and kept it chained up.* The power of creation was captured when the Dragon Ilyrion fell.

The Dragon Kahg knew the truth. Vindrash was not dead, nor lost, nor had she fled the world. She had gone into hiding. Kahg was the only dragon she trusted. She may trust him, but now he was not certain he trusted her. He and the elders believed they had discovered the true nature of the Vektia dragons. If so, Vindrash had not exactly lied to the dragons. She had just not told them everything.

He eyed the Dragon Fala flying high above the waves, shimmering orange and red.

"So you are the mighty Dragon Kahg," Fala taunted him, her voice booming. "Come do battle with me, mighty Kahg."

"You are the traitor dragon, Fala," Kahg returned.

Fala laughed in disdain. "Traitor? What have I betrayed?"

"Our Dragon Goddess, Vindrash," said Kahg.

Fala hovered in the air, did not fly immediately to attack him. She was probably delighted with her own importance, glad to talk about her favorite subject—herself. She would be eager to proclaim her views on life to this old dragon, who was too weary or too cowardly to engage her in combat.

Kahg was keeping watch on Sigurd's ship, which was slowly if steadily pulling away. Kahg could see Fala was tired. He would keep her in conversation, allowing her to tire herself still further.

"Humans!" Fala snorted a gout of flame. "Look at them on board my ship, running about pissing themselves at the sight of my glory."

"Why do you serve them?" Kahg asked.

"I *use* them, I don't serve them," Fala said with scorn. "I pretend to go along with the whims of Raegar, who stupidly believes he is my master. But, unlike you, mighty Dragon Kahg, I do the humans' bidding because I am being well paid. The humans have promised me jewels. They have a treasure vault filled with them."

"Have they given you any jewels yet?"

"No, but they will."

"And what does the god Aelon promise you?" Kahg asked.

"Is that his name?" Fala asked languidly, flying lazy circles above Kahg's head. "There are so many gods tromping about heaven these days I don't know one from the other. I care for no gods, any gods. Why should I? They have no care for us."

That much is true, Kahg thought bitterly.

"You know that if this Aelon succeeds in driving out the Old Gods, we dragons are next," he said. "We are a threat to Aelon's power. He will kill us or drive us off and then seal the entrance to this world."

"That old cow Vindrash *would* say that, wouldn't she?" Fala sneered. "Anything to keep us subservient. Aelon proclaims that he will welcome dragons to his world."

"Gods lie," said Kahg.

Fala shook her head. Flames rolled off her crest. "I grow weary of all this talk," she said, annoyed.

"You are just plain growing weary," Kahg said dryly. He cast a glance down at his humans. They were well-trained, bracing themselves for the fight, trusting in their dragon. "For days you hauled that war galley across the sea from Sinaria. And now you think you have energy enough left to do battle."

Fala was angry. "Very well, coward dragon, Kahg. We will see who is weary when I slay you and set fire to your ship!"

"Which is what you should have done in the first place, you silly twit!" Kahg roared, laughing.

Fala shrieked at him, furious, and dove down at Kahg. Her wings trailed fire, her breath roared flames that seared Kahg's scales. The pain was not severe, but it made him angry. Kahg roared and then ducked his head into the ocean, as though he were trying to douse the fire. He sucked in a belly full of seawater, raised his head, and spewed the water at his foe.

The blast struck Fala in the chest and sent the

startled dragon reeling. Her wings flapped wildly as she tried desperately to maintain altitude. Kahg sucked in more water and hit her again. The second blast flipped her over and knocked her from the air. Fala plummeted into the sea, steam rising from her floundering body.

Fala thrashed and fought to keep from sinking as white, foaming waves broke over her head. She choked and coughed and sputtered. Waves struck her repeatedly, slamming into her from behind, crashing over her crest.

Kahg watched with grim amusement as the young dragon paddled her legs like a dog, struggling to keep herself afloat. She glared at Kahg in rage. Her jaws worked. She opened her mouth to roast him alive. A wave hit her in the nose and she began to cough and choke.

"Your human is in trouble, Fala," Kahg advised. "You had better return to him. And you might tell him, by the way, no experienced Bone Priestess on board a ship in the middle of the ocean would ever make the mistake of summoning a fire dragon, especially when confronted by a dragon formed of water."

Kahg added in scathing tones, "And no intelligent dragon would ever permit it."

Fala started to say something, but nothing came out except seawater. She thrashed her legs and flapped her wings and managed, after a few failed attempts, to drag her heavy body up out of the waves. Water poured from her like rain.

Aelon's Triumph was in almost as sad a state as

its dragon. The war galley wallowed in the sea, surrounded by pieces of broken oars floating on top of the water. Raegar was on the foredeck yelling at his dragon, exhorting her to continue her attack.

Fala shook her head sullenly, sending down a flurry of water, refusing to obey. The young dragon had been made to look foolish, her pride wounded. She undoubtedly hated the Dragon Kahg with all her being, but she was too exhausted to fight. Kahg watched her fly off slowly, heading toward the nearest shore to rest and recover, leaving Raegar to shout after her in helpless rage. When men on his ship raised a cheer as they watched the dragon depart, Raegar swore at them and then ordered them to raise the sail.

"This is not over between us," Fala snarled over her shoulder.

"Come back when you grow up," Kahg told her.

On deck, his humans were celebrating, laughing at the dragon's humiliation and jeering across the water at Raegar. The human, Skylan, was urging Kahg on, urging the dragon to attack.

The other humans in the ogre ship were in no danger; they were putting more and more water between their ship and *Aelon's* so-called *Triumph*.

The Dragon Kahg considered his options.

Skylan stood on the deck of the *Venjekar,* his sword in hand, thrilled with the thought of avenging himself on his treacherous cousin. Raegar had counted on the strength of his dragon to destroy his enemies. He had never imagined that she could be defeated, or that his men would turn on him. Raegar was out here on the sea alone, with a ship full of demoralized troops. The fearful sight of the Dragon Kahg bearing down on them would unnerve them further.

Behind him, the godlord's ship, at the sight of the fire dragon, had slowed, keeping well out of the way. The vague outlines of a plan formed in Skylan's mind. He would send Kahg to destroy Raegar's ship in full view of the ogres. After that, Skylan would sail in triumph back to the ogres. He would offer them friendship while the Dragon Kahg circled overhead, letting them know what would happen to them if they declined. He would ask them to take Keeper's body, fulfilling his vow to his friend. Then he would boldly demand that they escort him safely to the ogre homeland.

"I will make up some reason," he said, explaining his plan to Aylaen. "I will tell them I've come to talk peace with their godlords. We will find the Vektan Torque and steal it back. But first"—Skylan gripped his sword—"I will settle my score with Raegar."

He realized suddenly that the *Venjekar* was slowing.

"What is the dragon doing?" Skylan asked angrily. "Tell Kahg to maintain course! We're going to fight—"

He saw the expression on Aylaen's face. "Now what's wrong?"

"The Dragon Kahg won't fight," said Aylaen. "He says we are in no danger and he won't risk the Vektia spiritbone for some petty human desire for vengeance."

The *Venjekar* was turning, maneuvering through the water.

"Kahg says we are going home."

Aylaen's eyes glistened with sudden tears. She lowered her head, averted her face.

"No!" Skylan cried. "He can't do that! We have a chance . . ."

His words died. He looked at Sigurd's ship, sailing north, up the coastline. Heading home. Skylan thought of his homeland. He thought of his father, the fields and the forests, fishing in the clear bright streams, playing games on the frozen lake. To bask in the warmth of a fire on a snow-silent night. To hear the laughter of his people as they gathered together in the Hall.

The two threads of his wyrd, one long, the other cut short. He remembered his dream. The serpents of Oran, the armies of Oran were marching to destroy his people.

Skylan would meet up with Sigurd, the two ships would sail home. Then he would wed Aylaen and she would be Kai Priestess. He would be Chief of Chiefs and this time he would try to be a wise and worthy chief. He would lead the Vindrasi in their fight against the armies of Aelon and when Aelon had been defeated, Skylan would raise a mighty army, command many dragonships that would sail to the ogre lands and beyond to find the Vektia spiritbones.

"We are going home," said Skylan. His spirit seemed to soar over the waves, carrying him to Vindraholm.

CHAPTER

9

Treia, forgotten in the excitement, had fled down into the hold. Frustrated and upset, fearful Skylan would kill her, she paced restlessly, sometimes stopping to watch what was going on through a chink in the wooden planking. She had rummaged through the supplies of food and weapons she herself had provided to the Torgun warriors as part of a plot to lure them to their deaths until she found a knife, which she used to whittle away at the chink until she had a good view of Raegar's ship—though with her poor eyesight, all she could see was a smudge on the ocean.

And all she could think about was Raegar.

Was he thinking of her? Did he know she was on board the ship? Had he come to rescue her? Or had he come to accuse her for summoning the dragon that had destroyed his city and his hopes and dreams?

"It was not my fault, my darling," she whispered, restlessly twisting the fingers of her cold hands as she paced the deck. "I was tricked. Hevis tricked me into summoning the dragon. Hevis knew I wouldn't be able to control it. This is his doing."

Treia tried to ignore the fact that she had not given Hevis his sacrifice. The god had demanded that she kill someone dear to her. In return, he would grant her the power to summon the Vektia dragon. Unfortunately, Treia's choice of victims were sadly limited. She hated her stepfather, despised her mother, and intensely disliked all of her kindred clan. That narrowed her selection to two people: her lover, Raegar, and her sister, Aylaen. At that point, the choice was easy.

Treia loved Raegar with a soul-consuming passion. She would have sacrificed herself before him. Treia had loved Aylaen because Aylaen was the only person who loved her. Now that love was gone, and Treia hated her sister. Aylaen had been marked for death and she had perversely gone on living, ruining Treia's deal with Hevis.

"Except that Hevis never truly had any power to give," Treia muttered bitterly. "He gave me the ability to summon one of the Vektia dragons, when all the time he knew that in order to control one, I had to summon all five. He tricked me! None of this was my fault. Yet I am the one being made to suffer."

Treia stared longingly through the hole in the hull at her lover's war galley and cursed the gods who had given her such poor eyesight. The ship was a fuzzy, wood-colored blur. By squinting, she thought she could discern Raegar at the prow near the head of the dragon. She could tell it was him because he was taller by far than the people of Sinaria. Being Vindrasi, he was fair-complected, whereas the Sinarians were brown-skinned. And Raegar was bald, his head shaved in the manner of the priests, and he was wearing armor—both his bald head and his armor gleamed in Aelon's blessed light.

Treia heard Skylan give the order for the *Venjekar* to chase and attack the war galley. Her lip curled. He was bluffing. He would never risk his own precious skin, nor that of his darling Aylaen. He wouldn't risk harming the Vektia spiritbone, now that he had one in his possession.

She watched Raegar summon his Dragon Fala, sending her to slay Skylan and all the rest of the fools, and her heart thrilled. That would be an end to her ordeal. She would be reunited with her lover. Watching Raegar stroking the neck of the carved dragon that graced the prow of the war galley, Treia couldn't help but wonder why Raegar had kept secret the fact that a dragon had come to serve him.

"If he truly loved me, he would have told me . . ."

The thought pained her. As a Bone Priestess who had summoned dragons before, she could have given him advice.

Such as never summon a fire dragon over water.

Treia watched in agony as the fire dragon burst into life above the war galley and watched with gloomy foreboding as the young dragon flew toward the *Venjekar.* Treia could almost hear the Dragon Kahg chuckling as the wet and demoralized young dragon flew away.

What now? Fear clutched Treia. Raegar was attempting to quell the panic on board his ship and hoist the sail. From the deck above, she could hear Skylan ordering the dragon to proceed with the attack.

Treia smiled in satisfaction. She could always count on Skylan's stupidity and his arrogance. Raegar and his soldiers would make short work of Skylan.

And then the ship lurched beneath Treia's feet. The *Venjekar* slowed and began to change course.

"No!" Treia gasped, as she caught sight of Raegar's ship dwindling in the distance.

"We are going home." Aylaen's voice came down from above, echoed hatefully in the shadows of the hold.

Treia picked up the knife.

The Dragon Kahg was not about to make the same mistake Fala had made. He left the sailing of the *Venjekar* to the humans aboard the ship. He remained with the *Venjekar* in spirit—his red eye was a fiery slit in the dragonhead prow. He left his physical body, returning his spirit to the spiritbone.

The wind blew steadily. The sea was unsettled, lead-colored, and restless. Oily waves slapped the hull from all directions, tossing salt spray over the bow. Skylan shouted at Farinn to help him and together they raised the *Venjekar*'s sail, while Acronis took the tiller.

The sail flapped and then filled. The wind caught the *Venjekar* and carried the ship through the waves and Skylan breathed easier. He looked back at the ogre ship. They had caught the same wind and were chasing after him. He would win this race; his ship was lighter and more maneuverable, and he was a better sailor. Still he didn't like to see that triangular sail dogging him.

"Why don't they give up the chase and go home?" Skylan wondered aloud, annoyed.

"Because they'll never make it home," said Acronis. He pointed at the ogre vessel. "Their ship is taking on water. It's sinking beneath their feet. It's not us they want. It's our ship."

"By Torval, you're right!" Skylan said, studying the ogre ship.

He was about to add, "They'll never catch us—" when Wulfe gave a shrill, gurgling shriek. The piercing sound was inhuman and dreadful and Skylan nearly leaped out of the ship.

His heart pounding, Skylan rounded furiously on the boy. "Damn it, don't ever do that—"

Wulfe had gone white beneath his tan. He pointed, his hand shaking.

Treia stood holding Aylaen, pressing a knife blade to her neck.

"Lower the sail," Treia ordered.

"Skylan, don't—" Aylaen began, and then gasped as Treia pricked her throat with the knife. Blood glistened on her skin.

"Farinn, lower the sail," said Skylan, not taking his eyes off Treia.

Farinn ran to obey. The sail fell in folds. The *Venjekar* wallowed in the restless waves. Skylan glanced at Raegar's ship, *Aelon's Triumph,* now gaining on them. The ogre ship was gaining, too, but Raegar's ship was faster and would reach them first.

"I've done what you asked, Treia," Skylan said. "Let Aylaen go."

"Give me the spiritbone of the Vektia," said Treia. "If you don't, I'll kill her."

"He can't give it to you," said Aylaen. "He doesn't know where I hid it. If you kill me you'll never find it."

Treia glowered and jabbed Aylaen with the point of the knife. Blood flowed down her neck. Skylan could see that Treia meant what she said. In another moment, she would cut Aylaen's throat.

"I'll give you the spiritbone, Treia," said Skylan. "Aylaen, tell me where it is."

"I won't!" Aylaen said stubbornly, through gritted teeth.

"Aylaen," Skylan pleaded, "this is not worth your life. Tell me—"

He was interrupted by a growl, low and rumbling, primal and savage, sending a shiver through Skylan, raising the hair on his arms. Wulfe had disappeared. In his place was a beast—a wolf with yellow eyes and gray, scraggly fur. The wolf opened his mouth, his lip curled, revealing sharp fangs. His ears flattened back on his head. His tail swept slowly from side to side. He made no sound. Breaking into a lope, he ran at Treia, who stared at the man-beast with wide, terrified eyes.

Aylaen twisted out of her sister's grasp. The knife blade sliced her neck as she escaped. Skylan met her, caught her in his arms.

The wolf had Treia penned like a sheep in the fold. She was backed into the bulkhead and there was nowhere to run. The wolf growled menacingly and slowly advanced, one paw after the other. Treia screamed and moaned.

"Wulfe, no! Stop!" Aylaen cried. "Don't hurt her!"

The wolf snarled and crouched, one foreleg raised, staring at Treia with yellow eyes. The wolf's lips parted, his mouth opened, his teeth gleamed. He stole a step nearer.

Treia shrieked and threw the knife wildly at the wolf, then grabbed hold of the rail and pulled herself up onto it. She hung precariously a moment, staring into the gray sea. The wolf lunged at her, jaws snapping. Treia gave a panicked cry and leaped into the waves. Aylaen ran to the side and leaned over the rail, trying to see what had become of her.

Acronis steered the ship near the place where Treia had jumped. The *Venjekar* rolled sluggishly in the waves. Treia was nowhere in sight. Skylan was thinking she must have drowned, when her head suddenly broke the surface of the water. Treia floundered, gulping water and coughing. She looked up at Aylaen and then looked in the direction of Raegar's ship. She couldn't see *Aelon's Triumph* for the waves that were rising and falling all around her. Skylan could see it. The ship was close enough he could see Raegar without the need for Acronis's magic glass. Raegar could see them as well.

Treia's now heavy robes were pulling at her. She raised her arms and tried to cry out. A wave swamped her and she went down. Aylaen gave a little gasp and covered her mouth with her hand.

Treia resurfaced. Her face was white and streaming water. She choked and gagged. Her eyes pleaded for help.

The ogre ship had also gained on them. It was near enough now that Skylan could hear the god-lord shouting orders.

The ogres and Raegar can fight over us, Skylan thought grimly.

He grabbed one of the wooden oars and threw it down to Treia.

"Hold on!" he cried, and began to strip off his armor, ready to jump in.

He was astonished to feel Aylaen's restraining hand on his arm.

"Don't," she said.

"I can't stand by and watch a woman drown," Skylan said gruffly. "Not even Treia."

"She won't drown," said Aylaen.

Treia had managed to flounder her way through the waves and was now clinging to the oar.

"Remember when Zahakis was chasing us and you threw Acronis into the water," Aylaen said.

"You told us that Zahakis would be forced to stop chasing us to save him. You were right. We escaped."

Aylaen looked back toward Raegar's ship. "He'll stop to save her."

Skylan was doubtful. "Are you sure Raegar loves her enough to stop to rescue her?"

"She summoned the Vektia dragon," said Aylaen. "Even if he doesn't love her, she's useful to him." She shrugged. "But, yes, odd as it may seem, I do think he loves her."

Treia clutched her oar, bobbing in the water.

"Farinn, raise the sail!" Skylan ordered. "Acronis, take us back on course."

Treia heard and she glared at them with such fury in her eyes that Skylan marveled the sea didn't start to boil. Raegar stood at the prow of the war galley, pointing to Treia, directing the helmsman to guide the war galley toward her.

The *Venjekar* came into the wind, gathering speed. The ogre ship had gained on them, but the *Venjekar* was once more bounding over the waves. With this wind, Skylan would soon leave the ogres and Raegar behind.

Aylaen gingerly put her hand to her neck and drew back her fingers, covered in blood.

"She meant to kill me," Aylaen said. "She would have, if Wulfe hadn't—"

She stopped, looked around in alarm. "Skylan, where is Wulfe?"

Skylan had been concentrating on his foes and forgotten the fae child, the man-beast. Skylan looked around the deck. He didn't see the boy and wondered if the wolf had run down into the hold and, if so, would he have to go down there after him?

He took a step and then saw Acronis pointing.

Wulfe was curled like a wild thing on a pile of rope, his head to his knees. He was naked and shivering, but so exhausted he didn't even feel the chill. Skylan walked over to stare down at him. This wasn't a boy. This was a monster. He glanced at Acronis, who shook his head, not in anger, but not sure he believed what he had seen. Farinn looked sick.

"He could kill us all," said Skylan.

Aylaen knelt down beside Wulfe and brushed the hair out of the boy's eyes. "But he didn't. He saved my life. Take him below. Let him sleep."

Skylan lifted Wulfe in his arms. The boy stirred, but didn't wake as Skylan carried him down into the hold. The bedding was soaked. At least here the boy was out of the wind. Aylaen rummaged through sea chests until she managed to find a relatively dry shirt. She wrapped the shirt around Wulfe. He woke a little, blinked in confusion, mumbled something, and lay down, yawned, and closed his eyes.

Aylaen and Skylan stood together, staring down at him. Then Aylaen shivered and Skylan put his arm around her and drew her close.

"I love you, Aylaen," said Skylan. "I can never take Garn's place . . ."

Aylaen lifted her head.

"You have your own place in my heart, Skylan. I have loved both you and Garn since we were little."

She sighed and added, "I think I loved you more. But loving Garn was easier. Loving you . . . You made it difficult."

Skylan hesitated. "When I asked before if you would marry me, you always said no."

"I said no because you never 'asked,' " Aylaen told him. "You demanded that I love you. You expected me to fall into your arms, like all the others."

Skylan thought back and smiled ruefully. "I was a fool."

"Yes," she said, smiling.

"Yes, I was a fool or yes, you will marry me?"

"Both," said Aylaen.

Their fingers twisted, locked.

"From this moment, our two wyrds are one," she said.

Skylan felt truly happy. He wished he could stay here forever. But nothing ever lasted forever. He thought of his two wyrds, one long. One short.

"Skylan!" Farinn shouted. "Come look!"

"You should stay here, bandage that wound," Skylan told Aylaen.

"It's stopped bleeding," she said. She paused, then said, flushing in embarrassment, "I know this sounds stupid, but I need to make certain Treia's safe."

He kissed her, standing at the bottom of the ladder.

"Skylan!" Farinn shouted.

"I'm coming," Skylan called back.

He and Aylaen went up together.

"Look. You were right," said Farinn triumphantly. "Raegar's stopped to save her."

Raegar was on deck, directing operations. Two men who could swim were in the water, tying a rope around Treia's waist. She held fast to the rope with her hands and several of those aboard the galley, including Raegar, hauled her up over the side and onto the deck. Once she was safely aboard and the men who had saved her were back on the ship, Raegar stood on the deck, his gaze fixed on the *Venjekar*.

Skylan picked up the spyglass and put it to his eye. He had to search for the galley as the sky and the sea bounced around, up and down, making him dizzy. Then he found the galley and he found Raegar. He seemed so close Skylan could have reached out and slugged him.

The two gazed steadily at each other.

Raegar looked about as bad as Skylan knew he himself must look. Raegar's armor was wet. His shaved head, with the tattoo of the serpent of Aelon, glistened with sweat. He was grim with anger and frustration and fatigue. Raegar had lost his dragon. His crew was on the verge of mutiny. He had no choice but to sail back to Sinaria.

A half-drowned and half-dead Treia came into view. She tried to put her arms around Raegar. He shook her off.

"He's probably thinking he made a bad bargain," Skylan commented to Aylaen.

He continued to watch as Treia seized hold of Raegar's arm and said something to him. She held up her hand, the fingers spread wide.

Five fingers spread wide.

"The secret of the Vektia. She *does* know it," said Skylan.

"And now so does Raegar," said Aylaen.

The guards escorted Treia below decks. She went meekly, her head bowed, now and then casting her lover a backward glance. Raegar paid her no heed. He was still staring at the *Venjekar*.

"Mark my words," said Acronis from his place at the tiller. "That man will be Emperor of Oran."

Skylan snorted in disbelief. "Raegar was a slave. A foreigner. Your people despise him."

"And yet," said Acronis, "they will follow him."

"They're not following him now," said Skylan. "He's lucky they don't throw him overboard."

"He's suffered a setback," said Acronis. "He was once, as you say, a lowly slave and he rose to become a Warrior-Priest. Mark my words. Emperor."

Skylan recalled uneasily the dream, the winged serpents, the armies of Oran invading his homeland. With all five spiritbones, Raegar would rule the world. He knew the secret and so did Aelon.

Those two are a long way from having all five, Skylan thought to himself.

In the distance, Raegar raised a clenched fist. Even so far away, his voice boomed across the water. "I call down Aelon's curse upon you, Skylan Ivorson!"

Skylan laughed because Aylaen was watching. He shouted back, "I would call down Torval's curse on you, Raegar, but the god is busy with more important matters!"

Skylan lowered the spyglass. He looked up at the sail, filled with wind. He looked at Raegar's ship, dwindling in the distance. He looked at the ogre ship, still too near, but now falling behind. He looked to the north, to the far horizon.

Let Aelon do his damnedest.

"We're going home," said Skylan.

CHAPTER 10

Skylan discovered he was becoming accustomed to using the spyglass, though he still didn't like it. He trained the glass on the ogre ship. He could see the godlord pacing back and forth on the deck, watching the *Venjekar,* the ship Bear Walker needed to save himself and his men.

The ogre's face was twisted in a scowl. He could see plainly that his slower, heavier ship could never catch the *Venjekar*. His ship had sunk lower in the water. It would soon go down and the ogres would go down with it.

Skylan thought of Keeper, his friend. He had tried to fulfill his vow, return him to his people. He had failed. Keeper would understand. Skylan would explain it to him when they were together in Torval's Hall.

The sun was high above them, beating off the water. The heat shimmered on the waves. Bear Walker unhooked the paws of his bearskin cloak and flung it away from him. As he did so, Skylan caught sight of a flash, as of sunlight striking gold. He caught his breath. He remembered another time he had seen that same flash—sun gleaming off gold. He had been on the field of battle.

The flash was there and then it was gone. The godlord had turned to speak to the shaman.

"Turn around, you bastard!" Skylan muttered beneath his breath. He kept the glass to his eye.

The godlord flung out his arm, pointing at the *Venjekar*. The shaman started waving his gourd at the ship, probably working some of his foul magic. Skylan paid the shaman scant attention. The sun shone directly on the ogre, on the gold he was wearing around his thick neck.

A wave hit the *Venjekar*. Skylan's arm jerked with the movement of the ship. The glass slipped from his eye and he lost sight of the godlord. Swearing, he braced himself against the rail, jammed the spyglass into his eye socket, and stared so intently his eye began to water. He caught only a brief glimpse, before the godlord left the rail and walked off.

A brief glimpse, but that was enough.

Skylan lowered the glass. He had seen all he needed to see—a torque made of heavy gold formed in the shape of two dragons, their tails intertwined, their heads facing each other. The two dragons held between them a spiritbone set with a sapphire.

The Vektan Torque.

Skylan had been prepared to sail halfway around the world to the ogre nation to retrieve the stolen Vektan Torque. And here it was.

On the neck of an ogre.

On a ship that was sinking.

If he didn't act swiftly, the Vektan Torque would be on the neck of a dead ogre on a ship lying at the bottom of the sea.

Skylan raised his eyes to heaven. "Torval, I can't do this! They have twenty ogre warriors to my four, five counting a fey child who can turn himself into a wolf. You can't ask this of me!"

Skylan waited, but he heard only silence and the slapping of the waves against the hull. He looked back at the ogre ship to see the sunlight gilding the water with gold.

Skylan looked up at the Dragon Kahg. The dragon's eyes seemed to shine with a golden glint.

"You, too," he muttered.

Skylan heaved a sigh and yelled.

"Bring the ship about!"

Acronis and Farinn and Aylaen all started talking at once.

"What are you doing? We're going home!"

Skylan shook his head.

"No," he said, "we're going to save the ogres."

They stared at Skylan in stunned disbelief. Before any of them could move, the Dragon Kahg took it upon himself to bring the *Venjekar* onto the new course, sailing toward the ogre vessel that looked to be lower in the water every time Skylan glanced at it.

Aylaen had watched and listened in shocked silence until the ship was under way and then she sucked in an angry breath and came storming at Skylan.

"*What* do you think you are doing?" she demanded. "Are you *still* trying to prove you are a man by chasing death? You will get us all killed—"

"The ogres have the Vektan Torque," said Skylan in flat, unemotional tones.

Aylaen gaped, the rest of her tirade forgotten.

"Bear Walker is wearing it around his fat neck," Skylan continued. "And his motherless dung heap of a ship is sinking, and if that whoreson godlord sinks with it, the Vektan Torque will lie forever at the bottom of the sea."

"How is that possible?" Aylaen asked in a strangled voice. "You must be wrong."

"Take the glass. See for yourself."

Aylaen grabbed hold of the spyglass and brought it to her eye. She gazed through it for a long time. Then she lowered the glass slowly.

"You're right. He is wearing it." Aylaen sounded dazed. She looked at Skylan in dismay. "What are we going to do?"

"Ask Kahg," said Skylan with a grim glance at the dragon.

Aylaen shivered in the bright sunshine. "The dragon knows you want him to attack the ogres, but that would put the spiritbone at even greater risk. He cannot recover the spiritbone. Only we can do it."

Her eyes filled with tears. "Damn it! This isn't fair!"

"Aylaen, I'm sorry—" Skylan reached out to comfort her.

"I'm not blaming you," Aylaen said wearily.

"It's just . . . we were going home . . ." She evaded his grasp and disappeared down into the hold.

Skylan sighed deeply. He longed to go comfort her, but he had to keep his attention focused on the ogres. Bear Walker and the shaman and several ogre warriors were gathered at the prow, watching the *Venjekar* and gesturing wildly, confused and alarmed at Skylan's sudden change of course.

Acronis looked questioningly at Skylan. "This Vektan Torque. A bit of gold jewelry. Is that really worth risking death at the hands of the ogres?"

"The Torque belongs to the Vindrasi," said Skylan. "It is sacred to our people. There are five Vektia dragons like the one that destroyed your city. We took the spiritbone of one of them from Treia. That 'bit of gold jewelry' holds the spiritbone of a second."

Acronis raised an eyebrow. "Ah, I see." He scratched his jaw. "Do the ogres know how to summon this Vektia dragon?"

Skylan had not considered this possibility.

"I'm assuming they don't," he said. "Otherwise they would have used the second Vektia dragon to attack Sinaria. But that's another reason to recover the Torque. We can't risk having them find out."

"How did they get hold of this spiritbone?" Acronis asked. "You said it was sacred to your people."

"The Vektan Torque was given to our people at the beginning of the world by the goddess, Vindrash. A cowardly chieftain—Horg, by name—traded the Torque to the ogres in return for saving his own hide."

Skylan did not tell the rest of the story—how he had fought in single-hand combat with an ogre godlord, killing him and recovering the Torque, only to lose it to the shaman and his foul magicks.

Wulfe came up on deck, tugging irritably at the shirt that was too big for him.

"What did you do to make Aylaen cry?" Wulfe asked, scowling at Skylan.

"We were going to go home," said Skylan. "And now we're not."

"You wouldn't have made it anyway," said Wulfe. "This shirt itches. Do I have to wear it?"

"Yes," said Skylan. "What do you mean we wouldn't have made it?"

"The oceanaids warned you to leave." Wulfe scratched and squirmed and wriggled.

Skylan snorted. "What did your fish friends say was going to happen?"

"They're not fish!" Wulfe said, offended. He cast a wary glance at the dragonhead prow and said in a whisper, "Kahg knows."

"Knows what?" Skylan asked.

"What's coming!" Wulfe hissed. "That's why he was sailing away."

"Then why did the dragon turn back?" Skylan asked, then he realized he already knew the answer. "The Vektan Torque. The dragon won't leave because of the spiritbone."

Wulfe shrugged, not interested. "I'm going to go tell Aylaen I hate this shirt."

Skylan cast an uneasy glance at the dragon, hoping for a sign, a reassuring flicker of the eye. But Kahg wasn't communicating. Aboard the ogre ship, the ogres were gesturing and pointing, and once again Bear Walker had to chase them away from the ship's rail.

The waiting was hardest. A tense silence fell over the small group on board the *Venjekar*. Aylaen brought food: bread and olives. Skylan ate because his belly demanded to be fed, not because he had any appetite. The vague shape of a plan was forming in his mind. It wasn't much of a plan, but at least it was better than nothing.

Wulfe had returned with Aylaen. She had found him a different shirt, one made from linen instead of wool.

"You and I need to talk," said Skylan to the wolf-boy.

Reaching out, he ruffled the boy's hair, a gesture of affection that startled Wulfe.

"What'd you do that for?" he asked suspiciously.

"Thank you for saving Aylaen," said Skylan.

"I didn't do it for you." Wulfe rubbed his hands vigorously over his head to restore his hair back to the way it had been. "I did it for her."

"Thank you," said Skylan. "But don't do it again."

Wulfe regarded him through narrowed eyes. When he saw that Skylan wasn't angry or accusing, Wulfe ducked his head. "I can't help it."

"I think you can," said Skylan quietly.

"My daemons tell me to do it!"

"Don't listen."

"It's hard!" Wulfe mumbled.

"I know," said Skylan. "I've had to quit listening to mine."

Wulfe stared at him and then gave an abrupt nod. "I'll try. But I don't promise."

He wandered off to go stand by the rail, staring out at the sea and occasionally wiping his eyes. Acronis had been listening and when Wulfe had gone he came over to talk to Skylan.

"I am right in thinking I did see that boy change himself to a wolf."

"Yes, sir," said Skylan. "Like those wolves that attacked us in Sinaria. The wolves that weren't wolves. If you ask the boy, he'll tell you it's a curse from his grandmother, the Faerie Queen."

Acronis shook his head. "It doesn't make sense, you know. It's not scientifically possible."

"Yet you saw it," said Skylan.

"Yet I saw it," said Acronis.

The *Venjekar* was now near enough to the ogre ship that Skylan ordered Farinn to trim the sail, slowing their speed. He guided the *Venjekar* to within hailing distance, yet out of spear range.

"What are you going to do?" Aylaen asked, attempting to sound calm. She had once more put on the Sinarian armor and buckled the sword of Vindrash around her waist.

Acronis was wearing his armor and his sword. Farinn was holding a battle-axe Skylan had given to him and trying to look as if he knew how to use it. Wulfe paced nervously, like a dog in a cage. Keeper lay beneath the sailcloth, peacefully sleeping the final sleep, waiting for Skylan to fulfill his promise to take him home.

"Pray to Torval," said Skylan. Touching the amulet, he shouted across the sea. "Bear Walker! I did what I promised. As you can see, I chased off your enemy, the Sinarian war galley. I have proven my friendship."

Bear Walker did not immediately answer. He was understandably suspicious. He looked from Skylan to Raegar's ship limping back to Sinaria. The godlord had witnessed for himself the battle between the two dragons. He had seen Skylan's dragon defeat the dragon of his foes. Bear Walker had also seen Skylan's ship start to leave.

The godlord grunted and shouted at Skylan, "Why did you turn around and come back?"

Skylan had anticipated this question, which was a logical one. He was prepared with his answer. "When I saw that your ship was sinking, lord, I came back to help."

"I don't know what you're talking about," Bear Walker said, glowering. "My ship is not sinking."

"You are taking on water, lord," said Skylan. "Is it possible you don't know?"

"I know," said Bear Walker, shrugging. "We are working to plug the leak."

Skylan could tell by the glances the ogres at the rail gave one another that the leak-plugging was not going well. Bear Walker glared at them, doubtless warning them not to say a word.

"I am skilled in ship-building, lord," said Skylan. "To prove my friendship, I will come aboard to help patch the leak."

Bear Walker was at first amazed, and then gave a loud guffaw. "What if I save you the trouble and take your ship?"

Skylan shrugged. "What if I sail away and let you drown?"

"You won't," Bear Walker said smugly. He put his hand on the Vektan Torque, made a show of stroking it. "You want this gewgaw I wear. *That's* why you came back."

Bear Walker grinned at Skylan's discomfiture.

"My shaman, Ravens-foot, told me the story. He says that your chief, a human named Horg, gave the ogres this gift as a mark of respect. You challenged the godlord to a battle and when you lost to him, you tried to steal the Torque—"

"Your whoreson shaman lies!" Skylan cried, losing his temper. "I fought your godlord in single combat and I killed him!"

"You're not helping!" Aylaen warned.

The ogres were angry, shouting that he lied, that no human was a match for a godlord.

Skylan thought swiftly. "The reason I was able to kill him was because our gods had cursed him!"

The ogres fell silent, listening. Ogres were respectful of the gods, all gods, even those they did not worship. Skylan remembered how Keeper had urged Aylaen to fight for the honor of her goddess, Vindrash.

"Horg had no right to give the ogres the Torque,"

Skylan continued. "It did not belong to him. The Torque belongs to the Vindrasi people. It was a gift to us from the gods. When Horg stole it, the gods cursed him."

Bear Walker tore the Torque from his neck. "Are you saying this thing is cursed?"

"Horg died a terrible death," said Skylan gravely. "The godlord who wore the Torque after Horg died a terrible death. Your shaman knows the truth. Ask him!"

Bear Walker turned to Ravens-foot, who began spluttering, probably protesting that Skylan was trying to trick them. Bear Walker's face darkened.

"Now *you* are wearing the Torque and misfortune has dogged you, Bear Walker!" Skylan pressed home his advantage. "Your raid ended in disaster. Your ship is sinking. The gods' curse is on you!"

The ogres on board the ship backed away from Bear Walker. The godlord eyed the Torque, then shoved it at the shaman. Ravens-foot shook his gourd at it and edged away. Bear Walker was left standing all alone, the Torque in his hand. He looked from the Torque to the foaming waves.

"He's going to throw it in the sea!" Aylaen gasped.

"Give me the Torque!" Skylan yelled hastily. "When the Torque is in my hands, our gods will lift their curse from you."

Bear Walker mulled this over. He wasn't stupid. He didn't trust Skylan and yet he didn't have much choice.

"You will patch our ship?" he asked.

"I will. I swear by Torval!" Skylan vowed. "Let me come aboard."

Bear Walker ordered his men to toss down a rope, which they did with alacrity. Skylan smiled reassuringly at Aylaen, who was watching unhappily.

"Pray to Vindrash for me," said Skylan, taking hold of the rope. "You are in command while I'm gone."

"Me?" she said, startled.

"If something happens, you and Kahg sail the *Venjekar* home. You can meet up with Sigurd."

"I've found you, only to lose you," Aylaen said in sorrowful tones.

"You haven't lost me yet," said Skylan, grinning.

He gave her a swift kiss on the cheek and then began to climb the rope, hand-over-hand. He had gone only a short distance when Wulfe seized hold of his ankle.

"It's coming!" Wulfe yelled frantically. "It's coming! It's almost here!"

"Let go, damn it!" Skylan swore, twisting on the rope and trying to kick at the boy, who was holding on to him with a strength born of terror. "Aylaen, Farinn, get him off me!"

Before they could grab him, Wulfe let go. Skylan continued his climb. Wulfe stood on the deck, staring up at him, his face contorted in fear. Skylan hesitated, remembering the time Wulfe's oceanaids had warned him a storm was coming. Skylan hadn't listened and his ship had been caught out at sea in a raging tempest.

The sky was clear. But the sea was unsettled, shining with a greasy, oily sheen. Suppose Wulfe was right, and something bad was coming.

"All the greater urgency for me to get my hands on the Vektan Torque," Skylan said grimly.

Several ogres offered to help Skylan, seizing hold of him—armor, sword, and all—lifting him up bodily and heaving him over the rail with as much ease as if he'd been the scrawny Wulfe. Once on board, Skylan could tell by the feel of the ship—sluggish and foundering—that it was taking on water at a rapid rate. He feared it was too far gone to save. He'd do what he could, however. He'd made a vow to Torval and he meant to honor it. *After* he had the Torque.

He walked over to greet Bear Walker. The two exchanged pleasantries. Ravens-foot, the shaman in the feathered cape, shook the gourd at Skylan, who stared at the shaman coldly and rested his hand on the hilt of his sword.

"I am here, as I promised," said Skylan. "Give me the Torque. The curse will be lifted."

"You can have the damn thing," said Bear Walker.

He held out the Torque. The gold shone brightly in the sunlight. The two dragons, holding the spiritbone between them, seemed to be watching Skylan with their jeweled eyes. His heart swelled with pride and pleasure.

He started to grasp hold of it. "Thank you, Torval . . ."

But before he could finish his prayer, the sea boiled. A horrible smell, as of a barrel of rotting fish, and enormous tentacles, gray and scaly and as big as mighty oak trees, shot up out of the water. The tentacles wrapped around the ogre ship. The Torque fell from his hand. Before Skylan could think or catch his breath or panic, the tentacles dragged him, the ship, and the ogres beneath the waves.

CHAPTER 11

The Aquin commander and her troops were on routine patrol near the City of the Third Daughter, when they received a report that a gigantic kraken had been sighted in their territory. The report came from several extremely excited naiad (fae folk who dwell in the sea, known by humans as oceanaids), and was therefore suspect, especially since kraken were not known to hunt in these waters. The commander, Neda, nonetheless decided she had better investigate.

She communicated the news to her patrol through a series of squeals and whistles used by the Aquins to communicate beneath the water. Since they might have to swim a far distance without being able to surface for air, the Aquin people made use of their breath-masks, devices concocted of large clamshells containing a specially grown seaweed that exchanged stale breath for fresh oxygen. The clamshell attached to the back of the swimmer with straps. A mask fit over the nose and mouth. A tube fed the oxygen supply to the swimmer.

The Aquins were a race of humans who lived in cities beneath the sea. Many tales were told about them, particularly among seafaring people, but much of the information in these tales was not true. For example, Aquins did not have the upper bodies of humans and the lower bodies of fish. They did not have gill slits, nor could they breathe water. The tales were true when they told that the Aquins were a peace-loving people who kept to themselves, avoiding the wars and disputes that raged among their land-dwelling cousins. The tales also spoke truly when they said that Aquins were known to come to the rescue of sailors who were washed overboard or swimmers who found themselves out beyond their depth, saving them from drowning.

Commander Neda questioned the oceanaids—not an easy undertaking, for the silvery-scaled, silvery-haired fae were all gesturing and bubbling and screeching in confusion. At length she was able to determine that not only was a kraken in the vicinity, it was attacking two ships. She dispatched several of her warriors to fetch more of the breath-masks, in the unlikely case that there were survivors, and set out with her patrol.

The Aquins came upon an astonishing sight—an enormous kraken, the largest they had ever seen. And below the kraken, guarding one of the ships, was a dragon.

The Aquins had never seen a dragon, though they knew of them, for of all the land-bound races the Aquins felt most closely connected to the Vindrasi, a sea-faring people who roamed the oceans in their dragonships. For a moment the Aquins could only stare, awestruck, at the dragon that had his body twined protectively around a ship with a dragonhead prow. Seeing several humans and ogres in dire peril, Commander Neda ordered her warriors to do what they could to save them.

The sea boiled. Tentacles whipped. One moment Skylan was standing on the deck of the ogre ship, reaching for the Vektan Torque. The next he was plunging into the roiling waves.

He was an experienced swimmer, as were most Vindrasi sailors, and had learned when young not to panic. Open your eyes, no matter how badly it stings, try to find the surface. The problem was the segmented armor, weighing him down. He managed to unhook the straps holding it on, letting the armor sink to the bottom. Next to go was his sword and sheath. Peering through a faint reddish tinge, Skylan searched for Aylaen and his comrades. Broken timbers, flailing, panic-stricken ogres, and the murky water made it impossible to find them. He had to worry about finding air to breathe and thrust his way through the water, kicking and pulling himself upward toward the distant sunlight.

He was almost there when he saw the sea monster that had attacked them. The kraken's elongated orangish-colored body was easily as long as the *Venjekar*. The sea monster had two huge yellow eyes, one set on each side of its bulbous head.

Eight arms extended from its head along with the two incredibly long tentacles that had seized the ogre ship and crushed it like an eggshell.

A single yellow eye fixed on Skylan. Terrified, he pulled himself through the debris-laden water as fast as he could. The kraken flashed toward him with horrific speed. A tentacle whipped out from the kraken's head and seized Skylan by the leg. Round cups on the tentacle adhered to his flesh. Myriad sharp teeth sank into him, sending splinters of agony through his body. The kraken began to reel him in like a fish on a hook, hauling him through the water toward the kraken's razor-sharp beak.

Skylan had no weapon. He beat on the tentacle with his fists, striking it again and again, without effect. His lungs were bursting, but it seemed likely he was going to end up being torn apart by the beak. His strength was failing. He could not hold his breath any longer. He brought Aylaen's face to mind. He would take her with him into death. He opened his mouth . . .

Strong arms seized hold of him. A woman slapped a mask made of leather that smelled strongly of fish over his face and thrust a tube into his mouth. The leather of the mask stuck to his skin, something sticky inside molding itself to his flesh. He fought the woman, for the mask, covering his nose and mouth and eyes, made him think she was trying to suffocate him. Her hands held him firmly. A face, floating in front of him, wearing the same kind of mask, motioned to him to breathe.

Skylan didn't have any choice. Either breathe or die. He gasped and was surprised and relieved to feel blessed air flow into his lungs. The woman strapped something onto his back. She pointed to what appeared to be a clamshell she wore on her own back, with a tube leading to the mask on her face. His brain was fuzzy, but he gathered this was what was enabling him to breathe. Dizzy and light-headed, he could do nothing for a few moments except breathe and stare through the portion of the crystal mask over his eyes, allowing him to see beneath the water as strange-looking warrior women attacked the kraken with spears and tridents.

With their sleek glistening bodies and rapid movements they reminded him of dolphins. He could not count their numbers, for they swam and darted about so swiftly he might have been trying to count a school of fish. He guessed there must have been about thirty of them, armed with spears and another weapon that resembled a pitchfork.

Working as a team, some of the warriors jabbed the kraken's grappling arms with the three-pronged weapons while others used the butt end of their spears to beat on the monster's head or make threatening motions at the kraken's eyes. The warriors did not appear to want to kill the kraken, only to force it to flee.

The kraken shot out a jet of ink that turned the water black. The kraken's arms and tentacles flashed around Skylan, striking him and seizing his rescuer, a tentacle wrapping around her waist, knocking loose the clamshell and dislodging the tube. Bubbles trailed out of her mouth as she fought to free herself, stabbing the tentacle with a knife.

The warrior women attacked the kraken in earnest, stabbing their spears and tridents into the head and arms. Trails of black blood spiraled up into the water as the warriors fought to free their comrade. Whenever they came close to her, the kraken lashed out with its arms, knocking away spears and sending warriors flying as it drew the woman it had captured toward its razor-sharp beak.

She was weakening, Skylan realized. She had lost her breath-mask and was running out of air. He grabbed hold of a loose spear and swam toward the struggling warrior. He stabbed at the tentacle with the spear, but the kraken didn't even seem to notice. If Skylan couldn't beat the kraken, he figured he'd join it. He wrapped his arm around the tentacle, putting his body between the warrior and the kraken's maw.

He had no idea if his plan would work. If not, the razor-sharp beak would rip them both apart. He held on grimly, waiting until the kraken opened its maw to suck them both inside. Skylan stabbed upward with all his strength, driving the spear into the inky darkness, praying to Torval he hit something tender.

The kraken gave a violent jerk. Arms flailed

wildly, tentacles whipped, flinging Skylan and the warrior about until finally it released them. Drawing its tentacles and arms close together, the kraken gave up the fight and swiftly swam away. Skylan would have gone after the wounded kraken to kill it, but the warriors appeared satisfied with having driven it off. Several warriors came to the aid of their comrade, placing a mask over her face and helping her breathe. One swam to Skylan and replaced his mask, which had been jostled in the fight with the kraken.

Skylan sagged in the water, barely able to keep his arms and legs moving. He was bleeding freely from numerous round wounds inflicted by the teeth in the kraken's suckers. His one thought was Aylaen and his friends. He had to find out if they were safe. The woman warrior floating in front of him made clicking sounds that he could hear through the water. Apparently she was talking to him in some sort of fish language. He had no idea what she was saying.

He motioned that he was going to the surface and began to swim that direction. The warrior woman seized hold of his arm and pointed off in a different direction. Skylan shook his head, not wanting to seem ungrateful, but intent upon going to find out what had become of Aylaen and the *Venjekar*. The woman refused to release him. Skylan was angry and tried to free himself. Ten or more women surrounded him, spears and tridents aimed at him.

These people must be the Aquins, he thought to

himself. The Vindrasi told tales about the Aquins, a harmless and gentle people known to save drowning victims. Except that these women did not appear to be either gentle or harmless. They regarded him with suspicion, enmity. The woman who had hold of him gestured to two of the warriors, who grabbed his wrists and bound them with what looked like seaweed.

He was immediately aware that the tales were mistaken when they described the Aquins as half-human, half-fish. He decided they were three-quarters human and one quarter fish. The Aquins had arms and legs like his. Their hands were webbed, with skin in between the fingers and thumbs, and their feet had long, webbed toes that made them look more like flippers than feet. Their rib cages were unnaturally large, their limbs slender and lithe.

He thought at first that they had skin that was a mottled blue-gray in color until he realized they were wearing lightweight armor made of fish-skin leather. Their own skin color was a pale green. Their hair color ranged from black to a greenish blond worn in a single braid that floated behind them. They wore helms made of the same kind of leather as their body armor, fitted close to their heads. All of the warriors were women. He looked but could not find any males.

His savior-captors swam off with him, carrying him between them, propelling themselves through the water with their flipper-like feet. He had no idea where they were taking him and no way to ask. He could see the sun shining on the surface that was perhaps three fathoms above him. Some of the warriors had removed their clamshell breathing masks and, swimming to the surface, they took a deep breath, then dove back down. He watched in amazement to see that they remained below water without drawing another breath for a long time and he began to understand why their rib cages were abnormally large. They must have huge lungs.

And then he saw the *Venjekar,* perched on a reef, with the Dragon Kahg keeping guard beside it. The ship was, for the most part, intact. The mast had snapped off. The hull looked to be undamaged, at least from what Skylan could tell at first glance. The dragon's eyes were fiery red. His wings fanned the water and his tail lashed. When he saw Skylan he bared his fangs. Kahg was still angry. He must have protected the ship from the kraken. Skylan was sorry he had missed seeing that battle. The warrior women were wary of the dragon and careful not to approach. They carried Skylan as close to the ship as they dared and asked by pointing to it and then pointing at him if the ship was his.

Sick with fear, Skylan could not at first respond. No one was on board the *Venjekar*. Bodies of ogres lay among the shattered remnants of their ship. One of the bodies was covered in black feathers. The shaman would not practice his magicks any more. Skylan looked for the godlord, hoping he might find the Vektan Torque, but the godlord had been dressed like the other ogre warriors and he could not tell one body from the next. Skylan did find Keeper's body, still partially wrapped in the sailcloth, lying near the *Venjekar*. Skylan sighed. He had apologized to Keeper so many times he had no apologies left. They would have a long talk in Torval's Hall.

Were his people alive? Had they been rescued by the Aquins? Or were they lying dead in the ship's hold? Skylan tore free of his captors and tried to swim for his ship. He was clumsy and slow in the water and the Aquin warriors caught him with ease. Angry and frustrated, he kicked at them and struck out with his bound hands.

The woman Skylan took to be the commander clicked and whistled a command. One of the warriors removed something from around her waist, untwined it, revealing a net made of seaweed and weighted with shells. She tossed the net over his head and shoulders and it settled around him. Two of the warriors cinched the net shut at his feet.

Enraged, Skylan tried to free himself from the net by tearing at the rope with his hands. The tough, fibrous green rope would not give. He wriggled and kicked and succeeded only in entangling himself in the net. The woman watched him with amusement. At length, realizing he stood no chance of escape and was only making himself look foolish, he ceased struggling.

One of the warriors had spotted something of interest, apparently, for she dove down and now was rummaging about the wreckage of the ogre ship. He saw something glint brightly. She plucked the Vektan Torque from among the debris and, turning it over in her hand to admire it, brought it to her commander. The commander stared at the Torque, then shifted her gaze to Skylan.

He gestured to the Torque and then thumped himself on the chest, indicating—he hoped—that the Torque belonged to him. The commander snorted; he could see the bubbles flowing from her nose. Keeping fast hold of the Torque, the commander motioned for her warriors to resume their journey.

The women pulled Skylan, trapped in the net, through the water. He twisted his head to look back at the dragon. Kahg's eyes flickered. He was staying with the ship.

Skylan was helpless. He was a prisoner and he could do nothing except go wherever his captors were taking him. He was more worried about Aylaen and his friends than about his own fate. He kept reminding himself that the Aquins had saved his life. He clung to the hope that they had saved Aylaen and the rest.

He looked at his surroundings. He was in a different world, a world he never knew existed. As a boy, Skylan had gone diving for clams and oysters in the cold waters around his homeland. He had never seen sea life as beautiful and varied as this, and despite his anxiety for Aylaen and his people, he gazed in awe and wonder.

Fish of many colors, more colors than the rainbow, glided and darted and flitted about undulating plants or hid among the rocks and coral. Wide chasms opened up beneath him and were suddenly gone. Spiny black sea urchins poked out from beneath rocks. Creatures like globs of wet flour aimlessly floated about, ugly tentacles dangling down from their bodies.

The women hauling his net slowed and drifted to a halt. More warrior women, coming from a different direction, were joining up with them, and there was a great deal of squealing and clicking and whistling between the commander and this new contingent. These women had hold of something that was wriggling and writhing in their grip. Skylan thought at first it was some sort of fish and then realized it was Wulfe.

The boy waved at him and, breaking loose, swam toward him, kicking and paddling in the water. The warriors let him go, making no effort to stop him. Wulfe was grinning widely, enjoying himself. It took Skylan a moment to realize the boy was not wearing a breath-mask, nor was he holding his breath. Bubbles flowed from his mouth.

Wulfe was not alone. He was surrounded by women of startling beauty, with silvery skin and long silver hair that twined about their naked bodies. These were oceanaids, nymphs who lived beneath the sea. They flowed around the boy, fawning over him, moving gracefully with the currents. Some of the oceanaids drifted on their backs. Others twisted and spun in exuberant play with others, who were undulating like porpoises.

The Aquin commander appeared highly annoyed at the sight of the oceanaids and made emphatic gestures, as if asking why her warriors hadn't chased them off. The warriors pointed at Wulfe, who was now swimming around Skylan, laughing to see him caught in a net and making fish faces at him.

Skylan was so relieved to find the boy that he shoved to the back of his mind the idea that Wulfe could apparently breathe water as easily as he breathed air. Desperate to find out about Aylaen, Skylan tried to rip the mask from his face to ask, though it seemed likely he would drown in the attempt. The mask was tightly stuck and before he could remove it he was stopped by his captors, who gestured sternly at him. Skylan motioned frantically back in the direction of the *Venjekar*. At first Wulfe didn't know what he wanted and blinked at him in confusion. Skylan was growing frustrated and angry, when Wulfe suddenly grinned. He mouthed Aylaen's name and made a motion of his hand to indicate her red curls and pointed at the mask Skylan was wearing.

Skylan sagged back in the net, weak with relief. Wulfe mouthed the names of Acronis and Farinn, pointing at the mask and then pointing at the net in which Skylan was trapped. He made a motion of having his wrists bound together.

Skylan understood that Acronis and Farinn were prisoners, like he was. Wulfe had not said the same about Aylaen. Skylan wondered what had become of her, where they were taking her, where they were taking him. Even if Wulfe knew, he and Skylan had reached the limit of their ability to communicate. The Aquin commander had succeeded in shooing away the oceanaids. The lovely nymphs held out their hands to Wulfe, urging him to come join with them. Twisting about in the water, Wulfe waved at Skylan and then swam off.

Apparently a boy who could change himself into a wolf could also change himself into a trout.

Fatigue and pain, awe and confusion and disbelief rushed at Skylan like warriors in an opposing shield wall. He had no weapons to fight them and he sank beneath their onslaught. Weary in body and spirit, he reconciled himself to the fact that he could do nothing except let the thread of his wyrd spin out as it would, go where it may.

BOOK 2

CHAPTER 12

Raegar looked powerful and magnificent standing at the prow of the war galley, his clenched fist raised to heaven, calling down the curse of Aelon upon the *Venjekar,* the dragonship that had humiliated them. The men on board the war galley were impressed and they watched in silence to see if Aelon would respond.

Nothing happened. The ship sailed away, bound on a course that would carry Skylan and the Vektia spiritbone back to Vindraholm. The soldiers—Temple guards, Aelon's chosen—either didn't think much of Aelon or they had lost faith in his Warrior-Priest, for they cast dark glances at Raegar and muttered among themselves. Though he was a Warrior-Priest, he was also an outsider, a foreigner, and he had conjured up a dragon, a dangerous and terrifying beast. Most felt they were lucky the dragon had not slain them all.

Raegar was a Vindrasi. He was accustomed to fighting alongside dragons and he had not, as Acronis had predicted, given any thought as to how the Sinarians aboard his ship would react to the sight of a dragon, especially after they had witnessed a dragon rain down death and destruction on their city of Sinaria. The fools had cheered when the dragon flew off in ignominious defeat. Then Raegar had been forced to waste precious time fishing Treia out of the sea. After that, the sailors had refused to continue their pursuit of the *Venjekar*. They were going home to their families—if they had any families left. Raegar had urged Captain Anker, commander of the Temple guards, to force the sailors at sword point to continue sailing the ship in pursuit of the *Venjekar*. In answer, Captain Anker had thrown his sword onto the deck.

"You do it," he'd said to Raegar, and walked off.

Raegar realized he had been made to look foolish. He'd lost all the political capital he'd gained in Sinaria. He needed to win it back and, with Aelon's help, he would.

Raegar paid no attention to his men. He continued to watch Skylan, his fair-haired cousin, beloved of the gods. Beloved of old, toothless, decrepit gods. Raegar had faith in Aelon. He waited to see what would happen.

The *Venjekar* slowed. The ship was turning, sailing off on a new course—heading for the ogre ship that had been dogging it. Raegar was puzzled and wary. What was Skylan up to? Was he plotting to join with the ogres and come after *Aelon's Triumph*? Raegar raised the spyglass. He was not an experienced sailor, but even he could tell that the ogre ship was sinking.

"By god! Look at that!" Captain Anker shouted. His face was pale beneath his weather-beaten tan, his eyes wide and staring. Men all over the ship were crying out in alarm. Raegar shifted the spyglass in time to see the enormous tentacles of the kraken wrap around the ogre ship and crush it. Another tentacle seized hold of the *Venjekar* and dragged it beneath the waves. The water boiled furiously for a moment and then grew calm. Nothing was left of either ship except a few pieces of cracked timber.

Raegar lowered the spyglass. He did not turn around.

"Praise Aelon!" he cried.

All he heard was silence and then came the sound of men dropping to their knees. A few shouted, "Praise Aelon," but most were too awed to speak.

Raegar turned around slowly, gazing at the soldiers and sailors who, moments earlier, had reviled him and who now were regarding him with almost worshipful respect. Treia, wet and bedraggled, stood with her mouth open, blinking, stunned.

"Witness the power of Aelon!" Raegar cried with a sweep of his arm. "He has destroyed our enemies with a single blow! We will sail back to Sinaria, praising Aelon's name, and we will bury our dead and rebuild our city! For Aelon's glory!"

"For Aelon's glory!" the men cried.

The sailors went to work with a will. Aelon granted them a fair wind. They had no need of rowers, which was good, since many of them were injured and their oars broken.

Raegar was well pleased with himself and with

Aelon. He was in an excellent mood and disposed to be generous to Treia. She had been the cause of the disaster that had leveled Sinaria and killed thousands, that was true. But if it hadn't been for this disaster, Raegar would still be a Warrior-Priest, carrying out the dirty work of Priest-General Xydis.

Now Xydis was dead. Raegar had long nurtured the ambition of one day rising to the office of Priest-General. The road to the fulfillment of his ambition had been long and winding and steep, blocked by rock falls and gaping pits. Holding the body of the Priest-General in his arms that terrible night, Raegar had seen the road to success suddenly flatten out, with almost all impediments swept away. The god, it seemed, was pleased with him. True to the fighting spirit of the Vindrasi, he stood on the smoldering rubble of his city and wondered how he could use this to his advantage.

The survivors would be left in disarray, bewildered and terrified, in desperate need. They would be searching for someone to lead them and, with the Priest-General dead and the Empress dead and no heir and no appointed successor, Sinaria was up for grabs.

Captain Anker stood before him, head bowed. He humbly begged Raegar's pardon and asked what he could do. Raegar waved a magnanimous hand.

"I'm going below," he announced. "Summon me when we reach port."

He walked across the deck, feeling all eyes on him, feeling the respect, the fear. Word would spread when they reached Sinaria. The people would hear how Raegar had asked Aelon for a miracle and the god had granted his request.

He stood for a moment, basking in the sunlight, and then he went below to deal with Treia.

CHAPTER 13

Treia had been as astonished as any man on board *Aelon's Triumph* to witness Raegar summon a sea monster from the deep and send it to destroy Skylan. She looked at Raegar, blinking at him with her weak eyes, and saw that he had changed. He was no longer a former slave, a foreigner, the hound beneath the table of great men, begging for scraps. He had attained greatness himself. He was, if not a god, godlike.

And where does that leave me? Treia wondered in despair.

As if in answer, when one of the soldiers asked Raegar what they were to do with her, he said coldly, without so much as a glance, "Take her to my cabin."

The soldier escorted Treia to a small room below deck, shoved her inside, and closed the door and barred it. She peered around in the dim light, searching for dry clothes, for she was wet and cold and shivering. She found a robe, one of Raegar's, that was much too big for her. She wrapped up in it, cocoon-like, lay on the cot that served as a bed, and wondered fearfully what would become of her.

She fell asleep and woke with a start to the sound of heavy footfalls, and the bar on the door lifted. Treia sat up, quaking. Raegar entered the room and stood frowning at her.

She tried to speak, but her throat closed. Raegar said not a word. He stood staring at her, coldly.

Treia cringed. "Thank you for saving me, my love."

"Don't call me your love!" Raegar said angrily. "You betrayed me! I heard the name of the god to whom you prayed when you summoned the dragon. Hevis was the name. You prayed to one of your savage, pagan gods and brought disaster upon us all!"

He paused, eyeing her, then said harshly, "Or perhaps, in your eyes, it wasn't disaster. Perhaps you count the destruction of Sinaria a victory!"

"No! Oh, no, dearest!" Treia cried, alarmed. She reached out a shaking hand. "I wanted only to please you. I was desperate to please you. So desperate . . . I could not tell you the truth."

"And what truth is that?" Raegar sneered.

Treia gave a weary sigh. "Aelon has no control over the spiritbones of the Vektia. Torval placed within the Five the power of creation in order to protect that power and keep it out of the hands of any other god who might try to usurp it. In order to gain the knowledge of the ritual to summon the Vektia dragon, I had to go to Hevis.

"If anything, he betrayed me," she added bitterly. "Hevis promised the dragon would destroy the ogres. I had no idea the dragon would go rampaging through the city, destroying everything in its path. But now that we know the secret of the Five, my love"—she spoke the word timidly, greatly daring—"you know how to gain this power for yourself."

"For Aelon, you mean," said Raegar.

"Yes, for Aelon, of course," Treia said meekly.

"Explain to me again this secret and what it means and how you came to discover it," said Raegar.

He had been standing, looming over her, but now he sat down. Treia explained, recalling Skylan's conversations with Aylaen, how Vindrash had given him the clue to the secret of the Five.

"The goddess was forbidden to tell him outright, because of the immense power that such knowledge gives to those who acquire the spiritbones. She had to drop clues, encourage him to think of it himself."

"Then how do you know Skylan is right?" Raegar asked, frowning.

"Because it makes sense. It is logical," said Treia. "Torval splits the power between the Five and then gives them to Vindrash, who makes certain the Five are separated, distributing four among the gods for safekeeping and giving one to the Vindrasi people. We know from past experience that other attempts to control one of the dragons led to destruction. Why go to such lengths to keep them apart? Because the Old Gods are weak and do not dare risk bringing them together for fear some stronger god will seize them."

"As you say, it makes sense." Raegar gave a

frustrated shrug and added testily, "But I do not know what good knowing the secret about the Five spiritbones does us when we now have zero."

"One is aboard the *Venjekar,*" Treia said. "The other . . ."

She paused, her voice trailed off. She stood unmoving, lost in deep thought.

"What?" Raegar demanded impatiently.

"The second spiritbone, the one the ogres stole from us. The *Venjekar* was sailing northward when Skylan suddenly altered course. He had the chance to escape the ogre ship, but he went back, risking almost certain death. Why?"

"Why does my whoreson cousin do anything?" Raegar snorted. "He wanted glory. To be a hero."

"I am not so certain, my love. I recognized one of the ogres on board that ship," said Treia. "It was the shaman in the black feather cape. He was with the ogres when they attacked our village. And he was the shaman who stole the Vektan Torque from Skylan. If the shaman was there—"

"Then maybe the Vektan Torque was with him!" Raegar exclaimed, bounding to his feet in excitement. The next moment, he threw himself glumly back into his chair. "Which means that now two of the spiritbones are in the belly of a kraken."

"Aelon sent the kraken," said Treia softly. "Aelon will lead you to the spiritbones, even though they lie far below the sea."

Raegar sat silently, ruminating, then he rose again to his feet and began to rove restlessly about the small cabin.

"Why am I talking of spiritbones? I must think of Sinaria. We must provide the survivors with food and clothing and shelter or Sinaria will be a city peopled only by ghosts. I sent messengers to the other cities in Oran, requesting aid, but it will be weeks before that can reach us. In the meantime, there is so much to do—"

"And you are the person to do it," said Treia.

She crept over to him and slipped her arms around him from behind. He did not return her embrace, but he did not push her away.

"When you called down Aelon's curse on Skylan," Treia said. "I saw you shine with the god's glory."

Raegar stirred and smiled, pleased to recall his moment of triumph. "Aelon's spirit was with me. I felt it."

"I saw the light surround you," Treia went on, glad to please him. "I saw it shine from you. All men on board the ship saw it."

Treia nuzzled her cheek against his back. "And when we return to Sinaria, everyone will see you shining with the god's light. You are destined for greatness, my love. You are Aelon's chosen. You will be the next Priest-General."

Raegar sighed. "That is my dream, but I am a long way from fulfilling it. I will have to prove myself to the people, to the other priests. There is Thanos, Xydis's son . . ."

"You won't need to prove anything," Treia said softly. "You won't need to worry about Thanos. You know the secret to the Five, the secret that will give Aelon the power to vanquish his rivals. Your god needs you, my love. Aelon will raise you up."

"I believe in Aelon. I have faith in him," said Raegar. He turned to face her. "But what if the priests refuse to support me? Thanos was being groomed to be Priest-General. The god might choose him. I will look the fool. The priests will laugh at me, mock me. I will lose all that I have gained."

"And what is that?" Treia said earnestly, clasping his hands in her own. "What have you gained? Their respect? Bah! Xydis made you a Warrior-Priest only to use you, manipulate you. You waded in the muck so that he could keep his boots clean. To him and to the others, you will always be an oaf, a savage, a slave. You will prove them wrong! You and Aelon! You have nothing to lose, my love. And *all* to gain."

Treia was not beautiful, not even particularly attractive. She was nearsighted and had developed a squint. Her face was pale and unsmiling, tended to be severe. She was thin, spare, her breasts small. Raegar often questioned why he was drawn to her. She knew the reason—in her weak eyes, he shone with the god's light.

"I love you, woman!" Raegar said huskily. "Aelon knows why, for you are a devious, conniving witch."

"That is why you love me, my dear," said Treia gently. She was still a little overawed by him, but she quickly added, "And that is why you will marry me."

"Marriage?" Raegar drew back from her.

"The Priest-General should be married, my love," said Treia. "Marriage will give you respectability, shelter you from scandal. Remember the rumors that circulated about Xydis, his bastard son . . . ?"

Raegar remembered. He stood eyeing her, chewing on his lip.

"I will not tie you down," said Treia, and deep within, she sighed. She knew she could not tie him down. "You know that. You know you can trust me." She lowered her eyes. "And perhaps there will be children . . ."

"I will consider it," said Raegar, but she saw that she had won him over. He grinned at her and, seizing hold of her, he sat down on the chair, with her on his lap. "As for babies, let us practice making one now."

Treia smiled and kissed him. Their love-making gave pleasure to them both. Refreshed, Raegar went back above deck to see how *Aelon's Triumph* was faring. The sailors reported that if the breeze held, they would reach Sinaria the next day. He paced the deck, plotting and scheming, while belowdecks Treia did the same. When darkness fell, he returned to her.

They shared a meal, and he told her of his plans. She made suggestions to which he listened and approved. They made love again and lay together on the cot that was scarcely big enough for two. Raegar was drowsy, wanting to sleep.

Treia caressed his chest and said, "For my bride gift, I would like the spiritbone of the Dragon Fala."

Raegar grunted and tried to roll over. "It is early to be talking of bride gifts."

Treia kissed his ear. "You know nothing of dragons. You summoned a fire dragon over water!"

Raegar stirred in displeasure, but he was too tired to argue.

Treia continued, soft and persuasive. "I have spent my life studying dragons. I thought all those years studying to be Bone Priestess were wasted, but now I know differently. This was Aelon's plan."

Raegar opened one eye, half-turned his shoulder.

"Marry me, my love," said Treia. "Give me the Dragon Fala, and nothing and no one can stand in your way."

Raegar gazed at her intently. As she playfully traced the serpent tattoo on his head with her finger, she could follow the thought process going on beneath it. He saw the wisdom of her words. He didn't know anything about dragons and now the Dragon Fala was off sulking somewhere. He had no idea how to get her back. What was more, he was flattered by the idea that Aelon had planned this union all along; that Aelon had been grooming her, making her ready for him. Marrying her would ensure her loyalty, bind her to him. And marriage did not mean that he had to remain faithful. Treia understood that, though she did not like it.

"The dragon will be your bride gift, my love," Raegar said. "And now, let me get some sleep."

He closed his eyes and nestled his head on her breast and was soon snoring. Treia held him close and gloried in her triumph. She thought, a little sadly, how easily he could be manipulated.

"This could be a problem," Treia said to him as he lay deep in slumber. She kissed his cheek. "But don't fear, my own. I will watch out for you. I will protect you from those others who would flatter and seduce you."

The wedding would be simple, she decided. And it would be soon.

CHAPTER 14

Following the disaster that had befallen their city, the Warrior-Priests of Aelon went out among the people and tried to help. They found to their dismay that no one wanted their help. In fact, many wanted them dead. Searching for someone to blame for the catastrophe, the people latched on to Aelon, the god who had failed to protect them from the ogres and the terrors of the Vektia dragon. The survivors turned their rage on the priests, who were forced to retreat beneath the onslaught and take refuge in their enclave.

Trapped inside their own Shrine, the priests of Aelon looked at each other and wondered what to do now. Warrior-Priest Raegar had taken charge at the height of the terror. They had welcomed his swift, decisive leadership and many had spoken of him as being the next Priest-General. Raegar had been absent several days now. He had purportedly taken a war galley to sea to finish off the ogres and some said he was most likely dead. Among the loudest of these was a young Warrior-Priest named Thanos, who had been Xydis's closest friend, his confidante, and his bastard son.

Xydis had been grooming his son to succeed him as Priest-General. Thanos would have been in the arena with Xydis and the Empress that fateful day Treia summoned the Vektia dragon and might well have died there with his father and so many others, for he had been invited to sit with the Empress in her box which had collapsed on top of her. He had been suffering from a severe head cold, however, and had been forced to decline. The Empress disliked being around sick people.

As it was, Thanos had been knocked unconscious when the roof of his father's house collapsed, but he had escaped serious injury. When he came to his senses some time later, he had been forced to dig his way out of the rubble. Once free, he went immediately to the Shrine, arriving shortly after Raegar had left to chase ogres.

Thanos found the members of the Council of Warrior-Priests in a state of confusion bordering on panic. Xydis was dead. The Empress was dead and had left no heir. They were quarreling over what to do. Some said they should go among the people to help, whether the people wanted them or not. Others said they should stay where they were and pray to Aelon for guidance. Still others advocated they should take up arms, to be ready when the mobs attacked.

Everyone was relieved to see Thanos. They were all glad to turn to him with their problems, eager to hear his council. Thanos was an attractive man, tall and well-built. He had the good fortune to resemble the statue of Aelon that stood in the rotunda of the public Shrine. His face was chiseled, his brow prominent. He was Xydis's son, born out of wedlock, though since his mother had died birthing him, her identity was only rumored, not known. Thanos had been raised in the church. He knew all its secrets. He confidently expected to succeed to the position of Priest-General.

Thanos was fond of good food, good wine, and bad women. He had the ability to keep his appetites under control, however, hidden from the public eye. He was a well-spoken young man, good-looking, charming, shrewd, and ambitious. Thanos was fortunate that his own faith in Aelon had not been shaken by the terrible events, because he had no faith to shake. Thanos did not believe in Aelon or any other god. He believed in himself.

Thanos apologized for being late. His excuse was that his house had fallen down on top of him. The priests were shocked to see the great gash in his head and urged him to go back to his bed. Thanos said the pain was nothing. He was here because he was needed. They told him, sadly, of his father's death. He bore up well at the news, saying that grief would come later, they must now deal with this terrible emergency. All of them were talking at once, arguing and yammering. Thanos listened as best he could through the throbbing pain in his head. His glance strayed to the bronze doors that led to the private offices of the Priest-General. No one was permitted to enter the bronze doors without the Priest-General's knowledge and permission. Beyond those doors was the dark and mysterious chamber of the Watchers and the treasure vault.

The bronze doors were wide open.

"Where are the guards?" asked Thanos, alarmed.

The priests all turned to follow his gaze. Not a guard in sight.

The Warrior-Priests, led by Thanos, rushed in a body through the bronze doors only to find themselves in pitch darkness. The halls were always shadowy, dimly lit by thin shafts of sunlight slanting down from skylights in the ceiling. Today the sky was dark. The smoke of burning obliterated the sun. Aelon's blessed light had gone out. Thanos sent men back for torches.

He crept through the dark hallway until he came to the room of the Watchers. Aelon's light still burned in this room, as small fires sputtered atop the water bowls. The Watchers still occupied their places, receiving messages from Aelon's chosen who had gone forth to bring the light of the god to the benighted world. Thanos and the Warrior-Priests stopped to stare in amazement at the Watchers, who were continuing to work in quiet calm, as though nothing had happened.

"Do not disturb them," said Thanos softly.

He continued down the hallway until he came to stand in front of the steel doors of the treasure vault. A Warrior-Priest guarded this door day and night. Anyone wanting to enter had to ask Aelon for permission.

The steel door was smooth, unadorned. The door had no handle, no means to open it except by Aelon's grace. When the god granted the suppli-cant's prayer, the door would rise noiselessly into the rock wall above. When those inside the vault departed, the door dropped down and sealed shut.

Thanos and the other priests stood in the light of the torches, staring at the steel door and at the body of the Warrior-Priest that lay in front of it.

"I know this man," said one. "Kleitos was on guard duty the night the dragon struck."

"How did he die?" asked another. "He wasn't attacked. His sword is still in his scabbard. There's no blood, no wound."

"I know," said the first priest grimly. "See how he lies with his hand stretched toward the door. He was trying to break inside. Aelon struck him down!"

Thanos eyed the body. He had no doubt that the priest was right. Kleitos was going to take ad-vantage of the confusion and terror to help him-self to some jewels and a golden chalice or two. Thanos did not believe that Kleitos had suffered from heavenly retribution. Far more likely he'd set off the trap meant to deter thieves. If they searched the body, they'd find a poisoned dart lodged in his belly or a poisoned needle in his finger.

"We should open this door," said a priest. "Check to see if we have been robbed."

Thanos looked up expectantly at the others only to find them looking at him.

"You must pray to Aelon, Thanos," said one of

the Warrior-Priests. "Xydis meant for you to be his successor. All of us know that. Aelon will open the door for you."

Thanos sneezed. The sudden violent movement caused his head to throb. He pressed his hand to his pounding forehead and wished he had stayed in bed where he belonged. Now they were all expecting him to fall to his knees and pray and the door would open.

Thanos had seen Xydis standing in front of the door, praying to Aelon. He had seen the door open for him. Xydis had claimed this was the god's blessing. Thanos had outwardly agreed. Inwardly he'd been offended. Did his father truly think him that simple? Thanos had done a little investigating on his own and discovered the hidden mechanical device that opened the door, though he could not find out the secret to how it worked. Thanos had known better than to ask his father, for Xydis either was or pretended to be a pious man and Thanos did not want to suffer through yet another sermon on his sins.

He had kept his eyes open and whenever he had entered the vault in company with his father, Thanos would surreptitiously nudge stones to see if any were loose, press his foot on various tiles, look for tiny latches or other mechanisms concealed in the wall. He had never found anything, but he knew such a device existed. Thanos looked at the corpse and was thankful he had never given in to the temptation to go poking about the door in search of it.

The others were waiting impatiently for him to

begin to pray. Thanos heaved a sigh and shook his head, a motion that caused boulders to roll around the inside of his skull.

"Only the Priest-General can open this door," he said.

"But there is no doubt, Thanos—"

"You will certainly be chosen—"

Thanos started to shake his head again and stopped himself in time. "It would not be right. Aelon must not be robbed of his choice."

The others agreed, except for one who insisted that the treasure might have been stolen.

"I believe we can rest assured that the treasure is safe. As the unfortunate Kleitos discovered, Aelon stands guard here," said Thanos. "We have our own work to do. We must tend to our wounded and bury our dead."

He apportioned out duties. When the priests had all departed, only Thanos and the Head of the Council of Warrior-Priests, a middle-aged man named Atemis, stood in front of the steel door. The priests had carried off the body of Kleitos, taking him to the mass grave they were digging for their dead. Thanos would have liked to have examined the corpse, see if he could discover the cause of death, but he feared the others would grow suspicious. The cause of death, in their eyes, was the wrath of the god.

"You should go to your bed, Thanos," said Atemis kindly.

Thanos thought longingly of his bed, gave it up with regret.

"Someone must enter my father's office," said Thanos. He would not ordinarily have referred to Xydis as his father, but he could trust Atemis, who had been his father's best friend. "Examine his papers. Burn any that are private or . . . um . . . potentially damaging."

"That can wait," said Atemis. He was a good man, but a dull one, not particularly quick to catch on.

"Not if you fear the Shrine will be attacked," said Thanos.

Atemis understood at last. He cast Thanos a grave glance. "I would say you would be the best suited to that delicate task, but you are in pain—"

"I will undertake it," said Thanos, and he added with a wry smile, "I am not being noble or heroic, I assure you, sir. My head hurts as much lying down as sitting up and the work will distract me."

"You are a wise young man, Thanos," said Atemis. "You will make an excellent Priest-General."

"When will the Council meet to make the selection?"

"After your father's funeral." Atemis looked uncomfortable. "The deliberations might take some time."

"Why?" Thanos asked, surprised. "Has someone else stepped forward to claim the position?"

"You have no rivals, but there are those who think you are too young and others who question your dedication to the Church. You have been frequently absent from Sinaria—"

"Traveling on the business of the Church," said Thanos. "I was my father's emissary on such occasions."

"We are all aware of that, but there are those who will bring that up." Atemis gave a meaningful cough, then added, "If, for example, someone searching his office were to find a missive in which Xydis made his wishes regarding his successor known—a letter to a friend, perhaps. There would then be no question."

Thanos smiled. "Thank you, Atemis. I am certain such a document might be found."

Atemis departed with a prayer that Aelon would restore Thanos to health. Thanos lit an oil lamp and entered his father's office and gazed in some dismay at the myriad scrolls stacked on racks, tucked in baskets, nestled in cubbyholes. He thought with a groan of reading through them all in search of a letter naming him heir and was momentarily sorry he'd volunteered for this duty.

Far easier, as Atemis had obliquely suggested, to forge the letter. His father had relied on a number of scribes, so Thanos did not even have to copy the handwriting.

"But what will that gain me?" Thanos muttered to himself. "I could be named Priest-General tomorrow and then what? Everyone will expect me to pray open that damn door."

Thanos did not for one moment believe that Aelon could reach down from heaven and open that door. But if that was true . . . If beyond all rational thought and logic, there happened to be an Aelon, the god was not likely to open the door to the treasure vault for Thanos, a nonbeliever.

Thanos looked morosely at the scrolls, hundreds of them, all on display, all in plain sight for anyone to read. What of the scrolls that were *not* on display?

Thanos sat down in the comfortable chair and placed the oil lamp on the desk. Xydis had been a cautious man, a man of sense. The writings in full view of the public would be mundane, dealing with the day-to-day business of the Church. Thanos could safely leave those to the scribes to catalog.

He needed to find the work dealing with the underside, the dark underbelly of the Church. Thanos knew all about it. His father had made no secret of it to him. Thanos had even undertaken some of the work himself. The accounts of bribes paid and received, sums given to assassins, the names of spies, as well as the money taken in from the slave trade, smuggling, and various other enterprises the Church decried in public and profited from in private. Such records must be hidden somewhere, and with them the secret to the vault.

Thanos closed the door to the office, locked it, and set to work. His first task would be to create a scroll naming himself as successor. The scroll did not take long to compose. He placed it among the others, hiding it well, but not too well. His second was to find the hidden chamber where the hidden records were stored.

He was exhausted. His nose was still clogged,

his headache becoming unbearable. He found a Warrior-Priest to stand guard, and, since he had no home to go to, he wrapped himself in a hooded cloak and entered the ruined city, heading to the home of one of his favorite whores. He was delighted to find she was still alive and in desperate need of comfort.

Thanos returned to the Shrine early the next day, walking the streets of Sinaria before dawn. Survivors slept in the streets. A few were awake, searching without much luck through the rubble for whatever they could find. He stopped a moment to watch. He would help these people. He would rebuild Sinaria and it would be grander and better than before. He would do this not in the name of Aelon, but in the name of Thanos. Priest-General Thanos. Emperor Thanos. He liked the sound of that.

He went on to the Shrine, which had escaped the wrath of the dragon unscathed. He looked at the impressive building, at the dome from which shone the god's light, and he thought with amusement of the old tale that Aelon would permit only the faithful to enter his sacred precincts. Thanos had been coming and going to the Shrine all his life and Aelon had never once struck him with a rock, much less a thunderbolt.

Thanos was greeted with pleasure by the priests. Atemis was there and informed him that the funeral for Xydis and the other Chosen of Aelon would be held today.

Back in his father's office, Thanos searched for

the hidden compartment and eventually found it—a trapdoor located in the floor beneath a rug underneath the desk. He was about to open the door when he was summoned to attend the funeral.

Thanos replaced the rug and the desk and went to do his sad duty as a son and bid his father farewell. Thanos had respected Xydis, if he had not loved him. Thanos had kept his father in the dark about his whoring and carousing. Thanos had worked hard to please his father and make him proud. He felt no regret, no guilt. Thanos had been a good son; about as good a son as Xydis had been a good father.

The funerals for the Priest-General and the Empress and the hundreds of other church officials who had died in the night were held hastily and in private. In the light of this new day, survivors were roaming the streets, looting any building still standing, including the Palace. They had not yet summoned enough courage to attack the Shrine, but the Warrior-Priests feared it was only a matter of time. The bodies were placed in a mass grave and hurriedly covered over.

Standing in the broiling sun, forced to endure the stench given off by the bodies, Thanos had to suffer through a great many sermons and speeches. He was called upon to speak a few words himself. He lauded Xydis to the heavens and then urged the priests to cease to grieve for those who were now safe with Aelon and turn their attention to the living who needed their help.

As Thanos was hastening back to the office, Atemis caught up with him. Thanos greeted his friend.

"You will be pleased to know that I found a scroll expressing my father's wishes. I do not think we should make it public yet—"

"I would not wait too long," said Atemis. "I have just received word that Warrior-Priest Raegar has returned to Sinaria. His war galley sailed into the docks this morning."

Thanos wiped his streaming nose on his sleeve. "Good for him," he said offhandedly. He was eager to return to the office.

"Not so good for you," said Atemis.

Thanos heard the grim note in the man's voice and paused. "What? Why? You think I have something to fear from Raegar? He is a slave, for god's sake!"

"They are saying Raegar performed a miracle," said Atemis.

"What did he do?"

"He summoned a sea monster in Aelon's name."

Thanos laughed out loud and then put his hand to his aching head. "I have work to do, Atemis. Forgive me, but I must go."

"Indeed you do have work to do, Thanos," said Atemis in ominous tones.

Thanos hurried off. Summoned a sea monster! He would have chuckled over the notion again, but laughter made his head hurt.

CHAPTER 15

Raegar was not greeted by cheering crowds when he entered Sinaria. He was not wreathed in laurel, nor received with accolades by the people in the arena. He was greeted by the stench of death, the wailings of mourners, the screams of the wounded. His war galley had to be hauled by its sailors onto a beach because the docks had been destroyed. Raegar posted guards on the ship, fearing that people desperate for shelter would try to steal the lumber.

He paid the rowers for their services in supplies from the galley; food being more valuable than gold these days. He ordered Captain Anker—a much more respectful Captain Anker—and soldiers to escort him and Treia back to the Shrine grounds.

Raegar's return was a triumph, though he did not know it at the time. Those who had been aboard *Aelon's Triumph* talked excitedly of their experiences at sea, telling in awed and reverent tones of how Raegar, the Warrior-Priest, had first summoned a dragon to fight for them (conveniently forgetting that they had been terrified and threatened to mutiny). He had then called down Aelon's curse upon two enemy ships and moments later an enormous kraken rose from the sea to drag both ships under.

The tale grew in the telling, as tales will. The kraken was soon as large as the palace and then became two krakens and so on. The enemy ships were more numerous until it was well known throughout the city that Aelon had destroyed the entire ogre fleet with an army of krakens and dragons. In all the tellings, one thing remained constant—the name of Raegar. Sailors and soldiers talked of his courage in facing the enemy. They spoke with tears in their eyes of how he had rescued the woman he loved from the fiends who had thrown her into the sea to drown. They talked of his faith in Aelon and how the god must love him.

The survivors of Sinaria needed hope and they needed a hero and in Raegar they got both. The fact that he had once been a slave added to the legend that was growing around him. He had known poverty and misfortune and loss. He was one of them. Raegar might not have been greeted by cheering crowds on his return, but the day after he could not walk the streets without being surrounded by admirers.

After debarking the galley, Raegar and Treia left with their escort for the Shrine in the early afternoon, a journey that should have taken only a short time on the well-paved roads of Sinaria. The roads were in ruins, however; impassable in many places, blocked by bricks and stones from buildings that had collapsed. Raegar and his soldiers stopped on the way to help shift wreckage and open the roads and to dig out trapped survivors.

Raegar used his great strength to lift heavy beams or move huge chunks of stone. Treia used her healing skills to aid the wounded. As they worked, the soldiers who escorted them told the tale of the kraken. Raegar was modest and gave all the credit to Aelon. Treia watched the people watching him with something akin to adoration and she began to think that what had seemed misfortune in summoning the Vektia dragon might turn out to be good fortune after all—at least for her and Raegar.

Thanos was meeting with the Council of High Priests when a messenger arrived from Warrior-Priest Raegar, saying that he had returned safely and would report to them as soon as he was able to reach the Shrine. The messenger related the exciting story of the dragon and the kraken, of Aelon's curse and the sinking of enemy ships.

Thanos, looking around the table, saw the priests listening in awe. Here was another candidate for the office of Priest-General. For not every member of the Council favored Thanos. He had made his share of enemies over time. What man does not? He had assumed these priests would be putting forth another candidate, but he had not been much worried. He had the scroll that proclaimed him his father's successor. Who could compete with that?

Apparently Raegar and a miracle.

Xydis and Thanos had often had a chuckle at Raegar's expense. Xydis considered Raegar a loutish brute, useful for his connections with the shadowy underworld of Sinaria. A former slave desperate to be accepted in a society that would never accept him, Raegar would do anything for a word of praise and the vague hint that he might be destined for great things.

Thanos listened to the talk and outwardly smiled and inwardly gnashed his teeth. He was in an untenable position. He dared say nothing against Raegar or suggest that this talk of miracle-performing kraken was downright silly, lest he should appear to be petty, jealous, or, worse, apostate. Thanos had to loudly praise Aelon for Raegar's safe return all the while heartily wishing the man were at the bottom of the ocean.

When the meeting ended Thanos did not stay to hear more about Raegar. He returned to the office of the Priest-General to continue going through his father's things. His enemies questioned that Thanos should be left there on his own. His friends, among them the powerful High Priest, Atemis, said that as Xydis's son and the probable next Priest-General, Thanos had every right to be there.

Unfortunately, Thanos had not found what he sought—the secret to opening the door to the treasure vault. He had read through most of the secret documents he had discovered in the cubbyhole beneath the desk and although he had learned a great deal that was highly informative, particularly regarding just how much wealth the church had amassed behind that bronze door, he had no idea how to obtain it. He remained hopeful, however, and continued reading.

By the time Raegar arrived at the Shrine, the political winds were blowing up a gale. He dismissed his escort, sending them off with Captain Anker to the makeshift barracks, their own having burned down. He kept Treia by his side and both of them knew the moment they entered the Shrine that they were walking into a storm. He was welcomed with rapturous gusts by some, who crowded around him, eager to shake his hand; a few of the more fulsome actually asked for his blessing. They talked openly of presenting him as a candidate for the office of Priest-General. Raegar was basking in the warmth of this breeze, when he was struck by a chill blast. High Priest Atemis came (slowly) to greet Raegar. The high priest said he had thanked Aelon for Raegar's safe return, adding that Raegar would of course want to wait upon Thanos, who was in the office of the Priest-General, to pay his respects to the man whom Xydis had named as his successor.

Treia flashed Raegar a warning glance and squeezed his hand. He had no need of her silent counsel. He had been expecting that Thanos would challenge him for the office. Thanos had probably never imagined that Raegar would be challenging him.

Raegar had known Thanos for a long time. In fact, Raegar knew more about Thanos than Thanos suspected. Raegar's friends in the underworld kept him well-informed. Thanos paid his whore enough to buy her secrecy. He never thought of paying off the man who "protected" her or her children, who would regularly report on "Mama's visitors." Raegar could have used his knowledge to discredit Thanos to the priesthood, but he feared that if he did, his own dealings with Sinaria's criminal element would come out.

By ordering Raegar to come to him, Thanos was making a bold move. If Raegar acted upon Thanos's orders, Raegar would be conceding that Thanos had a right to give orders.

Raegar was covered with the dirt and sweat and blood from his labors among the people. His face was drawn with fatigue and yet he spoke with an air of quiet dignity that impressed even the High Priest.

"I have been working to free survivors who were trapped in the rubble," Raegar said. "I am exhausted from this and from my venture out to sea. I would not presume to greet Warrior-Priest Thanos before I have washed and changed and rested. I will be in my quarters. If Thanos has need of me, he can wait upon me there."

Raegar gave a respectful bow and then left, in company with Treia, who held her head high. The High Priest listened to the talk among the other priests regarding Raegar. Their opinion of him was unanimously favorable. The High Priest carried Raegar's response to Thanos, curious to see how he would react to Raegar's refusal.

Thanos shrugged. He would have been surprised if Raegar had come to him. Thanos handed over the scroll naming himself as successor.

"I found it quite by chance," he said.

Atemis did not read it, but stood tapping it thoughtfully on the desk.

"What's the matter?" Thanos asked.

"I believe Raegar has a good chance of becoming Priest-General."

Thanos sniffed and wiped his nose. "Raegar is a valiant warrior. I believe his people are known for their savagery in battle. But he has an inflated idea of his own importance if he considers himself worthy of being Priest-General. Such ambition in a former slave would be laughable were it not so sad."

"That may be true," said Atemis. "But many on the Council are impressed by him. The people who are now gathered in the streets outside the Shrine grounds are no longer here to attack us, but to cheer Raegar. He has restored their faith."

"What do you suggest I do to counter this?" Thanos asked, preoccupied with his search.

"If you could perform a miracle, in full view of the Council—"

"And do what?" Thanos asked. "Summon squid? Lift a house?"

Atemis frowned. "You need to take this seriously."

"Very well." Thanos sighed. "What do you suggest?"

"The priests are wondering why you have not yet prayed to Aelon to unseal the door to the treasure vault," said the High Priest.

Thanos was tired. His head hurt. His throat was sore. He lost patience.

"Given the fact that gangs have threatened to attack us, hasn't it occurred to those fools that Aelon might be smart to keep the damn door shut?"

Atemis gave Thanos a shrewd look. "Aelon should not wait too long."

Thanos muttered something and went back to his search. He drew out the last scroll, glanced over it, saw that it was nothing but a ritual prayer to Aelon asking his blessing on the newly anointed Priest-General. Thanos was about to toss it aside when something odd in the prayer caught his attention. He started from the beginning, read it more closely.

"Simple, yet elegant. Aelon, if I believed in you, I'd get down on my knees in thanks," Thanos remarked.

Treia was afraid she was losing Raegar. She tried talking to him about Thanos, but he said curtly he was too tired to discuss the matter with her. She wanted to share his bed, but he said that would be unseemly. She brought up their wedding, asking him to set a date. He said he had too much to think about.

He told her go to her own rest in the small cell where she lived with the other priestesses of Aelon. When she left, he would not even kiss her. Raegar had changed. He *did* shine with a god's light. He was confident, strong, and she needed a way to strengthen her hold on him.

She went to her cell, but not to sleep. She dressed in the plain robes of a novice priestess of Aelon, drew her cowl over her head so that she would not be noticed, and went back to the Shrine where priests and priestesses had gathered to talk about the choice for the new Priest-General. Treia glided silently from group to group, listening to what was being said.

For the first time, Treia heard about the sealed bronze door and the death of Kleitos. Many were wondering openly why Thanos had not asked Aelon to open it. Treia listened, intrigued. An idea formed in her mind. She left word with the porter at the monastery where the unmarried Warrior-Priests had their quarters that she needed to speak with Raegar. He would find her in the garden near the Fane of the Spirit Priests.

Surrounded by fir trees, the garden was secluded and quiet. No one was around. The Fane of the Spirit Priests had been abandoned, the priestesses fleeing first the threat of ogres and then the threat of mobs. Treia sat on a wall of lichen-covered gray stone. The air was hot and humid. In her own land, summer would be ending. The days would be warm, but there would be a touch of coming winter in the chill air of night.

Treia had always hated winter. Raegar had assured her winter never came to Sinaria, never brought frostbite, starvation, howling bitter winds, killing snow.

Treia had no desire to ever go back to Vindraholm. She liked Sinaria, its heat, its abundance, its wealth. She didn't much like the people of Sinaria, but then Treia didn't much like anyone.

Treia's opinion of the gods was peculiarly her own. Raegar believed in Aelon with all his heart and soul. He viewed Aelon with awe and reverence, knowing him to be an immortal being who came to this world to bring the light of his glory to those walking in darkness. If Aelon's bright light blinded some and scorched others, that was due to their imperfections, not the god's.

Treia viewed all gods as immortal hucksters peddling their wares to gullible humanity. She drove a hard bargain for her faith. She was not about to give any god something for nothing. Sometimes, as she had with Hevis, Treia made a bad deal and learned not to make that mistake again. She liked the god Aelon, seeing him as a god with a practical turn of mind, ambitious, clever, cunning. She could work with a god like that.

Time passed. The sun was sinking and Raegar had not come. Treia wondered with a pang if he was going to ignore her summons . . . and she was filled with relief and gratitude when she saw him striding up the path. Raegar was wearing the robes of a Warrior-Priest. He was much refreshed and thinking more clearly following a good meal and a long sleep. He greeted Treia with a kiss, then, looking about and seeing they were alone, started to draw her into the bushes.

Treia stopped him. "We need to talk, my love. How is the successor to the Priest-General chosen?"

"If Xydis had lived, he would have named his successor on his deathbed. If the Priest-General dies before he can name his successor, the matter goes to the Council of Priests."

"There is talk that Xydis left a letter stating that he chose Thanos. It was found among his things in his office."

Raegar grunted. "Not surprising."

"Does Aelon have a say in the selection of the Priest-General?" Treia asked.

"Of course." Raegar looked shocked that she could even ask the question. "The Council prays to the god to guide the decision."

Treia clasped hold of Raegar's hand. "Then it is clear, my love. The god has already chosen. Aelon wants you to be Priest-General."

"Thanos would disagree," said Raegar dryly.

"I spent the afternoon in the Shrine, listening to the talk," said Treia. "The priests are impressed. You took charge in a time of crisis. You set out to sea to drive away the foe. You called down the wrath of Aelon upon your enemies. You came back a hero and yet you were not too proud to help those in need."

Raegar was pleased. "They are saying that of me?"

"That and much more," Treia assured him.

"And what do they say of Thanos?"

Treia shrugged. "That he is the son of Xydis."

Raegar laughed and kissed her on the neck.

"Time for love-making later," Treia said, wriggling away from him. "I found out something else, something of importance. You need to listen and decide what to do.

"The great door to the treasure vault remains sealed. The priests have prayed to Aelon to grant them the power to open it, but the door remains shut. One man died, they say, trying to force it open. Aelon struck him down."

"Only the Priest-General is given the power to unseal the door," said Raegar. "He prays to Aelon, who opens the door with his hand."

"That's just it, my love," Treia said softly. "If Aelon wanted Thanos to be Priest-General, Thanos would be counting jewels in the treasure vault now, instead of reading letters in his father's office. They say that High Priest Atemis himself has asked Thanos to pray to Aelon to open the door and Thanos refuses."

"With good reason," said Raegar sternly. "He is not Priest-General."

"You are too trusting," said Treia with a fond smile. "The door is trapped. Thanos is searching through his father's papers for the secret to the mechanism that will safely open it. Once Thanos has found it, then he will pray."

Raegar was displeased. "A mechanism! You speak sacrilege. The door opens at Aelon's command."

"*I* know that, my love," Treia said soothingly. "You and I have faith in the god. But others are skeptical. Rumor has it that this Kleitos died trying to open the door. From what I hear, he was not praying when he made the attempt."

"You think *I* should pray to Aelon to open the vault door. But I am not Priest-General. Aelon struck down Kleitos because the god was angered by his disobedience."

Treia sighed inwardly. Raegar was such a child sometimes. He would not disobey the god's command. She was certain there was some sort of mechanism. She did not believe the god truly raised and lowered the door. Whatever the truth, the question remained: how was the door to be opened if no one knew the secret? After all, the wyrds of gods and men are intertwined and it was men who built that door.

"When a new Priest-General is named, does he undergo some sort of ritual?" Treia asked.

"In the Mount of the Revelation is the holy cavern where the god appeared to the Sacred One who first brought the light of Aelon into our midst. The new Priest-General must undertake a journey to this cavern and offer himself to the god."

"That has to be the answer," Treia murmured. "That is where the god reveals the secret. Only the Priest-General is allowed inside the cavern?"

"The candidate must pass tests set by the god

r wedding gift, the necklace holding the spir-
e of the Dragon Fala, rested on the table. The
ng was crude and unlovely, for it had been
e in haste. After receiving the spiritbone, Rae-
had taken the bone to one of the local jewelry
kers with orders that it be made into a pen-
nt. He could not afford gold or silver and so the
weler had used bronze. A misshapen dragon
ith a lumpy tail held the spiritbone in four claws.
igh Priest Atemis had frowned at it during the
eremony and was overheard to make a remark
about "savages and their strange customs."

Treia snuggled into the warm robe and picked up the spiritbone and lovingly caressed it. Ugly though it might be, the spiritbone was hers. The Dragon Fala was hers.

Treia had never liked the Dragon Kahg because she knew the dragon did not like her. Treia had not wanted to be a dragon priestess. She'd been essentially sold into the Kai priesthood by her mother in return for the gods healing her father. The gods had not held up their end of the bargain. Her father had died and Treia had lived the life of a slave.

What was once a curse was now a blessing. Holding the spiritbone of the Dragon Fala in her hand, Treia smiled derisively. She would use the Vindrasi priestess's own teachings to destroy them.

Treia spoke to the dragon's bone as she ran her fingers over it and watched the bright blur that was the candle flame reflected in the bronze. She spoke

to prove himself worthy. He must enter alone. No one else is permitted to accompany him."

Treia twined her fingers around his and said softly, "Thanos will come to the Council armed with his father's blessing. You must come armed with Aelon's. You must be the one to take that journey."

"How do I prove to the Council that I have the blessing of the god?"

"With the help of your wife," said Treia coyly. "And my bride gift—the spiritbone of the Dragon Fala."

When she had finished explaining her plan, Raegar said, "I want to be Priest-General, but I don't want to gain the office by trickery—"

"You know as well as I do, my love, that Thanos is using tricks of his own," Treia said, annoyed.

"His wrong does not make me right," said Raegar sententiously. He drew his hand away and rose to his feet. "Besides, the Dragon Fala is angry. She will not come."

"She will come if Aelon commands her to come," said Treia.

Raegar paused to look down at her.

"What do you mean?"

Treia pursued her advantage. "The Dragon Fala pledged her assistance to Aelon because she believes in the god and wants to serve him. Right?"

"That is true," said Raegar.

"If Fala comes when she is summoned, she will do so because Aelon commands her. Because Aelon wants you to be Priest-General. This is not a trick. This will be your test to see if the god has faith in you."

Raegar mulled this over. Treia did not give him much time to think.

"We must act immediately, my love," she urged. "Thanos is even now working to build up support among the Council."

"And what if the Dragon Fala does not appear?" Raegar asked. "I will look a fool in front of the people and the Council."

Treia rested her hands on his chest and looked into his eyes. "You say you have faith in Aelon, my love. Either you do . . . or you don't."

Raegar and Treia were married that night in a simple private ceremony conducted by Atemis, the High Priest of the Council. Raegar was resplendent in his armor. The bride was dressed in the modest robes of a novice. Her only adornment was a necklace made of silver and amethyst and bone.

"A bride gift from my husband," said Treia. She added demurely, "And from Aelon."

CHAPTER 16

Treia lay in her bridal bed, waiting te she was certain Raegar was either passed out—he had celebrated by consu great deal of wine. They had consumma marriage, and while she waited she passed th hoping that they had conceived a child. She ne yet another link in the chain she had wound arc Raegar. A son would be the strongest yet.

She wanted a baby. A son to nurture, to raise son who would love her and only her.

Treia poked Raegar. He gave a drunken grur ble, but did not move. He was always a heav sleeper, even without the wine to dull his senses Treia slid from the bed, padded softly across the room. Wrapping herself in a robe against the night's chill, she sat down at the small table in one of the two chairs in their small dwelling.

Now that she and Raegar were married, they had been permitted to move into quarters for married couples: two bare, cold, cell-like rooms.

"Never mind," said Treia, lighting a candle. "We won't be here long. We will be moving into the grand palace belonging to the Priest-General."

softly, so as not to disturb Raegar, who must not hear what she was about to do.

"I need to talk to you, Fala. I know you are upset. You must forgive my husband." Treia's heart thrilled as she said the word. "Raegar was not trained as a Bone Priestess and he did not know what he was doing. I understand. I spent years studying the art of working with dragons. I—"

"And who are you?"

The voice came from the spiritbone.

"I am Treia, wife of Raegar," she responded.

"You have been trained as a Bone Priestess. Do you, then, worship the Dragon Goddess of the Kai, the one known as Vindrash?" Fala's voice was cold and harsh.

"I prayed to Vindrash. I knew no better. I now pray to Aelon."

"You pray to him. Do you worship him?"

Treia heard a sneer in the dragon's voice, as if Fala was prepared to accept Treia's weakness, but would always secretly despise her for it. Treia felt as though she understood the dragon. She hoped the dragon would understand her and decided to risk telling the truth.

"Perhaps I will offend you, Dragon Fala, but there should be no secrets between us," said Treia. "I honor and I respect Aelon, but I do not worship him. I do not worship any god. How could I, when I see gods acting out of conceit and ambition and greed, laid low by the same faults and follies as they claim to abhor in man."

The Dragon Fala was silent for a long moment and Treia feared she had made a mistake.

Then the dragon said, with a chuckle, "You are wise for a human, Treia. Wiser than the male you have taken for a mate, since we are both speaking the truth. I entered this realm for one reason: to search for young dragons to form a clan of my own. I refused to ally myself with the Old Gods. Their wyrds are frayed and tattered and will soon break. I was approached by both the Gods of Raj and Aelon. Both wanted me to join with them.

"I considered both. The Gods of Raj came late to the table and found nothing but leftover races: the ogres and the Cyclops and the goblins. I considered choosing them."

"Why is that?" Treia was forced to ask politely, though she was impatient to embark upon her plan. The Dragon Fala apparently liked to chat.

"Because of the Cyclops, a race that is most promising. They are humans who paint a third eye, known as the 'world eye' on their foreheads. This eye is magical and gives them special powers of insight into the human soul. Then, too, the Cyclops have always honored dragons. The entrance to our realm is located in a mountain in their land. The Cyclops worship the Gods of Raj and venerate them."

"You rejected them, apparently," said Treia, keeping an ear cocked, listening for Raegar and wishing the dragon would hurry this along.

"The Cyclops are shepherds and farmers. They

are not explorers. They build no ships. They dislike war and fighting. They are content with what they have, with no desire to go raiding their neighbors. That is of little use to me. I wanted to travel the world to acquire the jewels in which reside baby dragons.

"Aelon offered me the chance to explore the world with a war galley, as well as the jewels in the Church's treasury that turned out to be dragons. A bargain I trust you and the god will honor."

Treia sighed with relief. She could not have asked for a better opening.

"*I* would honor it, as would my husband, Raegar. We are both Vindrasi and we understand how to work with dragons." Treia shook her head sorrowfully. "Unfortunately, Aelon grants control of the treasure vault to only one man and that is the Priest-General. The office remains vacant since the untimely death of the last Priest-General. A successor has not yet been chosen. Raegar would be honored to accept the position—"

"Then let him be Priest-General and be done with it," said the Dragon Fala.

"The matter is not that simple," Treia said with deep regret. "The choice of the Priest-General is left to men. The other man vying for the post is the son of the last Priest-General, Xydis. Many on the Council are planning to select him. For all we know, Aelon himself may incline in that direction."

"I know this Xydis," said the Dragon Fala, angered. "Raegar sought payment for me in the form of certain fine gems he had seen in the vault. When he attempted to obtain them, Xydis refused, claiming he had received no instructions from the god."

"I promise you, Dragon Fala, that if Raegar is named Priest-General, you will have first pick of all the jewels that come into the treasury."

"We could leave the choice to Aelon," said Fala.

"We could . . ." Treia shrugged.

Fala chuckled again. "Let me hear your plan."

"You must keep this secret," Treia warned. "My husband must not know. He is a pious man and would not understand."

The Dragon Fala agreed to cooperate. Dragon and Bone Priestess parted on the best of terms.

After the dragon was gone, Treia remained seated at the table, dreaming of the future. She was shocked to realize that for the first time in her life, she was happy. She was married to the man she adored. A man who would rise to great heights in this world, and she would rise with him. She was thinking about this, smiling contentedly, when the candle's flame flared up with a sudden hiss that made Treia start.

She was about to trim the wick when she was horrified to see eyes in the flame. Treia's mouth went dry; her breath stopped. She gripped the table with both hands to support herself or she would have fallen from the chair.

Hevis, god of fire, lies, and deceit, gazed at her from the fire.

"What . . . what do you want?" Treia whispered through trembling lips.

"We made a bargain. I gave you what *you* wanted—the power to summon the Vektia dragon. You owe me. You promised to sacrifice one you love."

"Aylaen is dead," Treia said, shivering. "I promised you she would die and she did."

"You didn't kill her."

"I tried! That horrid fae boy attacked me before I could . . ." She stopped, choked by terror.

The god's eyes burned.

"Excuses! You seek to weasel out of your bargain with me."

Treia wilted beneath the heat. "Please, give me more time . . ."

"You have nine months. Or the choice of the sacrifice is mine."

The candle guttered, the flame flashed out. The god vanished, leaving Treia shuddering. Nine months. What could that mean? She had to kill someone she loved . . . Nine months.

"Oh, god!" Treia moaned, clasping her hand spasmodically over her belly. "Oh, god, no!"

She nearly fainted when she heard footsteps.

"It's the middle of the night," Raegar grumbled, coming up behind her. "What are you doing?"

Treia drew in a quivering breath, then pushed herself up from the table.

"I couldn't sleep . . . for joy . . ." Treia gulped. "Come, let us go back to bed."

She walked unsteadily into the bed chamber and crawled beneath the blanket. Raegar plunked himself down beside her.

"Damn, woman, you're freezing! Your body is like a block of ice." He laughed. "I'll warm you."

He began to run his hands over her body. His touch usually thrilled her, but now she felt sick to her stomach. Her skin crawled. She tried to claim she was too tired, but he was awake now and filled with desire. Treia stiffened.

"What's wrong with you?" Raegar said angrily. "This is our wedding night."

"You . . . you have so much work to do tomorrow," Treia stammered. "You should be rested . . ."

"I will rest. After this."

He drew her to him. She yielded to him, but when they were finished, Treia curled up into a ball. His seed was in her womb. Hevis's curse would see to that. Treia choked back her sobs.

Nine months. She had nine months to find a sacrifice, or either her baby or her husband would die.

to prove himself worthy. He must enter alone. No one else is permitted to accompany him."

Treia twined her fingers around his and said softly, "Thanos will come to the Council armed with his father's blessing. You must come armed with Aelon's. You must be the one to take that journey."

"How do I prove to the Council that I have the blessing of the god?"

"With the help of your wife," said Treia coyly. "And my bride gift—the spiritbone of the Dragon Fala."

When she had finished explaining her plan, Raegar said, "I want to be Priest-General, but I don't want to gain the office by trickery—"

"You know as well as I do, my love, that Thanos is using tricks of his own," Treia said, annoyed.

"His wrong does not make me right," said Raegar sententiously. He drew his hand away and rose to his feet. "Besides, the Dragon Fala is angry. She will not come."

"She will come if Aelon commands her to come," said Treia.

Raegar paused to look down at her.

"What do you mean?"

Treia pursued her advantage. "The Dragon Fala pledged her assistance to Aelon because she believes in the god and wants to serve him. Right?"

"That is true," said Raegar.

"If Fala comes when she is summoned, she will do so because Aelon commands her. Because Aelon

wants you to be Priest-General. This is not a trick. This will be your test to see if the god has faith in you."

Raegar mulled this over. Treia did not give him much time to think.

"We must act immediately, my love," she urged. "Thanos is even now working to build up support among the Council."

"And what if the Dragon Fala does not appear?" Raegar asked. "I will look a fool in front of the people and the Council."

Treia rested her hands on his chest and looked into his eyes. "You say you have faith in Aelon, my love. Either you do . . . or you don't."

Raegar and Treia were married that night in a simple private ceremony conducted by Atemis, the High Priest of the Council. Raegar was resplendent in his armor. The bride was dressed in the modest robes of a novice. Her only adornment was a necklace made of silver and amethyst and bone.

"A bride gift from my husband," said Treia. She added demurely, "And from Aelon."

CHAPTER 16

Treia lay in her bridal bed, waiting tensely until she was certain Raegar was either asleep or passed out—he had celebrated by consuming a great deal of wine. They had consummated the marriage, and while she waited she passed the time hoping that they had conceived a child. She needed yet another link in the chain she had wound around Raegar. A son would be the strongest yet.

She wanted a baby. A son to nurture, to raise. A son who would love her and only her.

Treia poked Raegar. He gave a drunken grumble, but did not move. He was always a heavy sleeper, even without the wine to dull his senses. Treia slid from the bed, padded softly across the room. Wrapping herself in a robe against the night's chill, she sat down at the small table in one of the two chairs in their small dwelling.

Now that she and Raegar were married, they had been permitted to move into quarters for married couples: two bare, cold, cell-like rooms.

"Never mind," said Treia, lighting a candle. "We won't be here long. We will be moving into the grand palace belonging to the Priest-General."

Her wedding gift, the necklace holding the spiritbone of the Dragon Fala, rested on the table. The setting was crude and unlovely, for it had been done in haste. After receiving the spiritbone, Raegar had taken the bone to one of the local jewelry makers with orders that it be made into a pendant. He could not afford gold or silver and so the jeweler had used bronze. A misshapen dragon with a lumpy tail held the spiritbone in four claws. High Priest Atemis had frowned at it during the ceremony and was overheard to make a remark about "savages and their strange customs."

Treia snuggled into the warm robe and picked up the spiritbone and lovingly caressed it. Ugly though it might be, the spiritbone was hers. The Dragon Fala was hers.

Treia had never liked the Dragon Kahg because she knew the dragon did not like her. Treia had not wanted to be a dragon priestess. She'd been essentially sold into the Kai priesthood by her mother in return for the gods healing her father. The gods had not held up their end of the bargain. Her father had died and Treia had lived the life of a slave.

What was once a curse was now a blessing. Holding the spiritbone of the Dragon Fala in her hand, Treia smiled derisively. She would use the Vindrasi priestess's own teachings to destroy them.

Treia spoke to the dragon's bone as she ran her fingers over it and watched the bright blur that was the candle flame reflected in the bronze. She spoke

softly, so as not to disturb Raegar, who must not hear what she was about to do.

"I need to talk to you, Fala. I know you are upset. You must forgive my husband." Treia's heart thrilled as she said the word. "Raegar was not trained as a Bone Priestess and he did not know what he was doing. I understand. I spent years studying the art of working with dragons. I—"

"And who are you?"

The voice came from the spiritbone.

"I am Treia, wife of Raegar," she responded.

"You have been trained as a Bone Priestess. Do you, then, worship the Dragon Goddess of the Kai, the one known as Vindrash?" Fala's voice was cold and harsh.

"I prayed to Vindrash. I knew no better. I now pray to Aelon."

"You pray to him. Do you worship him?"

Treia heard a sneer in the dragon's voice, as if Fala was prepared to accept Treia's weakness, but would always secretly despise her for it. Treia felt as though she understood the dragon. She hoped the dragon would understand her and decided to risk telling the truth.

"Perhaps I will offend you, Dragon Fala, but there should be no secrets between us," said Treia. "I honor and I respect Aelon, but I do not worship him. I do not worship any god. How could I, when I see gods acting out of conceit and ambition and greed, laid low by the same faults and follies as they claim to abhor in man."

The Dragon Fala was silent for a long moment and Treia feared she had made a mistake.

Then the dragon said, with a chuckle, "You are wise for a human, Treia. Wiser than the male you have taken for a mate, since we are both speaking the truth. I entered this realm for one reason: to search for young dragons to form a clan of my own. I refused to ally myself with the Old Gods. Their wyrds are frayed and tattered and will soon break. I was approached by both the Gods of Raj and Aelon. Both wanted me to join with them.

"I considered both. The Gods of Raj came late to the table and found nothing but leftover races: the ogres and the Cyclops and the goblins. I considered choosing them."

"Why is that?" Treia was forced to ask politely, though she was impatient to embark upon her plan. The Dragon Fala apparently liked to chat.

"Because of the Cyclops, a race that is most promising. They are humans who paint a third eye, known as the 'world eye' on their foreheads. This eye is magical and gives them special powers of insight into the human soul. Then, too, the Cyclops have always honored dragons. The entrance to our realm is located in a mountain in their land. The Cyclops worship the Gods of Raj and venerate them."

"You rejected them, apparently," said Treia, keeping an ear cocked, listening for Raegar and wishing the dragon would hurry this along.

"The Cyclops are shepherds and farmers. They

are not explorers. They build no ships. They dislike war and fighting. They are content with what they have, with no desire to go raiding their neighbors. That is of little use to me. I wanted to travel the world to acquire the jewels in which reside baby dragons.

"Aelon offered me the chance to explore the world with a war galley, as well as the jewels in the Church's treasury that turned out to be dragons. A bargain I trust you and the god will honor."

Treia sighed with relief. She could not have asked for a better opening.

"*I* would honor it, as would my husband, Raegar. We are both Vindrasi and we understand how to work with dragons." Treia shook her head sorrowfully. "Unfortunately, Aelon grants control of the treasure vault to only one man and that is the Priest-General. The office remains vacant since the untimely death of the last Priest-General. A successor has not yet been chosen. Raegar would be honored to accept the position—"

"Then let him be Priest-General and be done with it," said the Dragon Fala.

"The matter is not that simple," Treia said with deep regret. "The choice of the Priest-General is left to men. The other man vying for the post is the son of the last Priest-General, Xydis. Many on the Council are planning to select him. For all we know, Aelon himself may incline in that direction."

"I know this Xydis," said the Dragon Fala, angered. "Raegar sought payment for me in the form

of certain fine gems he had seen in the vault. When he attempted to obtain them, Xydis refused, claiming he had received no instructions from the god."

"I promise you, Dragon Fala, that if Raegar is named Priest-General, you will have first pick of all the jewels that come into the treasury."

"We could leave the choice to Aelon," said Fala.

"We could . . ." Treia shrugged.

Fala chuckled again. "Let me hear your plan."

"You must keep this secret," Treia warned. "My husband must not know. He is a pious man and would not understand."

The Dragon Fala agreed to cooperate. Dragon and Bone Priestess parted on the best of terms.

After the dragon was gone, Treia remained seated at the table, dreaming of the future. She was shocked to realize that for the first time in her life, she was happy. She was married to the man she adored. A man who would rise to great heights in this world, and she would rise with him. She was thinking about this, smiling contentedly, when the candle's flame flared up with a sudden hiss that made Treia start.

She was about to trim the wick when she was horrified to see eyes in the flame. Treia's mouth went dry; her breath stopped. She gripped the table with both hands to support herself or she would have fallen from the chair.

Hevis, god of fire, lies, and deceit, gazed at her from the fire.

"What . . . what do you want?" Treia whispered through trembling lips.

"We made a bargain. I gave you what *you* wanted—the power to summon the Vektia dragon. You owe me. You promised to sacrifice one you love."

"Aylaen is dead," Treia said, shivering. "I promised you she would die and she did."

"You didn't kill her."

"I tried! That horrid fae boy attacked me before I could . . ." She stopped, choked by terror.

The god's eyes burned.

"Excuses! You seek to weasel out of your bargain with me."

Treia wilted beneath the heat. "Please, give me more time . . ."

"You have nine months. Or the choice of the sacrifice is mine."

The candle guttered, the flame flashed out. The god vanished, leaving Treia shuddering. Nine months. What could that mean? She had to kill someone she loved . . . Nine months.

"Oh, god!" Treia moaned, clasping her hand spasmodically over her belly. "Oh, god, no!"

She nearly fainted when she heard footsteps.

"It's the middle of the night," Raegar grumbled, coming up behind her. "What are you doing?"

Treia drew in a quivering breath, then pushed herself up from the table.

"I couldn't sleep . . . for joy . . ." Treia gulped. "Come, let us go back to bed."

She walked unsteadily into the bed chamber and crawled beneath the blanket. Raegar plunked himself down beside her.

"Damn, woman, you're freezing! Your body is like a block of ice." He laughed. "I'll warm you."

He began to run his hands over her body. His touch usually thrilled her, but now she felt sick to her stomach. Her skin crawled. She tried to claim she was too tired, but he was awake now and filled with desire. Treia stiffened.

"What's wrong with you?" Raegar said angrily. "This is our wedding night."

"You . . . you have so much work to do tomorrow," Treia stammered. "You should be rested . . ."

"I will rest. After this."

He drew her to him. She yielded to him, but when they were finished, Treia curled up into a ball. His seed was in her womb. Hevis's curse would see to that. Treia choked back her sobs.

Nine months. She had nine months to find a sacrifice, or either her baby or her husband would die.

CHAPTER 17

Treia had recovered from her fright by the following morning. The nightmarish encounter with Hevis had been just that—a nightmare brought about by drinking too much wine. She was being foolish, overreacting. She and Raegar had coupled many times before and he had yet to get her with child. She had work to do and she could not allow any distractions. She would not think of it now.

As Raegar dressed in his finest robe and put on his ceremonial armor, she showed him the spirit-bone, explained what to do, what to say, how to say it.

"Where will you be?" Raegar was shaving his head and face with a razor, viewing his reflection in a small bronze mirror. "Won't you be with me? You are my wife now."

"No, no, my love," said Treia. "This is your moment of glory. I don't want to be a distraction."

Raegar shrugged, not much caring. Treia saw this and felt a pang. Never mind, she thought. I am his wife. That is all that matters.

"I will be watching from some quiet place," Treia said. "And praying to Aelon."

Raegar scraped at his jaw. "The god is with me. I feel his presence."

Treia handed him a cloth to mop his face.

"The god loves you," said Treia, helping him adjust his armor. "And now, you must take a walk through the city. Show yourself to the people. Ask for their support."

Raegar did as she suggested. He rode through the streets in a chariot and was pleased and astonished to find the people shouting his praises, surrounding his chariot, wanting to touch him, asking for his blessing. Cheering throngs escorted Raegar to the Shrine. Treia, disguised in her cloak, wearing the spiritbone around her neck, made her solitary way to an old shrine where she and Raegar had often met to make love.

The shrine was small and run-down. Hidden among trees, the shrine was dedicated to a lesser god in the pantheon, a god whose name no one knew or cared to know. Made of stone, the building was dark, dank, and shadowy. No one was here, as Treia had foreseen. Everyone had gathered to find out the decision of the High Council.

Treia picked up a handful of mud from the soggy ground and then entered the shrine. Choosing a dark corner, she knelt down on the ground and took off the spiritbone. She covered the bone with mud and began to chant the words that would summon the dragon.

The High Council of Warrior-Priests was meeting in the domed Shrine of Aelon to consider the two candidates for the office of Priest-General. No one was quite sure of the proper protocol, for none of them had ever been faced with this unique situation; the Priest-General had always named a successor before he died. They opened the session with prayers to Aelon, asking for the god's guidance, and then the two candidates were asked to come forth to state their claims.

Thanos, as the son of the late Priest-General, was given the honor of speaking first. He had recovered from his cold and the effects of a cracked skull. He began by praising Raegar, which everyone thought was generous. He then modestly gave the High Priest the forged scroll naming himself as his father's choice to be Priest-General, saying that he was humbled to know how well his father thought of him. He finished by explaining some of his plans for the future of the church and the rebuilding of the city of Sinaria. Since these plans would increase the wealth and power of the priests, they were consequently well received.

The council asked friends of the candidate to offer their assessment of him. They proclaimed Thanos to be a man of honor and intelligence, possessing wisdom far beyond his years. They also added, pointedly, that he was a Sinarian.

Raegar was then invited to speak. Most of the council considered this a formality, a sop thrown to the people of Sinaria, who were gathered outside the Shrine, shouting Raegar's name. High Priest Atemis introduced Raegar by first cautioning the members to guard against succumbing to the will of the masses, who, like children, did not always know what was good for them. After some faint praise, acknowledging Raegar's heroics during the past crisis, Atemis invited Raegar to speak.

Raegar's speech was brief. He was not a Sinarian, that was true, but he asked if the worship of Aelon was limited only to Sinarians. He trusted this was not so, since the church had priests of all races now, working to bring everyone in the world out of the darkness and into Aelon's light. Selecting him, a Vindrasi and a former follower of the old, failed gods, to be Priest-General would show people the world over that Aelon and his church was all-inclusive. Everyone, from human to ogre, was welcome. He concluded with a statement that astonished them all.

"I say to the members of this honored council that Aelon has already chosen his Priest-General. The god has chosen me. He gave me the power to summon the kraken that attacked our enemies and dragged them beneath the sea."

Before the Council could recover from their shock at this temerity, Raegar called as witnesses the men who had served aboard *Aelon's Triumph*. They came forward, led by Captain Anker, who gave a stirring account of the kraken flinging its tentacles around the two ships, the sounds of ogres screaming in terror, the cracking and rending of timber, the horrible gurgling as the ships went under and, finally, the awful silence left behind.

The members of the council were impressed. Thanos and High Priest Atemis exchanged glances. Thanos rose to say that while this show of Aelon's power was truly wonderful, it did not prove that Aelon had chosen Raegar as Priest-General. Aelon performed miracles every day.

Up until now, Raegar had been feeling dubious about Treia's plan. Was he demanding too much of the god? Seeing the looks the High Priest and Thanos exchanged, Raegar knew beyond doubt that Treia was right. These two were conspiring to take over the priesthood. Raegar believed with all his heart that Aelon had made his choice. Aelon had given him the power to summon the kraken and these two were intending to thwart the god's wishes. Raegar's doubts vanished.

The council was about to vote when the shouts of the people gathered outside the Shrine of Aelon changed to wails and cries for help.

One of the Shrine guards raced inside.

"My lords!" he cried. "Another dragon!"

Raegar left the Shrine in company with the other priests. They stared up in horror, adding their panicked shouts to those of the populace. A dragon flew overhead. She was greenish-gray in color and not nearly as large as the Vektia dragon, but one dragon looked much the same as another to the terrified.

People called upon Aelon to save them. The priests either called upon Aelon or looked about for some place to hide. Raegar stepped forward. He towered over the masses. His armor gleamed in the sunshine. He lifted his hands to the heavens and thundered out the name of Aelon.

Hidden in the shrine, Treia hugged the spiritbone to her breast and smiled to think that this would mark the beginning of her husband's triumph.

Thanos sat in his chair in the Shrine. He was alone; the others had all rushed out to either see the dragon or flee from it. He had known the moment the dragon appeared that he was finished.

Xydis had told Thanos that Raegar's lover, a Vindrasi woman, had the power to summon dragons.

This woman is going to summon a dragon of immense power that will drive out the ogres and save the city, Xydis had told his nephew. She will be doing the bidding of Aelon.

"Of course she will," Thanos murmured.

He rubbed his forehead. The aching had returned.

"I can't denounce Raegar because I have no proof," he said softly. "No one will believe me."

Atemis had gone outside with the other Warrior-Priests to confront the dragon. He returned, looking for Thanos.

"Here you are." Atemis was displeased. "You should have gone with us. The others will say you are a coward."

Thanos looked up with a smile. "Does it matter now what they say?"

Atemis regarded Thanos with a grim expression, then shook his head. The sound of cheering shook the walls.

"I assume the dragon flew down from heaven at Raegar's command and knelt at his feet?"

"Something like that," Atemis said sourly.

"So Raegar has yet another miracle."

"A trick! He staged it. That wife of his—"

"Rather like me forging the scroll naming my father's successor," said Thanos. He spread his hands. "Don't you see, my friend. It's all a trick. The secret to opening the vault door. The dragon appearing at the right moment. There is no Aelon. Never was. Never has been."

Atemis stared at Thanos in shock. "You can't mean that!"

"Oh, I do, I assure you." Thanos shrugged. "Now, my friend. I've made it easy for you. You can cast your vote for Raegar with a clear conscience. As for me, I must take my leave. I have packing to do and not much time in which to do it."

"You're leaving the city?"

"I am," said Thanos. He started to walk off, then turned back to say, "You might consider taking a trip yourself. Priest-General Raegar will not look kindly upon those who opposed him. And I know from reading my father's missives that Raegar knows how to deal with his enemies."

Atemis, considerably shaken, promised to give the matter thought. He did not think too long.

Later that day, after the dragon had flown away in peace and Raegar had been acclaimed a hero by the populace, he was named Priest-General by a vote of the Council of Warrior-Priests. The vote would have been unanimous, but two members were missing.

That night, men wearing dark cloaks armed with knives entered the dwellings of both Atemis and Thanos.

They found no one at home.

CHAPTER 18

The next morning, Raegar was busy packing, preparing for his journey to the sacred mountain. Treia stood watching him forlornly.

"Please take me with you," she begged him. "I don't see why I can't come."

"It is forbidden," said Raegar. "I must go alone. The mysteries of Aelon are revealed only to the Priest-General."

"You can enter the cavern alone," said Treia, who had no desire to delve into the mysteries of Aelon. "I could keep you company on the journey."

"I need to be alone to pray," said Raegar. "To meditate and commune with the god."

That was the truth, but not quite all the truth. He and his retinue would be stopping for the night at villages along the way; villages with lovely Sinarian women eager to please the new Priest-General.

Treia knew why he didn't want her to come. She tasted the bitter bile of jealousy and wanted to spit it in his face. Her calculating mind cooled her passion. She could never win such a battle and she was not about to allow Raegar to ride off with the memory of a shrieking shrew for a wife. That would only make him all the more eager to find solace in the arms of a woman who "understood him."

Raegar loved her, though not as much as she loved him. He needed her. They made a good team. He would always treat her well, never beat her, which was more than her own mother could say. Treia would have to reconcile herself to the fact that there would always be other women.

"But in the end, you will come home to me," she said.

"Where the hell else would I go?" said Raegar, laughing.

He gave her a smacking kiss. He was in an excellent mood. Treia responded with a strained smile and a stiff-lipped kiss that brushed his cheek. Raegar picked up his gear and was headed out the door when she ran to him and flung her arms around him and kissed him fiercely.

"Be careful!" she pleaded, clinging to him. "Come back to me safely."

"I will," he said, startled. "What's the matter? You haven't been yourself, ever since our wedding night. You're not with child, are you?" he asked, teasing.

"Of course not," Treia said crisply. "Now you had better be going. You have far to ride before the sun sets."

He bade her farewell and hastened to mount his horse, planning to ride as many miles as he could while there was still daylight. She smiled and waved good-bye as long as she could see him and then she went back inside.

She had a great deal of work to do. She must supervise their move into the palace of the Priest-General and select the fabric for new, elegant robes suited to her high station. Mindful that she and Raegar must continue to court the goodwill of the populace, she had arranged to lead a delegation of priestesses into the city to help alleviate the suffering of the people.

And now that Raegar was leaving, she would be alone to deal with all these responsibilities. True, she had servants to help her now, but they were merely servants. She had no friend in whom she could confide. No one to advise her, help her. Treia was an outsider, a Vindrasi "savage." The other priestesses obeyed her only because she was the wife of the Priest-General. They had never accepted her as one of them. They had never tried to befriend her. Treia didn't care. Her own people had never liked her, not even her own sister. Only Raegar loved her, understood her.

Treia had work enough to keep her well occupied. She would wear herself out so that at night, when she went to sleep, she would be so exhausted she would not dream the fiery dreams that had been plaguing her since she had made the bargain with Hevis.

Raegar enjoyed his ride through the countryside. He was riding a splendid horse, with a leather saddle of the finest quality. His one regret was that he was not wearing the resplendent armor of the

Priest-General. Raegar was so large the traditional jewel-encrusted ceremonial armor did not fit him. He had to make do with his own plain armor until new armor could be made.

He had no worries about traveling alone. Captain Anker had sent soldiers ahead to make certain the road was clear of bandits and beggars and to apprise the people of the villages en route of the coming of the new Priest-General.

Raegar stayed the nights in the homes of the wealthy. He was flattered and treated to the finest of everything from wine to women. He met with the leaders of the local Church and listened to their complaints and promised he would solve all their problems.

The journey took about a fortnight. He reached the Mount of the Revelation at sunrise, meeting up with Captain Anker and his men in the foothills at the beginning of what was known as the Trail of Deliverance. A marble statue of the god Aelon stood in the center of the trail. The god wore his battle armor and held a spear in his hand. The spear was real, the haft made of polished oak and the spear tip of steel.

"It is said that if anyone tries to walk the Trail of Deliverance without the god's sanction, the statue will plunge his spear into the man's heart," said Captain Anker.

Raegar looked at the spear and at the face of the god, cold, hard, implacable, the marble eyes that stared off into eternity. Raegar's gut knotted. Aelon had chosen him. Aelon had proved that by sending the Dragon Fala to crawl to Raegar on her belly. Deep, deep in his soul, Raegar knew Treia and the Dragon Fala had plotted this between them. He had known and he could have forbidden it. He had allowed them to go ahead with their plan.

He had tricked Aelon.

If Raegar had been alone, he would have turned around and ridden back home. Captain Anker and his soldiers were all watching him expectantly. If he passed the statue without being pierced to the heart by a spear, they would carry word to Sinaria. If not, they would carry his body.

And if he proved a coward and refused to walk the trail, they would ride off and leave him. He could never go back to Sinaria. He would be jeered, derided, left to beg in the streets.

"After all," men would say, "what do you expect? He was a slave."

Raegar thanked the captain and his men for their service. He ordered them to take with them the two pack mules loaded with the valuable gifts he had received from the villages along the way.

The captain and his men prayed with him and then they waited. Raegar's armor was polished. He had shaved and bathed in a chill stream and dressed himself in his best robes. He wore his breastplate, adorned with Aelon's serpents, and girded on his sword. He got down from his horse and knelt at the foot of the statue and asked Aelon's blessing and then, drawing in a breath, he walked past the statue.

Those few steps took a lifetime. He longed to break into a panicked run, but forced himself to walk slowly, with confidence. Sweat rolled down his body and his head and ran into his eyes. He kept walking, every moment expecting to feel the steel tip of the spear slam into his back.

He heard the soldiers cheering and only then did he realize he was safe. He stood at the beginning of the trail that led up the sacred mountain. Aelon had given Raegar his blessing.

Raegar staggered. He almost sank to his knees in relief. He leaned a moment with his hand on a tree trunk and spoke a heartfelt prayer. Then he straightened and turned to wave to Captain Anker and his men. They cheered again and waved back and then they rode off to carry the news.

Raegar was elated. The knowledge that he was Aelon's chosen filled him with joy. He felt strong enough to run all the way up the mountain. He had a long way to go, however, and he needed to conserve his strength. After a time, he was glad for the slow pace he'd set.

The path was narrow and covered with a layer of brown needles that had fallen from the sheltering pines, which made it difficult to find. The fir trees clustering thick around the trail filled the air with a sharp invigorating scent. The needles pricked Raegar's flesh. The path was like one of Aelon's serpents, he thought, winding back and forth upon itself, sometimes rearing upward toward the summit and then inexplicably plunging down into crevices.

Raegar had a good sense of direction, but soon even he was confused as to where he was. He could not see his way and had no idea how far he had to go. He was hot and tired, and the needle scratches on his arms stung. Coming upon a cold mountain stream, he took off the breastplate and unbuckled his sword and dropped them to the ground. He drank his fill, splashed his head and neck with water, and sat down on a boulder to rest and think about what he should do.

The sun had climbed high in the sky. He had been walking this path since dawn and he had no idea where he was, if he was close to his destination or far, far away. He had not brought any food, for he had figured to dine at Aelon's table. Raegar had the sudden, sickening fear that Aelon had spared his life only to let him die lost and starving on the mountain.

Sighing, he stood up and prepared to go on. He left the heavy breastplate on the ground, slung his sword belt over his shoulder, and slogged up the trail. He grew so tired he paid no attention to where he was going. He could think only of putting one foot in front of the other. And then something hissed.

Raegar stopped dead.

The serpent was in front of him, coiled up on a sun-warmed flat rock on the trail. The serpent hissed again, forked tongue flicking from its mouth.

The serpent was sacred to Aelon. Raegar couldn't kill it. Yet the bite was deadly. The serpent blocked his way. Raegar had to get past it. The trees and underbrush were so thick, he couldn't go around. He feared that if he stepped off the trail, he would never find it again.

This was a test. One of the tests set by the god for those who dared ascend the mountain.

Raegar drew his sword. The serpent suddenly raised up and made a darting motion. Its fangs missed Raegar by a finger's breadth. He was hot and sweating and cold and shivering all at the same time. He prayed to Aelon, repeating the god's name over and over. And then he had an idea.

He laid the sword in front of the serpent.

The snake's head sank back down amid the shining coils of its body. The serpent no longer threatened him.

Raegar, quaking, began to slowly and carefully shuffle past the snake. He watched the serpent, who watched him, slit eyes following his every move. The snake did not strike. It let him pass safely. He cast a regretful glance back at his sword lying on the trail, sighed, and kept going.

And there, before him, was a cave.

Raegar was so amazed he stumbled back a step or two, for the cave seemed to have sprung up from nowhere. He approached it warily, expecting to find yet another guardian. He looked about carefully, searching for traps. No one guarded the cave. He found nothing around it but dirt and rock and trees. Raegar's eyes filled with tears. He paused a moment to thank the god with all his heart and then he walked into the cave, into cooling darkness.

He fell to his knees and sank into a deep sleep.

Raegar woke to light shining in his eyes. He sat up swiftly and looked around. He was no longer in a cave. He was in a chamber such as one might find in the Empress's palace, sumptuously and exquisitely decorated. Beautiful rugs carpeted the floor. Silk curtains lined the walls. Couches with velvet cushions were placed artfully here and there. Small tables made of rosewood stood beside the couches. The scent of jasmine filled the air.

Raegar rose to his feet. He was so tall his head nearly brushed the ceiling. He searched for a door, but if there was one, it was concealed behind the curtains. Raegar listened, but he could hear nothing. He had no idea what to do. He was uneasy. This was certainly not what he had expected.

He was about to peep behind a curtain, see if he could find a way out, when the smell of jasmine grew stronger. The curtains parted and a woman walked through them.

Raegar sighed as he gazed upon the most beautiful woman he had ever seen. She was Sinarian, with long black hair that fell in languorous curls down her back and over her shoulders. She had large dark eyes and her skin was golden brown. She wore a gown that looked as if it had been spun from cobwebs, held by golden clasps shaped like serpents at her shoulders; the gown was of such gossamer fabric as to be daringly revealing.

She carried a silver cup in one hand and a wine jar in the other. She placed the cup on one of the tables, poured the wine, and then lifted the cup and held it out to Raegar.

"Your journey has been long and difficult," she said in a voice that was deep and rich and hauntingly melodious. "You should drink this."

He could only stare at her. Desire welled up in him. Desire strong and urgent.

The woman flushed a dusky rose color. "I am sorry. I should have introduced myself. I am Kea, Aelon's consort. The god sent me to welcome you."

Raegar gave an inward groan. Aelon's consort. He stammered something about being honored to meet her and took the wine and swallowed it in a gulp.

Kea drew near. He tried to back away and bumped into a couch. Her black eyes seemed to swallow him.

"My lord said I was to help you pass the time until he arrived." Kea's red lips curved in a smile. "He may be some time in coming."

Raegar broke out in a sweat. He wanted this woman more than he had ever wanted any woman in his life. He had felt no compunction about enjoying himself with other men's wives. But not the consort of his god.

He said, in a shaking voice, "I do not mind waiting alone. Though I thank you for your offer." He made a clumsy, fumbling bow.

"Are you certain?"

Kea lifted her hands and unfastened the golden serpents. The diaphanous fabric slid down her body and lay in a heap at her feet. Kea stood naked before him. She smiled at him, warm and inviting.

Suddenly Raegar was angry. Bending down, he picked up the gown and thrust it at her.

"You should be ashamed to so dishonor your lord and master. Cover yourself and leave!"

Yet even as he held the gown out to her, he dared not look at her. Fearing his resolve would weaken, he stared at the floor. Rippling laughter caused him to raise his gaze. Kea was dressing herself, settling the gown over her shoulders, attaching it with the golden serpent pins.

"I am pleased with you, Raegar. You are a man of honor. You passed the final test. It is good to have a Priest-General in whom I can place my trust."

Raegar gazed, dumbfounded, his jaw slack, his mouth hanging open.

"Who are you, Lady?" he asked thickly.

She laughed again. "You should know me, Raegar. You pray to me often enough. I am *your* lord and master. My name is Aelon."

CHAPTER 19

Raegar was in a state of paralyzing shock, unable to absorb the fact that the powerful god he had worshipped was a woman—a beautiful and desirable woman. Aelon had seen that her Priest-General needed time to come to terms with this astonishing revelation and she had mercifully left Raegar alone to recover himself. When Aelon returned, she was dressed more chastely in a gown of soft lamb's wool.

"Sit down," she said. "We have a world to discuss." Reagar learned that his god was still powerful, and that her ambition and hunger for power was as vast as the universe.

Aelon and Raegar made plans for what they would do when Aelon had driven out the other gods and gained sole control of this world and its people. This conversation lasted for days, though Raegar was so busy he never noticed the passing of time. When he and the Sinarians conquered the world, they would build immense cities, using the labor of slave-races such as the ogres and the Cyclopses. Raegar's armies would destroy the fae, whom Aelon considered undisciplined and dangerous troublemakers. She would banish all dragons who refused to pay her homage and work for her. The rebellious Vindrasi would have to be eradicated.

"They will always be loyal to the Old Gods," Aelon said. "Even if the Old Gods are dead and gone, the Vindrasi will refuse to worship me."

Raegar, humbled and reverent, listened to his god in awe, enthralled by her vision.

"I lack one thing in making my dream a reality," said Aelon. She fixed her gaze upon him. "The power of creation. Torval, curse him, has hidden it away. Fortunately, now we know where. I need the spiritbones of the Five Vektia dragons."

Raegar's exultant feeling evaporated.

"I take it then that this is the only reason you chose me to be Priest-General, Lord God," he said bitterly. "Because I have knowledge of these spiritbones."

Aelon understood that he was hurt, his pride wounded. She took hold of his hand in hers and drew near him. The scent of jasmine, warm from her body, filled his nostrils.

"Do this for me," said Aelon softly. "Find these spiritbones for me, bring them to me, and I will reward you. You will *not* be Priest-General . . ."

Raegar sighed deeply and shook his head.

Aelon squeezed his hand. "You will be Emperor."

Raegar lifted his head, gazed at her in astonishment.

"Kings of all the nations in the world will bow down before you," said Aelon. "They will send you tribute, do you homage. As Emperor of the New Dawn, you will dwell in a magnificent palace, high in this very mountain. And there, in a room known only to ourselves, I will visit you."

Aelon smiled. She was beautiful when she smiled. She lingered on the word "visit" and he saw—or hoped he saw—her true meaning in her eyes. He stared at her in dumb adoration, then, with a wrench, he tore his hand from her grasp, stood up, and walked a few paces away.

"I would give my life to do whatever you asked of me, Lord God Aelon, but I must tell you the truth. I cannot give you spiritbones." Raegar shook his head. "Four of them are missing and one lies at the bottom of the sea. Recovering it would be impossible—"

"Oh, as to that," Aelon interrupted with an air of nonchalance, "*two* of the spiritbones are in the sea. Retrieving them should not be difficult."

Raegar stared at her. "Two?"

"Your wife, Treia, was right when she said that Skylan went back to retrieve the Vektan Torque from the ogres. I like your wife, by the way. I admire her ambition and her ruthless nature. The time may come when she has to be removed, however. Do not worry," Aelon added, seeing Raegar's eyes widen in horror, "nothing will happen to Treia until after the birth of your son."

"My son . . . ," Raegar breathed. "Then I am to have a son?"

"You will need an heir," said Aelon. "A son with the blood of warriors in his veins."

Raegar swelled with pride. He could already see himself cloaked in purple, crowned in gold, sifting through casks of jewels.

"Of course," said Aelon, "all this is contingent upon the recovery of the Five spiritbones. We have or soon will have two. The problem lies in finding the other three. Where they are, I fear, I cannot tell you. The Old Gods have hidden them well."

"Pardon me for asking, Lord God," Raegar said hesitantly, "but how am I to gain the two that are beneath the waves?"

"The spiritbone of the Vektia that was in the possession of the god, Sund, is inside the hull of the *Venjekar*. The fae child hid it there. The other, the Vektan Torque, is in the possession of the Aquins, who have also taken your cousin, Skylan Ivorson, prisoner."

"My whoreson cousin is dead," said Raegar. "He was killed by the kraken."

"Ivorson survived. Everyone on board the *Venjekar* survived, including the woman named Aylaen, your wife's sister."

Raegar was stunned. "How is that possible? I saw the kraken smash the ship—"

"With the gods, all things are possible." Aelon said. "The Old Gods are battered and bloodied, but they are not defeated. This time, however, they will not win. I have worshippers among the Aquins. With their help, you can recover both these spiritbones."

"And I will use them to find my cousin, Lord God," said Raegar harshly. "So long as Skylan lives, he will be a danger to us. He needs to be put down like a rabid dog."

Aelon shrugged, a movement of her shoulders that caused her breasts to stir beneath the thin fabric of her gown. Raegar found himself staring at her hungrily and he flushed and tore his gaze away.

"Your cousin is not the danger. Kill him or not as you choose. The one who truly concerns me is the woman, Aylaen Adalbrand."

"So must I kill Aylaen?" Raegar asked in a low voice.

"On the contrary," Aelon said coolly, "you must do everything in your power to keep her alive."

Raegar was relieved. "I will obey your command, Lord God. If I could ask why . . ."

"When I have the Five spiritbones, I will need a Kai Priestess to summon the dragons."

"I beg your pardon for saying this, Lord God," said Raegar. "Though I have tried many times to introduce Aylaen to your glorious light, she has refused. She is very stubborn."

"Bring her to me," said Aelon. "She will do my bidding. She will have no choice."

"I live to obey, Lord God," Raegar vowed. He hesitated, started to speak, then stopped, clearly uncomfortable.

"There is something on your mind," said Aelon. "Speak the words in your heart."

Raegar flushed. "I do not know if I dare, Lord God."

"Nothing you say will offend me."

"You test every Priest-General—"

Aelon nodded. "The Test of the Spear proclaims your commitment and courage. The Test of the Serpent reveals your wisdom and cleverness. With the final, the Test of Temptation, I see every man's weakness and I offer him what he most desires."

Raegar's flush deepened at the word *weakness*. He lowered his eyes and spoke in gruff tones. "I know I am weak when it comes to women. A man has needs," he added defensively. He looked at her, saw her regarding him with cool dispassion. His skin burned, but he stammered on. "You are so . . . so beautiful, Lord God. The most beautiful creature I have ever seen. You offered yourself to me. If . . . if I had accepted your offer. If I had tried to make love to you—"

"I would have sent your ashes back to your wife in a very small box."

Raegar shuddered. He thought how close, how very close, he had come to destruction, and he was sick to his stomach, his body drenched in cold sweat. He feared for a terrible moment he was going to vomit on his god.

"You made a vow in my name to be faithful to your wife," said Aelon relentlessly. "Yet even now you look at me with lust in your heart."

Aelon rose to her feet. He was tall, but she seemed to tower over him.

"You will be true to that vow, for by being faithful to her, you are faithful to me. You must learn discipline, control your 'needs.' "

Raegar sank to his knees and clasped his hands.

"Forgive me, Lord God," he said wretchedly. "I will be faithful to you. I swear."

"Bring me the Five spiritbones. Bring me the Kai Priestess of Vindrash. Keep my mysteries. Keep my secrets. Keep every vow you make in my name. Do all this for me, and you will be rewarded. *Well* rewarded," Aelon said softly. She reached out to touch his cheek. "I might even give you what you want most."

Raegar fell to his knees and kissed the hem of her skirt. Aelon traced her fingers over the serpent tattoo on his head and then, leaning over him, she kissed the serpent. The touch of her lips swept over him like fire. The tattoo was branded on his soul.

"I am yours, Lord God Aelon!" Raegar cried, and he prostrated himself before her, his large body shaking with sobs.

"Yes, Raegar," Aelon said, smiling in satisfaction. "You are. And you always will be."

CHAPTER 20

Raegar returned to Sinaria and this time he was received with all the honors accorded to a new Priest-General. He first went to his home, embraced the astonished Treia, and, lifting his wife in his arms, took her with him in the chariot. As they rode through the streets of Sinaria, people threw flowers and cheered until they were hoarse. When Raegar finally reached the Shrine of Aelon, he assembled the priests in front of the steel door to the treasure vault and, in full view of all, he prayed to Aelon. The steel door rose slowly and ponderously. The priests cheered, some more loudly than others, for there were still those who had their doubts about their new Priest-General. They were careful to keep those doubts to themselves, lest the men in the black cloaks pay them a nocturnal visit.

Finally, late that night, Raegar and Treia entered the magnificent dwelling of the Priest-General. Men had worked feverishly during the time Raegar had been gone to repair the mansion. Raegar dismissed the servants and his guards, saying he wanted to be alone with his wife.

Slowly and ponderously, Raegar got down on his knees before her.

"I ask your forgiveness, Treia," he said.

"My love! Don't do this. You're frightening me," Treia said nervously. "What is the matter with you?"

"I was wrong," said Raegar quietly. "I have not been faithful to you, to your love. By breaking my wedding vow to you, I broke my vow to the god. Aelon chastised me and made me see I was wrong. You are my wife and the only woman who will share my bed."

Treia regarded him intently. Raegar looked different. He sounded different. He sounded like a man in love. But he wasn't pledging his faith to her. He was pledging his faith to his god.

Treia had always been jealous over Raegar. She had seen the way he looked at other women. She had seen the way he looked at Aylaen, her own sister. At least, Treia had told herself with satisfaction, he would always came back to her bed. Now, even in their bed, Raegar would not be with her.

Treia noticed a subtle change when Raegar referred to the god, not using "he" or "his." As a wife is said to know in some mysterious way that her husband is having an affair with another woman, Treia knew that something had happened between Raegar and this god of his. If she did not know the truth, she knew him well enough to come close to guessing it.

"I may not win this battle," Treia muttered beneath her breath, "but I will not stop fighting. He is mine, do you hear me, Aelon. I can give him something that you cannot!"

Treia staggered and seemed faint. Raegar caught her in his arms, lowered her into a chair, and shouted for the servants to bring wine.

"Forgive me, Wife," said Raegar. "I did not mean to upset you. I thought this would make you happy."

Treia managed to force her stiff lips into a smile. "You did not upset me, my husband. You made me very, very happy. Especially now. I did not want to say anything, because I am not sure. It is too soon . . ."

"Then it is true!" Raegar cried jubilantly. "I am to have a son!"

Treia stared at him in astonishment. "How could you know that the baby will be a boy?"

"Aelon told me. Aelon is all-knowing," said Raegar. "Blessed be the name of Aelon."

Treia gnashed her teeth.

"Can I do anything for you, my love?" Raegar asked solicitously. "Fetch you something to eat? A cushion for your feet?"

"Sit here and talk to me," said Treia. "Tell me of your meeting with the god."

"I may not speak of such mysteries," said Raegar grandiosely. "But I have been granted leave to tell you some news that will gladden your heart. Your sister, Aylaen, is alive!"

Treia stared at him in shock. She couldn't believe this news. She went so pale that Raegar was worried.

"I'm sorry. I should have prepared you."

Treia gulped some wine and the color returned to her face. "How can Aylaen be alive?" she asked warily. "I saw the kraken drag the *Venjekar* down beneath the waves. All aboard must have drowned."

"Skylan is beloved of Torval," said Raegar. "Aylaen is the priestess of Vindrash. The Old Gods carry on the battle, though their power weakens daily. Aylaen is alive and I know where to find her and the spiritbones of the Vektia. Aylaen treated you badly, but she is your sister and I know you love her despite her faults."

"Love her," Treia repeated with emphasis. "I do love my sister and I am thankful she is alive. I would give anything to see her. Where is she?"

"Ah, the answer to that is complicated," said Raegar, scratching his jaw. "You will find this hard to believe . . ."

"Tell me," said Treia.

"Skylan and Aylaen were saved by the Aquins."

"The who?" Treia blinked.

"The Aquins. The people who live beneath the sea."

Treia burst into laughter.

Raegar regarded her coldly. "You mock your husband."

Treia hastened to stifle her mirth. "I am sorry, my love, but it sounds too fantastic. The Aquins are creatures of myth—"

"They are real," said Raegar in stern tones. "Aelon has proclaimed it."

"Oh, then, very well, I must believe . . . ," Treia murmured dutifully.

She wanted to believe. She wanted this news to be true. She prayed for it to be true. The god to whom she prayed was not Aelon.

"And now, Wife," said Raegar fondly, "I have been longing for a fortnight to take you in my arms."

He kissed her and carried her to their bed.

The two made love, though not really to each other. The body Raegar caressed was the voluptuous body of the god. Treia saw in her mind the face of Hevis.

If Aylaen was alive, the god would have his sacrifice.

Raegar had an overwhelming amount of work to do. He had to supervise the rebuilding of the city of Sinaria, which had already begun. Thus would he let the people know that Aelon had neither forgotten nor abandoned them. He had to consolidate his power base and select a new High Priest, the previous one having hastily departed. He had to receive delegates from the kings of the other cities throughout Oran, all of whom would by vying to be named Emperor, since the throne was now vacant.

Raegar grinned inwardly. He had a candidate in mind—himself. Raegar announced that he was taking the matter of naming a new Emperor under "prayerful consideration." As he prayed, he would work to acquire the Five Vektia spiritbones. Once he did that, all prayers would be answered.

Aelon had told him where to look for Aylaen and the spiritbones—beneath the sea. Raegar had been annoyed with Treia for laughing at the idea of people living beneath the sea. He didn't like to admit it, but his annoyance was aimed partly at himself. Humans living like fish? The thought came to him that Aelon was deceiving him. He didn't like to believe it. He wanted to believe in the god and in the god's promises. He couldn't help himself. He doubted.

The Watchers would be able to assist him, alleviate his doubts. Or laugh at him.

Raegar and Treia stood in the doorway of the room where the Watchers did their work, waiting for the priest known as the Flame Master.

In the large, darkened, hushed room, priests sat cross-legged on the floor. In front of each priest was a silver bowl, plain and elegant, filled with water. Each priest concentrated on his bowl. Occasionally gouts of flame would rise up from the water and when this happened, the priest leaned closer and listened to the voice of one of Aelon's priests as the man spoke into a bowl of water, perhaps asking a question, passing on information to another priest, sending urgent news. At times, a Watcher would rise to his feet and hasten over to the Flame Master asking for guidance. The Flame Master would either instruct the priest in a voice that was barely above a whisper or she would send one of her runners to a scribe. Not even the Priest-General could interrupt the work of those whose task it was to communicate with Aelon's priests the world over.

And perhaps the world under.

The Flame Master rang a small gong. At the melodious sound, another priest emerged from an inner room and came to take over. The Flame Master rose to her feet and went out to confer with Raegar.

"Priest-General," said the Flame Master, bowing.

She was a middle-aged woman, of medium height, corpulent, with shrewd eyes and a masterful air that cowed both the new Priest-General and Treia.

As a Warrior-Priest, Raegar had often made use of the Watchers, especially when he had been a spy on his own people, the Vindrasi. He had passed on information about them, about the Old Gods. He had used the Watchers to betray his cousin, Skylan, into slavery. Raegar had never had occasion to enter this sacred room, however, and he was nervous and overawed.

"What is your need, Priest-General?" the Flame Master asked.

The use of the title and the woman's deference bolstered Raegar's confidence. He drew Treia forward.

"My wife's beloved sister has been lost at sea," said Raegar. "We are expecting our first child," he added with pardonable pride, "and I fear that her grief will harm the unborn babe. Aelon has given me to know that Treia's sister, Aylaen, is safe with the Aquins."

Raegar spoke nonchalantly, as if one discussed people living beneath the sea every day. He watched the Flame Master closely. If the woman's lips so much as twitched or her brow raised, Raegar would know Aelon had lied to him.

To Raegar's vast relief, the Flame Master smiled at Treia, offered congratulations on the news of the child, and said she understood Treia's concerns.

"Please accompany me," said the Flame Master, adding quietly, in soft rebuke, "First, remove your shoes."

Treia and Raegar hurriedly took off their shoes and, uncertain what to expect, accompanied the Flame Master, threading their way among the kneeling Watchers, who were intent upon gazing into the silver bowls and paid them no heed. The Flame Master led the two to a small room set off from the main chamber. Beautiful tapestries covered the room's walls. A fragrance of cedar filled the air. The room had no furniture. A silver bowl filled with water; a golden flask, adorned with serpents; and an oil lamp made of silver and encrusted with jewels were arranged on the floor. The only light came from the small, unwavering flame of the oil lamp. The Flame Master brought forth several cushions, placed them on the floor, and then gestured for Treia and Raegar to be seated.

"Is this your private chamber, Flame Master?" Raegar asked, glancing around the room with admiration. "If so, I thank you for allowing us to make use of it."

The Flame Master bowed. "This is *your* private chamber, Priest-General. Whenever you want to speak to your priests, Worshipful Sir, you have only to summon them."

Raegar was mystified. "But how do I do that, Flame Master? When I was a priest, the Priest-General never asked to speak to me."

Treia squeezed his hand and Raegar knew immediately he'd said something stupid.

The Flame Master was careful not to smile. "The Priest-General would not have wanted to interfere with your duties, I am certain. You would speak to your priests only on matters of extreme importance or in an emergency."

"Ah, yes, of course," said Raegar, blushing at his mistake.

"When you want to summon one of the priests, you speak to the Watcher in residence, who will then summon the priest. Pour the sacred oil upon the water. Ask Aelon's blessing and light the flame. Speak the name of the priest three times. The Watcher will appear."

Raegar cleared his throat. "If you could . . . uh . . . remind me of the name of the High Priest of the Aquins—"

"Ceto, Worshipful Sir," said the Flame Master.

"Ah, yes, of course," said Raegar.

He glanced triumphantly at Treia and was gratified to see her looking awed and even dazed.

The Flame Master rose to her feet. "If you no longer have need of me, Priest-General, I will leave you to conduct your business in private."

"Thank you, Flame Master," said Raegar.

He squatted awkwardly down before the silver bowl and motioned for Treia to join him. She did so nervously and with some trepidation. Raegar lifted the flask of holy oil, offered a prayer to Aelon, and poured the oil carefully upon the water. He took a wooden taper, touched the tip to the flame, and waited for the taper to catch fire. He then lowered the flame to the oil floating on the surface of the water.

The flames spread across the water. Raegar spoke the name of the High Priest of the Aquins three times. The flames on the water began to swirl and rise up, forming a small cyclone of fire in the center of the bowl. The heat washed over them. Treia gasped and drew back. Raegar sat gazing intently into the water.

A face appeared, startling Raegar. The face was a pale green in color with greenish-blond hair adorned with seashells.

Treia gasped and stared at Raegar in slack-jawed astonishment. Raegar was inordinately pleased. He so rarely had the chance to impress his clever wife.

"I am Raegar, the new Priest-General," he said to the Watcher.

"We heard of the sad death of Xydis. We extend our condolences. What is your will, Priest-General?" the Watcher asked.

"I wish to speak to Ceto, High Priest of the

Aquins," said Raegar. He hesitated, then said, "I am speaking to a member of the Aquin race, is that right? You . . . uh . . . live beneath the sea?"

The Watcher seemed amused, but too respectful to do more than give a very slight smile. "We reside in the City of the Fourth Daughter, Worshipful Sir. The city itself is not beneath the sea. Our cities are built in the interior of atolls. But we Aquins have an abiding love for the sea and spend much of our time there. Please wait while I fetch her, Worshipful Sir."

She was gone but a few moments, then another face appeared in the water. Ceto was also a woman. Raegar had never heard of a woman being High Priest, but he did not want to appear ignorant by asking any more questions.

The High Priest bowed. "I am here at your command, Priest-General. How may I serve you?"

Raegar had to gather his scattered wits. The truth was, he had not expected to be talking to a person who lived underneath the ocean. Treia, beside him, was no help. Generally glad to put herself forward, she was mute with amazement.

"My wife has a dearly beloved sister who was on board a ship when it was attacked by a kraken. My poor wife, who is carrying our child"—Raegar was becoming fond of announcing that—"is beside herself with grief. We were hoping that through the miracle of Aelon, your people have rescued this woman and her companions."

The High Priest gave a grave nod. "Rumors have reached us that several land walkers were saved from a kraken by those who live in the City of the First Daughter. I paid little heed to such gossip, not knowing at the time that these people might be of importance. I will find out what I can and return to you with information."

"The man's name is Skylan Ivorson. The woman's name is Aylaen Adalbrand. We are most interested in the welfare of the woman," said Raegar.

"Of course," said the High Priest, as if that were a given. "I will be in contact."

The face vanished. The flame went out, leaving Raegar and Treia sitting in the dimly lit darkness. They waited for their eyes to adjust, then Raegar rose to his feet and solicitously assisted Treia.

"You no longer doubt the power of Aelon," said Raegar.

"No, my love," Treia murmured. Her hand on his arm trembled.

Raegar was pleased. Treia had always seemed cynical about Aelon. He was glad to hear her finally speak of the god with reverence.

BOOK 3

CHAPTER 21

The Norn, three sisters who rule the destinies of gods and men, sitting beneath the World Tree, spin the wyrds of men. As Raegar's thread runs through their gnarled twisted fingers, the Norn laugh over the follies of those whose lives they hold so loosely and carelessly. Raegar's wyrd seems made of golden thread these days and spins headlong toward glory. Beneath the sea, the wyrds of Aylaen and Skylan, Farinn and Acronis and the Dragon Kahg seem to have slipped off the wheel, for time slows beneath the sea. The Norn keep fast hold of these mortals, however, twisting and tangling and binding together and cutting apart.

Aylaen woke from a horrifying dream of tentacles rising up out of the water and wrapping around the *Venjekar,* Kahg roaring in fury and sinking his fangs into a tentacle and the mast breaking, falling . . . to a more horrifying reality of pain in her head, and being held underwater by strange-looking women who were trying to smother her by pressing a mask over her nose and mouth. When Aylaen fought and tried to tear the mask off, the women took hold of her hands and would not let go.

Aylaen breathed deeply and kept breathing. The pain and terror subsided, replaced by dazed wonder to realize that she was far below the surface of the sea, being carried along to some unknown destination by the women who had . . . saved her life. Gradually, Aylaen began to think the horrible dream had not been a dream at all. The *Venjekar* had been attacked by a sea monster. The Dragon Kahg had fought it off. The mast had fallen on top of her and that was the last she remembered until waking up in another world.

She could see very little of her surroundings, for the water was dark and murky, the women far below the surface where the sunlight could not reach. They carried small, translucent globes that gave off an eerie bluish-white glow, which they used to find their way. As Aylaen went along, she began to worry. What could have become of Skylan and the others? She was alone; the women had carried her off, away from the ship and her friends. Having saved her life, the women appeared to have taken her prisoner.

Legends and tales of the Aquins came confusedly to her mind. They were half-fish, half-human—who saved sailors from drowning. She had awakened from a dream to find herself in a bard's song, only these women did not have scales or fins, though they swam as gracefully and rapidly as dolphins.

Aylaen could not communicate with her captors, two of whom held her fast and linked arms around her. Three more women swam near, carrying the globes and their weapons. The flow of the saltwater over Aylaen's body had a soothing effect. She slipped into a kind of trance, as though her mind and body had parted company.

At length the water began to grow brighter. The sea floor appeared to be rising. She looked up. Sunlight filtered down from above, illuminating the world beneath the waves. Aylaen gazed about in awe and amazement at the marvels around her: plants swaying with the motion of the water; fish glowing as though they were lit by flame; other fish more colorful than birds, flashing and swooping by or gazing at her with goggle-eyed uninterest. And all of it in almost complete silence.

The quiet was comforting, unlike the silence of an abandoned house that weighs heavily upon the spirit, nor the awkward, uncomfortable silence of two who can find nothing to say. Nor was the silence frightening, like the whispering, rustling silence of the woods at night. The silence of the sea was tranquil, restful, and all the more amazing for the motion and activity and life.

Only a few months ago, Aylaen had never given a thought to what lay beyond her own forests and fields and mountains. All that had changed. She had seen wonders and horrors, the giants of the Dragon Isles, the teeming city of Sinaria, the great stadium of the Para Dix, and now a world beneath a world. She had known death and loss and grief. She had loved and lost and found that love could come again. She looked back on the Aylaen who had considered walking the short distance to Owl Mother's remote cabin an adventure and viewed her former self with pity for her ignorance mingled with regret for its loss.

The Aquins swam with her to the surface, removed their masks, and looked about. Aylaen blinked, dazzled by the sunshine. She tried to take off the mask, to ask questions, but the Aquins stopped her.

"We have surfaced only to gain our bearings, Vindrasi Lady," said one of the women. Her speech was rapid and darting, like the fish, but Aylaen understood her.

"We are taking you to our city," the Aquin added, pointing to a small dome-shaped island covered with trees. The island looked like a green mound rising out of the water.

Aylaen could see no signs of a city, no other dwellings or buildings, and she wondered what the woman meant, but she was too sick with fear for Skylan and the others to pay much attention. Desperate to find out what had become of them, Aylaen pointed to herself and then held up five fingers, hoping to make the Aquin understand that there had been five people aboard the ship.

"You are asking about your males," said the Aquin. Her voice grew stern. "We saved two of them, an old man and a young man. They are being held until our Queen has made her judgment regarding you. I believe the commander of our forces, Neda, saved another human, a male who had been caught by the kraken. He will be held with the others."

Aylaen sighed softly in relief. She asked about the fifth, making a sign to indicate someone smaller than the others, a child.

The Aquin stared at her with a frown, not knowing what she meant. Then, suddenly, she raised her eyebrows.

"Do you mean the fae child, the prince? He was with you?"

Aylaen had no idea what the Aquin meant by a prince, but she nodded her head.

"We assumed he was with the oceanaids," said the Aquin. "He swam off with them."

Aylaen wanted to ask more, but the Aquin told her curtly they were supposed to rendezvous with their commander in the city. They started to drag Aylaen back underwater, but she resisted.

Finally, one of the Aquins removed her mask. "Tell me where you are taking me," she said.

The Aquin again pointed to the island. "We are taking you to our city, Lady."

"I see no city," said Aylaen. "I see only an island with nothing on it. Am I to be marooned there? Left to die?"

The Aquins stared at each other, momentarily perplexed, then they suddenly began to laugh.

"The island that you see, Lady, is actually the top of a mountain. Our city is not on the island," the Aquin said. "Our city is built *inside* the mountain. The entrance is beneath the water. Come with us, Lady, and you will see wonders few land walkers ever experience."

Aylaen didn't have much choice. They treated her with respect, but she was still their captive. They dragged her down under the water again and continued on their way to the city that was beneath the water, inside a mountain.

The Aquin commander was waiting for them in front of the underwater entrance to the city—a cave-like opening in the side of the mountain. The opening was guarded by a portcullis made not of iron, but of the teeth of some gigantic sea creature that had been driven into the rock. The teeth were set far enough apart to admit humans to swim through them, though only a few at a time.

The Aquin commander took charge of Aylaen at the gate, indicating that the others could go about their duties. She drew Aylaen into the opening. Swimming past the huge teeth, Aylaen felt as though she were entering the maw of some gigantic sea monster.

Once inside, Aylaen and the commander broke the surface of the water. The commander removed the mask from Aylaen's face. Aylaen was glad to breathe normally again and she drew in deep breaths and gazed around in wonder at beauty that pierced her heart.

The commander introduced herself as Neda.

"Welcome to the City of the First Daughter, Vindrasi Lady."

Aylaen could only stare. Aquins told her that the City of the First Daughter had been carved out of the interior of the mountain by the hand of the Sea Goddess. The city was built in levels that ascended up the interior walls in a spiral like a nautilus. Roads cut into the rock ran from one level to another. Houses and shops of various shapes and sizes lined the roadways, all of them facing out over the water, for the sea formed a vast lake in the center of the city. Shafts of sunlight shining down through skylights illuminated the city from above, while openings in the rock just beneath the surface of the sea caused the sunlight to shine through the water, suffusing the water and the cavern with radiant blue light. Groves of bamboo grew on the upper levels, directly beneath some of the skylights, and small patches of greenery grew beneath others. Aylaen would later discover that these green patches were small fields and orchards where the Aquins grew fruit and vegetables.

The city was filled with people, some walking along the paths, while many others swam in the water.

"I understand you are taking me to the Queen," said Aylaen. "Is the palace far?"

"Some distance," said Neda. "The palace is located in the mountain's interior." Giving Aylaen an appraising glance and seeming to see for the first time that Aylaen was faint with exhaustion, the commander added, "We will travel in skiffs."

The skiffs to which she referred were similar to wooden rafts. There were a great many of them gliding across the surface of the water. Female Aquins stood at the back, steering and propelling the skiffs by means of long poles that they thrust into the water, shoving them off the floor of the cavern. Other Aquins sat on the skiffs, dangling their feet in the water, or standing at their ease. The commander raised her voice and shouted; an empty skiff immediately headed in their direction.

Ropes of seaweed hanging from the sides allowed people to pull themselves out of the water and onto the skiff. Neda pulled herself aboard the skiff with ease.

Aylaen grabbed hold of the rope and tried to pull herself aboard. Her arms ached. Her legs were limp from fatigue. She fell back into the water. Neda saw her distress and reached down her hand, helped pull her on board. Aylaen sat on the skiff, shivering in her wet robes, and gazing in amazement at this strange and wonderous city.

A group of Aquin women swam over to the side of the skiff to stare and giggle at Aylaen, who stared back at them. The women were pointing and commenting on what Aylaen was wearing and Aylaen was staring and blushing at what the Aquin women were not wearing, for many of the women were bare from the waist up, while others wore only what looked like a flimsy shift that revealed more than it concealed.

In the city she saw, for the first time, the male Aquins. Two men were riding on a skiff traveling in the opposite direction. The men were taller and heavier than the women, though with the same fine, light bone structure. They wore nothing but loincloths. They had long hair, which they wore braided.

One of the men had a bundle strapped to his body. Aylaen saw that he was carrying a baby. The man caressed the child lovingly, patting the baby's back soothingly when the child began to whimper. The two men were chatting. Both men stopped talking to stare curiously at Aylaen as they passed. A frown from the commander caused both men to shrug and turn away, resuming their conversation.

Looking around, Aylaen saw many Aquin males with small children strapped to their chests. Other men were shepherding groups of young children along the walkways or supervising their play in the water. Still others could be seen carrying baskets or bundles. Aylaen saw one man outside a dwelling wielding a broom.

Aylaen looked from the broom-wielding male to the commander seated on the raft, armed with her spear, and realized dazedly that this world was all upside down. Men took care of babies while women fought sea monsters. She tried to imagine the Vindrasi men sending their women out to fight while they stayed home to keep house. She almost laughed out loud at the thought.

Commander Neda instructed the skiff's pilot to take them to the palace. The pilot and Neda were the only two passengers on the boat. Seeing that the pilot was busy attempting to steer the skiff among the swimmers, Aylaen asked the commander what had become of Skylan and the others.

"Your males have been taken to prison to await the judgment of our Queen." Neda fixed Aylaen with a narrow-eyed and penetrating stare. "Her Majesty will want to know why you have invaded our realm."

"Invaded!" Aylaen gasped, shocked. She wrapped her arms around herself, trying to keep warm and wondering at the Aquins, swimming in the water, wearing practically nothing. "We did not invade your realm. None of us had any idea your realm was even down here. We were attacked by the kraken that dragged us below the water."

"We know you Vindrasi," said Neda coldly. "We have been rescuing you people for centuries. Your males are warriors who delight in raiding your neighbors. You came here in one of your dragonships, which your dragon is now guarding. For all we know, it was your dragon that attacked the kraken. Your males will be taken to the dungeons for safekeeping until our Queen decides your fate."

"Dungeons!" Aylaen was growing angry. "I tell you again, we are not invaders. I want Skylan and the others to be with me when I come before the Queen."

"To meet Her Majesty?" Neda snorted. "Never."

"Then take me to the dungeons with them," said Aylaen boldly. "They are my friends. Skylan is my . . . my betrothed." She had never said the word before now and she blushed.

Neda seemed to consider this. "He is courageous, I will say that for him. Though he appears to me to be willful and stubborn." She shrugged. "Still, perhaps he will give you strong daughters."

Aylaen did not know what to make of this remark and eventually decided the commander was jesting, though she had to admit the stern-faced woman gave no indication of ever having made a jest in her life.

The skiff glided beneath a series of arched stone bridges spanning the water. The cavern narrowed at these junctures, then opened up again to reveal another chamber of dwellings connected by roadways cut into the stone walls.

"How many people live here?" Aylaen asked.

"Perhaps five thousand. We are one of the smaller cities."

"Are there more cities like this beneath the sea?"

"Twelve cities, each ruled by a descendent of the twelve daughters of the Sea Goddess, Akaria."

"Daughters of the Sea Goddess," Aylaen repeated, astonished. "Our people know nothing of this."

Neda shrugged, as if nothing concerning the land walkers could surprise her.

"The Sea Goddess Akaria became enamored of a human male, a Vindrasi warrior. She gave him the ability to breathe under water, like we Aquins, and brought him beneath the sea to live with her. She built him a grand palace and bore him twelve children, all of them female. The Vindrasi was not content. He wanted a male child and he coupled in secret with a Vindrasi female, who bore him a son. When the Sea Goddess found out he had been unfaithful, she changed him and his mistress and the son into hippocampus—half horse, half sea monster—and forced him and all his descendants to serve her. She gave each of her daughters a magnificent city and summoned the Aquins, who had been scattered all over the world, to live within them."

"So that is why this city is named 'First Daughter,' " said Aylaen.

"Each city is named for the daughter who founded that city," said Neda. Her eyes shone with a fierce pride. "That was centuries ago and in all that time, the Twelve have never gone to war. Unlike you land walkers, who spill your own blood constantly, no Aquin has ever died at the hands of another."

Neda's expression darkened. She added in low tones, almost to herself, "Though that may change."

"Why is that?" Aylaen asked.

Neda was tight-lipped, however, and would say nothing more. She seemed not to hear Aylaen when she asked her other questions, even innocent ones, but sat in brooding silence.

The skiff slid beneath yet another stone arch and entered the largest chamber yet.

"The palace of our Queen," said Neda proudly.

Shafts of sunlight poured down from various skylights set in the walls, all of the beams converging on the palace of the Sea Queen that stood on an island in the center of a blue-green lagoon. The walls of the palace were of many colors: pink and orange, black and gray, they glittered in the sunlight. The palace was simple in design, consisting of four walls in a square with a round tower at each corner. A great many large windows admitted the sunlight and salt-tinged air.

Aylaen gave a soft gasp at the extraordinary beauty. Neda eyed her approvingly and explained that the palace was fashioned from granite and the sheltering walls were striated with sparkling mica.

The skiff docked at the island on which the palace stood. Neda and Aylaen were met by Aquin female guards, who saluted the commander and stared rudely at Aylaen. Neda spoke to one of the guards, relaying Aylaen's demand that her males were to join her. The guard first frowned, then looked shocked and disbelieving but said she would consult Her Majesty.

Neda led Aylaen into a garden filled with exotic flowering plants; the perfume suffused the air. The palace was not very large, not nearly as large as the palace of the Emperor of Sinaria. Neda explained that only the Queen, her consort, two young daughters, and a few servants resided here.

"There are rooms for guests," said Neda. "You will be accommodated here while the Queen determines your fate."

"And my menfolk?" said Aylaen. "And the fae child, Wulfe?"

"I have sent one of the guards to make this strange request of yours. We will see what Her Majesty says. Do not get your hopes up," Neda added grimly.

Aylaen sighed. She felt very much alone in this strange and beautiful world. She missed Skylan's strong comforting presence, Acronis's wise counsel, Farinn's quiet cheerfulness. She even missed Wulfe who, though his unpredictability made her nervous, was rarely daunted by much of anything except the Dragon Kahg.

Thinking of the dragon, she wondered what had become of the *Venjekar*. She hoped the ship was close. As beautiful as she found this world, she did not want to remain here long. This world might be beautiful, but it was not home.

Aylaen ran her hand through her wet hair to drag it out of her face. She glanced down at her sodden clothes and thought that she must look like a drowned rat.

"I am a Kai Priestess of my people, a queen in my own right," Aylaen said proudly. "My betrothed is the chief of our people."

Neda was startled by Aylaen's proclamation and eyed her suspiciously. "You made no mention of this before."

"You took me prisoner. For all I know, you might have intended to hold me hostage for ransom," Aylaen returned.

"And now you trust me," Neda said with a snort.

Aylaen looked around at the slanting rays of sunlight glinting on the palace and sparkling on the water, at the red of the roses in the garden and the pink-red coral in the clear waters below, the gold and silver and many-colored fish swimming amid the gently waving plants.

"You could not live in such beauty, create such

beauty, if you did not have such beauty in your souls," Aylaen said softly.

Neda was surprised by the answer. A sad smile touched the thin lips.

"Once that might have been true . . . ," Neda said. She shook her head and sighed.

The guard returned to say that Her Majesty was not holding audience this day. The Vindrasi female was to be given quarters in the palace. As for the males, the Queen would consider the request.

Aylaen was not pleased. She was about to insist that she wanted to see the Queen now, then reflected and kept quiet. She did not want to sound like an impatient, petulant child. And, she thought, the delay would give her a chance to rest and put on some dry clothes.

"When will I see Her Majesty?" Aylaen asked.

Neda shrugged. "Whenever Her Majesty decides. Come with me."

Neda escorted Aylaen past the guards at the palace entrance, which was a gate made of stone decorated with shining tiles set in a fanciful mosaic portraying all manner of sea life. As Aylaen walked past the guards, she noticed that this palace had no fortifications. The gates were not barred and stood open to the world. She recalled what the commander had said about the Aquins living in peace for centuries.

The inside of the palace was much like the outside. Sunlight streamed through the windows and skylights. A long, wide hall led to a large round chamber with a domed ceiling. Two staircases, spiraling upward, one on Aylaen's left and one on her right, led off the hall. The hallway was bare of all furnishings, with no furniture, tapestries, or paintings. The walls and floors had been polished, bringing out the natural colors of the granite and glittering mica striations.

A female servant met them at the entrance. Aylaen was relieved to see that this servant was more appropriately clothed, although the fabric was lightweight and seemed very flimsy to her northern eyes. She waited while the servant and the commander conferred. The servant then turned to Aylaen and told her that she would be taken to her room and provided with every comfort.

"Her Majesty has agreed that your menfolk will be present at the audience tomorrow," Neda said in a dour tone that sounded disapproving. "I will bring them."

"Thank you," said Aylaen. "And thank you for your care of me."

Neda touched her hand to her forehead in what was apparently a salute, then departed. The servant bowed respectfully and gestured for Aylaen to accompany her. She led Aylaen into a tower and they walked up one of the spiral staircases to the top. They arrived at a door with a lock made of brass, the first metal Aylaen had seen in this realm. The servant unlocked the door with a brass key and they entered a large round chamber. Six doors opened off this central chamber. The servant explained that these were the palace's guest rooms and bathing room.

She led Aylaen through one of the doors into a small room with a pool of fresh water in the center. This was apparently the bathing chamber. Aylaen washed off the salt, which was starting to make her skin itch.

After Aylaen had bathed, the servant took her to one of the bedrooms, elegant in its simplicity. There was a bed constructed of teak. A chair and a small table also of teak stood by a window through which the sun shone brightly.

The servant brought Aylaen a gown made of fabric that she learned later was made of bamboo. Like everything in this world, the gown, a caftan, was comfortable and simple, gliding over the shoulders and buttoning down the front with pearl buttons. Men and women both wore caftans over loincloths wrapped around the hips.

On the table was a bowl of odd-looking fruit and a pitcher of what looked like fresh water. The fruit did not appear to be edible until the servant showed Aylaen how to peel away the outer rind to find sweet, juicy pulp beneath.

"Is there anything else I can do for you, Vindrasi Lady?" the servant asked, hovering near the door.

"I would like to see Her Majesty now," said Aylaen, trying again.

The servant smiled and shook her head.

"That is not possible. Her Majesty spends this day with her children and her consort. Besides, forgive me for saying so, lady, but you look very tired. You should rest."

The servant drew curtains across the window and then glided silently out of the room and shut the door behind her. The doors to the single rooms had no locks. Aylaen walked stealthily out of the room, into the central chamber, and tried the tower door, but it was locked.

Aylaen went back to her room, frustrated. The bed looked wonderfully inviting, but she was too worried about Skylan and the others to sleep. She was worried about the *Venjekar,* the dragon, and the precious cargo, and wondered what had become of the ogres and the Vektan Torque. She walked over to the window and she wondered if she could climb through it and escape. The room was at the top of the tower, however. The garden was a long, long way down. The air smelled of sea salt and flowers.

Aylaen flung herself on the bed. As she tried to decide what to do, her body made the decision for her: she fell asleep.

CHAPTER 22

Skylan's experience of the City of the First Daughter was not nearly so comfortable or awe-inspiring as Aylaen's. The dungeons were located in a part of the caverns separate from the city and consisted of a few rooms gouged out of the stone walls. No prison door slammed shut behind him, and no iron bars blocked his escape. He was not chained to the wall in iron manacles. The Aquins kept their prisoners inside nets suspended from a hook in the ceiling. A soft glow filtered down from skylights.

Skylan had been angry before his arrival and now, left trapped in a net like a mackerel, he was raging. His hands and arms and feet were scratched and bloody from trying to claw through the net. He was hoarse from demanding to know where Aylaen was and shouting challenges to fight that fell on deaf ears. The female Aquin guards standing in the entryway outside the prison cells paid no heed to him except to occasionally glance at each other and roll their eyes in amusement, which only infuriated Skylan more.

"You might as well relax, Skylan," said a familiar voice. "You are only wearing yourself out."

Skylan glanced around. He had been so intent upon trying to gain his freedom that he had not paid any attention to his surroundings. He saw with relief that Acronis and Farinn were in the same cell, trussed up in nets of their own. Skylan shook the net in frustration and then slumped down. His gyrations caused the net to spin and swing from side to side.

He had been on the ogre ship when the kraken attacked. He asked what had happened on board the *Venjekar*. Acronis explained that the kraken had attacked the *Venjekar* and the Dragon Kahg had attacked the kraken.

"Not much of a fight," said Acronis. "The dragon sank his teeth into one of the kraken's arms and the creature let go and swam off. The mast fell on Aylaen, but she was not badly injured," he hastily assured Skylan. "Farinn flung himself on her."

"I owe you a debt I can never repay," said Skylan, looking at Farinn, who lowered his eyes and blushed.

"You should be grateful to the Aquins," Acronis was saying. "They saved our lives. Both Farinn and I would have drowned if the women hadn't put those amazing masks of theirs over our faces so that we could breathe."

"They saved us only to make us prisoners. Do you know where they have taken Aylaen?" Skylan asked. "I tried to find out, but that she-devil of a guard refused to tell me."

"Perhaps because you were threatening to rip off her head," said Acronis dryly. "The commander took Aylaen to the palace for an audience with the Queen."

"Then I should be with her!" Skylan said, starting to grow angry all over again. "I am Chief of Chiefs! Here, you: I want to see your Queen!"

Two Aquins had entered the prison cell. The two were male, Skylan realized after a moment. He had difficulty telling them from females because they were dressed in long gowns with flowing sleeves. The men carried baskets and drinking flasks made of fish skin. One had a bundle strapped to his chest.

"Finally!" Skylan exclaimed, seizing hold of the net and staring eagerly down at the men. "Tell those women of yours that I demand to see your Queen! I am Chief of Chiefs of the Vindrasi and yet these women treat me like a slave!"

The two men looked at each other and began to laugh.

"He demands to see the Queen," said one in mocking tones.

"I am certain Her Majesty will be highly honored," said the other.

"I will rush over to the palace at once and tell her," said the first, and the two laughed again.

Skylan's face burned. He shook the net. "I am Chief of Chiefs of my people. That means I am king. They have taken Aylaen, my woman, to see the Queen. If anyone talks to the Queen, it should be me."

The men grinned and shook their heads, then handed the prisoners flat cakes made of ground wheat and gave them each a flask of fresh water. Skylan was parched, his mouth seemed coated with salt, and he drank thankfully. When the man drew close to the net, Skylan saw that the bundle the male Aquin carried was a sleeping baby.

"Now I understand," said Skylan bitterly. "You, too, are a slave."

The man smiled. "I am sorry. You use that word for a second time. I am not familiar with it. What does it mean?"

"A person who is owned by another person," said Skylan. "Someone who is not free to do what he chooses. He must do another's bidding."

"Such a concept is unknown among my people," the Aquin said, "though it occurs to me now I have heard that you land walkers commit such atrocities."

"If you are not a slave, why must you carry around that baby?" Skylan asked.

The man appeared mystified by the question. "He is my son. I carry him because I am his father."

The Aquins picked up the empty baskets and made ready to go, promising to bring them more food the next day.

"Why is the child in your care?" Skylan persisted. "Are you a widower? If so, there must be women who can tend to the boy."

The man caressed the child, stroking his head tenderly. "We believe it is only logical that the strongest in society protect the weakest."

"Our women care for our children," said Skylan.

The man raised his eyebrows. "It is a wonder your people have managed to survive."

As the two left, they stopped to exchange some words with the female guard on the way out. The woman kissed the child the man was carrying, then kissed the man on the cheek.

Skylan sat down in the net. Trying to find a comfortable position and failing, he ate his bread in silence.

"A matriarchal society," said Acronis.

"A what?" Skylan grunted.

Acronis smiled. "Matriarchal. A society run by women. Women are the rulers. They are the warriors. The men stay home to guard and nurture the children. He was right. Their way of living makes sense, if you stop to think about it. The strongest protects the weakest."

Skylan found this concept baffling. "Yet their women claim to be the warriors. Do the women fight battles while the men stay home to suckle babes?"

Acronis yawned widely and made himself as comfortable as was possible trapped in a net. The light was fading, night falling. Farinn, with the ease of youth, had gone to sleep long before this.

Acronis closed his eyes and gave another yawn. "Perhaps these people are peace-loving and need no warriors. Perhaps there are no wars for them to fight."

Skylan pondered this notion. He recalled that the Aquin warriors had not killed the kraken. They had driven it away with jabs from their spears. Thinking of the kraken made him recall those hellish moments when he thought he was going to drown. He shook the thoughts from his mind and tried to find some sort of comfortable way to position himself in the net.

That being impossible, he settled himself as best he could, thinking and worrying about Aylaen, and drifted off into an uncomfortable slumber.

Skylan woke with an aching back, a stiff neck, and itching all over. The prison cell was dimly lit with the coming of dawn. Guards entered, lowered the nets, and escorted the prisoners one by one to a pool where they were allowed to bathe and perform ablutions. The women took away their clothes, which were stiff with salt water, and gave each of them one of the odd-looking robes and a loincloth to wrap around their hips. Farinn was abashed in the presence of the women, who grinned when they saw him blush in shame for his nakedness.

Once they were dressed, they were not returned to the nets. They were given food and drink and informed that the Aquin commander was coming to speak with them.

"I would advise you to be diplomatic," said Acronis. "If you want to see Aylaen."

Skylan grudgingly admitted that this was probably sound advice, but all his good intentions went up in smoke the moment Commander Neda entered the prison cell. Skylan jumped to his feet.

"I want to see Aylaen. I want my ship. And the fae child. The boy who was with me? Where is he?"

"You make a lot of demands for a man who spent the night in a net," said Neda coldly. "Your Queen is in the palace. She is safe and well. As for your ship, it is harbored outside the city. You need not worry about it. We are hardly likely to steal it," Neda added wryly. She shrugged. "The last I saw of the fae child, he was with the oceanaids."

"I want to see Aylaen," Skylan said insistently.

"Your Queen has requested that you attend her; *our* Queen has approved her request," said the commander. "You and the others will accompany me to the palace."

"Queen?" Skylan was puzzled. This was the second time she'd referred to a queen. "What Queen—"

Acronis gave a cough. "She means Aylaen," said Acronis.

"Aylaen? But she is not—"

Acronis cleared his throat with a loud *argh-um*.

Skylan took the hint and did not speak again to the Aquin commander. He smiled reassuringly at Farinn, who was looking frightened and overwhelmed, and praised him again for his bravery in saving Aylaen. Farinn smiled, pleased, and relaxed.

The commander went to summon her warriors.

"What is this about Aylaen being a queen?" Skylan asked Acronis.

"As I said, in this society, women are the rulers. Aylaen must have said something that led them to believe she was a Vindrasi ruler. You need to support her," Acronis admonished him.

"Even though I am Chief of Chiefs, I should pretend that Aylaen is my ruler?" Skylan frowned.

"Does that bother you?" Acronis asked with a slight smile.

"Women rule the household and raise the children. Men govern and fight the wars. That is how the gods intended," said Skylan. "These people have got everything backward."

Acronis was now chuckling. Skylan wondered why.

CHAPTER

23

The throne room of the palace was located in the center beneath a domed ceiling decorated with a mosaic that portrayed colorful fish, whales and dolphins, and coral. An opening in the ceiling admitted air and sunlight. The only furniture was the Queen's throne, which was made of teak adorned with seashells and twelve blue-green sapphires set in a semicircle above the Queen's head.

A male Aquin, presumably the Queen's consort, was present when Aylaen entered, along with three young women, who must be the Queen's daughters, by their resemblance to their mother. The eldest was perhaps Aylaen's own age and that made Aylaen uncomfortable. Would this woman take her seriously or dismiss her as a child? The Queen introduced herself as Magali and her husband as Tai. He regarded Aylaen with a penetrating gaze and spoke a few words to the Queen. She rested her hand on his briefly, then he and the daughters left the room.

Aylaen stood alone at the far end. She was

nervous. She did not want to give offense, yet she intended to be strong, deny these foolish charges that they were invaders, and free herself and her people, and her ship. She adopted a stance that she hoped appeared bold and self-confident, yet tempered with respect.

Queen Magali was perhaps in her forties. Her face was smooth and youthful, though not untouched by care and worry. She wore the simple caftan of her people, no jewels, no golden crown, and only a circlet of seashells that held back her hair from her face. The Queen's expression was serious as she regarded Aylaen, yet there had been a sweetness in her smile when she had spoken to her husband and children that made Aylaen's heart warm to her. As their business commenced, however, the Queen was no longer smiling.

"Come forward," Queen Magali commanded.

Aylaen walked to within a few feet of the throne and stopped. Was she supposed to bow, kneel? She decided she would not kneel; that would appear too servile. Before she could do anything, the Queen motioned her nearer.

"Give me your hand."

Mystified, Aylaen drew close to the throne and stretched out her hand. Queen Magali took hold of her hand, pressed it, turned it over, ran her hand over several calluses before releasing her.

Queen Magali's eyes were cold. "A hand that wields a sword. You were wearing a sword when my warriors found you."

The Queen gestured and a servant entered, carrying Aylaen's sword, the blessed sword of Vindrash.

"Is this weapon yours?" the Queen asked. She seemed disapproving.

"It is mine," Aylaen answered, adding defensively, "your warriors carry weapons, Your Majesty."

"My warriors do not carry swords. They carry the trident and the spear in order to fend off sea predators, such as sharks and kraken," said the Queen. "We do not kill even these predators if we can help it. We do not kill each other. We do not believe that the goal of a man's life is to die with a sword in his belly and the blood of another on his hands."

Aylaen was startled. She had never heard the Vindrasi described in such terms. She was about to angrily defend her people when she realized that Queen Magali was simply stating the truth. To die a hero with his sword in his hand was a warrior's dearest ambition. Those like Skylan's father, who grew old and died in their beds, were looked upon with pity.

Aylaen realized suddenly she had been standing for long moments in brooding silence and she feared the Queen might think she was sullen or obdurate. She flushed and said, "I did not mean to be rude—"

Queen Magali smiled slightly. "I have been following your thoughts in your eyes. The fire in your eyes, ready to defend your people. The lowering of your eyes, the fire quenched by doubt. The widening of your eyes in wise, sorrowful understanding."

"I am not certain I understand anything anymore, Your Majesty," said Aylaen, suddenly feeling very young and vulnerable.

"Tell me your story," said Queen Magali.

Aylaen drew in a deep breath and wondered where to start. She didn't want to talk about the Vektia dragon and so she began her tale when they were out at sea.

"Our ship was dragged beneath the waves by a terrible sea monster, Your Majesty," said Aylaen. "The mast fell . . . I was drowning and I don't remember anything else until I was able to breathe again with a mask on my face and your warriors tending to me . . ."

"And what of your dragon?" asked the Queen with an intent look. "You Vindrasi have sailed our seas in your dragonships for centuries. We have rescued your people from drowning down through the ages. And this is how you repay us—by invading our realm."

"You misjudge us, Your Majesty," said Aylaen. "We were made slaves by the Sinarians and managed to escape. We were returning to our homeland when we were attacked by the kraken." She spread her hands. "If you know Vindrasi, you know that if we were going to invade, we would have had many warriors on our ship and many ships at our command."

"The Vindrasi delight in battle and conquest," said the Queen in grim tones. "You were allied with the ogres. The kraken attacked an ogre ship that was near yours and we found the body of a dead ogre godlord on the deck of your ship. A powerful dragon serves you. You have with you a faerie princeling who commands his fae followers to serve you. What are we to think?"

"A faerie princeling?" Aylaen repeated, mystified. "Do you mean Wulfe? Why, he's just a boy—"

A boy who can change himself into a beast. Aylaen decided it would be best to let that drop. She stopped and tried to think.

"The ogre godlord was a friend of ours who died on our ship. We were going to return his body to his people and that was why we were with the ogres. Your Majesty, we are far, far from the Vindrasi homeland. We have no intention of invading your realm. To be honest, we had no idea your realm even existed!"

"You come at the command of your god, Aelon," said the Queen in ice-rimmed tones.

Aylaen was about to indignantly deny this accusation, when the thought came to her that this could be a trap. Queen Magali and her people might be followers of Aelon, hoping to inveigle her into denouncing the god. Aylaen's next words might doom her and her companions. She should tread lightly, feel her way, be diplomatic.

"The hell with that," Aylaen said to herself wearily. She and her people had done nothing wrong except to be attacked by a sea monster that, for all she knew, this Queen had sent to kill them.

"If you know the Vindrasi as you claim, Your Majesty, then you know that we have always worshipped the Old Gods. I am a priestess of Vindrash. The goddess gave me her blessed sword. The goddess has been at my side since I was a child. I will be true to Vindrash as she has been true to me."

Queen Magali looked thoughtful. She tapped her fingers on the teak arm of the throne. Aylaen could not tell from the woman's expression if the Queen believed her or not.

A servant entered and whispered something to the Queen, who nodded and said, "Bring them before me." The servant departed. The Queen turned to Aylaen.

"Your menfolk are here."

Aylaen was filled with thankfulness and relief and dismay all at the same time. If there was ever anyone in this world who had no idea how to tread lightly, it was Skylan Ivorson. Aquin guards entered, followed by Skylan, who shook loose of his captors and came crashing into the throne room like a storm-driven wave. Rudely ignoring the Queen, Skylan hurried to Aylaen and took hold of her hands.

"Are you all right?" Skylan moved to embrace her and whispered in her ear. "These people have the Vektan Torque!"

Aylaen stared at him, astonished.

"Say nothing," Skylan admonished. "Go along with me."

He drew back and cast the Queen an angry glance, then asked Aylaen abruptly, "Have these people harmed you?"

"I am fine, Skylan," said Aylaen, wondering uneasily what he was planning. "Her Majesty has been most gracious to me."

"Well, Her Majesty hasn't been gracious to me," said Skylan furiously. "I've been treated like a goddamn slave."

He turned to the Queen, who was tight-lipped with anger at his insult.

"Please, Skylan," said Aylaen, "Let me handle this—"

Skylan ignored her. Throwing back his head, he announced proudly, "I am Skylan Ivorson, Chief of Chiefs of the Vindrasi. I speak as Chief of Chiefs, from one ruler to another, and I demand that you set us free! We have done nothing wrong. And I insist that you return to us our property—the golden torque your warriors found."

His words boomed around the dome of the throne room and went nowhere. They seemed to fall to the floor with a thud. If a kraken had then appeared to drag Aylaen down to the bottom of the ocean, she would have been grateful. No one spoke. Skylan glared around defiantly.

Queen Magali turned to Aylaen.

"Is this male your husband?"

Aylaen bit her lip. "He is . . . he is my betrothed."

"So he is unmarried. That explains his lack of manners," said the Queen. "He claims to be a ruler of your people. Is that true?"

"I do not lie!" Skylan said heatedly.

The Queen cast him a cool glance and indicated Aylaen was to answer.

"Skylan is Chief of Chiefs of the Vindrasi, Your Majesty. That is equivalent to a king."

"And you are their priestess," said the Queen.

"Yes, Your Majesty."

"I am a priestess of my people," said the Queen. "Who are your other menfolk? Let them come forward."

The guards had brought in Acronis and Farinn. Aylaen introduced them.

"Legate Acronis. He is from Sinaria—"

"A Legate no longer," said Acronis with a deep bow. "My past is gone. I am Acronis, Your Majesty. And I am glad beyond telling to be in your beautiful realm."

The Queen seemed pleased by this, for she smiled at Acronis. Her gaze turned to Farinn, who turned red to the ears and gave a nervous bow.

"Farinn Grimshaw," said Aylaen.

"A Vindrasi warrior," said Skylan.

Farinn stood staring at the floor. He very slightly shook his head.

"He is a bard, a poet," Aylaen said.

Farinn cast her a grateful glance.

"Poets are much revered among my people," said the Queen.

She shifted her gaze at last to Skylan. "You may be a king in your realm, but not here. Your queen will speak for you. Go stand with the other men.

And be warned. If you do not hold your tongue, you will be escorted from the room."

Skylan looked blank, completely stunned, as though he'd been hit by a lightning bolt. Aylaen felt a surge of laughter bubble up inside her. She worked to suppress her mirth, fearing if she once started laughing, she would end up in tears.

She put her hand on his arm. "Skylan, please do this, for my sake."

Skylan gave her a withering look. "You want me to go stand with your other 'menfolk'!"

"Skylan, please!" said Aylaen.

"We have to get the Torque back and get out of here," said Skylan.

Wearing that obstinate look she knew all too well, he turned on his heel and went to stand with Acronis and Farinn. Skylan faced the Queen, his chin jutting out, his arms crossed over his chest. The rage in his eyes could have set the sea boiling.

Aylaen was sweating. She felt drained and exhausted and tried to think what to say. The Queen regarded her thoughtfully, then gestured to a servant who brought forth a box made of seashells studded with gemstones. The Queen opened the box. Aylaen saw the glint of gold, the Vektan Torque. The Queen was about to draw the Torque from the box when Commander Neda entered the throne room.

"I need to speak to Your Majesty," she said. "The matter is urgent."

The Queen beckoned Neda to come forward.

The commander spoke to her in low tones. The Queen's jaw set. Her mouth tightened.

"They come in peace?" she asked.

Commander Neda whispered.

"They will be permitted to enter," said the Queen.

By her expression, the commander did not like this decision. She hesitated a moment, seeming to hope the Queen would change her mind. The Queen had no more to say on the matter, however. Commander Neda saluted and walked off. The Queen shut the box and handed it back to the servant.

"Leave us," she said. The servant and the box and the Vektan Torque disappeared.

The Queen's gaze went back to Aylaen and lingered on her. Aylaen had the unsettling feeling that whatever dire news the commander had brought had something to do with them.

A delegation of five women entered the throne room. They bowed to the Queen, who inclined her head with cold politeness. Aylaen felt her stomach clench. The women wore armor bearing an all-too familiar insignia, that of a serpent biting its own tail: the symbol of Aelon. Aylaen cast a sidelong glance at Skylan. His blue eyes were fixed on the armor. He stood braced, tense, his hand reaching unconsciously for the sword that he had lost when the ship sank beneath him.

The leader of the delegation stepped forward. "We come to Queen Magali of the City of the First Daughter with a message from her cousin, Queen Thais of the City of the Fourth Daughter."

"The delegation from my cousin, the Queen of the City of Fourth Daughter, is welcome," said the Queen in a frozen tone that indicated quite the opposite. "What message do you bear from my cousin?"

The leader glanced at Aylaen. "Queen Thais commends you on the capture of these land walkers. You are undoubtedly aware that they are dangerous people, wanted criminals. We have come to relieve you of the burden of their care. Give them to us and we will see to it that they are returned to the city of Sinaria and given into the custody of Priest-General Raegar."

Aylaen turned to Skylan in shock. He looked at her and shook his head. His fist clenched.

"You claim these people are dangerous," the Queen was saying to the Fourth Daughter's delegate. "What charges are leveled against them?"

"The woman is an evil sorceress who summoned a dragon that destroyed much of the city of Sinaria and killed many hundreds of its citizens."

"Raegar is a lying bastard!" Skylan shouted, forgetting he was supposed to remain silent.

The Queen cast him an angry glance and then looked to Aylaen. "I warn you, Madame. If you cannot keep these menfolk of yours under control, I will have them removed!"

"I will speak to him, Your Majesty," Aylaen said.

She walked across the floor, conscious that all the women were staring at her. Aylaen was flushed and hot with embarrassment and anger, fear, and confusion. To make matters worse, Skylan was regarding her as though she were the enemy. Aylaen came to stand before him and spoke in a low voice.

"If we were standing in the shield wall, I would obey your commands. I would not argue with you or make you look small because you are Chief and we would be fighting for our lives. For now, Skylan, these people take me for the Chief. We are fighting for our lives."

Skylan's mouth tightened. A muscle in his jaw twitched. He kept his arms crossed and did not look at her.

"I have often put my trust in you, Skylan," Aylaen said, resting her hand on his arm. "Today, you need to put your trust in me."

Skylan's blue-eyed gaze softened. He gave a small nod and said quietly, "I am here if you need me."

Aylaen sighed and turned back to face the Queen.

"Skylan speaks the truth, Your Majesty. I did not summon the Vektia dragon."

"She has the artifact she used to summon the dragon in her possession," the leader of the delegation stated. "The artifact is a bone from a dragon."

The Queen's cool gaze went to Aylaen.

"Is this true?"

Queen Magali had seen the Vektan Torque. She had held it in her hand. She knew about the Dragon Kahg. Aylaen guessed that the Queen knew she had been holding the bone of a dragon in her hands. Aylaen would not lie, but she could not tell all the truth.

"I did not summon the dragon, Your Majesty," Aylaen repeated. "I used the blessed sword of the goddess, Vindrash, to destroy it."

"You see, Your Majesty, she does not deny she has the artifact," said the delegate. "These dragon bones are dangerous. This woman is dangerous, as are her heathen gods. You put your own realm at risk by allowing her to remain here. Give her and her savage men to us, Your Majesty, to be returned to Sinaria."

The Queen sat in silence for long moments, seeming to consider. Aylaen held her breath. She did not dare look at Skylan, but she could sense his presence, strong and reassuring, and she was comforted.

"I need to study this matter, take it under consideration," said Queen Magali at last. "Thank my cousin, Queen Thais of the City of the Fourth Daughter, and tell her that I will send her my answer in a fortnight."

"My Queen will be not be pleased with the delay," said the delegate, glowering.

"I am sorry to incur my cousin's displeasure," said Queen Magali calmly. "But if these prisoners are as dangerous as you claim, I could not in good conscience hand them over to endanger your people. My commander will escort you out," said the Queen, nodding to Neda.

Bowing stiffly, the delegation stalked off, accompanied by Commander Neda and her guards.

The Queen again sat silently on her throne, absorbed in her thoughts. Her unfocused gaze found Skylan. A new thought seemed to come to her.

She eyed him steadily and then asked, "Are you, by any chance, the one known as Torval's Fish Knife?"

CHAPTER
24

Skylan gaped, his jaw going slack. "No one knows about that! I never told anyone!"

He looked back at the Queen, his voice hardening. "What do you mean, Your Majesty? How do you know me by a name given to me by the gods?"

The Queen sighed deeply. "I must think about this."

Without another word, she rose and walked away, leaving them to stare after her in astonishment.

"Wait!" Skylan called. "You can't just walk out! What about the Torque—"

But he was talking to no one. The Queen had left the throne room. Swearing, Skylan ran his hand through his hair in frustration.

"Do you know what is going on?" he asked Aylaen.

She shook her head. Seeing guards approaching them, Skylan rounded on them.

"You're not taking me back to that dungeon!" he said.

"You are to be given quarters in the palace, near your Queen," said the guard.

"My Queen," Skylan repeated, smiling at Aylaen. He fell into step beside her, the guards leading the way. "I behaved like a rampaging boar. I am sorry. It's just . . . this is all so strange and I feel so helpless. At least our ship is safe. If we could reach it, we could escape—"

"Not without the Vektan Torque," said Aylaen.

"That's right," said Skylan, brooding. "I forgot."

"So why are you called Torval's Fish Knife?" said Aylaen.

Skylan gave a shame-faced smile. "Back on the Dragon Isles, I once asked Vindrash arrogantly if Torval thought of me as his sword. The goddess laughed at me and said I wasn't a sword. I was nothing more than a knife Torval used to gut his fish."

Aylaen smiled. "You were insulted."

"I was then," said Skylan. He added somberly, "I've learned a lot since."

"But not how to hold your tongue," Aylaen said, grinning.

Skylan shook his head morosely. "I do not understand these people."

"I remember where I've heard that about the fish knife," said Aylaen. "When we were in the Temple with Garn's spirit, Vindrash said she was going to bet Torval's fish knife against her shining sword. I had no idea what she was talking about."

"You, of course," said Skylan.

Aylaen blinked at him, startled. "Be serious."

Skylan took hold of her hand. "I am serious. You are her 'shining sword.' The blessed sword of Vindrash."

"I fear my blade is dull and blunted," said Aylaen with a sigh.

"And I am a broken fish knife," said Skylan. "You spoke to the Queen before I arrived. What did you talk about? Why doesn't she set us free? Why is she keeping us here?"

"She accused us of invading her realm by the command of Aelon," said Aylaen. "I told her we followed the Old Gods. She said she was a priestess, but she did not say of which god. I do not think, from what we have seen, that she worships Aelon."

They were climbing the spiral stairs and both paused to look out one of the many windows. The sun was starting to sink. The lagoon's blue glow was touched with pinks and oranges. Glints of mica sparkled. Aquins walked along the far shore or strolled on the paths that wound up the cliff side or sailed upon the shining water in boats or swam with flashing strokes that sent ripples spreading.

Their guards did not hasten them, but stopped when they stopped. Farinn had charmed one of his guards, a young woman who looked to be in her mid-twenties, who could not seem to take her eyes off him. Acronis was talking volubly with his two guards, asking questions about their lives, their city. His guards were smiling, glad that he was taking an interest in their people.

"The Legate is an unusual man," said Aylaen, following Skylan's gaze. "We were his slaves with reason to hate him and he made us love him. And now he has endeared himself to his captors."

"Acronis is a fair and honest man," said Skylan. "He opens himself to new ideas. That's why Raegar and his priest friends hated him. They could not tell him what to think."

"So Raegar is Priest-General now," said Aylaen. "That will make Treia happy."

"And the first thing he does is come after us," said Skylan. He scratched his chin, puzzled. "How did he know we were alive and where to find us?"

"Aelon's priests have many ways to communicate with each other and he has spies and followers everywhere, even below the sea. They must have passed on the information."

"So why don't you think this Queen worships Aelon?"

"When Queen Magali spoke Aelon's name, she sounded as though she had bitten into a rotten apple. She seemed to want to spit it out."

"You trust her?" Skylan asked, regarding her with a slight frown.

"I trust her and I like her," said Aylaen. "I think she is fair and she is honest. What is more important, our gods trust her, Skylan. How else could she know about you and Torval?"

Skylan shook his head, not convinced.

"Our gods are fighting the battle in heaven," Aylaen said earnestly. "They are battered and bloodied, but they fight on and they are helping us as best they can. Perhaps we were brought here for a reason."

"So we were nearly drowned and then killed by a kraken for a reason," Skylan said.

"Everything we do is for a reason," said Aylaen. "Perhaps you were brought here so that you can learn to care for babies."

Skylan was about to protest indiginantly, and then saw her smile. He took hold of her hand.

"It is good to see you happy again."

The palace was quiet. From outside came the sound of the water lapping on the shore. The tranquility of this lovely realm seeped into both of them. Aylaen drew near Skylan.

"Come to my bed tonight," Aylaen whispered.

Skylan's body stiffened. He swallowed and stared out the window and then, clearing his throat, he said quietly, "No. Not until we are wed. Our son will be Chief of Chiefs. He must be born in honor. When you are my wife, I will come to your bed."

"Then let us wed here," said Aylaen.

Skylan was astonished.

"The Queen can marry us." Aylaen seemed pleased with her idea. "She is a priestess. She can wed us."

"Right before she sends us to Raegar," said Skylan with a grim smile.

"I do not think she will do that . . . Oh, Skylan, listen to me. I feel like our wyrds are like balls of yarn rushing down a hill, unwinding as they go.

We will reach our end far too fast. Because I did not know my own heart, I have already missed too many moments of joy with you. I would not miss any more."

Pain darkened Skylan's eyes. Aylaen's voice faltered. "If . . . if you want to wed me . . ."

The pain was gone, replaced by almost blinding joy.

"I have made so many mistakes in my life," Skylan said. "Loving you is the only thing I got right. I will speak to the Queen tomorrow."

"No," said Aylaen. "*I* will speak to the Queen."

Skylan laughed. One of the guards ordered them to keep moving. They had been standing there long enough. Arms twined around each other, Aylaen and Skylan continued slowly up the stairs. Acronis and his guards followed, still talking companionably. Farinn, conscious of the admiring gaze of the young woman, lost his footing, tripped, and stumbled. She was at his side to steady him. Blushing and self-conscious, he did not know where to look and tripped again.

The mood was shattered by Wulfe, who came running into the palace with a couple of guards in pursuit. He was half-naked and wet and slippery as an eel. He raced up the stairs, his bare feet slapping.

"Hey, Skylan," he shouted gleefully, "I've been running all over the palace looking for you!"

The Sea Goddess, Akaria, stood in a hidden alcove, covered by a decorative frieze, and looked down upon the group on the staircase. From her vantage point, she could hear and see all they did and said. Another goddess, wearing a dented breastplate stained with blood and chain mail whose links were pierced and broken, stood beside the Sea Goddess looking down on the mortals below.

"I do not think much of Torval's Fish Knife," said Akaria. "Any number of gods must want him dead."

"As Skylan concedes, he has learned a lot, though his lessons had to be beaten into him."

"So Sund is seeking to kill him. Why did no one tell me Sund had turned traitor?"

"If you had not been off sulking in your grotto, you would know what has happened in the world," Vindrash admonished.

"I was mourning the death of my daughter," said Akaria sullenly. "What has this arrogant and rebellious mortal to do with our future?"

"Sund was the only one of us with long sight. He could look into the future and see what was to come. Of course, since our wyrds are bound with the wyrds of men, Sund saw many futures, all constantly shifting. He chose among the many, finding the most probable, and relating that future to us. In the beginning, he chose wisely. But when we foolishly did not heed his counsel, Sund grew angry and embittered. The darkness in his soul caused him to see only those outcomes that are bleak and unhappy."

"And what did Sund see that sent him running to Aelon?" Akaria asked.

"Sund foresaw that if Skylan Ivorson recovers all Five of the Vektia Dragons, he will use them in the battle against Aelon. The Five would destroy Aelon and save the world from the tyrant god."

"And that is bad?" Akaria frowned.

"So it would seem," said Vindrash somberly. "For if Skylan recovers the Five and drives away Aelon, Sund sees nothing for us."

"What does that mean, Dragon Goddess?"

Vindrash gave a small shrug. "Impossible to tell. Perhaps the world is saved, but we are no more."

Akaria stood brooding. "You want me to give them the third Vektia spiritbone."

"Sund gave Aelon the spiritbone of the Vektia in the belief that Skylan and Aylaen would not fail to obtain the Five. Aelon's ambition led him to use the Vektia dragon to try to defeat the invading ogres and strike a blow at his rivals, the Gods of Raj. Aelon nearly ended up destroying himself and in an ironic twist of the thread, the Vektia spiritbone fell into Aylaen's hands. The very fate Sund had attempted to avoid came to pass. Your Sea Queen has in her possession the Vektan Torque, the second of the Five."

"And you want me to tell them where to find the third," said Akaria. She turned to face Vindrash. "If our doom and theirs lies in the Five coming together, why do you want to bring this doom about?"

"We are not very good gods," said Vindrash.

"Speak for yourself!" Akaria snapped.

Vindrash shook her head. "I was wrong to hide away the power of creation. I did so because I feared other gods might seize it, use it against us. But that left a void, and creation's opposite, destruction, rushed in to fill it. Once, long ago, the races of the world prospered and lived in peace. Now they are at each other's throats."

"There has never been war among the Aquins. Never has one Aquin shed the blood of another in battle," Akaria said. "If Queen Magali refuses to give into the demands of Aelon's followers, our long-time peace will end in bloodshed. This Fish Knife is expendable. There are always more where he came from."

"The evil was slow in finding its way to you, Akaria," said Vindrash. "But it has come. Turn Skylan and Aylaen over to Aelon, and we are doomed."

"It seems we are doomed no matter what we do," Akaria said, and she burst out crossly, "Why did you bring them here, dump them in my lap?"

"I did not," said Vindrash. "I was trying to help them reach Vindraholm."

"Aelon's work, then."

"Aelon sent the kraken to kill them. It was your people who saved them," Vindrash pointed out.

"Force of habit," Akaria muttered. "We are always saving land walkers, and small thanks we get for it! But if not you and not me and not Aelon, then who?"

"The Gods of Raj," Vindrash suggested.

Akaria gave a bitter laugh. "Their ogres lie dead at the bottom of the sea."

Vindrash was silent, then she said quietly, "There are those we have forgotten. The dragons."

CHAPTER 25

Farinn Grimshaw had seen sixteen summers—barely. He had just passed his sixteenth on this voyage. He was an orphan and had moved to Luda to live with his mother's sister's family after his parents were killed in a forest fire. Caused by lightning, sweeping through tinder-dry underbrush, the fire had roared through the woods, consuming the house and his parents, trapping them inside before they could escape.

Farinn had not been home or he would have met the same fate. Unable to sleep, he had left his bed and gone out to roam the hills and listen to the song of the stars, the song of the night.

Farinn had been a disappointment to his parents. He was termed lazy, for instead of planting or weeding or minding the cattle, he was often caught staring dreamily at nothing. His father had taught him to wield a battle-axe and to hold his shield and to stand with other warriors in the shield wall because every man must know these things.

Farinn had joined the Torgun in the shield wall

when they fought the ogres. He had taken his place, standing shoulder-to-shoulder with his fellow warriors, their shields overlapping, gripping his axe, waiting for the foe to attack. He had done the same, gripping his axe, when they faced the giants on the Dragon Isles. He had gripped his axe, but he had yet to strike his first blow.

He wasn't a coward. He had been terrified, but he had not run away. He had waited with a grim and desperate courage for some enemy to attack him, but strangely, though the battle swirled all around him, the fighting never touched him.

It was then that he realized the gods were saving him for something larger. And when he began to hesitantly and tentatively string words together to describe the battle with the giants or to compose the lay for the death of Garn or sing of Skylan's battle with the fury in the Para Dix, Farinn had thought at first the gods had spared him to tell the tale of Skylan Ivorson, the Chief of Chiefs of the Vindrasi. Later Farinn would come to realize the gods wanted him to tell their own tale, how the wyrds of men and gods are bound together. That knowledge would only come long after he had sung the final verse.

Skylan and the other men did not know what to make of Farinn. Because he was so quiet, they tended to forget he was around. Farinn liked it that way. When the men thought no one could hear them, he listened. When they thought no one was looking, he saw. Farinn did not judge. That was not his place. He crafted the song in his mind and repeated it to himself again and again and again, so that he would not forget. But this meant that if he died, the song would be lost, never to be heard. That was why he was learning to write down the song, so that others would remember, even if he was not there to sing it.

Caught up in his dreams and songs, Farinn did not pay much heed to girls, mainly because girls did not pay much attention to him. He had soft brown hair and mild brown eyes and once he'd overheard two giggling girls saying he looked like a cow. He was slender without much muscle, for when other boys his age were practicing their fighting skills, he would sit beneath a tree, his eyes closed, humming to himself. Girls thought him odd, as did boys.

The young Aquin guard did not consider him odd. She could not think he looked like a cow, since it was unlikely she had ever seen a cow. She walked up the stairs by his side, regarding him with an interest that even he, in his naïveté, could see was admiring.

"My name is Kailani," she said. "What are you called?"

Farinn mumbled his name and was then forced to repeat it when she said she hadn't heard.

Kailani was lovely. Her beauty was strange and exotic and she found him attractive, too, though he could not imagine why. Of all the marvelous and wonderful things in this amazing place, fish and flora and fauna and oceanaids and breathing air under water, the fact that this beautiful young woman had taken a liking to him seemed the most marvelous, the most wonderful.

Farinn had first seen Kailani when she had slipped into the palace to join the other guards. She was flushed from running and avoided the commander's eye, leading him to believe she was late for duty. Kailani had been fortunate. The delegation from the City of the Fourth Daughter had arrived at that moment, distracting Commander Neda.

Farinn had felt Kailani's eyes on him all during the meeting in the throne room. He was trying to pay attention to what was being said and done, trying to commit it to memory for the song. But Kailani's gaze was distracting.

When the Queen abruptly left them and the guards were ordered to escort them to their quarters, Kailani latched on to him. Skylan and Aylaen were in the lead. Skylan always took the lead. He could no more have walked in the rear than he could have flown through the air. Aylaen, with her long strides, easily kept up with him. Wulfe joined them, the fae child, a constant marvel to Farinn, who wasn't sure if he liked him or not, keeping close to Skylan, talking about his oceanaids. Farinn and his guard walked behind the three of them, while Legate Acronis lagged after all the rest, asking, observing, listening, taking it all in to, as the Legate would have said, "tell Chloe." Farinn felt a wistful envy at the father's love for his daughter, a love that not even death could conquer. A love he had never known.

Sometimes Skylan would glance back at Farinn to see if he was all right and give him a reassuring smile. Skylan had been touched when Farinn had chosen to stay with him instead of returning home with the others. Farinn had seen, with the keen eyes of the poet, that Skylan thought Farinn had stayed out of loyalty. Farinn loved and admired Skylan and he was glad to think that he'd pleased Skylan and that was why Farinn would never divulge the truth. He had stayed for the song.

Unfortunately, Farinn was finding it hard to think of the song right now. The staircase narrowed as it spiraled upward and Kailani moved close by his side, so close that they would bump into each other. When that happened, Farinn was keenly aware of the firmness of her hip, the touch of her fingers brushing his arm. The way she smiled at him, a secret, knowing smile, told him she knew what he was feeling.

When they reached the top of the stairs, a guard unlocked the door with the brass lock and then separated the "guests." Each was given a room in the tower wing. His room was small, and contained a bed, a chair, and a table. Each room had its own door leading into a central area. The individual doors could not be locked. Once Farinn and the others were inside, the guard told them she would lock the outer door and she and her comrade would take up their posts outside it. She implied that this was for their protection, but there was no doubt in anyone's mind that they were prisoners.

Skylan offered to keep Wulfe with him. He and Aylaen parted with loving looks. Farinn was too busy with his own love song to notice. When Kailani escorted Farinn to his room, which was next to Skylan's, Farinn was startled to feel Kailani's fingers twine around his.

"I want to be with you tonight," Kailani whispered. "If you want me, that is."

Her hand squeezed his. Her eyes smiled into his. Farinn felt his heart swell with love. He longed to say something clever, something intelligent, but he couldn't think of a single word. He was as giddy as the night he'd rashly joined in a drinking game with Sigurd and Bjorn.

Farinn must have made his meaning known, for Kailani smiled with pleasure. The guard yelled at her impatiently to come away. Kailani squeezed his hand again and then turned and ran.

Farinn sat down on the bed, but he did not see it. He was floating somewhere far above it in a dream of desire.

For once in his life, the song had gone clean out of his head.

Farinn watched impatiently for night. Darkness filled his room. He sat waiting eagerly, yet when the knock came on his door, he was paralyzed. He could not move until the second, impatient rapping. Farinn sprang from the bed and flung open the door.

Skylan stood there.

Farinn blinked at him.

"I came to see if you were all right," said Skylan.

"Oh, uh, yes, I am . . . um . . . fine . . ." Farinn stammered to a halt.

"Are you sure?" said Skylan, regarding Farinn with a slight frown.

Farinn tried to look as though nothing was the matter and apparently failed, for Skylan suddenly laughed and clapped him on the shoulder.

"You sly dog! You were expecting someone else to knock at your door, weren't you? Someone a lot better looking than I am. What is her name?"

Farinn flushed more deeply and thought he should deny this, but he'd never been good at telling lies.

"Kailani," he mumbled.

Skylan said with a wink, "I saw her. She is a beauty. Have your fun, lad."

Skylan left, still laughing. Farinn closed the door. He had never been so humiliated. Desire drained out of him and he thought he would simply crawl into bed and pull the blanket over his head and die of shame. When the knock came again, he almost couldn't bring himself to answer it. Then he feared that would be rude. He opened the door.

Kailani stood there. She was not wearing her armor. She was not wearing much of anything, just the loincloth twisted around her slender thighs. Her skin was wet and so was the cloth. Her body glistened in the light. She reached out and took hold of his hand. "Come with me! Quickly, before anyone sees us."

Farinn could not take his eyes off her. Yet he hesitated. "Where are we going?"

"Somewhere secret," Kailani breathed. "Somewhere we can be alone. Just the two of us."

Farinn was still uneasy. "I can't leave. The guards—"

"Silly!" Kailani giggled. "I'm your guard."

Farinn looked back at his bed. "We could stay here—"

"The walls are thin. Everyone would hear us," said Kailani. "The guard would come to see what was going on. If we were discovered . . ."

"What would happen?" Farinn asked nervously.

"Nothing would happen to *you*," Kailani said.

"I don't want to get you into trouble . . ." Farinn started to back away.

"I like being in trouble!" Kailani whispered.

She pressed close to him and twined her arms around him and kissed him. Taking hold of his hand, she led him out of his room and into the center area.

The night was dark. He could see nothing but Kailani seemed to know where she was going. Cautioning him to be silent, she led him through the darkness. He followed her, his heart pounding with the thrill of the adventure and the touch of her hand. She stopped and he bumped into her.

"Where are we?"

"A secret passage that leads out of the tower," she whispered. "The door is hidden."

She spoke words that were foreign to him and

let go of his hand. Bright light flared, dazzling his eyes, and then it vanished. He heard a creaking sound, as of the door opening, and Kailani had hold of his hand once again.

"Be careful," she cautioned. "There's a step. Don't fall."

He slid his foot onto the step. Putting out his hand to steady himself, he encountered a stone wall. He heard Kailani whispering again and the creaking sound again; the door closing. He felt her fumbling about in the darkness and then a soft, glowing light flared. Kailani was holding one of the lanterns he'd seen the Aquins carry.

The two were pressed together at the top of a long staircase that plunged almost straight down through the stone walls. The staircase was so long, Farinn could not make out what lay at the end. He looked over his shoulder. The door was indeed hidden. He reached out his hand, touched what seemed to be rock, cold and slightly damp.

"What was this used for?" he asked wonderingly.

"An escape route," Kailani answered. "In case the palace ever came under siege, which it never has in all the history of our people." She gave his hand a squeeze. "Now it's used only by servants or lovers."

They walked cautiously down the uneven stairs, with Kailani taking the lead, guiding Farinn with a touch of her hand.

"You used a magic spell to open the door," he said.

He was growing increasingly uncomfortable, perhaps because he did not know any warriors who knew magic. He had never before been in a building with a magic door.

Kailani glanced over her shoulder. Her hair clung to her bare skin. "A simple rune spell. Everyone in the palace knows it."

She stopped on the step beneath him and looked up at him. Her eyes were wide and beautiful and yearning.

"Don't worry, Farinn," she added, guessing his thoughts. "You will be back before morning. You will never be missed."

Farinn bent to kiss her, slipped, and nearly fell down the stairs. She caught him and they both laughed.

"Make haste!" she whispered, her breath hot on his face. "I cannot wait for our pleasure."

She began to run down the stairs heedlessly. Farinn plunged recklessly after her, tripping and stumbling and hoping he would not break his neck. He had never before felt like this—wild and bold and exhilarated, as though he had burst free from himself and was soaring toward heaven. The song, his song, crashed and thundered in his head.

The staircase came to an end with an abruptness that caused Farinn to almost pitch headfirst into a stream of water, black and swift.

"Run-off from the rain that falls on the top of the island. We collect it to use for drinking and to water the groves and gardens," Kailani explained. "From here, we will swim. Take off your caftan."

She drew near him and her fingers tugged on the buttons. "Let me help . . ."

Farinn grasped her hands and kissed her. The caftan slid to the wet rock. She laughed and jumped into the water and pulled him in after her.

The current was fast and carried Farinn along. He couldn't see and he would have been nervous if the water had been deep, but he could touch the bottom with his feet. Kailani swam beside him, twisting and rolling like an otter.

"Enjoy the ride," she said to him. "There are streams like this throughout the city. The current will carry us through the sluice gate and out into the sea."

Farinn tried floating on his back and finally let himself relax and revel in the moment. He found pleasure in surrendering himself to the current, letting it carry him along. Kailani set the lantern upon the water and he was amazed to see it float. The light swirled in the eddies and bumped up against them. Farinn was delighted. He would put this in a song, but only a song for himself. No one else would ever hear it. Except, perhaps, Kailani.

"Where are we going?" he asked, and realized suddenly he didn't care.

"To Lover's Cove," said Kailani. "It is really only a cave, but it is filled with hundreds of little nooks and hideaways, perfect for those seeking privacy." She added with a little sigh, "Privacy is something hard to come by in our city."

"Why is that?"

"Our dwellings are small and overcrowded. We live on top of one another. Our life spans are long. The only threats we face are accidents, disease, and predators. Families may have as many as four generations living beneath one roof."

Kailani shook her head. "But our peaceful ways may come to an end. War is inevitable, I fear. The followers of Aelon are trying to force his worship on everyone and there are those like our Queen who are faithful to the Old Gods."

Farinn held out his arm as they floated down the swift-moving stream and showed Kailani the long, jagged, snake-shaped scar. "Back in Sinaria, the priestesses of Aelon cut our flesh and embedded us with magical crystals. If we did anything or thought anything Aelon did not like, the god punished us."

"Truly?" Kailani's eyes were wide, startled. "Aelon can do that?"

"The pain of disobedience was like plunging my arm into hot coals," said Farinn, grimacing. "When we escaped, Skylan used the blessed sword of Vindrash to cut out the crystals. Our blood washed away the god's hold over us."

Kailani caught the lantern as it floated past. She took his arm and held the light to examine the scar. She ran her fingers along it. Farinn flinched at her touch.

"I'm sorry," Kailani said, concerned. "Does it still hurt?"

"The memory of it," said Farinn. "But we won't think of such things now."

She splashed water in his face. Playing like children, they floated together down the stream, kicking with their feet and sometimes coming together to kiss, their mouths filling with water, which only made them laugh more.

The current slowed, the stream widened. Kailani drew away from him. By the light of the lantern, he could see a gate made of the enormous teeth of some sea creature embedded in the stone wall. The teeth were set close together, leaving barely enough room for him and Kailani to slither between. Fortunately Farinn was thin for a Vindrasi or he would have been forced to dive under the teeth.

"The sluice gate will not repel invaders," Kailani said. "But it will slow them down. A man built like your chief would never make it!"

Beyond was the sea, inky black.

"That is our destination," said Kailani, indicating a cavern in the distance, the opening glimmering with a faint phosphorescence. "The way is not far. I have brought you a breathing mask."

She helped Farinn put the mask over his face and attached the clamshell to his back. He felt an instant's panic when he could not breathe through his nose, but relaxed when he drew air into his lungs. Kailani did not use a mask. She began to swim, flashing through the water as fast as a porpoise. Farinn was a strong swimmer, but slower, burdened with the clamshell, and he soon lost sight of her. He could see the lantern she was carrying, however, and he swam toward the light.

His thoughts were on Kailani and taking her into his arms and his desire building and then the sweet release. When he felt an arm wrap around his waist, he thought it was Kailani, teasing him. Farinn was about to laugh in response, but then there were more arms, strong hands clasping him.

He was not a warrior, at least by Skylan's standards, but Farinn had been trained to fight—his father had seen to that. Farinn lashed out at his captors. He kept his wits and made his punches count and he managed to hurt one of them, for he heard a grunt of pain. Something hard, like the butt end of a spear, slammed into his gut. Farinn doubled up, groaning. When the pain eased, he raised his head and saw Kailani, treading water quite close to him, holding the lantern, lighting the way.

"Don't fight them," she advised him. "You will only get hurt."

A bitter taste flooded Farinn's mouth. Kailani's seduction had been a ruse, a trick to lure him out of the palace and into this ambush, though why they wanted him he could not imagine. He was only a poet.

"Where should we take him, Kailani?" one of the warriors asked.

"I will guide you," she answered. "I'm sorry, Farinn. I didn't mean . . ."

He looked away, unable to stand the sight of her. The lantern light wavered and then she swam off.

Overwhelmed with shame, Farinn sagged listlessly in his captors' arms, the fight knocked out of him. He could not hear his song and wondered if he would ever hear it again.

CHAPTER 26

Aylaen was walking a path through the forest, a familiar path. The time was winter. The trees were bare of their leaves, the evergreens green and white. The path was covered over with snow, but she knew where she was; the path led to the house of Owl Mother.

Aylaen was bewildered. She didn't know why she was on this path, because she didn't want to visit Owl Mother. She was back home and she wanted to go to her own mother. Aylaen tried to turn back, but no matter which way she turned, she always ended up on the same path. She came to a halt outside Owl Mother's ramshackle house.

The day was gray and silent, the thick, heavy silence that comes with the snow. A smudge of smoke rose from the chimney, and a light burned inside the window. The snow was trampled, marked with the footprints of animals.

Aylaen knocked loudly on the door.

"Owl Mother! It's me, Aylaen. I've come home. Let me inside!"

The door opened. A baby dragon stood on the

threshold. The dragon's wings lifted and its crest flattened. When it opened its mouth and hissed, Aylaen gasped and fell back in shock. Owl Mother hobbled over, flapping her skirts at the dragon and chiding it.

"Get back to the fire, you silly beast. You'll catch your death!"

The baby dragon ran off. Aylaen stared after it in astonishment. She did not accept Owl Mother's invitation to enter, but remained standing on the threshold.

"Come in, child," Owl Mother called from the smoke-tinged, warm darkness. "Don't worry about the dragon. She can't fly; she has a torn wing."

"I've never seen a baby dragon," said Aylaen, awed.

"Not many have, child. Mostly the parent keeps the babies safe in their own world. I've no notion how this one came to be here. She may be an orphan who wandered through the portal."

Aylaen still hovered on the threshold and Owl Mother scowled.

"Why did you knock if you don't plan to come in?"

Aylaen flushed. "Forgive me, Owl Mother, I will visit you another time. Now I want only to go home and I can't find the way . . ."

"Come inside. You are letting in the cold," Owl Mother chided her.

Owl Mother had seen over seventy summers. Her hair was white as the frost. She wore a wool dress and a heavy shawl wrapped around her shoulders and tied behind her back. A fire crackled in the fireplace, and the room was invitingly warm.

Aylaen entered the house reluctantly. Everyone knew that Owl Mother was a little mad. It was said she consorted with the fae.

Owl Mother closed the door on the cold and the snow. The old woman motioned for Aylaen to sit down in a chair by the fire, first shooing away a seagull perched on the chair's back. The seagull flew off with an annoyed squawk. The baby dragon was curled up on a pile of straw before the fire. The dragon's eyes gazed steadily at Aylaen. The seagull took refuge in the rafters and cleaned its beak with its foot. Aylaen remained standing.

"Owl Mother, I need to find the way home . . ."

"So do we all, child. Sit yourself. Someone wants to talk to you. He's come a long distance."

"Talk to me? How did anyone know I would be here?" Aylaen asked, bewildered.

"Because we are always where we need to be," said Owl Mother, a cunning glint in her eye.

A small oil lamp stood on a table. By the flame's light, Aylaen could see the dragon's red eyes gleam and the seagull's black eyes glisten. Owl Mother's eyes were dark and did not reflect the light. Aylaen sat down in the chair.

A tapestry covered one end of the room. The tapestry was very old and portrayed warriors in strange-looking armor battling each other. Aylaen had been forced to learn to sew and she could appreciate the work that had gone into the tapestry. Owl Mother walked over to the tapestry and with her wizened, clawlike hand drew it aside.

A man sat on a low three-legged stool. He rose when he saw Aylaen and stood facing her. He was tall and once must have been well-built, strong, and muscular. His heavy shoulders were now stooped, his muscles grown flaccid, and his skin hung from his arms. His face was deeply creased, and the corners of his mouth sagged.

His eyes were strange and arresting. Large and gray, the eyes were red-rimmed, watery, sunken in his head and constantly in motion, roving back and forth, shifting this way and that. He spoke to her, but he did not look at her. He searched, watched, always watching.

Aylaen rose to confront him. She knew this man, or rather, knew this god.

"I see you recognize me," he said, not looking at her.

"You are Sund the traitor!" said Aylaen.

"I am Sund," said the god. The corners of his mouth rose a moment in what was the memory of a smile. "I am pleased you know me, Daughter."

"Do not call me Daughter!" Aylaen said angrily. "I am not daughter to one who betrayed his comrades and his people!"

"Too many eyes are watching you, Daughter," said Sund. "Too many ears are listening to every word you speak. Too many hands carry knives to kill you. I needed to meet you where we would both be safe."

"You wasted your time," Aylaen said curtly. "I have nothing to say to you."

Sund would still not look at her. His eyes roved back and forth; the side of his mouth twitched. "Your small mortal eyes can see no farther than your own nose. You have no way of understanding me. I make allowances."

Sund shrugged his heavy shoulders. "I did not bring you here to hold discourse with you, Daughter. I brought you here to tell you what you are going to do."

Aylaen shook her head. "My small mortal eyes may not be able to see into the future, but I know that if I was *meant* to do what you are going to *tell* me to do, you would not need to tell me to do it."

Owl Mother chuckled. Sund's gaze roved through the future, always searching and sifting through the myriad threads of the wyrds of men and gods.

"You know where to find two of the spirit-bones of the Vektia dragon. You will be given the opportunity to obtain a third. You will take the two you have now and destroy them. You will destroy the third should it come into your possession."

"Destroy them!" Aylaen repeated, not believing she had heard him right. "The Vektia bones hold the power of creation. If I destroy them I destroy the ability of the gods to create!"

"Precisely. And lacking that power, Aelon and

the Gods of Raj will grow bored and depart. They will leave the world once more to us. If you attempt to use the Five, you will lose control. Torval, Vindrash, all of us will be destroyed. Aelon will gain control of the power of creation. And the first thing he will do with it will be to slaughter you and your people."

Aylaen was distracted by Owl Mother, who was seated at the table, playing with a small wooden spinning top, a toy made to entertain small children. Owl Mother gave the top a twist with her hand and set it spinning on the table. The top spun and spun and then began to slow down and wobble. Finally, it fell over, rocked for a moment on its side, and ceased to move. Owl Mother folded her hands in front of her and winked at Aylaen.

Sund was not watching Owl Mother, yet he saw her, for he scowled. Owl Mother rolled her eyes and twiddled her finger around her head.

"That is one future," Aylaen argued. "One among the many."

"No, Daughter," said Sund, "it is the one."

Sund's roving eyes rested on her at last. She looked into the wide and terror-filled eyes and realized with shock that the god's fear had driven him to madness.

"I have tried to kill Ivorson and thus far I have failed," Sund said. "His wyrd is strong and Torval protects him. But though Skylan is the one who finds the Five, it is you who will use them."

Sund clenched his fist. "Promise me that you

will destroy the Vektia bones, and all will be well between us!"

"I cannot make such a promise," said Aylaen, trembling.

"Know this, then, Daughter," Sund said, his voice deep and shaking with rage. "If you bring the power of creation into the world, you yourself will lack it. Your womb will be barren. No children will be born to you! This I have foreseen."

"You are mad!" Aylaen cried.

"Your sister, Treia, is carrying Raegar's child," Sund continued relentlessly. "Her son will become Emperor of the Oran nation. Her son will grind his boot into the necks of the Vindrasi. I know this. I have seen it all. This is what will come to pass if you do not destroy the Five!"

Aylaen shrank away from him. She had to hold on to the back of the chair, where the seagull had perched, to keep from falling.

"Ivorson says his son must be born in honor." Sund gave a hollow laugh. "His son will not be born at all! His seed will fall on dry, cracked ground."

Aylaen could not bear to look at him and she covered her face with her hands. The baby dragon hissed in fear.

"Many wyrds," Sund shouted. "Many wyrds wrapped together into one doom . . ."

And then all was quiet.

Slowly, Aylaen drew back her hands. Owl Mother let fall the tapestry. The god was gone.

"He is mad," said Aylaen.

Shivering uncontrollably, she moved her chair closer to the fire. The dragon edged over to make room for her. Owl Mother took off her shawl and draped it around Aylaen's shoulders.

"Sund was distraught over the death of the Sea Goddess's sister, Desiria," said Owl Mother. "He foresaw her death and he tried to warn Torval and Vindrash and the other gods, but they would not listen. They believed they were invincible . . ."

"Will what Sund threatened come true?" Aylaen asked, chilled. "Will I be barren?"

Owl Mother filled a horn with mead and handed it to Aylaen.

"Drink this," said Owl Mother. "I will cast the rune stones."

Aylaen drank the sweetly bitter mead and warmth returned to her body. Owl Mother drew from her belt a tattered and greasy leather pouch, opened the pouch, and took out six stones worn smooth from much handling. On one side of each stone was a rune. The other side was blank. Each of the six runes had meaning and were read together to reveal the future. Owl Mother dumped out the stones on the table and began to mix them with her hand.

Aylaen stirred in her chair.

"I only want to find my way home," Aylaen said.

"You know the way," said Owl Mother.

Aylaen realized she did know the way. Why then did she feel lost?

"If Sund, a god, cannot see the future, how can a bunch of rocks predict it?" Aylaen asked.

"Close the door tight when you go," said Owl Mother, mixing the stones. "Or else the wind blows it open."

Aylaen gazed down at the stones on the crude, rough-hewn table polished by loving hands rubbing oil into the wood.

Owl Mother indicated the stones with a nod. "Pick them up. And cast them down."

Aylaen hesitated, then did as she was told. She held the stones tightly for a moment, then threw them onto the table with a jerk.

"Humpf," said Owl Mother. "Never seen that before."

Five of the stones came up blank. Only the sixth had fallen rune-side up.

"What does that mean?" Aylaen asked nervously.

"Only one choice brings victory," said Owl Mother. She pointed to the sixth rune. "That is the rune for Death."

"You talk in riddles," said Aylaen shakily. She was sorry she had stayed. But still she did not leave. "Will I be barren?" she demanded. "The stones were supposed to tell me that."

Owl Mother shrugged. "The stones have said all they can say. If they didn't answer your question that was because you didn't ask it. And now the vision is ended. You must go."

"Vision? What vision?" Aylaen asked.

Owl Mother took hold of Aylaen's elbow and steered her toward the door.

"This isn't a vision," Aylaen protested, frightened. "I'm home. I want to see my mother."

Owl Mother yanked open the door. A gust of cold air blew inside. The dragon whimpered in displeasure and curled up tightly, tail wrapped around her nose. The seagull swooped down from the rafters, flying so near Aylaen's head she ducked with a startled cry. The seagull sailed into the wind and perched in a tree. Aylaen shivered with the cold.

"I can tell you this much," said Owl Mother. "Sund seeks to frighten you. Have faith in yourself and in that young hothead, Skylan. So far he's turned out better than I imagined." Owl Mother gave a shake of her head as though finding that hard to believe.

Owl Mother raised a gnarled finger. "And remember this, child. Love is never barren. Now before you go, give me back my shawl."

Aylaen unwound the shawl and handed it to Owl Mother. The old woman shoved Aylaen out the door, then shut it with a bang that woke her.

Skylan lay in his bed in the small room they had given him. Wulfe was in the room with him, curled up in a corner, sound asleep, feet and hands twitching. Skylan was wide awake, gazing into the darkness that for him was as bright as sunlight with happiness.

Aylaen loved him. She was to be his wife.

Skylan closed his eyes and he could still see the sunlight that seemed to glow throughout his being. He pictured their children. Their firstborn would be a son. They would name him Garn. He would have his mother's red hair and his father's fighting spirit. Skylan would teach his son how to use a sword and shield, how to take his place in the shield wall. He would teach his son to hunt, sail, and fish. He would teach his son, too, how to be a good chief. Skylan imagined his joy as he laid his newborn son in his grandfather's arms, beseeching Norgaard's blessing. Such a moment would help make up for the pain Skylan had brought his father.

Their second born would be a daughter. She would be a redheaded, saucy little imp who could reduce him to pudding with a look from her green eyes. They would name her Dawn and he would teach her to fight, as well, for women must know how to defend their home and children. His little daughter would nestle in his arms and fall asleep with her curly head on his breast. She would be as beautiful as her mother and as brave and courageous. The young men would be wild about her, but she would scorn them all. And when the time came for him to give her to another man—though Skylan could not imagine there would be any man worthy of her—she would hold fast to Skylan's arm and whisper that she would always love her father best.

And at night there would be Aylaen. She would be there to love him, to tease him, to chide him and scold him. And at the end, Aylaen would hold him in her arms as his eyes closed upon the world. He would wait for her in Torval's Hall. The afterlife would hold no joy until she was with him.

Wulfe gave a violent sneeze that jolted Skylan from his dreams. Smiling, he rolled over and went to sleep.

Owl Mother sat in her cabin. The baby dragon lay at her feet. The seagull perched upon the arm of her chair.

"You gods," Owl Mother grumbled. "You're all mad, as far as I'm concerned. Is it any wonder I would rather spend my time among the fae? They know how to enjoy life."

"They will not enjoy life if Aelon takes control of the world," said Akaria. "We gods put up with their nonsense. Aelon will not. He views them as dangerous."

"He views you as exceedingly dangerous, Owl Mother," Vindrash added. "I wish you would come to live with us in Torval's Hall."

Owl Mother snorted. "Maybe in the old days, when Torval knew how to throw a feast. Not now. His gloom turns the ale sour."

The dragon smiled and rested a clawed foot gently upon Owl Mother's boot.

"I thank you for warning us of Sund's scheming, Owl Mother."

"I still think we should have stopped him," said Akaria with a vicious snap of her seagull beak.

"We should not have let him threaten the mortal. Aylaen will give in to her fear and all will be lost."

"We needed to hear what Sund had to say," Vindrash said, adding with a sigh, "He may be mad, but he still sees the future. I have faith in Aylaen. She will be a worthy guardian of the Five."

"I am not impressed," said Akaria dismissively.

"The two of you must go," said Owl Mother, pushing herself up out of the chair. "Some of us have work to do. I have a sick calf to tend to at the Jorgesons'."

She began to gather together her stock of herbs and poultices. The two goddesses, in their true forms, gazed down at the casting stones that still lay where they had fallen on the rough-hewn table: five blank and one marked with Death.

"What do you suppose it means?" Vindrash murmured.

"That a bunch of rocks cannot predict the future," said the Sea Goddess.

CHAPTER 27

Aylaen sat on her bed, watching the coming of day, hearing Sund's words.

Destroy the spiritbones . . .

The Vektan Torque. Made of solid gold, adorned with jewels, the Torque had been given to the Vindrasi people centuries ago by the hand of the Dragon Goddess, Vindrash. The Torque was the most valued treasure the Vindrasi possessed. Countless warriors had given their lives to protect it. Skylan had fought an ogre-chief to keep it. Aylaen imagined taking a hammer to the Torque, smashing the spiritbone of the Vektia dragon, pulverizing it, crushing it to dust and scattering the dust to the winds. She might as well smash the heart and soul of her people.

"I can't do it," she said softly.

Yet . . . to be barren! To never give Skylan a son to bring him honor, a daughter to bring him joy. And there was her sister, pregnant with Raegar's son! A son destined to grow up to rule the Vindrasi!

Aylaen pressed her hand on her belly, her fingers clenched.

Owl Mother might say love was never barren.

Skylan would love her. Aylaen was certain of that. He would always love her, but he would be unhappy that she could not give him children. He would never say anything to hurt her, but she would see the pain in his eyes when he watched other fathers playing with their children. He had already fathered sons, so he would know that she was the one at fault. If Aylaen was barren, Skylan was entitled by law to take a son by another woman into his home.

Aylaen was jolted from her unhappy reverie by the door opening. She had the impression that someone had been knocking for a long time. She rose to her feet.

"I thought perhaps you were asleep," said the servant. "The Queen summons you."

"Thank you. I will come now," said Aylaen, hastily wiping her eyes.

She glanced at Skylan's door as she passed, thought of saying something to him. She decided to let him sleep. He would want to come with her and she was not yet ready to face him. She had to decide what to do.

The servant did not take Aylaen to the throne room, as she had expected, but outside the castle to the garden. She found the Queen on her hands and knees, pulling weeds from the flower bed. Seeing her, Queen Magali rose and dusted the dirt from her hands and smiled at Aylaen's look of astonishment.

"I enjoy working with my flowers, watching

them grow," said Queen Magali. "They are like my children—"

Aylaen felt a spasm of pain. She bit her lip. The Queen regarded her with concern. "Are you unwell?"

"I had . . . a bad dream," said Aylaen. She managed a smile. "I worked in the fields in my homeland." She held out her hands. "These calluses do not come from fighting men with my sword. They come from battling weeds with a hoe."

Queen Magali laughed, then grew somber.

"Come walk with me, Aylaen. I misjudged you," she said. "I was too quick to believe Commander Neda when she told me you had come to invade our realm. I prayed to the Sea Goddess, Akaria. She and I have made a decision. We will not turn you or any of your people over to the priests of Aelon."

"I am grateful, Your Majesty," said Aylaen. "Though I fear that this decision will mean war for your people. I am sorry to have brought this trouble on you."

"Trouble was here long before you came," said Queen Magali with a sigh. "My cousin, Queen Thais, is ambitious. She has been promised rich reward by Aelon if she brings all the other cities under her sway. I fear war is inevitable. Which means that you and your friends are in danger. You should leave immediately. My warriors will escort you and your friends to your ship."

Queen Magali beckoned to one of the servants,

then started to walk away. Aylaen stared after her in dismay.

"Your Majesty, I cannot leave without the Vektan Torque," said Aylaen. "The Torque belongs to my people. It is sacred to us."

Queen Magali turned to face her, her expression cold.

"I have only your word for that," she said. "My warriors found the Torque on the floor of the sea."

"I can explain what happened," said Aylaen. "The ogres were going to attack Vindraholm. The former Chief of Chiefs was a coward. He bartered away the Torque to save his own life—"

Queen Magali made a dismissive gesture. "I do not have time for bard's tales. I have given you leave to go, Vindrasi Lady. You said you wanted only to return to your homeland. You are free to do so. But the Vektan Torque remains with me."

"Then so do we, Your Majesty," said Aylaen angrily. "Those who came with us are free to go, but neither Skylan nor I will leave without the Torque."

"You are clearly troublemakers. Perhaps I should hand you over to Aelon after all," said Queen Magali.

"You must do what you think best, Your Majesty," said Aylaen. "The Vektan Torque belongs to our goddess and our people. I will not be like that coward Horg. I will not barter away the Torque to save my own life."

Queen Magali raised an eyebrow. "The Torque

is sacred because it holds one of the spiritbones of the Five Vektia."

Aylaen blinked, not knowing what to say. She realized a moment too late that her very silence had spoken for her. She tried to repair the damage. "I . . . I don't know what you mean, Your Majesty. I have never heard of the Five—"

Queen Magali smiled. "Do not ever try to lie, Aylaen. You are no good at it."

Aylaen flushed and bit her lip. Queen Magali sat down on a bench made of bamboo. She motioned Aylaen to sit beside her. Aylaen did so, gingerly, warily, keeping her distance.

"I did cast my net to ensnare you, Aylaen," said Queen Magali. "Do not fear. You escaped. You chose to stay, rather than save yourself. That told me much about you."

"And why did you need to know anything about me?" Aylaen asked, annoyed and angry.

"Because I have it in my power to give to you a trust sacred to my people," said Queen Magali. "I had to know first if you were worthy of my trust. I know all about the Five spiritbones of the Vektia. I hold one of them in my care. For many generations, the Queen of the City of the First Daughter has kept the spiritbone safe. The First Daughter was the Sea Queen's eldest child and she passed the spiritbone to her daughter and so on down through the generations. But now war is coming to the twelve cities. We will fight, but we are not strong. Many of the other cities are allied against us. If we fall, the spiritbone might end up in the hands of Aelon."

The Queen fixed with Aylaen an intense, penetrating gaze that seemed to turn Aylaen inside-out, lay all her secrets bare.

"The Sea Goddess has given me permission to send the spiritbone with you," said Queen Magali. "Will you pledge to keep the spiritbone of the Sea Goddess safe?"

Aylaen could not speak. Her chest was tight, she couldn't breathe for the pain. She closed her eyes for a moment. There had never truly been any doubt. Just one little selfish qualm and that was soon over.

"The Five Vektia spiritbones do not belong to me, Your Majesty, nor do they belong to you. They belong to all the people of this world. If they come into our possession for a time, it is only so that we may hold them as a sacred trust. I pledge my life to keep the spiritbones safe, as the goddess Vindrash is my witness."

"Even though the god Sund might curse you," said Queen Magali.

"None of us knows the future, Your Majesty," said Aylaen steadily. "Not men. Not gods."

"Vindrash chose her sword wisely," said Queen Magali.

Aylaen gave a little sigh.

Skylan paced about the room, chafing at his imprisonment, his inability to do anything. Earlier in the morning, he had gone in search of Aylaen, only to be told by the guards that she was with Queen Magali. Skylan had insisted that he should also be in the meeting, but the guards had only rolled their eyes and told him to go back to his room or be hauled off to the dungeons again.

Skylan had returned in a bad mood.

"Why are you stomping about?" grumbled Wulfe, sitting up from where he'd been sleeping on the floor. "You woke me up."

"Aylaen's meeting with the Queen," said Skylan.

Wulfe shrugged and yawned. "Why are you mad about that?"

"She should have taken me with her," said Skylan. "This could mean war and war is man's business, not women's."

"War?" Wulfe leaped up, alarmed, and started for the door.

"Where are you going?" Skylan demanded.

"You will put on your sword," said Wulfe. "I don't like you when you're wearing your sword."

"I don't even have a sword to put on," said Skylan bitterly. "Mine is somewhere at the bottom of the ocean."

Wulfe shook his head, not believing him. "War means swords. I'm going back to the oceanaids."

"Wait!" said Skylan. "If you're going back, you can take a message to the Dragon Kahg for me."

Wulfe scowled. "The dragon doesn't like me."

"He likes you," said Skylan, exasperated. They had been through this before. "If the Dragon Kahg didn't, he would have thrown you overboard long ago. Tell the dragon that we are in danger and he needs to be ready to take us out of here. Will you do that?"

"The dragon doesn't like me," Wulfe repeated sullenly.

Skylan shook his fist at him. "So help me, Torval—"

"I'm going," said Wulfe.

"Will you tell the dragon?"

"Maybe . . ."

Wulfe darted out of the room. Skylan heard the boy banging on the locked door, demanding to be set free. The guards were glad to accommodate the fae child, the "princeling" as they called him with a laugh. Skylan resumed his pacing, only to be interrupted again by Acronis.

"I was hoping Farinn was with you," said Acronis.

"I haven't seen him," said Skylan shortly.

"He's not in his room. His bed hasn't been slept in. I can't find him anywhere."

Skylan went to look for himself. Farinn's room was certainly empty. The bed was rumpled, but no one had slept there.

"The young fool! I knew that young woman who was flirting with him was coming for a tryst with him, but I never thought he'd be crazy enough to run off with her!"

Skylan swore and ran his hand through his hair in frustration, trying to think what to do. "She was one of his guards. He said her name was Kailani. They had to go out through that door. The other guards must have seen them. You're friendly with these people. Go ask the guards what they know."

Skylan remained in Farinn's room, searching for clues as to what had happened to the young man. Acronis returned to report.

"The guards claim that no one has passed through the door except the Queen's servant and Aylaen. They said there are hidden passages in the palace. Farinn and his lover probably slipped out through one of those. They don't know any warrior named Kailani, but she could be new. They laughed and added that the boy would return a man."

"I hope they are right," said Skylan, though he remained unconvinced. "I am his commander. He should not have left without telling me."

"He's sixteen," said Acronis. "And I don't imagine he was thinking much about you last night. The Aquins said they would search for him. We must leave it to them."

Skylan did not want to leave this to the Aquins, but there wasn't much he could do. He went back to his room to worry about Farinn and fume over Aylaen, only to find her waiting for him. She was tense and pale and Skylan forgot all about Farinn, and that he was angry with Aylaen. She closed the door and turned to face him.

"What is wrong?" he asked her the moment the door had closed. "Have you been crying? Did the Queen upset you? Is she going to hand us over to Raegar? By Torval, I will—"

"Skylan, let me speak!" said Aylaen desperately.

"If you don't, I will lose my courage. First, the Queen is going to give you the Torque. On our wedding day . . ."

"But this is wonderful—"

"Wait! Yesterday, you wanted to marry me," said Aylaen, her voice trembling. "I said I would, but now—"

Skylan turned livid. He forgot about Farinn, forgot about Raegar. "Tell me you have not changed your mind!"

"No, Skylan," said Aylaen softly. She took hold of his hands. "But I must give you a chance to change yours. Last night, Vindrash sent me a vision."

She related the dream, told him everything. "Sund wants me to destroy the Vektia spiritbones. If I do not, he claims that I will be barren. That you and I will never have any children of our own."

"It was a dream, Aylaen," said Skylan.

Aylaen shook her head. "I have had these visions before, Skylan. I am a Kai Priestess. Vindrash gave me her sword. She speaks to me."

Skylan would have said something, but Aylaen put a finger on his lips. "I have to say one thing more. I thought about doing what Sund asked, Skylan. I thought about destroying the dragon bones of the Vektia. I couldn't. Not even to save our happiness."

Aylaen looked into his eyes. Skylan brought to mind the picture of the son he had imagined, the picture of the little daughter with the red curly hair. He watched them fade away like the mist and then he gathered Aylaen to him and held her close.

"*You* are my happiness, Aylaen," he said. "The threads of our wyrds are so tangled together, not even the gods could unravel them. I cannot say what the future holds for us. But with you as my wife, I do not fear it."

CHAPTER 28

The morning of his wedding day, Skylan eyed with disfavor the long caftan the Aquins had given him to wear. A warrior was wed in his best clothes, a man's clothes. Skylan thought back to his first marriage, the ill-fated union with Draya. He looked backward through time at a Skylan he barely knew—a callow youth, arrogant and proud, thinking only of himself, never of others.

"I treated Draya shamefully," Skylan said softly, overcome by guilt and remorse. "I deserved the punishment meted out to me by the gods. I do not deserve the reward of such happiness I will be given this day."

He took hold of the silver amulet of Torval he wore around his neck.

"I swear to you, Torval, I have learned from my mistakes. I will be worthy of your trust."

Skylan wanted to wear his own clothes at his wedding. His shirt and breeches had been taken from him and he had no idea what the Aquins had done with them. He tried to think of a way to ask that would not insult them. He gave a sudden, rueful grin.

"Not so long ago, I wouldn't have given a damn if I insulted anyone," he said to himself. "Garn would be proud of me."

Skylan grew somber, thinking of his friend.

"I hope, Garn, that you are not angry with me for marrying Aylaen," Skylan said. "When we meet in Torval's Hall, we should meet as brothers. I could not bear to lose your friendship, not even for Aylaen's love."

A knock on the door startled him.

Skylan answered the door, half-expecting to find Garn there, for Skylan's mind was centered on his friend. Instead he faced a male Aquin, an older man, with a grave expression, dark hair that was gray at the temples, and deep-set eyes. He was tall and muscular and wore a caftan of fine cloth, light blue in color, trimmed in deeper blue with pearl buttons set in gold.

"I am Tai," he said, by way of introduction, "King of the Aquins. I come to bid you joy on the day of your wedding."

Skylan was impressed. The king spoke with dignity; his bearing was regal. Skylan would be happy to stand beside Tai in a shield wall, if only he could get the image out of his head of this Aquin male carrying babies around in a pouch.

"I am Skylan Ivorson, son of Norgaard," said Skylan. "Chief of Chiefs of the Vindrasi, which is similar to a king among our people." He said this not to impress the man, but to let the Aquin king know they were on equal footing.

"Is there any way in which I can be of service to you?" King Tai asked.

This was the perfect opportunity to ask about his clothes. Skylan opened his mouth, and was interrupted by Acronis.

"I wish you joy on this day, Skylan," said Acronis, smiling broadly. "If your marriage to Aylaen brings you half as much joy as my marriage brought to me, you will be a blessed man."

"Thank you, sir," said Skylan earnestly. "Any sign of young Farinn?"

Acronis shook his head. "He has not returned."

King Tai heard this exchange with concern. "What has happened? Is the young man missing?"

Skylan explained, adding that they had not said anything yesterday, because they thought Farinn had gone off with a comely young warrior woman. He added that the Aquin warriors had promised to search for him.

King Tai smiled. "The young are ruled by their hearts. I will go ask the guards if there has been any word of him."

King Tai stepped out of the room. Once he was gone, Skylan shut the door and seized hold of Acronis. Keeping an eye on the door, in case King Tai returned, Skylan said urgently, "You have to tell him. I don't want to insult him, but I won't be married in a dress!"

Acronis raised his eyebrows. Skylan jerked his thumb at the caftan lying on the bed.

"Ah, of course," said Acronis.

"I am good with a sword," said Skylan. "But when it comes to words, I'm likely to cut off my own hand."

Acronis promised he would undertake the task.

King Tai's return ended their conversation.

"The warriors have not found the young man," King Tai said. "They went to Lover's Cove, but there was no sign of him there. There is no need for concern yet," he hastened to add.

"The two could be almost anywhere. If you knew the name of the young woman or something about her—"

Skylan shook his head. At the moment, he could not even describe her very well. He had been thinking only of Aylaen.

"The warriors will continue to search. Let us not worry," said King Tai. "Nothing should mar the happiness of this day."

Skylan decided the king was right. He could do nothing for Farinn now except to wait. And today he was to be married to the woman he had loved all his life. He nudged Acronis.

"Which brings me to broach a rather delicate subject, Your Majesty," said Acronis. "I know nothing of the customs of your people—though I would be so pleased to learn about them, if ever you had time—"

Skylan nudged Acronis again, this time harder.

"As I was saying," Acronis continued, "Skylan is to be wed this day and while he is respectful of your ways, it is natural that he would like to be wed according to the customs of his people. He would like to be wed in his own clothes, with his chain mail and helm—"

"They are on my ship," said Skylan. "And a sword. I lost mine in the fight with the kraken, but you might find one on my ship. Aylaen told me that your queen has her sword in her possession."

"Chain mail! Swords!" King Tai was astonished and displeased. He asked sternly, "Why do your people bring death to a wedding?"

"The sword doesn't have anything to do with death," said Skylan. "The sword means that I vow to take my wife under my protection, to guard her with my life. I place my ring on the tip of my sword and offer the ring to my bride. Aylaen places her ring on her sword and offers it to me, meaning that she vows to fight life's battles at my side."

"You people view life as a battle?" King Tai regarded Skylan with wonder.

"Life is hard for the Vindrasi, Your Majesty," said Skylan proudly. "To die in battle with my hand on my sword's hilt is the highest honor a man can attain. I will go to Torval's Hall and there spend the afterlife in revels with my fellow heroes, both friend and foe, and with my beloved wife when she comes to join me."

"Remaining alive to care for one's family is the highest honor we Aquins can attain," said King Tai. "To die peacefully in old age, surrounded by those we love, frees the soul to return to the sea from which we all come . . ."

Skylan considered this was only to be expected

of people who lived among fish. Fortunately, he did not speak his thought aloud. Another thought had struck him.

"A ring! I'm talking about rings on swords and I don't have a ring to give Aylaen."

King Tai smiled. "Do not worry about the rings. I came to ask if you would accept these rings as gifts from Her Majesty and myself, and I have brought you this."

Inside the box was the Vektan Torque and two rings. The wedding rings were made of ivory delicately carved to symbolize the threads of his wyrd and Aylaen's twisted together. The rings flanked the Torque, one on either side.

"How appropriate," Skylan murmured, pleased.

He left the rings in the box. They would be used in the wedding ceremony. He lifted the golden Torque, adorned with the spiritbone of one of the Five. He thought of all the Chiefs of his people who had worn it before him. He thought of the sacred trust that he was taking on himself, and he remembered with shame the first time he had put the Torque around his neck, claiming it for his own, when he had sworn to Torval he would give the position of Chief to his father.

Torval had punished him by taking the Torque away from him. Perhaps now the god was telling him that all was forgiven. He placed the Torque reverently around his neck.

Before, when he had worn the Torque, he had not noticed the weight. Now he felt the heaviness, not of the gold, but of his responsibility.

"I will try to be worthy, Torval," Skylan said softly.

King Tai was discussing the wedding plans with Acronis. "We have arranged the ceremony for noon, if that is agreeable. Our Queen herself will perform the ceremony in the name of Akaria, the sea goddess."

"If we could also pray to Torval—" Skylan began, then stopped when he saw Acronis's brows shoot up.

"We know *of* Torval," said King Tai politely. "We do not pray to him."

He bowed to Skylan and walked out.

"Imagine," said Skylan, shuddering. "Dying in bed so weak you cannot stand up and then spending your afterlife among fish. What a strange people. I cannot believe we worship the same gods."

"The Aquins are peace-loving," said Acronis with a smile. "They do not believe in war. In their entire history, which spans many centuries, no Aquin has ever killed another in battle."

"A strange people," Skylan repeated.

Skylan and Aylaen were wed in the shrine of the Sea Goddess Akaria. If they had been in their homeland, they would have been wed before the altar of Vindrash, the dragon goddess. The Vindrasi had always revered the Sea Goddess, however, for they were a seafaring people.

The shrine was located on its own small island that was surrounded by a shallow pool of sea water. The shrine was made of stone carved to resemble the two halves of a conch shell standing open, with the altar of the Sea Goddess in the center. The interior of the conch shells were lined with mother of pearl and shone with a rainbow radiance in the light of the noontime sun.

Aylaen wore the apron dress of her people, a new dress made of green wool embroidered with dragons, clasped at the shoulders by two golden dragon pins. Aylaen had been amazed when Queen Magali gave her the dress, wondering how the Aquin people had come by it, for there had been no time to make it.

"A gift from the Sea Goddess," said Queen Magali. "To go with your sword."

Skylan wore soft leather breeches and a leather tunic, gifts of the Sea Goddess, and his chain mail and his own sword, which the warriors had found lying near the *Venjekar,* both marvels to the Aquins. He also received another gift from the Sea Goddess. King Tai handed him a box of driftwood. When Skylan opened it, he laughed. Inside was a fish knife.

Acronis stood with Aylaen in place of a male relative. Skylan had been hoping to have Farinn by his side, but the young man had not yet returned. Wulfe did not attend the ceremony, either. Skylan was just as pleased. There was never any telling what the fae child might do or say. And so Skylan took his place alone in front of the altar.

He was standing there, waiting for Acronis to escort Aylaen, when he felt a presence by his side. Thinking Farinn had returned, Skylan turned to chide the young man. The words froze on his lips.

Garn stood next to him.

"My friend!" said Skylan, choked, his eyes dimming with tears.

"The two people I love best in this world are being wed," said Garn. "You did not think I would let a little thing like death stop me from standing with you."

Skylan and Aylaen spoke their simple vows of love and faithfulness, pledging them in the name of Torval and Vindrash and Akaria, the sea goddess. Skylan placed the ring on the tip of his sword and presented the ring to Aylaen. She took the ring, brought it to her lips, then slid it onto her finger. She drew her sword, the blessed sword of Vindrash, placed her ring on the tip of her sword, and presented the ring to Skylan. He took it, kissed it, and slipped the ring onto his finger.

Clasping hands, the two kissed each other decorously and then turned to face the King and Queen, who had been watching all this with amazement. They stared at them uncertainly, wondering what came next.

"And so we are wed," said Skylan, seeing their confusion.

Queen Magali smiled and looked relieved. She and King Tai wished the couple joy. Acronis whispered some words to Skylan and embraced Aylaen.

"I wish for you all the happiness I would have wished for my own dear Chloe," he said softly. "A father's blessing on you, my dear, since your own father cannot be here."

"In my homeland," said Skylan, "we would now celebrate with games and a great feast."

"In this, our people are alike," said Queen Magali, smiling.

Skylan and Aylaen left the shrine and boarded a small barge decorated with shells and flowers. No one was there to pole the barge and they were wondering how they were to reach their destination when they were surrounded by young Aquins, men and women, who took hold of the barge and began to pull it through the water. There was much jostling and splashing. The barge rocked precariously and, of course, in the end tipped over, throwing Skylan and Aylaen into the water to the delight of the crowd.

Skylan, in his chain mail and his sword, immediately sank, causing even greater mirth. The Aquins rescued him and hauled him, coughing and spluttering, to the surface. The young people swam with him and Aylaen to the palace, laughing and jesting. Such was their jollity that Skylan, though he feared his chain mail was ruined forever, could not help but join in the merriment.

The wedding feast was given by Queen Magali and King Tai. Skylan and Aylaen entered the chamber hand in hand, both of them dazed by their happiness. There were no long wooden tables such as the Vindrasi used for their feasts. The Aquin women sat on mats or cushions on the floor. The men served them, bringing in large trays filled with seashells that bore vegetables and fruits and rice.

Aylaen, seated on a cushion beside the Queen, laughingly ordered Skylan to bring her food. Skylan thought of his homeland, where Aylaen would be serving him, and he thought he should be angry, but he found he liked serving Aylaen.

The men were not all that different, he discovered, for as they were filling the plates for their women, they made the same ribald jests, teased Skylan about his prowess, and shared some of their wine with him. The wine was made from bamboo and he found it atrocious, but he drank it, not wanting to insult anyone.

He was thinking of this night, dreaming of taking Aylaen into his arms, and wondering when they could slip away without offending their hosts. Aylaen sat laughing and talking with the Queen and her daughters and other female members of the court. Skylan had risen and was going over to speak to her, to persuade her to come to their wedding bed with him, when Commander Neda entered the room.

She went swiftly to the Queen, who rose to meet her. They exchanged a few words. The Queen looked grim, her lips tightened. She motioned for Aylaen to join them. Aylaen listened and then turned, crying out urgently, "Skylan!"

He dropped the food and shoved aside the men and hurried to her side.

"It's Farinn," Aylaen told him. "He's been abducted. Aelon's followers are holding him hostage. Oh, Skylan, they threaten to kill him!"

CHAPTER 29

"Who has him? Who is threatening to kill him?" Skylan demanded.

"Aelon's followers," said Commander Neda. "They have taken the young Vindrasi to the City of the Fourth Daughter." She held a scroll case made of ivory in her hand. "I was given this. I assume it is their demands. Should I read it, Your Majesty?"

Queen Magali pressed her lips tightly together and gave a stiff nod. The commander drew out a sheet of paper made of bamboo and glanced swiftly through it, then began to read aloud.

"We gave our cousin, the Queen of the City of the First Daughter, fair warning that she should hand over to us the dangerous criminals she has in her care. She has chosen to ignore our warnings and refuses to heed our request. We have therefore taken it upon ourselves to apprehend one of these criminals ourselves. We demand that the Vindrasi Priestess and her mate, as well as their dragonship, be turned over to us by orders of Priest-General Raegar. If Her Majesty refuses our request, we will send pieces of this young man's body to his friends."

Aylaen turned in dismay to Skylan.

"I won't let that happen," he promised, putting his arm around her.

Commander Neda glanced at them, and then continued her reading. "If Queen Magali refuses our request, let it be known that a state of war will exist between our two kingdoms."

A stunned and disbelieving silence fell over the chamber. War—the word was almost unknown to these people.

"This may be some trick," said the Queen. "Do we have proof that they have taken the young Vindrasi?"

"My warriors have been searching for him, Your Majesty, and they cannot find him," said Commander Neda. "The young woman he left with gave her name as Kailani. No one serving in my ranks goes by that name."

"All this talk is wasting time," said Skylan angrily. "We must go after him—"

"And go where? And do what?" Queen Magali asked sharply. "Will you take on a thousand warriors?"

"If I have to!" Skylan retorted.

The Queen looked shocked. Aylaen rested her hand on Skylan's arm.

"I think we should find out the facts, Skylan. They may help guide us to Farinn."

"I know how to find him," Skylan said grimly.

Aylaen flashed him a glance and dug her nails into his flesh. Skylan fell silent.

Commander Neda summoned the troops who

had been given the charge of guarding the Vindrasi. Upon questioning, none of them could remember having ever seen the young man's guard before. She said that she had been newly transferred from the detail that guarded the city beyond the walls.

The two had left by a passageway off the tower rooms known as the old stairs. They found the caftan Farinn had been wearing.

"We found it on the landing beside the Crystal Stream," the guard reported.

"No one told me this!" Skylan said, growing angrier still.

The guard shrugged. "We thought he had gone for a swim with his admirer. We did not think that he could possibly be in any danger."

"This woman must be a follower of Aelon, sent here to lure your young friend out of the palace," said the Queen.

"How could she know her way around? How could she know of secret passages?" Skylan demanded, glowering.

"Our city is open to all," said the Queen. "Any Aquin may enter and find welcome." She sighed, sorrow darkening her eyes. "And now one has betrayed us. Her people ambushed your friend and took him captive."

"I blame myself, Your Majesty," said Commander Neda. "I saw this woman among the guards and the thought came to me that there was something not right about her. I was busy at the time and I did not pursue my doubts."

"I am the only one to blame," Skylan said impatiently. "Farinn is young and naïve. I should have warned him to be careful. Instead I wished him joy of his conquest! And since I am to blame, I will go to this City of the Fourth Daughter where Farinn is being held prisoner and bring him back."

He glared at the Queen. "Unless, of course, you intend to give in to their demands, Your Majesty. In which case, there will be war between us." Skylan rested his hand upon the hilt of his sword.

The Queen's eyes flashed with anger. She rose to her feet. "Our course of action will be determined by what is best for our people, Vindrasi. Not by threats of violence!"

Acronis walked over to stand beside Skylan. "Apologize," he said.

"But—" Skylan sought to argue.

"You were in the wrong," said Acronis. "What if the situation was reversed? What if your people were being threatened? Put yourself in her position."

Skylan could not possibly understand a people in love with peace, a people who had never known war. He could, however, understand what it meant to decide the fate of those who looked to him for leadership. Queen Magali had been placed in a terrible position and he was, in some respects, responsible.

"Your Majesty," he said in a softer tone, "I do apologize. Before you make any decision or reply to the terms of Priest-General Raegar, I ask to speak to you and the commander of your forces in private. I believe that I may have a way out of this dilemma, a way that does not involve bloodshed."

Queen Magali gazed at him and then shifted her gaze to Aylaen. "You are the wife and head of the household. What do you say to his proposal?"

Aylaen reached out to Skylan and took hold of his hand. She smiled at him and said softly, "My husband and I—we stand together."

The Queen dismissed the court. The Aquins left to carry word of the crisis to the rest of the population. Fear and unease flowed through the city, as neighbor told neighbor. Queen Magali could hear the murmurings that washed like the waves upon the shores of her palace. She stood at the window gazing out upon her city.

She had asked for a moment alone to consider her decision. The Vindrasi, Skylan, had proposed a plan that used the ploys of Aelon's followers against them. He and a group of warriors would disguise themselves as Aelon's followers.

To the Queen's surprise, Commander Neda was in favor of the Vindrasi's plan. "I believe it will work, Your Majesty."

"But this Skylan is a man. How can he disguise himself as a warrior?" the Queen asked.

"I have heard a rumor that the Priest-General has ordered that men be trained as warriors and taken into the army," said Commander Neda.

The Queen was astonished. "Is this true? Are they mad? Who protects the children?"

The commander shrugged. "I do not know, Your Majesty."

"Leave me for a moment. I must think about this."

In truth, Queen Magali didn't need to think about it. She knew what she had to do. She was trying to find the courage to do it. As she stood at the window, her husband came to stand by her side. He took her hand and brought it to his lips. Queen Magali rested her head on his chest and he clasped his arm around her.

"Our way of life, that has endured for so many centuries, is ended," she said sadly. "No matter what the outcome of this mission, there will be war."

"Peace ended with the death of the Sea Goddess's daughter," said King Tai. "We tried to close our eyes to the truth then, but the flames now burn too bright for us to ignore. We must open our eyes and look ahead with courage."

"My store of courage is very low, I fear," said the Queen. "I would put my faith in the gods, but I have the feeling the gods are putting their faith in us."

"Perhaps that is not such a bad thing," said King Tai, striving to be cheerful. "Mortals and gods should work together. The world belongs to all."

"While there is a world . . . ," Queen Magali said.

Aylaen's wedding night was not exactly what she had dreamed it would be. With the wedding celebration abruptly ended, she and Skylan first consulted with the Queen. Skylan explained his plan. Her Majesty listened and said she would consider it. Skylan wanted an answer immediately, but he was forced to wait.

"Go be happy together while you can," said Queen Magali, gently dismissing them. "Spend your wedding night together. We can do nothing until the morning anyway."

Skylan fumed and again went over his plan with Aylaen as the warriors escorted them back to their rooms in the tower. When they arrived, Skylan was so preoccupied that he started to leave her, saying he wanted to speak to Commander Neda.

Aylaen caught hold of his hand.

"You are my husband," she said. "Before you rush off to war, you have husbandly duties to perform."

Reaching up, she removed the Vektan Torque from his neck and laid it on the table.

Skylan stared at her. His breath came fast. He shut the door. She lifted her lips to his and he kissed her and before either quite knew what was happening, the two of them were on the bed. Their bodies merged like their wyrds; afterward, she laid her head on his chest.

"Perhaps we made a baby then," said Skylan.

"Perhaps we did," said Aylaen with a sigh that she took care he did not hear.

They lay in each other's arms, weary, but not wanting to end their joy by falling asleep. Skylan told her about his plan yet again. Aylaen listened and knew the pain of a woman whose man must rise from her bed with the dawn to take up his sword. This night might well be the only night they would ever have together. She interrupted his talk of battle by pressing her mouth over his.

Neither of them slept that night.

CHAPTER

30

Skylan rose well before dawn. When the first rays of the sun shone through the skylights, he and his small band of warriors set out. He was astonished and pleasantly surprised when Commander Neda told him she would not be leading this mission. He had foreseen arguing with the strong-willed woman. She said that she could not leave her duties at the palace, not in this time of turmoil. Her second-in-command, a woman named Manta, would lead the warriors. Skylan bristled at this. He knew considerably more about warfare than did people who had lived in peace all their lives.

"You are not going to war," said Commander Neda coldly. "You are going to rescue a friend. There is a difference. We are not as soft as you seem to think us, Vindrasi. Who was it saved you from the kraken?"

Skylan had no answer to that, or rather no answer that would not have offended her. Realizing he was wasting precious time arguing, he gave in. Manta led Skylan and her warriors along the same route Farinn and Kailani had taken in case they should come across any more evidence. They found nothing, however, no signs of a struggle. Farinn had come willingly with his lovely captor.

"They were likely waiting for him here," said Manta when they emerged from the sluice gate, pointing to the sea that lapped up on the rocks. "We patrol this area, but the abductors waited in the depths before surfacing to seize your friend."

Skylan glanced back at the sluice gate through which the water flowed into the sea. "You do realize that any enemy that wanted to attack you could easily dive beneath those teeth and enter your city. You should post guards day and night with some means to sound the alarm if they are attacked."

"All you Vindrasi think about is war," said Manta derisively.

"You Aquins should start thinking about war," Skylan stated grimly. "Because it is coming."

Manta fell silent as she regarded the aperture with a thoughtful frown. "I will mention this to Her Majesty on our return."

The six warriors under Manta's command were armed with spears made of bone, and all wore armor with the serpent emblem of the City of the Fourth Daughter. Craftsmen had worked all night to make the armor, which was crafted out of whale skin. Manta explained that they did not kill the whales; the mammals were sacred to the Sea Goddess. When they found a dead whale, they honored it by harvesting its skin and anything else they could use. The armor fit over Skylan's shoulders and chest and was laced under his arms. It was supple and lightweight, but surprisingly tough.

Since Skylan was bigger through the shoulders and chest than any Aquin warrior, the armor did not fit him well, leaving large gaps of unprotected flesh beneath his arms and exposing most of his midriff.

"He will fool no one," Manta complained to Commander Neda. "He should not go with us. He imperils the mission."

Skylan was ready to argue, then found an unexpected ally in Commander Neda. "The Vindrasi will only cause trouble if he is left behind. Besides, you need the Vindrasi. He is the only one who can find out where they have taken the young man. Just tell him to keep out of the light."

Because they had a long way to travel to reach the City of the Fourth Daughter, Manta and her warriors all wore the breathing masks, as did Skylan. He chafed at this, for the bindings on the clamshell attached to his back were tight and constricted his movement. He was constantly afraid he would tangle himself up in the tube that led from the clamshell to the mask and accidentally yank it out. His sword was useless under water. He tried swimming while holding a spear and nearly sliced open his foot. Skylan remembered with fond longing the shield wall, where a man stood on his own two feet, and battled in blood and died in the muck. He had to settle for carrying a bone knife, which he thrust into a leather belt he wore around his waist.

Manta and her warriors took to the water, gliding in gracefully, creating hardly a ripple. Skylan jumped into the sea with a great splash that made the women laugh at his clumsiness.

"We must go to my dragonship to talk to the fae child," said Skylan before putting on the mask. "Do you know where it is?"

Manta knew the location. The dragonship had been the object of much curiosity among the Aquins. Most of the people in the city had swum out to take a look at it. The Dragon Kahg kept watch over it; the red gleam of the dragon's eyes preventing people from approaching it. Skylan put on the detested mask and dove beneath the waves, following Manta's lead.

The ship rested on a coral reef, slightly at an angle. When the Dragon Kahg caught sight of him, his red eyes swiveled in Skylan's direction. Skylan motioned for the warriors to stay back. The Aquin warriors floated in the water, waiting for him. He searched for Wulfe, but could not find him.

The water was clear, gleaming with sunlight. The coral and the colorful fish and the waving plants were beautiful and Skylan thought that he would never be so glad in his life to be away from a place as he would from this realm, back into air and sunlight and dry land. He gave the Dragon Kahg a respectful salute as he swam past him. The dragon's eyes followed Skylan with his usual stern glower. Skylan had no idea what the dragon was thinking.

Skylan was frustrated. Wulfe was never around

when needed and always around when he wasn't. The boy might be down in the hold, since he was apparently part fish as well as half beast. If so, Skylan wasn't about to dive into the dark confined space beneath the water to look for him. He started to swim back to Manta and her warriors when something latched on to his leg.

Skylan's first panic-stricken thought was of the kraken and he grabbed his knife, ready to fight, and kicking at it with his feet. Whatever it was wouldn't let go. He looked to see a beautiful woman had hold of his ankle. Silver-white hair flowed over her silvery skin. The woman was laughing at him and gesturing to other oceanaids, who clustered about him, grabbing hold of his arms and tugging him along.

The oceanaids carried Skylan to the other side of the reef, where he found Wulfe playing with a large sea-going turtle. Skylan stared in amazement for a moment at the enormous swimming turtle, then beckoned to Wulfe to come with him. The boy was pleased to see Skylan and swam to where Manta and her warriors waited.

Skylan swam to the surface, or tried to. The oceanaids had twined their arms around him, fondling him and playing with his hair. He did what he could to fend off the teasing faerie folk, pushing away their groping hands as gently as he could. He dared not offend them, for he needed their help. He saw, out of the corner of his eye, the Aquin warriors grinning.

He broke through the surface, blinking in the

sunlight. Manta and her warriors surfaced with him. Wulfe bobbed up beside him. Skylan removed the tube from his mouth and tried to ignore the oceanaids, who were tickling his toes.

"Tell your fish friends to leave me alone," said Skylan irritably.

"They're not fish," said Wulfe. "They're fae, like me. And they're only having fun with you."

"I'm not here for fun," said Skylan grimly. "I'm here because I need your help. Farinn's been abducted and his captors are threatening to kill him. Your oceanaids see and hear everything that happens either on land or sea. Do any of them know where they took Farinn?"

"I like Farinn," said Wulfe. "He sings for me sometimes. He says I'm going to be inside his song. I've never been inside a song before. The song is about you—"

"We're not here to discuss a song!" Skylan said through gritted teeth. "Since you like Farinn, you need to help me find him. They're going to hand him over to Raegar."

Wulfe's eyes narrowed, glittering gold. "I'll ask them."

He dove back down, his butt sticking out, his scrawny legs flailing. Skylan saw him communicating with his oceanaids, who petted him and fawned over him.

"Where did you meet the princeling?" Manta asked.

"Why does everyone keep calling him that?" Skylan asked. "He's a scrawny kid."

Who can breathe underwater and turn himself into a wolf, Skylan thought, but didn't say aloud.

"Because that's what the oceanaids call him," Manta replied.

Wulfe had always claimed to be the grandson of the Faerie Queen. Skylan had always dismissed the claim as just another of the boy's outlandish tales, which had included the ability to talk to the dryads of the sea. Watching these dryads listening to Wulfe with obvious deference and adoration, Skylan wondered if the boy had been telling the truth. The idea made Skylan's head ache.

Wulfe swam back to the surface to impart his news.

One of the oceanaids' favorite pastimes was to watch the human lovers in the caves and several of the oceanaids had been swimming in the vicinity of the sluice gate the night Farinn had been taken. The oceanaids had been thrilled to witness warriors capture the young man and drag him away, this being more excitement than the oceanaids generally encountered in an evening.

"Do your friends know where they took him?"

The oceanaids knew. Intrigued by the abduction of the young man, they had followed the warriors. Farinn was being held in the dungeons of the City of the Fourth Daughter. The dungeons having no access by water, the oceanaids could not see what had become of him.

"They'll lead us there," said Wulfe.

"They'll lead *me* there," said Skylan. "You're not going."

"If I don't go, my friends won't go," said Wulfe with a sly smile.

"There might be fighting," said Skylan.

Wulfe hesitated a moment, then shrugged. "I'm still going. It's boring down here. There's only so much you can do with fish."

Skylan was about to order Wulfe to stay, then he had a thought. "Very well. You can come. I might need your magic."

"Magic?" Wulfe repeated, suddenly wary. "I don't know magic."

"I've seen you, remember?" Skylan said, exasperated. "Hot cinders raining down out a clear night sky. Jellyfish leaping out of the sea and grabbing a man's hand. Not to mention breathing underwater."

Wulfe gazed at Skylan through a thatch of long, wet hair. "My mother says if you Uglies know I do magic, you'll kill me."

"I haven't killed you yet," said Skylan, grinning. "Though I admit I've been tempted."

He reached out and playfully dunked the boy's head. Wulfe came up laughing and suddenly flung his arms around Skylan's neck.

"I love you!" Wulfe said in a low, fierce voice, giving Skylan a hug that nearly strangled him. The boy swam off, going back to his oceanaids, leaving Skylan to stare after him in wonder.

Manta had never been inside the City of the Fourth Daughter, but all the Aquin cities were built more or less along the same plan, which meant that the dungeons had probably been built some distance from the city proper.

"Your plan might work, after all," Manta conceded grudgingly.

"Then let's get started," said Skylan. "How far is this city?"

"About thirty miles," Manta replied.

Skylan's jaw dropped. "Thirty miles! We can't swim that far!"

"*We* could," said Manta, chuckling at Skylan's dismay. "Don't worry, Vindrasi. We have need for haste and so we will summon help."

Manta put her hands to her mouth and gave a call that Skylan could not hear. Within moments, twenty or thirty large dolphins arrived, swimming around them.

"The dolphins will aid us in reaching our destination," said Manta.

Skylan was dubious, thinking she meant he was to ride the dolphin like a horse, which brought hoots of derisive laughter from the Aquins. Manta showed Skylan how to grasp hold of the dorsal fin.

"Lie flat and hang on," she instructed.

Skylan took hold of the dolphin's dorsal fin as instructed. The dolphin's skin against his body was surprisingly smooth. He gave the dolphin's neck a tentative pat, as he would have his horse. The dolphin appeared to find this highly amusing, for the creature opened its mouth and lifted its head in what sounded like a chortle.

The Aquins, seeing Skylan was ready, gave orders to the dolphins, who swam ahead. Skylan's dolphin gave a flip of the tail and surged ahead so swiftly that Skylan nearly lost his grip on the fin.

Skylan found he had to adjust the position of his body to that of the dolphin to avoid hampering the animal's ability to swim. Once he figured out how to hold on, he found the rapid and effortless movement through the water exhilarating. He glanced back to see Wulfe swimming with a dolphin, surrounded by an immense number of oceanaids who darted around the boy like minnows.

Undoubtedly the strangest raiding party in the entire history of the Vindrasi, thought Skylan.

CHAPTER 31

Aylaen felt useless. Skylan had gone to rescue Farinn, leaving her behind to wait either for his safe return or news of his death or capture.

"Such is the fate of women," Aylaen said bitterly to herself. She stood in the tower room, gazing out the window, seeing nothing. In her mind, she was following her husband, trying to picture where he would be, what he would be doing.

Aylaen had wanted to go with Skylan but he had refused to take her, saying, quite rightly, that she should remain behind with the Vektia spirit-bones, one of which was on the Vektan Torque that she now was wearing. The other was hidden in the *Venjekar*.

"If I do not come back," Skylan had said to her. "You must go to the dragonship. The Dragon Kahg will carry you safely back to Vindraholm."

"You will come back," said Aylaen, adding with mock severity, "If you don't, I will come to Torval's Hall and slap you silly!"

Skylan had laughed heartily at this and kissed her and left her to stand gazing after him.

Aylaen turned from the window. "I can't stay here doing nothing," she muttered.

The thought came to her that she *could* do something to help Skylan. She could pray for his safe return. Aylaen returned to the small shrine where she and Skylan had been married. She was hoping to be alone and was at first disappointed to find Acronis there, using ink he had made himself from fruit to sketch the altar of the Sea Goddess on a scrap of cloth.

The Aquins, like the Vindrasi, had never developed a written form of their language. Again like the Vindrasi, bards kept the history of the Aquins in the form of song. Unlike the Vindrasi, whose songs were of courage and honor and heroes dying in battle, the songs of the Aquins were serene and tranquil, celebrating long lives well lived.

He rose when he saw her and gathered up his materials. "I will leave you to your prayers," he said.

"Wait," said Aylaen, halting him. "I have been cooped up in my room, listening to my own fears. The sound of your voice is a welcome change. I would like you to stay, sir, if you don't mind."

"Of course," said Acronis. "Don't worry, my dear. Skylan will be fine. The gods love him."

"Not all the gods," said Aylaen somberly, thinking of Sund.

Aylaen stood before the altar. She wanted to pray to Vindrash, but it occurred to her that she had never before spoken to the goddess. Or rather, she had spoken to Vindrash only in visions.

"Treia told me that the Kai Priestess Dharma talked to Vindrash incessantly, morning and night. She held intimate conversations with the goddess, as if they were friends." Aylaen frowned. "I don't think I want to be friends with the goddess. I'm a little afraid of her."

"I spoke to the gods when I was young," Acronis said. "I remembered thinking they answered me. The gods always speak to the young."

Aylaen didn't understand, but then Acronis was constantly saying things like that. She let the peace of the shrine settle into her soul and pondered what it meant to be Kai Priestess of her people.

"I am here because of a lie," she said abruptly.

Acronis was silent, waiting for Aylaen to continue.

She looked back in time, saw herself as someone she did not recognize.

"The ogres had stolen the Vektan Torque from our people. Skylan was going to set sail for the ogre lands to claim it back. He chose valiant warriors to take with him, including the man I loved. I could not bear to be left behind and so I cut my hair and told a lie in order that Skylan would be forced to bring me. I said I wanted to become a priestess of Vindrash and that sailing on this voyage was some sort of ritual. In truth, I did not want to become a priestess. I came because I was a foolish, selfish girl who could not bear to be left behind."

The course of our wyrds might have run so much differently if I had not come, Aylaen thought.

Garn might still be alive. She would never know. Those waves had rushed to the shore and receded and were forever gone.

Acronis rested his hand on her shoulder.

"It seems your lie was the truth, after all," he said.

"Skylan believed in me, even when I didn't believe in myself," said Aylaen. "I used to ridicule him for his faith, even as I secretly envied him. When I held the blessed sword of Vindrash in my hand I knew that I was her priestess. I knew then that I had always been her priestess. Poor Treia. She saw that Vindrash had chosen me and repulsed her. No wonder my sister hates me."

Aylaen drew the blessed sword that Vindrash had given her and placed it upon the altar. Kneeling on the cushions, she lifted her eyes and her voice to heaven.

"Blessed Vindrash, I believe you brought me here for a reason. I know that you walk with me, and I know that even though I cannot see the road ahead, you will guide me. I will strive to do my best to serve you and my people." Aylaen's voice faltered a moment, then she added firmly, "No matter what the cost."

She thought of Farinn, the shy, quiet young man who was learning to read and write so that he could give his songs to those who came after him. He was alone and captive in a strange place. He must be afraid. She thought of Skylan, risking his life and his happiness to save Farinn because the young man was Skylan's man and the Vindrasi stood together. She thought how proud she was of Skylan and how much she loved him. The prayers in her heart for him and for Farinn were too sacred to be spoken aloud, even if she could have spoken for her tears.

"Aylaen, someone is coming," Acronis said quietly.

Aylaen looked around and saw Queen Magali standing in the entrance.

"I am sorry to disturb you at your prayers," said the Queen, hesitating. "I will leave."

Aylaen rose swiftly. "Please do not go, Your Majesty. I am finished with my prayers. Vindrash knows what is in my heart better than I do anyway."

Queen Magali's gaze went to the sword lying, shining, on the altar. Aylaen flushed and removed it, slipping the sword back into the sheath she wore around her waist.

"Forgive me, Your Majesty. I did not mean to offend you or the Sea Goddess."

"Your ways are strange to us, that is true," said Queen Magali. "But our ways must seem as strange to you."

The Queen entered the shrine. She paused before Acronis, who bowed deeply.

"We have not had a chance to speak, sir. I am told you recently lost your young daughter." Queen Magali's voice was soft with sympathy. "My own children are a daily gift to me. I cannot imagine losing a child. My heart would be torn, never to mend."

"I wanted to die, Your Majesty," said Acronis

simply. "I tried to kill myself and when I could not, I asked Skylan to help me take my life. He had no reason to love me and every reason to hate me. Yet he refused. He made me see that Chloe would be ashamed of me if I took such a cowardly path."

"And that is why you are his friend?" the Queen asked.

"Chloe was all to me. My old life would have been empty without her. I sailed with young Skylan and his bride"—Acronis smiled at Aylaen—"and I have seen many wonderful and terrible and beautiful things. I plan to share everything with Chloe when she and I are together again in Torval's feasting hall."

"You are Sinarian. Your people worship Aelon. Yet you believe in our gods?"

"I have no choice," said Acronis, shrugging. "I met one, Your Majesty. The goddess Vindrash spoke to me. It would be rude *not* to believe in her, don't you think?"

The Queen blinked at this statement. Uncertain how to respond, she turned to Aylaen.

"I have yet to give you the gift, Aylaen," Queen Magali said.

"You mean the spiritbone—" Aylaen began.

The Queen swiftly interrupted. "The gift of which we spoke."

Aylaen gave a nod to show she understood the need for secrecy. "Do not think me ungrateful, Your Majesty, but I would like to wait until Skylan can be here with me."

"I fear that there may not be time," said Queen Magali. "War is inevitable. When Aelon's priests discover that the hostage has escaped, they will come here in force. You and Skylan and the others must be well away or you will be caught up in the fighting."

"I know Skylan. He will stay to fight with you," said Aylaen. "And I will stay with him."

Queen Magali smiled, touched and pleased. "At first I did not understand how a beautiful and strong young woman like you could possibly choose such an arrogant, outspoken, obstreperous male as this Skylan for your mate. I find I understand him better now. He will give you strong daughters, as strong as their mother."

Aylaen bit her lip and managed a smile. She was about to reply when Acronis said softly, "Keep talking," and slipped quickly out the door. Aylaen had no idea what to say. She stammered something and then fell silent. Queen Magali's face was pale, her lips drawn tight.

Acronis returned. "I heard the sound of shells crunching underfoot and feared someone was spying on us. I am afraid I was right. I caught sight of a woman sneaking about outside. I don't know who she was, for I could not get a good look at her. When she saw me, she ran away. She must have come up from the water, for she left behind a puddle where she was standing."

"A spy?" Queen Magali asked, amazed.

Acronis shook his head. He looked very grim. "I am sorry to say that I saw a glint of metal. The woman was carrying a knife. She was not a spy. She was an assassin."

"The evil is indeed upon us," the Queen said softly.

Aylaen stared at the Queen in dismay. "I am so sorry, Your Majesty. This is our fault—"

Queen Magali managed a smile and spoke loudly, her voice deliberately bright and cheerful in case anyone else happened to be eavesdropping.

"I have heard of your Vindrasi dragonships all my life, though I have never before seen one, Aylaen. I would like very much to visit your ship."

"I will be honored to have you as my guest, Your Majesty," said Aylaen.

Queen Magali took hold of Aylaen's hand and squeezed it tightly. "You must make ready to sail the moment your husband returns."

"I do not want to leave you in danger," Aylaen said, shaking her head.

"You will not," said the Queen. "The person with the knife was not waiting for me, Aylaen. She was waiting for you."

"But why?" Aylaen asked, startled.

"Sund knows you defied him," said the Queen. "He has told Aelon. Skylan may be the one to find the Five, but you are the only one who can summon the power. You are the one they most fear."

CHAPTER 32

The Dragon Kahg decided he liked living at the bottom of the ocean. All these years, he had sailed on top of the sea, riding the waves in the Vindrasi ships that carried his spirit with them, viewing with pity and disdain the lowly creatures forced to swim. Kahg could not imagine a life without flight, without the freedom to soar among the clouds, bask in the warmth of the sun.

He could have fled the *Venjekar* when the kraken attacked it, returning to his own realm. He chose to remain with the ship because the sacred Vektia dragonbone was hidden within the hull and he was determined to protect it. He was also determined to find out what had become of the Vektan Torque that held the second Vektia bone lost during the kraken attack.

The Dragon Kahg had used his magic to prevent the kraken from crushing the *Venjekar,* giving the ugly beast a powerful jolt when it tried to wrap its tentacles around his ship and biting its tentacles with his fangs. Kahg had chuckled as the kraken sullenly squirted a blast of ink in his direction before turning to find new prey.

The Dragon Kahg had been grateful to the Aquins who had come to the aid of Aylaen and the other humans. Kahg liked Aylaen far better than any other Bone Priestess who had served him over the years. The fact that he remembered her name marked his approbation. The dragon had even come to admire Skylan. Kahg had known so many Vindrasi warriors over the years, they all tended to blend together, but the dragon could remember Skylan's name most of the time.

As for the fae boy, Kahg was firm in his dislike or at least so he continually told himself, even as he allowed the fae child to live on board the ship. Whenever the dragon found himself growing amused by the boy's antics or taking too much interest in the gossip from those annoying oceanaids, Kahg would bare his teeth in a snarl that would send the oceanaids fleeing in squealing panic and the boy swimming off to hide in the hold.

The Dragon Kahg kept the *Venjekar* anchored to the coral reef and found he did not miss the blue sky or the sun or the gray clouds and the rain. He liked the stillness, the sunlit blue of the water, the hypnotic motion of the plants stirred by the movement of the waves. The storms that ravaged the world above had small effect on the world below. He knew such peace would not last long. In the interim, he was glad for the respite.

"Have you forgiven us, Kahg?"

Kahg shifted his gaze to the goddess Vindrash swimming alongside him. The goddess was in her dragon aspect, probably hoping to flatter him, appease him. She moved sinuously among the coral, her wings sleek by her flanks, her tail rippling. Kahg looked away. He gazed sternly straight ahead, pretending to be absorbed in watching a puffer fish.

"Have you forgiven us?" Vindrash repeated.

"Since you ask, no. You gods lied to us," said Kahg. "Not once, but many times over. First you say the spiritbones of Vektia come from five mighty dragons. The thing that destroyed Sinaria was not a dragon. Then you claim that it was the power of creation—"

"So it is," said Vindrash.

"But that is not *all* it is," said the Dragon Kahg. "Even now, you will not admit the truth."

Vindrash was silent a moment, studying the dragon. Then she said, "You have found out, haven't you?"

The dragon gave a shake of his mane that sent the small fish swimming off in panic. He was not willing to commit himself.

Vindrash sighed. "If you know the truth, Kahg, then you must understand why I darc not reveal it."

The Dragon Kahg considered this. Sighting some curious oceanaids hovering near, he snapped his jaws at them. The oceanaids cursed him roundly and angrily swam away.

Once he and the goddess were alone, Kahg said grudgingly, "Maybe I do understand. You thought that if we dragons knew the truth, we would try to seize these sacred bones for ourselves. Perhaps you were right. Perhaps we would have. But you might have given us the benefit of the doubt."

"We could not take the chance. We feared—"

"Fear!" The dragon snorted clouds of bubbles from his snout. "You gods are ruled by fear!"

"We acted for the best," said Vindrash.

"That's always the excuse," said Kahg.

Vindrash was quiet a moment, then said, "This, then, is the truth. The power of creation is stored inside the bones of Ilyrion. When the Five Vektia bones are brought together, the great dragon, Ilyrion, will be reborn. She will return to the world. We know this will happen, because Sund saw us all there, at the final battle. The great dragon, Ilyrion, fights at our side, as do you and the other dragons."

"And what is the outcome of this last battle?" The dragon did not like the sorrow in the goddess's voice. He swiveled his red eyes uneasily.

Vindrash shook her head. "All we know for certain is that whatever Sund saw drove him to madness."

"And still you send out your Fish Knife to find the Five? Even though they represent your own destruction?"

"Without Ilyrion, we have no hope of defeating Aelon and the Gods of Raj."

"Apparently we have no hope of defeating them *with* Ilyrion," Kahg growled. "So what do we do now?"

"We find the Five," said Vindrash, "and we hope."

CHAPTER 33

The City of the Fourth Daughter was almost identical to the City of the First Daughter, as least as far as Skylan could see. Like the City of the First Daughter, this city was also built inside an island in the middle of the sea; the only access to the city was far beneath the ocean's surface. The oceanaids, with Wulfe tagging along, led Skylan and the Aquin warriors to the location of the dungeon area and indicated with gestures that this was where they had seen the warriors drag the young Vindrasi.

Manta thanked the dolphins and dismissed them, asking them to come back when called. The sea around the Fourth City was alive with fish and Aquins, going about their daily routines, much as the streets of Skylan's village would be filled with people heading out to the crops in the fields or to the woods to hunt. Skylan noted the presence of a great number of warriors among the people of the Fourth City, many of them male. The men had their heads shaved and marked with the serpent tattoo he'd first seen on Raegar's head. He guessed that like Raegar, these men were Aelon's chosen—elite Warrior-Priests.

One group of Warrior-Priests was engaged in what looked to Skylan like mock battles. A warrior on land could hurl a spear at his foe. Below water, combat was entirely hand-to-hand and, interestingly enough, conducted without weapons. The warriors were being taught choke holds and various other means of subduing a foe without drawing blood. Skylan couldn't imagine why at first. A moment's thought provided the answer: pitched battle with armies of spear-wielding Aquins would end with both sides losing to the blood-seeking sharks. Skylan touched Manta's shoulder to draw her attention and pointed to the training session.

She and her warriors watched the male warriors with amusement, judging by their derisive sounding clicks and squeals. Skylan shook his head, envisioning large numbers of these Warrior-Priests launching a swift and deadly attack on the First City, seizing those outside the safety of the city walls and either killing them or taking them prisoner. Once this was accomplished, the army would then move inside the city and put their spears and knives to use.

Skylan could envision this, but Manta and the Aquin warriors could not. He was glad he had come, if for no other reason than he could warn Queen Magali of the danger and she could train her people to guard against it.

The presence of large numbers of male Warrior-

Priests ensured that Skylan and his warriors, wearing the armor adorned with the serpent, were not likely to be noticed—one small band among so many. Skylan kept close watch, but no one paid them any attention as the oceanaids led the group toward a cavernous opening below sea level.

Judging by the number of warriors gathered around it, Skylan assumed this must be their destination. Wulfe swam among the oceanaids. Manta tried, but, unlike the dolphins, the oceanaids were not about to be shooed away. They had never known such excitement and they swarmed around the warriors like silvery, voluptuous fish. Fortunately the Aquins were used to them and paid them no heed, ignoring them as they ignored the rest of the sea creatures that made this area their home.

Manta studied the terrain for long moments, then motioned Skylan to join her and the others in one of the many cavernous alcoves that dotted the island. Skylan broke through the surface of the water, took the tube from his mouth, and thankfully breathed air that didn't come through a tube.

"That entrance the oceanaids showed us leads to the dungeons," Manta confirmed. "Like our city, the dungeons are kept separate from the city proper. The young man will be well-guarded. How do you propose to free him? We will not fight," she added, frowning. "We will not shed the blood of another Aquin."

"Let's hope Farinn's Aquin guards feel the same," Skylan said dryly.

"We are not like you land walkers," Manta

said, offended by his sarcastic tone. "You think of nothing except ways to spill each other's blood."

"Right now, I'm thinking of my man who is being held prisoner inside there," said Skylan angrily. "You saw those warriors out there. What do you think they were doing? Playing games? Those warriors are being trained to kill. They are training for battle. The City of the Fourth Daughter is preparing to go to war—against your people."

"You see what you want to see," Manta insisted.

Skylan saw no point in arguing further. He swam over to talk to Wulfe.

"If I need your magic, what kind of magic spell will you cast?" Skylan asked the boy.

"Look at the bats up there!" said Wulfe, craning his neck.

"Wulfe, forget the bats. This is serious," said Skylan. "We're going inside the dungeon to rescue Farinn and I need to know what you plan to do with your magic."

"I don't know," said Wulfe. He shrugged. "Magic isn't something you plan. It's something that happens—like a sneeze."

Skylan glanced hurriedly at Manta and the other Aquin warriors, hoping they hadn't heard that the magic that might save their lives was like a sneeze. The Aquin warriors were huddled together, talking in earnest. Skylan hoped they were finally taking what he'd told them to heart.

Skylan gripped Wulfe's shoulder. "Going in there

will be dangerous, especially for you. If Raegar gets hold of you, he'll kill you—"

"He won't get hold of me," said Wulfe with a grin. "Maybe you, but not me."

Skylan gave up. He considered the situation and thought that of all the challenges he'd faced in his life, this was undoubtedly the greatest. He was entering a dungeon filled with Aelon's Warrior-Priests thirsting for his blood alongside a group of warriors who had vowed not to fight and a fae child who didn't know what spell he was going to cast because magic was like a sneeze.

Skylan touched the silver amulet at his neck and prayed. "Torval, I know you never venture into the ocean and I can certainly understand why, but if you could make an exception, I need your help!"

His prayer dispatched, Skylan swam back to Manta. "You know what to say?"

She looked annoyed. "We have gone over this many times."

"We have to get this right," said Skylan.

Manta sighed. "I am a messenger from Priest-General Raegar. He has ordered that the young man be taken to the Temple of the Spirit Priestesses"—Manta stumbled over this title—"so that they may restore the tattoo on the young man's arm that allows the slave to again receive the wisdom of Aelon's counsel."

Skylan nodded his head. "Good."

"But what if these worshippers of Aelon don't

have these Spirit Priestesses?" one of the warriors asked.

"They will," said Skylan with more confidence than he felt.

Logic dictated the presence of Spirit Priestesses among the Aquins. The Warrior-Priests were marked with Aelon's serpent tattoo and, at least in Sinaria, that could be administered only by the Spirit Priestesses. The danger was that the Aquins might call them by a different name.

"What if they hand over Farinn, then decide to send an escort with us?" Manta asked.

"I will deal with any escort," said Skylan.

The Aquins glanced at each other.

"You mean you will kill him," said Manta in cold and disapproving tones.

"Farinn is my man and he was taken from your protection," said Skylan in grim tones. "I'll try my best not to kill anyone, but I will do what I must to recover my man. If you don't like it, you can all swim back to your city. I'll go alone."

"With me," said Wulfe. "I'm going."

"The fae princeling is not coming!" said Manta. "He can wait for us here."

"He's coming," said Skylan.

The Aquins were not pleased about any of this.

"If something goes wrong, the boy will provide a diversion. Like I said," Skylan added, "you can all swim back home."

The Aquins exchanged glances.

"We will come with you. Our honor is at stake. If there is trouble, we will deal with it in our own way. Once you have your man, you will return immediately to the First City. The dolphins are waiting to carry you."

"Trust me, I don't want to stay down here any more than you want me down here," said Skylan. "The sooner I can breathe real air and feel the sun on my face, the better."

Manta's frowning gaze went to Wulfe. "About the fae princeling—"

"He's coming," said Skylan flatly. "He's here in case something goes wrong. And nothing's going to go wrong."

"Something always goes wrong," Wulfe whispered.

"Shut up," Skylan muttered, and put the breathing tube back in his mouth.

Skylan found himself in an unusual situation, one he didn't like. All his life, he had been in command. As a child of eight, he and Garn, Bjorn, and Erdmund and the other boys spent their leisure time forming a shield wall and charging into imaginary foes. Skylan had been their war chief then. He had been their war chief when he and his friends stood together in a real shield wall. Now, for the first time, he wasn't in command.

Manta had made it clear before they left on this mission that none of her warriors would serve under the leadership of a male and Skylan had been forced to agree to accept Manta as his commander or abandon the mission. Although he had boasted to the Aquins that he could do this alone, he hadn't truly meant it. He would have tried, of course, because Farinn was his man and he wouldn't abandon him, but he knew quite well he would have failed.

He climbed the stone stairs that led out of the water and up to the dungeon level, keeping in the rear, staying out of direct light, for he didn't want the guards to get a good look at him. The breathing mask on his face, the harness around his shoulders, the clamshell attached to his back, and the serpent armor over his chest provided some disguise, but anyone looking at him closely would see that he wasn't an Aquin.

He glanced over his shoulder, back down the stairs and into the water. Wulfe's head bobbed on the surface, along with the silvery heads of the oceanaids, trying to see what was going on. The oceanaids had no love for Aelon, according to Wulfe, who said they had heard about his depredations among the fae from their cousins, the dryads. The oceanaids had offered to help if there was trouble. Skylan, more frightened of this than he was of the Warrior-Priests of Aelon, had issued a strict order that the oceanaids were not to get involved. Wulfe had only grinned. Skylan had left the boy and his fae friends with the gloomy feeling he was doomed.

The dungeons of the Fourth City were exactly like those in which Skylan had been imprisoned, only larger. He could see the prisoners hanging in nets suspended from the ceiling.

Aquins were by nature a peace-loving people, fond of simplicity and order in their lives, and the dungeons were not very crowded, for not many Aquins broke the law. There was no thievery because the Aquins kept nothing of value to steal. The idea of murder, of one Aquin taking the life another, was impossible to imagine. Aquins who did break their society's few laws were brought before the Queen, who passed judgment on them, which meant they spent a few days in a net to think over their wrongdoing.

Skylan counted twenty prisoners hanging in nets, compared to no more than a few in the First City. Skylan guessed that the expansion of the prison of the Fourth City was occasioned by the need to lock up those dissenters who did not find Aelon to their liking. They were probably being held captive so the god could convince them of the error of their ways.

He quickly spotted Farinn, whose blond hair and fair skin stood out in contrast to the bluish-green skin of the Aquin prisoners. The young man was in the second cell and lay curled up in a ball of misery in his net, paying no heed to what was going on around him.

Having located Farinn, Skylan turned his attention to the guards. They were all males and one of them was a Warrior-Priest with the serpent tattoo on his head. Skylan sucked in a breath. The Warrior-Priest was wearing a sword made of brass, so that it would not rust. The sword hung from a belt around his waist. He had no sheath for it. Judging by the unblemished surface and high polish, the brass sword was brand new. The hilt was wrapped in leather, either whale or shark skin. The blade was slender, made to suit the hand of the lightweight Aquins. In a realm where a brass key was a rarity, this sword must be worth a fortune.

A Warrior-Priest with a valuable sword was no lowly prison guard, Skylan realized. This priest was a high-ranking officer. Why was he here? Skylan kept an uneasy eye on him.

Manta walked forward confidently, with a bit of a swagger. The Warrior-Priest advanced to meet her. Skylan had been taught from an early age to look at how a man, any man, handled his weapon. A friend could turn to a foe in an instant and then Skylan had better be ready to fight. He noticed without even being aware that he was noticing how the Warrior-Priest fidgeted with the sword's hilt. The man was unsure of himself, his grip shifting, trying to find a comfortable hold. When the Warrior-Priest walked forward, he got the blade tangled up in his legs and nearly tripped himself. Skylan grinned behind the mask. The sword was newly-forged and so was the swordsman.

The Warrior-Priest eyed Manta. "What are doing here? Did you bring a prisoner?"

Manta launched into her explanation.

"You have a Vindrasi prisoner," she said, and continued on with her speech. She stumbled again over the word "priestesses," which made Skylan wince, but otherwise she did well.

Skylan shifted his gaze from the priest to Farinn.

Manta had spoken loudly. The prison cells were quiet and Farinn could hear her quite clearly, especially when she said "Vindrasi prisoner" and mentioned the Spirit Priestesses. He remembered these women and the hateful tattoo. Farinn rose to his feet, his hands on the net.

Skylan shuffled a little nearer to the cell, to let Farinn get a look at him. Farinn clung to the net, straining against it as though he would rip his way through it, sucked in a deep breath, and shouted with all his might.

"Skylan, run! It's a trap!"

CHAPTER 34

So that's why the priest bastard is here," Skylan muttered to himself.

Manta and her warriors were in front of him, standing between him and the Warrior-Priest. The Aquins were startled, wary, wondering what to do. The Warrior-Priest cast his gaze over the women and gestured to the guards to take care of them. The Warrior-Priest circled around, coming for Skylan, who noted that the priest was having some trouble removing the sword's hilt from the belt loop.

Skylan took advantage of the man's delay. Skylan shoved aside Manta and ran to meet the Warrior-Priest. Skylan briefly considered grabbing Manta's spear as he dashed past her, decided his bone knife would serve him better. The Warrior-Priest saw Skylan draw his knife and smiled.

A novice warrior watches your weapon, Norgaard had taught his son. A skilled warrior watches your eyes. Skylan gave his ear-splitting war call, partly to intimidate his foe, but mostly to let Farinn know that they were going to be fighting their way out. Torval's name echoed and banged its way around the cavern, sounding so fearful it almost frightened Skylan. He waved his knife threateningly in the air, and jumped up and down, howling, trying to look and sound the part of a bloodthirsty Vindrasi.

The Warrior-Priest did not cow easily. He stood his ground, his sword in his grip, his hand unconsciously clasping and unclasping the hilt. His eyes were fixed on Skylan's wildly swinging knife. He was not watching Skylan's feet.

Skylan kicked the Warrior-Priest in the knee. The man's leg buckled and he went down. He dropped his sword, his hands instinctively reaching out to keep himself from falling. The moment the blade hit the stone, Skylan slammed his foot down on it. The priest stared up at him, his mouth open.

"Eyes, fool!" Skylan said, pointing to his own. "Next time, look at the eyes."

He kicked the priest in the head. The man toppled sideways and rolled over on his back with a groan, blood streaming. Skylan had probably broken his jaw.

He looked up to find Manta and her warriors and the Aquin guards standing unmoving, staring at him.

"Go free Farinn!" Skylan cried, and he tossed the bone knife to Manta.

She caught it more by reflex than because she knew what she was doing.

"Go!" Skylan shouted, and Manta came to her senses. She gave a brief nod and, calling to two of her warriors, ran into the cell where Farinn hung in his net.

Skylan snatched up his prize sword and turned to face the guards. The sword was lighter in weight than he liked and it was brass, not steel, but the weapon was well made. The sword was superbly balanced, the blade sharp. He made a few experimental passes with it, to get the feel of it and to drive back the Aquin guards, who apparently had been entertaining the idea of rushing him. At the sight of the gleaming blade and the deft way Skylan wielded it, the guards backed off precipitously.

Keeping one eye on the guards, Skylan bent down to swiftly unbuckle the sword belt and drag it off the Warrior-Priest. The belt was too small to go around Skylan's waist. He slung it over his shoulder. He named the sword Viper Tooth.

"Can I use my magic now?" Wulfe asked. "I thought of a spell my mother taught me. I want to try it out."

Skylan was startled to hear the boy's voice. He turned to find Wulfe standing right behind him.

"Guard them," Skylan said, pointing to the Aquin guards who were bunched up in a far corner.

"Can I use my magic?"

"Only if they move," said Skylan.

He looked into the cell to see Manta sawing with the bone knife at the net that held Farinn. Screams and shrieks and squeals came from below. Skylan ran to the stone stairs and looked down into the water. Aquin warriors had been waiting in ambush for him. The warriors were under attack by the oceanaids, who slammed the Aquins with waves, knocking them into the rocks, battering and buffeting them until they were eventually forced to retreat.

Silent slinking
sideways sliding
scuttling slithering

Wulfe began happily singing his song. Skylan paid no attention. The oceanaids had secured the sea route. He wondered how long it would be before the soldiers would come for them by way of land. Probably not long; they might already be on their way.

Skylan ran into the cells. Manta was hacking at the rope net with her knife, but not making much progress. She stared at the brass sword in his hand and then nodded in approval.

"We're not out of this yet," said Skylan. Issuing orders came so easily to him, he forgot he wasn't in command. "Warriors were lying in wait to attack us from the sea. The oceanaids stopped them for the moment, but I don't trust those fish-women. Wulfe's casting some sort of magic spell on the guards. I don't trust him either. More soldiers are probably coming from the land-side and could be here any moment. I need for you and your troops to go back in there and clear a way for us to escape."

Manta gave a nod. She handed the bone knife to him, glad to be rid of it. Summoning her troops, she turned to go back to the guard room.

"Manta," Skylan called, "I know you and your people won't take a life. But these Warrior-Priests don't have the same convictions. Aelon killed the daughter of your Sea Goddess. Remember that."

Manta's expression was unreadable. He had no idea what she was thinking or what she would do. Skylan would do what he had come to do. Save his man. He thrust the knife into his belt.

"Stand back!" he ordered Farinn.

Farinn backed up as far in the net as he could. Skylan swung his sword. The blade sliced easily through the rope, opening a good-sized hole. Farinn wriggled out and dropped to the ground. He faced Skylan and swallowed.

"I'm sorry, Skylan," he said, shame-faced.

"Later." Skylan clapped his hand on Farinn's shoulder and gave a rueful smile. "There's blame enough to go around. Now we're going to get out of here—"

"Ivorson! Skylan Ivorson! Don't leave us!"

The deep bellowing roar calling out his name caused Skylan to stare in amazement. The ogre godlord and his shaman were in a nearby cell, shaking the sides of the net and thundering for him to be set free.

"They were the ones who warned me about the trap," said Farinn, nodding at the ogres. "They overheard the guards talking."

Skylan had first-hand knowledge of ogre fighting skills. He would be glad to have them on his side.

"I thought you were dead," he said to the god-lord as he ran over to their net.

"We thought the same about you," the godlord grunted. "Will you free us?"

Both ogres were in a sorry state. They'd lost weight; ogres liked meat and lots of it. A diet of seaweed had nearly killed them. The shaman's black feather cape was almost completely denuded, with only a few scraggly feathers remaining. With his long, gangly legs now bare to the thighs, the shaman reminded Skylan of a molting heron. The shaman grimaced as though he were being forced to swallow bitter wormwood when he saw that he was going to owe his freedom to Skylan. The sha-man muttered something to the godlord.

"Your magic got us into this mess," the godlord told the shaman. "Stay if you want. I'm leaving."

"Stand back," Skylan warned.

The net was barely big enough to hold both ogres and they had nowhere to go. Skylan sliced his sword through the rope at the bottom, taking care to come as close to the shaman's foot as he could without actually cutting off a toe. As it was, the shaman let out a yelp and snarled at Skylan in fury.

Manta yelled his name. A series of loud splashes and a horrified bellow from the guard room sent Skylan running. He trusted the ogres would free themselves. He dashed into the guard room, slid to a sudden halt and caught hold of Farinn as he would have run past him.

The guard room was ankle deep in snakes.

Black snakes, water snakes, brown snakes, green snakes, all kind and manner of snake writhed and coiled and hissed and curled and slithered. Manta and her troops had fled, jumping into the water. The Aquin guards must have followed, for they were nowhere to be seen. The wounded Warrior-Priest had regained consciousness and was flailing about on the floor, trying to hurl off the snakes that were crawling over him.

Wulfe stood in the middle, snakes coiling about his shins, gaping in wonder. Catching sight of Skylan, the boy made a flying leap for him and climbed Skylan as he would have climbed a tree.

"Are any of those poisonous?" Skylan demanded.

"No. Yes. Maybe . . ." Wulfe had hold of Skylan around the neck, his legs around Skylan's waist. "It's not my fault. That stupid serpent on his head gave me the idea."

Skylan would have liked to ask the Warrior-Priest what he thought of serpents now, but there wasn't time. The godlord, coming up behind him, began to swear. The shaman gabbled. Skylan hoped to Torval the shaman wasn't going to cast one of his foul spells.

Their only way out was the sea and to reach the stone stairs they had to traverse the snake-ridden floor. And all of them were barefoot.

Skylan attached his sword to the belt loop and draped it over his head. Carrying Wulfe piggyback, Skylan jumped and hopped, trying to avoid snakes, looking for any patch of open floor. That proved impossible and he cringed, his flesh crawling, as he felt snakes wriggling beneath his feet. He could see them striking at him with their fangs and he waited grimly for the first signs that he had been poisoned. He and Farinn and the ogres leaped and staggered and swore and kicked their way across.

Skylan didn't bother with the stairs. Manta and her warriors were waiting for them below, as were the oceanaids, all of them fending off the snakes that were slithering down the stairs into the water. Skylan flung Wulfe into the sea and threw himself in after him. He surfaced to see the oceanaids surrounding Wulfe, laughing heartily.

Farinn jumped next. Skylan caught hold of him. The godlord landed with a gigantic splash and kept on going, sinking beneath the water. The shaman stood teetering on the edge, his fear of the water vying with his desire to escape. He either jumped or slipped, for he fell down clawing at the air and landed on his belly with a stinging splat. He went down with a strangled cry, leaving a trail of bubbles.

"You'll have to go rescue the ogres," said Skylan to Manta.

She shouted to several of her women, who dove down to find the ogres.

"The dolphins are waiting to carry you and your friend back to the First City," Manta told him. "You can take my breathing device for your friend." She divested herself of the clamshell and helped Skylan strap it onto Farinn.

"You are a brave warrior," Skylan said to her.

"So are you, Vindrasi," she said, adding with a sly smile, "for a male."

The Aquin warriors returned from the depths, bringing up the ogre godlord. His eyes were bulging, his face purple. He gave a great gasp when his head broke the surface and he hung there, too weak to do anything to help himself. The Aquins didn't dare let go for fear he would sink again. The shaman floated naked in the water. The dive had finished off his black feather cape.

"Will your people see to it these two reach land?" Skylan asked. "According to Farinn, they warned him of the ambush they had set for us. We owe our lives to them."

"We do not like ogres, but we do not let any living being drown if we can save them. Though I do think it is odd we found them here," Manta said with a frown.

Skylan was involved in readjusting the sword belt, trying to find a way to wear the sword so that the tip would not stab him or the dolphin carrying him back to the *Venjekar*.

"Why?" he asked. "What's odd?"

"I could have sworn I saw both of them lying dead at the bottom of the sea," said Manta.

"Ogres all look alike," said Skylan.

"Not one wearing black feathers," said Manta. She shrugged, not truly interested. "Perhaps I was seeing things."

Skylan did not have time to give the matter further thought. They had already lingered here too long. Panicked shouts and yells from the dungeon indicated that the Aquins who had entered from the land-side had discovered Wulfe's snakes.

"You looked really funny leaping around, trying to dodge snakes," Wulfe said with a giggle.

Skylan remembered the feel of snakes writhing beneath his feet and he shuddered.

"The next time I ask you to work a magic spell, just run a sword through me. It will be easier."

Wulfe frowned. "You know I can't touch iron."

Skylan hid his smile. "Swim back to Aylaen. Tell her to meet us at the *Venjekar*. And take your blasted oceanaids with you. Oh, and thank them for dealing with those warriors," he added grudgingly.

Wulfe swam off. The oceanaids waved goodbye; a few gave him fond pats, and then followed their princeling.

"The dolphins are here to take you back," Manta said.

"Thank you, Manta. For everything. I will pray to the Sea Goddess that war does not come to your people," Skylan said. "If you must fight, pray to Torval. He heeds the prayers of valiant warriors."

"I hope it does not come to that," said Manta fervently. "But I will remember. Farewell, Vindrasi, and good luck."

Manta and her warriors swam off, hauling the half-drowned ogres with them. Skylan instructed

Farinn on how to swim with the dolphins and was about to adjust the breathing mask on his face when an Aquin woman swam up from beneath.

"Kailani!" Farinn gasped, sank, and sucked in a breath that got mixed with water.

Skylan drew the bone knife. Kailani made a clicking sound and the dolphins left Skylan and swam to her. Farinn was choking and coughing, spitting out sea water.

"Put away your weapon, Vindrasi," Kailani said. "I mean you no harm and I might do some good. I ask only that you listen to me."

Skylan didn't have much choice. He had no way to communicate with the dolphins.

Farinn was flushed, both from near drowning and embarrassment. Kailani regarded him sadly. "I wanted to tell you I am sorry," she said, grasping his hand and keeping hold of it when he tried to pull free. "I do truly care for you. I was not acting. I wanted very much to make love to you."

Farinn cast an embarrassed glance at Skylan and kept his eyes lowered.

"You have had your say," said Skylan coldly. "If you do care about him, release our dolphins."

Kailani ignored him, spoke only to Farinn. "I thought about the story you told me about the tattoo and how Aelon inflicted pain if you did not heed his commands. It seems gods should want to ease our pain, not cause it. We inflict enough pain on each other."

Kailani's voice was filled with sorrow. She

reached out her hand to Farinn. "Will you forgive me?"

Farinn flushed red. He took her hand and she brushed his cheek with a kiss. She clicked commands to the dolphins, who swam back to Skylan.

"One thing more, Vindrasi," Kailani said, shifting her gaze to Skylan. "You were not the only target of the ambush. They knew you would come to rescue Farinn. While you are gone, they plan to kill your wife."

CHAPTER 35

Manta and her warriors carried the ogres to a small island, little more than a sandbar with a single tree, and left them in the shallow water.

"Sinarian fishermen ply their trade in the waters near here," Manta told them. "You will not be marooned here long."

This was not likely to bring much comfort to the ogres, who had invaded Sinaria and would likely be killed by Sinarians, not rescued. The two ogres did not appear to mind, however. They thanked Manta and her warriors and the shaman blessed them in the name of the Gods of Raj.

"Perhaps you might be interested in hearing more about the Gods of Raj," the shaman said.

Manta and her warriors rolled their eyes and left them.

The godlord and the shaman splashed among the ocean waves. Dripping wet, they trudged onto the beach and threw themselves down in the sunshine, puffing and blowing, glad to be out of the water. The shaman plucked off the last few black feathers of his cloak and tossed them aside. The godlord waved to a woman, who had been sitting at her ease in the shade of the lone tree.

"The way you two are carrying on, one would think you could actually drown," said the woman, leaving the shade to join them.

The woman was not an ogre. She was a human with skin as dark and glistening as jet. She had black hair that she wore in myriad small, tightly bound braids elaborately wound about her head and trailing down her back. She was slender and long-legged, dressed in a long leather tunic and leather boots. Her features were lovely, except for the astonishing fact that she had what appeared to be three eyes: two large and lustrous brown eyes placed on either side of her nose, where eyes should be, and the third eye, round and white-rimmed with a red iris, in the center of her forehead.

On closer observation, one could see that the third eye was painted on the woman's forehead. This eye was known as the "world eye" and the woman was a Cyclops, a race old as time. The world eye was painted onto the forehead when a male or female Cyclops came of age at sixteen. The world eye was said to give the Cyclops the ability to see inside the minds of others, and indeed the Cyclops race was noted and feared for their uncanny ability to know what others were thinking.

The realm of the Cyclops bordered the lands of the ogre kingdom. The two races had been at war over disputed territory along the border for so long that this land was known as the Bloodlands by both races. No one could remember a time when ogres and Cyclops had not been killing each other over it.

"You get accustomed to these mortal bodies," said the godlord. "You start to feel what they feel."

"And you have no right to talk," said the shaman, eyeing the Cyclops. "Once you took that body, you have not left it."

The godlord was not, in truth, an ogre godlord. He was not even an ogre. Neither was the ogre shaman. The Cyclops was not really a Cyclops. Manta had spoken the truth when she claimed to have seen the ogres lying dead on the bottom of the ocean floor. The two had fallen into the water when the kraken attacked their ship and had almost immediately drowned.

The three were gods, the Gods of Raj.

The Cyclops grinned, her teeth white against her dark complexion. She sank down with easy grace onto the sand. She wore earrings of gold and her head was decorated with beads and feathers that sparkled in the sunlight.

"You went down beneath the sea to meet these mortals who so terrify the mad god, Sund," the Cyclops said. "Did you succeed?"

"We did not find the woman," said the shaman. "But we spoke to the male. I forget his name."

"Skylan Ivorson," the godlord reminded him.

"What do you think of him?" asked the Cyclops.

"A dangerous man. He is loyal and brave, however, a man of honor," said the godlord.

"He is a young hothead," said the shaman.

"Who rescued us when he could have left us," the godlord pointed out.

The shaman shrugged and plucked a black feather off his arm.

"Sounds like a mortal Torval would like." The Cyclops gave a sardonic smile. "The question is: can this Skylan do what Sund fears he will do? Can he succeed in finding the Five spiritbones of the Vektia? And what do *we* do if he does? We might well be forced to leave this pretty world we found."

"As I have pointed out before now," said the shaman dryly, "we never missed the power of creation until we found out we didn't have it."

"That is true," conceded the godlord. "We have succeeded in eradicating many of the bloodthirsty practices that were destroying the ogres. Our followers are now thriving. Work continues, of course, but overall I am pleased with our progress."

"My mortals have accepted us and are adapting to our worship," said the Cyclops. "As you say, however, our work among them continues." She sighed deeply. "We are fighting against centuries of hatred and blood feuds and mistrust. The power of creation might prove useful."

"Our main goal should be to keep the power out of Aelon's grasping little hands," the shaman said grimly. "A thousand pities our attack on Sinaria failed. I fear the ogres will start to lose faith in us."

"We must prepare our shamans to deal with the outcry," said the godlord, and he heaved a sigh.

"And I fear once the Cyclops hear of the defeat they will take advantage of what they perceive to be the ogres' weakness to raid across the border," said the Cyclops.

The three sat in gloomy silence, broken only by the sounds of the waves lapping on the shore.

"Much work lies ahead of us," said the shaman. Slapping his bony knees, he rose to his feet. "I suggest we go about our business and let be what will be—for the moment at least."

"What of this Skylan?" asked the godlord. "He could be a threat to us."

The Cyclops brushed the sand from her tunic. Her golden earrings jangled as she laughed and tapped her forehead.

"Do not worry, friends. I will keep my 'eye' upon Skylan Ivorson."

CHAPTER

36

Aylaen had not been back to the *Venjekar* since the attack by the kraken. How many days had that been? She had no idea. She had lost track of time because in this world, time seemed brief as a heartbeat and long as forever. She wondered if the Dragon Kahg had remained with the ship and she was relieved to see the familiar sight of the red glint in the dragon's eye.

Queen Magali, with Commander Neda and her guards, accompanied Aylaen to the dragonship. The Queen made a graceful salute to the Dragon Kahg, who seemed pleased by the attention. The red in the eyes warmed.

Commander Neda did not seem that enamored of the dragon, for she posted warriors armed with spears and tridents at the prow with apparent orders to keep an eye on Kahg. The warriors attached themselves with tethers wrapped around the dragon's neck to keep from floating off. Aylaen had the impression Kahg found this more amusing than offensive.

Acronis was also with them. He followed the directions of one of the guards and tied himself to the dragon's neck. He drifted about on this tether, studying one of the Aquin lanterns, which he found fascinating. He peered into it, tapping on it to cause the glowing organisms inside to float around.

Queen Magali was not wearing a breathing mask. She indicated to Aylaen that they should swim to the surface, where they could speak. Commander Neda was going to accompany them, but the Queen, through clicking sounds, ordered the commander to remain with the *Venjekar*. Commander Neda was not pleased, but she had no choice except to obey.

Acronis looked at Aylaen, who made a gesture and nodded her head in the direction of Commander Neda, asking him to keep an eye on her. Acronis gave a small nod.

Aylaen broke through into the fresh air and sunlight. She took the breathing tube from her mouth, blinked her eyes at the brilliance and waited for them to adjust. Queen Magali swam up beside her.

The Queen glanced around to make certain they were alone. She reached down to a pouch she had been carrying with her and brought forth a bracelet made of twelve brass rings attached to a bar in the center and studded with emeralds and sapphires and pearls. The bracelet was meant to fit over the lower part of the arm, extending from the wrist to the elbow. Every ring was etched with various sea creatures: dolphins and whales and all manner of fish.

A bone was mounted on the bar in the center of

the bracelet. A dragon made of brass twined around the bone, holding it firmly to the bracelet with wings and tail. Jewels sparkled in the sunlight. Pearls shone with a lustrous radiance. Aylaen was so taken by the beauty she did not realize immediately that she was looking at the third Vektia dragonbone.

When she understood, she raised her eyes in wonder to meet the Queen's. Queen Magali took hold of Aylaen's hand to slide the bracelet onto her arm.

"May the Sea Goddess Akaria bless you," said Queen Magali.

"I will keep it safe aboard the *Venjekar,* Your Majesty," said Aylaen, removing the breathing tube to speak. "The Dragon Kahg will protect it. I thank you and the Sea Goddess for your trust in me. I will not fail you."

"I have something else for you," said Queen Magali. "I have been given permission to tell you where to find the fourth Vektia spiritbone. If I tell you, you must set sail immediately to find it."

"But . . . we were going home," said Aylaen, dismayed.

"And so you may, my dear," said Queen Magali. "No one would blame you."

"We could sail home and gather our forces and then go find the fourth spiritbone," Aylaen offered.

Queen Magali shook her head. "It would be too late. Sund seeks the fourth spiritbone, as do the forces of Aelon."

Aylaen let her thoughts linger on her homeland for just a moment, then let them slip away, like the seawater through her fingers. "Tell me where to find the fourth."

Queen Magali and Aylaen returned to the *Venjekar*. Aylaen carried the pouch, the bracelet safely tucked inside. Commander Neda and her guards were extremely relieved to see their queen return. The Dragon Kahg fixed his eyes intently on Aylaen.

She had been wondering where to hide the bracelet. When Wulfe returned and they were once again sailing in the sunlight, she would have him conceal the bracelet in his hidey-hole. Until then, she decided the best place to hide it would be in the hold.

The *Venjekar* was still underwater. Sunlight filtered down from above, but that would not light the darkness in the hold. Aylaen peered down into the black hole and feared she could not do it. She could not swim into the darkness. She might be trapped down there alone, unable to escape. She told herself that was ridiculous, the Aquins were here, Acronis was here. No one would leave her to die. Still, she had to take a few moments to bolster her courage before gesturing to Acronis to bring her the lantern.

Once down in the hold, she searched swiftly for a hiding place for the bracelet. She rejected the wooden sea chests that had been upended and overturned during the sinking of the ship, thinking that might be the first place someone would search. She hid the bracelet and the Vektan Torque, which she had been wearing, in one of the stone jars that had once held wine, sealing the jar with the lid.

Aylaen frowned at the jar, which seemed a very inadequate hiding place. The Aquins had brought Aylaen's possessions with them. One of the warriors had placed her things in the hold by her direction. Among these were her clothes and her sword. Not knowing what else to do, Aylaen picked up the blessed sword of Vindrash in its leather sheath and laid the sword in front of the jar.

Aylaen swam out of the hold, glad to be in the open once more. Commander Neda and the Queen conferred, their clicks and squeals resonating through the water. Aylaen swam over to where the spiritbone of the Dragon Kahg hung in its customary place on the prow. Aylaen placed her hand over the spiritbone, letting her heart speak to the dragon, telling him about the precious cargo they had taken aboard. She had no need to ask him to protect it. He would do so with his life.

The *Venjekar* had become the keeper of three of the Five Bones of the Vektia. And she knew where to find the fourth.

A warrior offered to tether Aylaen. She shook her head. She preferred to be free to swim about. She kept hold of the dragon, finding comfort in his nearness. Aylaen thought of Skylan and wished he would return. She was uneasy about this rescue attempt. She told herself she was being silly. She had confidence in Skylan. But he was in an unusual situation, quite literally out of his element, and the more she considered the abduction of young Farinn, the less sense it made. Something was not right.

Queen Magali made a sign to Aylean and then swam away, her guards and Commander Neda accompanying her. Aylaen and Acronis were alone. She was trying to take her mind off her worries by admiring the beauty of her surrounding, the red and orange coral, like branches of trees; fish as blue as the sapphires in the bracelet. A quiver ran through the dragon.

Startled, Aylaen looked up at Kahg. The red eyes were hooded, the fire banked. Aylaen searched swiftly for some hint of danger, but she could see nothing. She glanced at Acronis and her feeling of unease deepened. He was peering intently into the water that was unusually dark beyond the light of the lanterns.

Acronis turned to face Aylaen. He gestured frantically, pointing behind her, and began swimming toward her. Aylaen started to turn. She caught a glimpse of someone moving up rapidly through the water and then strong hands had hold of her, pinning her arms behind her.

Male warriors seized Acronis. Serpent tattoos on their bald heads glistened in the eerie lantern light. Aylaen guessed that if she turned, she would see the same on her captor. A Warrior-Priest yanked the breathing tube from Acronis's mask. Bubbles rose from his mouth. He tried frantically to grab hold of the mask. The warrior held it just out of his reach.

And then Commander Neda floated into view. Aylaen was relieved to see her, thinking the commander had come to free her. Aylaen's relief changed quickly to bewilderment and confusion. Commander Neda clicked commands. The Warrior-Priest holding Aylaen tethered her to the ship, tying a line around the dragon's neck. Aylaen yanked on the rope, trying to free herself. Commander Neda swam close to Aylaen. The commander pointed to Acronis, whose eyes were rolling back in his head, his movements starting to grow feeble. The commander touched the breathing tube in Aylaen's mouth and made a motion as of yanking it out. Her meaning clear.

Stop fighting or his fate will be yours.

Aylaen watched in dread as Commander Neda clicked and squealed more commands. The Warrior-Priests holding Acronis thrust the breathing tube back into his mouth. Acronis gasped for air and began to revive. The commander gestured to the hold and the Warrior-Priests swam that direction, dragging Acronis with them. Aylaen wondered why, for a moment, then realized they were going to search for the Vektia spiritbones. Either Commander Neda thought Acronis had seen where Aylaen had hidden them or they assumed he would have some idea of where to look.

Aylaen was sick with fear, not for herself, but that Aelon's priests would find the spiritbones. She had not had time to hide them that well. She trusted Acronis. He would never help the priests of Aelon, but even without his help, they would find them. She cast a frantic glance at the Dragon Kahg, but his eyes revealed only a faint glimmer of life. The dragon could not help her anyway. Magic or no magic, if he tried, Commander Neda would simply remove Aylaen's breathing tube and let her drown.

Her only hope now was Skylan, who was supposed to meet her at the *Venjekar*. He had been gone a long time. He should be back any moment now.

Commander Neda looked at Aylaen and smiled an unpleasant smile. The commander grabbed hold of Aylaen's hand and wrenched off her wedding ring. Commander Neda held it in front of Aylaen's eyes and then made a motion as of a knife gliding across her throat.

Your Skylan is dead.

Neda tossed the wedding ring away. The white ivory floated down through the water and landed on the deck. Aylaen watched it fall. They had bound her to the dragon, but they had not bound her hands.

Go to hell.

Aylaen grabbed hold of Commander Neda by her long braid and pulled hard, nearly yanking the hair out by the roots. The pain must have been excruciating. Commander Neda gave an involuntary gasp that expelled the air from her lungs, and lashed out at Aylaen, who hung on to the woman's hair with a deathlike grip. Warrior-Priests had to swim to Commander Neda's rescue, wrenching Aylaen's hands loose. The commander was forced to surface for air.

Loud clicks caused the Warrior-Priests to swiftly shift their attention away from Aylaen. Queen Magali appeared, swimming into view. The Queen's face was pale with fury. Commander Neda returned, diving back down to the *Venjekar*. She was startled to see the Queen, who was obviously astonished to see the commander. Queen Magali looked from Neda to the Warrior-Priests to Aylaen, bound to the dragon. Queen Magali swam close to the commander, propelling herself with angry strokes.

Although Aylaen could not understand the communication, she knew without doubt what the Queen was saying. Queen Magali demanded to know what was going on, demanded that the captives be freed and told the commander to send these followers of Aelon back to their own city.

Commander Neda did not immediately respond. The Queen's unexpected return had disrupted her plans. She was sullen at first, acting like a child caught in some mischief. Then Commander Neda made a sound, cold and harsh. She pointed at the Warrior-Priests who had hold of Aylaen and to more Warrior-Priests who swam out from behind the coral reef where they had been waiting. Queen Magali was alone, surrounded by her foes.

The Queen gave Commander Neda a look of

contempt and swam to Aylaen. The Queen fixed the Warrior-Priests guarding Aylaen with a glittery gaze, daring them to cross her. The men glanced at each other, uncertain. Queen Magali took advantage of their confusion to swiftly start to untie the tether that bound Aylaen to the dragon.

Commander Neda seized a spear from one of the Warrior-Priests. Queen Magali had her back to the commander. Aylaen shook her head frantically, desperate to make the Queen understand the danger. Aylaen even went so far as to start to take the breathing tube from her mouth. Queen Magali understood. She turned around to the woman who had been the commander of her guards for many years. The Queen did not speak. She did not have to. Her unspoken words burned in Aylaen's heart.

You were more than the commander of my guards. I counted you a friend. Will you now betray me?

Commander Neda hesitated, then she pressed her lips tightly together and lunged, driving the spear into the Queen's breast.

The breath rushed from the Queen's mouth. She held fast to the spear for a moment, staring at the commander in sorrow. Blood billowed from the terrible wound. The Queen went limp in the water.

Aylaen broke free of her captors and took hold of the dying Queen. She yanked the spear from the Queen's body and flung it away, then held the

Queen in her arms. The Queen gazed at her. Her lips moved, but only blood and a faint trail of bubbles rose from her mouth, staining the sea.

The bubbles ceased. Her blood darkened the water.

Commander Neda stared down, white-faced, at the woman she had murdered. She seemed overwhelmed by the enormity of her action. The Warrior-Priests were dazed, shocked, with no idea what to do. With no thought of what she was doing, Aylaen yanked the breathing tube from her mouth to shout words that no one could hear.

See this! See what you have done in the name of Aelon! See and remember!

Commander Neda came to her senses. The water was filled with blood. Next, the water would be filled with sharks. She grabbed Aylaen and thrust the breathing tube into her mouth, slapping her when Aylaen tried to drag it out again. Neda handed her over to the Warrior-Priests. This time they bound her hands and her arms and then dropped a net over her. Whistling to dolphins, the Warrior-Priests swam away, dragging Aylaen with them.

Aylaen looked back to the *Venjekar*. The dragon's red eyes blazed, bathing the Queen's body in lurid light. Acronis, swimming out of the hold alone, the blessed sword of Vindrash in his hand, saw the body and stared in horror and shock, then searched frantically for Aylaen.

She whispered a prayer, many prayers. A prayer

to Vindrash, who had protected the Vektia spirit-bones. A prayer to Torval that Skylan was not dead. A prayer to the Sea Goddess to say she was sorry, so very sorry.

Sharks, scenting blood, were already circling.

CHAPTER 37

Raegar, resplendent in his new armor, marked with the symbol of the Priest-General, a serpent twined about a sword, walked the deck of his dragonship. The afternoon sun was hot, but he basked in the rays with the keen enjoyment of one who remembered the bitter bite of winter's icy winds and the freezing darkness of long nights. He often reflected that it was Aelon's promise of warmth and light which had first drawn him to the God of the New Dawn. Raegar did not in the least miss his home in the north. He longed to return, but only as conqueror.

Raegar noted, as he walked the deck, how the sailors and soldiers were careful not to cross his path. If forced by the necessity of their work to do so, they would cringe, beg his pardon, and remove themselves as swiftly as possible. Looking around, Raegar saw respect in every eye and he thought to himself that it was about damn time.

So often in the past Raegar had looked into men's eyes and seen derision, disdain. His superiors had made use of him, even as they despised him. Xydis had laughed at Raegar behind his back, mocked him, promoted him so that Raegar could do the dirty work. Raegar had swallowed the insults and done their bidding, performed their demeaning tasks, soiled his own hands so that theirs would remain clean. He had all the while been faithful to his god and his god had rewarded him, giving Raegar the satisfaction of sweet revenge. His enemies in Sinaria had either fled before he could reach them or he had found them and they were now no longer a threat.

One enemy remained, an enemy that had no intention of fleeing. One enemy currently out of his reach. His cousin, Skylan Ivorson, who always seemed to find a way to make Raegar look bad in the eyes of both men and gods. A prime example was their last meeting. Raegar's dragon, Fala, had abandoned him. His men had mutinied. He'd been forced to retreat, leaving Skylan the victor. Aelon had sent a kraken to drag Skylan to a watery grave, but Skylan had been saved by Aquins loyal to the Old Gods and he was again the victor.

This time, by Aelon, Raegar would be the victor.

The lookouts had been scouring the ocean, searching for those they were here to meet. One gave a cry and pointed out to sea. Raegar could see heads bobbing in the water. He raised his spyglass and put it to his eye. Two Aquins swam into view. He saw bald heads and serpent tattoos, Warrior-Priests. With Aelon's blessing, they were here to deliver the goods.

Raegar directed the captain to sail toward them. This was the same captain, Anker, who had turned on Raegar their last voyage. Anker had since had a change of heart. He was now Raegar's most loyal subject. He gave Raegar a respectful salute and shouted orders. Sailors jumped swiftly to obey. The Dragon Fala had returned to the dragonship. Treia had given Fala's spiritbone to Raegar, with strict instructions on the proper way to summon the dragon. Treia had wanted to come, but Raegar would not hear of risking either his wife or the child she was carrying. Treia might have insisted, but the mere thought of swooping up and down on the waves made her nauseous. She had sent Raegar with her blessing and the reminder never to summon a fire dragon over water. The Dragon Fala invested the ship with wings, as it were, and *Aelon's Triumph,* now flying the flag of the Priest-General, sailed swiftly toward the waiting Aquins.

"Do you have her?" Raegar bellowed as they drew near.

"We have her, Priest-General!" a Warrior-Priest shouted back.

The ship slowed as it circled the men in the water. Soldiers and others who had no duties lined the rail to catch a glimpse of the generally reclusive Aquins, curious to know what business the "fish people" had with their Priest-General.

At first they thought the Aquins were handing over a haul of fish, for they asked that the sailors lower a rope with a hook. They attached the hook to a large net. The sailors heaved on the rope and hauled in the net. Water ran from it, cascading onto the deck. They lowered the net and then opened it to reveal a woman. She had some sort of odd mask over her face. She pried this loose, then flung the net from her and rose to her feet, blinking in the sunshine.

"Greetings, my dear sister Aylaen," said Raegar in pleasant tones.

In answer, his "dear sister" sprang at him, struck him in the chest, catching him off guard and sending him staggering. Aylaen ran past him, making a dash for the railing with the intention of jumping back into the sea.

Raegar roared a command and two men ran after Aylaen and dragged her back from the rail. They had hold of her by the arms. She kicked at them, trying to break free. The men on board the ship were grinning, for Aylaen's flimsy gown clung wetly to her body and all on board were enjoying the view.

This included Raegar, who could not take his eyes from her. He had always lusted after Aylaen. He could have her, too. He was master of this ship. He had his own cabin down below. She would have to submit to him. She would have no choice. She might actually enjoy it. He had long suspected Aylaen had a secret yearning for him.

He licked his lips and was about to give the order for his men to take her below. Clearly his men were expecting this; perhaps they were hoping that when he finished, they would get his leftovers. Then he remembered—his vow to Aelon. He had sworn to be faithful.

Raegar almost groaned aloud. He had been true to his vow up until now. He had been faithful to Treia and to Aelon, mainly because he had been too busy with affairs of state and the church to be unfaithful. This was the first time he had been truly tempted and he suddenly knew this was a test. Aelon was watching him and judging him. The thought was like jumping naked into a snowbank. Desire shriveled up and died.

"Find some decent clothing for this woman!" Raegar ordered, his voice rasping. He turned a cold gaze on Aylaen. "Cover yourself, Sister. You look like a whore."

He wondered what to do with her. He had been about to tell his men to take her to his cabin, but he feared if he was alone with her, the temptation might be too great. Aylaen might try to seduce him. After all, she had run off to sea dressed like a man.

"When she is dressed bring her to me here, on deck." Raegar walked over to stand at the prow. The dragon's head, rearing up over him, provided a suitable backdrop; it would remind Aylaen that he had risen in the world. Raegar gave orders to sail the ship back to Sinaria with all haste. The sooner he handed Aylaen over to Aelon, the sooner he was rid of her, the better.

Aylaen returned wearing the only clothes they had been able to find for her: a soldier's tunic. The tunic was short, barely covering her thighs. Raegar kept his eyes on her face. On his orders, one of the men brought a stool for Aylaen. She glanced at it and shook her head.

"You might as well make yourself comfortable, Sister," said Raegar. "The journey back to Sinaria is a long one."

"Don't call me that," said Aylaen.

She did not sit down. She did not look at him. She gazed stonily out to sea.

"Call you what? Sister?" Raegar smiled broadly. "But you *are* my sister now. Ah, but you don't know, do you? Treia and I were married. She is carrying my child, my son." Raegar spoke proudly.

A spasm of pain contorted Aylaen's face. Her eyes blinked rapidly. She said nothing.

"Treia will be pleased to have you join her. She worries about you—"

"My sister who tried to kill me?" Aylaen snorted.

"What are you talking about?" Raegar asked with an incredulous laugh. "Treia loves you."

Aylaen gave him a pitying glance. "You truly don't know, do you?"

"Know what?" Raegar was wary.

"My sister, your wife, the mother of your child, has blood on her hands. She poisoned the men who were on guard duty the night we fled Sinaria. She poisoned Keeper on board our ship. She tried to kill me by slitting my throat."

"I don't believe you!" said Raegar, scowling.

"Treia made a bargain with Hevis, god of lies and deceit. She promised to sacrifice someone she loved and in return he gave her the ability to summon the Vektia dragon."

Aylaen shrugged. "She failed to keep her bargain. Hevis will not forget. I would watch what she puts in my soup if I were you—"

Raegar struck Aylaen across the face. The blow was not hard, more shocking than painful. Aylaen tasted blood from a cut lip.

"You will not speak such lies about my wife," said Raegar, cold with fury.

Aylaen wiped the blood from her mouth. "Treia told you Aelon gave her the power to summon the dragon, didn't she? And you never thought to question that?"

Aylaen looked back out to sea.

Raegar had to take a moment to recover his composure. He had rarely been so angry. He didn't believe her, he reassured himself. But there was an ache inside him, a fear. He wanted to hurt her in return.

"If you are holding out hope that Skylan will come to your rescue, forget it. He is my prisoner," said Raegar.

Aylaen glanced at him and then looked away. Raegar smiled.

"He fell into my trap. I knew he would want to play the hero and rush off to save that young fool Farinn. My men were waiting for him. He was captured and he is being held in the dungeons of the Aquins."

Raegar was lying when he said this. He did not know for certain his cousin was a prisoner; Raegar had yet to receive the report from the Watchers. He could not see how his plan could have possibly failed, however, and so he took the liberty of stretching the truth.

Aylaen turned away from him. A tear trickled down her cheek. She whisked it away, but not before he had noticed. Jealousy twisted inside Raegar. He grabbed hold of her, yanked her around to face him. "You slept with Skylan, didn't you?" He gripped her arm so hard she cried out in pain. "I said you looked like a whore. Now you act like one. Garn's bed is scarcely cold before you jump into Skylan's—"

Aylaen's nails flashed toward his eyes.

"Stop it," Raegar ordered, "or I will hit you again and next time I'll break your jaw. Now sit down and listen to me!"

He threw Aylaen at the stool. She missed and stumbled and fell onto the deck. He made no move to help her, stood waiting as she picked herself up. Aylaen's green eyes smoldered. Her lip was starting to swell.

"Skylan will find you and he will gut you like the pig you are," she said.

"He will have trouble finding me when he is locked in a cell," said Raegar dryly. "I have gone to a great deal of trouble to find you, Aylaen. Aren't you curious to know why?"

"Go play with yourself," said Aylaen.

Raegar chose to ignore this. "You are greatly honored, Sister. The god Aelon has instructed me to bring you to the sacred temple in the mountain, there to stand before Aelon."

Aylaen gave a snort. "I don't believe you."

"Believe it." Raegar leaned back against the rail and smiled at her. "I have long desired you, Aylaen. You know that." He gestured. "I am master of this ship. I could take you below and ravish you and no one would lift a finger to stop me."

His voice hardened. "Once I would have done it. I still desire you. But you are safe. I will not touch you. Why do you think that is?"

Aylaen's eyes flickered with uncertainty.

Raegar looked out to sea. He drew in a deep breath and continued to speak, his voice soft with awe. "When I was made Priest-General, I came before Aelon. The god touched me, spoke to me, honored me. I vowed to Aelon I would be faithful to Treia and to our unborn son. I will not touch you. I will not harm you. Aelon commanded me to bring you to the mountain and I will do as my god commands."

"Why would your god want me?" Aylaen asked with seeming indifference. "I will be glad to tell Aelon what I think of a god who brings war to a people who have only ever known peace."

"Treia lost control of the Vektia dragon. You were the one who gained control and banished the dragon. You have the spiritbones. Three of them, if my spies are not mistaken."

"You and your god waste your time. I would never give the Five dragon bones to Aelon," said Aylaen.

"You don't need to," said Raegar. "Of course, if you did, Aelon would reward you. The god would give you whatever your heart desires. The god will see to it that you are not barren. The god will give you as many sons and daughters as you want."

Raegar had no idea where those words had come from. They had suddenly flashed into his head. He knew when he saw Aylaen's pale face that it was the god who had spoken.

"Aelon will even give you Skylan's life," Raegar said, pursuing his advantage. "Skylan will live long. His sons will be chief—"

"His sons will be slaves," Aylaen said, trying to sound defiant. Her voice trembled.

"If you remain stubborn and refuse to give Aelon the spiritbones," Raegar went on relentlessly, "the god will kill Skylan and keep you, the Kai Priestess, the only one who can bring the Five together, a prisoner. You will be locked up in the mountain fastness, alone, forever. Whether you are barren or not won't matter."

Aylaen stared past him.

"You have time to think things over," Raegar said. "The voyage to Sinaria will take several days."

Aylaen did not answer.

Pleased to think he had broken her at last, Raegar walked off. Before he went down to his cabin, he cast one last look at her.

Raegar sighed deeply and turned away. He hoped Aelon honored him for his willpower.

As Raegar sat alone in his cabin, he wasn't thinking of Aelon or of his lovely sister-in-law. He was thinking of Treia, wondering if what Aylaen had told him was true. Was Treia a murderer? A liar? A wicked heretic who had turned in secret to a pagan god, promised him a sacrifice?

Since Raegar was himself a murderer and a liar, he might have been more sympathetic. These are not qualities one looks for in a wife, however. Raegar loved Treia in his own way, as much as a selfish, arrogant, and power-hungry man could love anyone. He didn't want to believe Aylaen. Yet her accusation explained a lot he had wondered about.

He frowned deeply, stared at his hands, flexed his fingers.

"I have to keep Treia around only until my son is born." Raegar slowly clenched his fists. "Women often die in childbirth . . ."

CHAPTER

38

The journey through the sea back to the *Venjekar* seemed the longest journey Skylan had ever taken in his life. Longer than the journey that had brought him from childhood to manhood. He cursed himself, blamed himself. Raegar had set a cunning trap, based on Skylan's vainglorious need to be in the center of the action, and Skylan had rushed in with drums beating and banners flying.

Raegar had ordered the Aquins to abduct Farinn, because he was an easy mark and because Raegar knew Skylan would try to save him, leaving Aylaen and the *Venjekar* with the spiritbones alone and unguarded. Skylan berated himself. If only he had let the Aquins undertake the rescue! If only he had stayed with Aylaen and his ship, as was his duty.

"I am sorry, Torval," Skylan prayed as they sped through the water, hanging on to the dolphins. "Once again, I have failed you. Please, do not punish Aylaen. Let this mistake fall on me!"

He was relieved to see in the murky distance the red eyes of the dragon and the *Venjekar,* resting on the coral reef. His relief was short-lived. He and Farinn arrived to find the Aquin warriors in the midst of a desperate battle. The women had not forsaken their dead Queen. They surrounded her lifeless body, lying on the deck of the *Venjekar*, using spears and tridents to fend off ravenous sharks.

Acronis fought with them, wielding a sword. Skylan searched the deck, but he could not find Aylaen. He told himself she might be down in the hold, but he knew better. She would never run from a fight. Then he saw that the sword Acronis was wielding was the blessed sword of Vindrash. He looked at the body of Queen Magali and saw the gaping wound in her breast. Skylan knew with dread certainty that something terrible had happened to Aylaen.

The red eye of the Dragon Kahg flared at the sight of Skylan, almost as if pleased to see him. Skylan was too preoccupied to notice this, but he did remember to give the dragon a salute. Movement caught his eye. Wulfe, surrounded by his oceanaids, who were keeping the boy at a safe distance from the sharks. Sighting Skylan, Wulfe broke free and swam toward him, legs kicking, arms paddling like a dog. The oceanaids were all aflutter over his leaving and swarmed after him in a silvery wake.

The dolphins abandoned Skylan, sensibly fleeing at the sight of the sharks. Skylan fumbled for his sword, his movements clumsy underwater, the clamshell breathing device in his way. He cursed the water, the clamshell, himself. He motioned for Farinn to remain behind, and pointed at Wulfe.

Farinn nodded his head in understanding and caught hold of the boy and held fast to him.

Skylan was ready to fight his way through the circling sharks to reach Acronis, when the warm water in which he had been swimming turned suddenly cold.

Every living creature in the sea felt the change. Fish darted around in a frenzy, then fled. The sharks circled their prey, uneasy, yet reluctant to leave. The mysterious chill deepened, as though a stream of icy water were flowing into the sea. The sharks abandoned the fight and swam away. The Aquins felt the change and hovered near their Queen, glancing around uncertainly, not knowing what was going on, yet staying to guard their Queen.

Skylan swam to Acronis. Taking the tube from his mouth, he mouthed the word, "Aylaen?"

Acronis shook his head. Seeing the agony in Skylan's eyes, Acronis tapped his hand over his heart. Skylan at first had no idea what this gesture meant and then he understood. Aylaen was alive, her heart was beating. Acronis crossed his wrists, indicating shackles, and then pointed out into the water in the direction they had taken Aylaen. Acronis turned his sorrowful gaze to the dead Queen. Skylan understood. Queen Magali had died trying to protect Aylaen.

Skylan would go after Aylaen. He would find her if he had to circumnavigate the world. First, he had a duty to the dead.

I will always honor you, Queen Magali. I do not know where your soul will travel in your last journey, he thought. I pray to Akaria, goddess of the sea, that you find the blessed peace you did not find here.

"She will," said a voice. "I will take her there myself."

Skylan was startled to hear the voice beneath the waves. He looked up to see a woman standing over him. The woman's long white hair floated around her. Her beauty was marred by lines of grief and anger and deep-etched sorrow. Her eyes were the color of the sea in all its moods, green with mischief, blue with halcyon calm, gray with storm.

She was Akaria, the sea goddess, and with her was King Tai and his daughters. The king stared down in disbelief at the body of his beloved wife, then he gathered her in his arms and hugged her close. The daughters drifted in the water, huddled together, holding on to each other, unable to comprehend the terrible tragedy that had torn apart their family. Acronis covered his face with his hand, unable to endure the sight of such heart-rending grief.

This is my fault, Skylan thought in silent misery, knowing the goddess could understand the words in his heart. If we had not come—

The Sea Goddess shook her head. "I would like to blame you, Skylan Ivorson, for I do not think much of you or your god, Torval. War would have come with you or without you. The twelve cities lived at peace for centuries until the coming of Aelon. Now our peace is shattered. The people of this city will never forgive the murder of their Queen. There will be more bloodshed. I cannot prevent it."

King Tai bade the daughters kiss their mother farewell. He gave his wife a final kiss, lifted her body, then gently rested her in the arms of the Sea Goddess. Akaria would carry the fallen Queen back to her home.

She turned back one last time to face Skylan.

"Find the Five, Skylan Ivorson," said the Sea Goddess. "Summon the great dragon, Ilyrion, to drive Aelon from the heavens. My blessing goes with you."

The great dragon, Ilyrion . . . The Five spirit-bones had been the bones of the great dragon, Ilyrion. The bones in which Vindrash had hidden the power of creation. Bring the Five bones together . . . Summon the great dragon that once guarded a world until she fell to Torval. Ilyrion would come back to save the world she loved.

No wonder Sund was scared.

Kahg's eyes flared. Skylan and the dragon shared a moment's perfect accord. Both understood. It all made sense. They just had to bring this miracle about.

Kahg's eyes narrowed. He was eager to be gone. Desperate as Skylan was to be gone himself, to pursue Aylaen's captors, he waited in respect until the funeral cortege had passed beyond his view.

The sight of the king's grief-ravaged face haunted Skylan. As a warrior, he had always accepted the fact that he would never reach old age.

His wife would be the one to bid farewell to him as he set off on the journey to Torval's Hall. He could not imagine holding Aylaen's dead body in his arms, forced to go on living without her.

A hand closed over his hand. He looked down, startled, to find Wulfe gazing up at him. Wulfe gave Skylan's hand a squeeze and an awkward attempt at a reassuring smile. Skylan was touched. Wulfe squeezed Skylan's hand again and pointed up at the dragon.

Skylan looked to see the red eyes glaring fiercely down at them. The *Venjekar* shuddered and began to move off the reef. Skylan and Farinn and Acronis had time only to grab hold of the stump of the mast or trailing rope or whatever they could find and hang on as the angry Dragon Kahg lifted the *Venjekar* from below the sea.

CHAPTER 39

Held captive aboard the *Aelon's Triumph*, Aylaen sat huddled on the stool, two soldiers standing guard over her. She paid no heed to them. She told herself Raegar was lying to her, that Skylan was safe and well and would be coming after her. Common sense told her she was the one who was lying—to herself. Of course, Skylan had walked into an ambush. The abduction of Farinn made no sense otherwise. Skylan would fight. He would not allow himself to be captured, taken prisoner. He would fight until they beat him to the ground and then he would fight on until death overcame him.

At the thought, tears burned her eyes. Aylaen refused to let herself cry. She would not allow Raegar or these other men to see her be weak.

She was thinking of Skylan and afraid the tears might come anyway when she saw the guards behind her jump to attention. Raegar walked toward her. She rose to her feet, faced him with defiance. He was almost welcome. She could sink her grief in hatred.

Raegar gave her an oily, insinuating smile.

"Have you thought over Aelon's offer? The god is being magnanimous. I hope you have sense enough to appreciate it."

Aylaen snorted and started to turn away. He reached out, seized hold of her shoulder.

Aylaen bit him.

Raegar swore and snatched his hand back, blood welling from tooth marks in his fingers. Raegar's face flushed an angry red. Furious, he struck Aylaen, knocking her to the deck. She lay there dazed, her ears ringing, pain bursting in her skull.

Gritting her teeth, trying to focus her eyes, Aylaen pushed herself up off the deck. One of the guardsman reached to help her. Aylaen snarled at him and he drew back. She held fast to the rail and spit out the blood, hers and Raegar's.

"My stepfather hit me harder than that," she said, sneering.

Raegar's flush deepened to an ugly purple. He raised his hand again, fingers clenched to a fist. She had made him look the fool in front of his men and this time he might well kill her. Aylaen braced herself for the blow, but it never fell.

A rogue wave rose from a flat, calm sea and smacked the side of Raegar's dragonship. The vessel lurched, men staggered across the canting deck. Sailors who were still on their feet began to point and yell in terror.

The *Venjekar* rose out of the sea, leaping up from the waves like a whale, foam flying. The red eyes of the dragon blazed. Seawater ran in cascades from the prow and the hull and foamed beneath the keel. Seaweed hung dripping from the ropes and twined about the stump of the broken mast. The deck was empty. There was no sign of anyone living on board.

"Ghost ship!" one sailor yelled hoarsely.

"Come to claim us!" another shrieked.

The story was ancient and always the same, whether told by Sinarian sailors over wine, Vindrasi sailors over mead, or ogre sailors over fermented goat's milk. All told the tale of the ghostly ship that sailed the seas, searching for sailors to man her.

Aylaen could see that Raegar was as shaken as the rest of his crew, though not by a ghost ship. He was startled by the unexpected sight of the *Venjekar*.

The sky darkened, clouds roiled and flickered with lightning. The wind freshened. The sea grew leaden, waves rolling sullenly. The Sea Goddess was angry and grieving and not likely to be kind to *Aelon's Triumph*. Waves struck the dragonship from all directions. The ship bucked and twisted and corkscrewed.

Aylaen clung to the railing.

"Skylan!" she screamed, as the wind tore her words from her mouth. "Skylan!"

The hatch on the *Venjekar* rose. Skylan came running up from below, his brass sword in his hand. He was naked except for the loincloth worn by the Aquins and soaking wet, his long blond hair plastered to his head, his skin glistening. Farinn and Acronis followed him; both of them looking more like mermen than humans. Wulfe dashed up last, dancing and gibbering. They seemed a fitting crew for the ghost ship that had sprung from the waves. One sailor gave a wild yell of terror and leaped into the sea.

Others seemed likely to follow, preferring a swift death by drowning to an eternity sailing with this ghastly crew. Captain Anker swore and bellowed, trying to restore calm, shouting commands to which few sailors paid any heed. The soldiers, either more disciplined or less superstitious, drew their swords and drove the sailors to action.

"Archers!" Raegar yelled, pointing at Skylan and the men on the *Venjekar*. "They're not ghosts now, but they soon will be!"

The archers drew their bows and took their places at the stern. They tried aiming, but found it difficult to maintain their footing on the bounding deck.

Raegar turned and went lurching across the deck, racing for the prow. The spiritbone of the Dragon Fala swung from a hook on the dragon-head prow. Raegar was going to summon the dragon.

The *Venjekar* sailed closer, Akaria speeding the Vindrasi dragonship, even as she impeded Raegar's.

"Aylaen!" Skylan called to her. "Jump!"

"The oceanaids will save you!" Wulfe screeched.

The two soldiers supposed to be guarding Aylaen were picking themselves up off the heaving deck. Aylaen looked at Skylan and she looked back at Raegar.

His Dragon Fala had suffered a humiliating defeat the last time she had attacked the Dragon Kahg. Fala would be eager for a chance to have her revenge.

Aylaen hoped Skylan understood. She couldn't waste time explaining. She started to run after Raegar. A hand seized hold of her arm, dragged her back.

Aylaen turned to face her captor. Only one thought was in her mind. She must prevent Raegar from summoning the dragon. This man was trying to stop her and that couldn't be allowed. Resolve and determination filled her.

In that moment, Aylaen knew Torval's Madness.

All her life, she had heard about the Madness of Torval, the crazed power that fills warriors in battle. During this madness, a warrior is said to become one with the god. The warrior loses all sense of his own mortality. He tramples on fear and slays doubt. He runs toward danger, not away from it. He knows himself to be invincible.

Time slows for a warrior in Torval's Madness. The god gives the warrior the strength of his arm and guides his hand. The light of the god's wrath shines in the warrior's eyes, making him terrible. His foes cower before him and throw down their weapons and flee in terror.

The madness filled Aylaen. Time slowed. She saw the flash of lightning on the sea, the foam flicking from the waves. She felt the storm wind on her face, tasted salt on her lips. She watched the play of muscles in her forearm, the turning of her wrist, the graceful, gliding motion, the stretch, the reach, her fingers wrapping around the hilt of the guardsman's sword. She watched her hand grasping, tightening, pulling the sword free of the sheath. She stood tall and swung the sword with the god's might.

Blood sprayed her face. Someone screamed. The hand let loose of her arm. The bright fire of the god blinded Aylaen. She ran across the deck, as though she were running on a cloud. Faces with mouths wide loomed in front of her and she swung her sword and they disappeared in blood-red spray.

Raegar stood at the prow, reaching for the spiritbone. Aylaen was yet a few feet from him. She shouted to Torval, shouted the cry the war chief raises as he throws his spear over the enemy shield wall, warning his foe to prepare to die.

Raegar heard her. He turned in astonishment. His eyes widened in fear.

She saw herself in those eyes, her face and arms and legs blood-splattered, shining-eyed, wild and utterly consumed by madness. Raegar could do nothing for a petrified moment except stare at her as she came racing down on him, blood flying from her sword.

Terror drove him to action. He grabbed the spiritbone by the glittering golden chain with his left hand and fumbled to draw his sword with his right.

Aylaen jabbed her sword at the hand holding the chain. Raegar jerked his hand back to keep from losing it. Aylaen flung away the sword. She grabbed hold of the spiritbone, gave it a yank that broke the slender gold chain, and ran for the ship's side with the intention of jumping into the sea.

Raegar, roaring in fury, pounded over the deck behind her.

Aylaen clamped her teeth over the spiritbone and seized hold of the rail, pressing her hands into the wood to lift herself up and over. The rail was wet with salt spray. Her hands slipped. Before she could regain purchase, Raegar grabbed hold of her and dragged her back and flung her to the deck.

She landed on her hands and knees. The spiritbone fell out of her mouth, lying in front of her in a tangle of gold chain. Raegar made a grab for the spiritbone. Aylaen lunged, caught hold of it, and threw the spiritbone into the sea.

Raegar howled orders for men to go in after the spiritbone, floating on the surface of the black, turgid waves. No one obeyed. Furious, Raegar began to unbuckle his armor with the intention of diving in himself.

"No use, Your Worship," called Captain Anker, peering down into the water. "It's sunk."

Aylaen slumped wearily to the deck. The madness of Torval ebbed away, leaving her cold and shivering and sick to her stomach. Her hands and arms were sticky with blood. Her tunic was drenched. She was dimly aware of men shouting out a warning, but she was too weak to find out why everyone was rushing around in a frenzy of fear.

Someone loomed over her. Raegar gripped his sword. He meant to kill her.

Aylaen gave him a ghastly, bloodstained smile.

"Aelon wants me alive," she reminded him.

"I will send the god your soul!" Raegar snarled.

He lifted the sword.

The *Venjekar* rammed into the hull of *Aelon's Triumph*.

CHAPTER

40

Skylan stood at the prow of the *Venjekar,* forced to watch Aylaen's valiant assault on Raegar from a distance, unable to come to her aid, torn between fear for her and pride in her courage. The ship, powered by the angry Dragon Kahg, sped through the water. The waves flew past him, spray splashed over him. He pounded the rail with his fist and urged the dragon to travel faster, faster.

He ordered the Dragon Kahg to bring the *Venjekar* close so that he could board *Aelon's Triumph*. He watched Aylaen fling the spiritbone of the Dragon Fala into the sea and he cheered. Then he saw her fall and Raegar standing over her, his sword raised.

Skylan bellowed in outrage. The *Venjekar* was still some distance away, but he had to try to reach Aylaen, though with both ships leaping and rolling in the erratic waves, he knew in his heart he would never make it. He was about to climb up on the rail when Acronis shouted.

"Tell the dragon to ram them!"

Skylan looked up at the Dragon Kahg and realized he didn't need to tell the dragon anything.

The *Venjekar* was sailing straight toward *Aelon's Triumph*, bounding over the waves. Aboard Raegar's ship, the sailors saw their doom and they were crying out in terror and rushing for cover.

Then the *Venjekar* smashed headlong into the ship's hull.

Skylan flung himself to the deck. The shattering crash jarred every bone in his body. Wood splinters rained down on top of him. Skylan jumped to his feet in time to see the *Aelon's Triumph* mast snap off and fall to the deck, taking the sail down with it. The *Venjekar* had punched a hole in the hull. Water would be pouring inside. He could not see Aylaen or Raegar. The sail had landed on top of them.

"Acronis, you're with me. Farinn, stay with the ship!" Skylan yelled. "You stay with Farinn!" he ordered Wulfe, catching hold of the boy by the scruff of his neck as he was starting to jump.

Yellow eyes gleamed. Teeth glistened in the boy's mouth, sharp, elongated. Skylan was holding on to fur, not skin.

"I'll rip out his throat," Wulfe snarled, squirming in his grasp.

"I need you to stay here to guard Farinn."

Wulfe snapped at him, teeth leaving a thin trail of blood on Skylan's arm.

"Stay here, Wulfe," Skylan said grimly, "or I swear by Torval that you and I are finished."

He didn't wait to see if the boy obeyed him or not. Viper Tooth in hand, Skylan leaped from the *Venjekar* onto the slanting deck of the disabled

Aelon's Triumph. Acronis was behind him, carrying Aylaen's sword, guarding Skylan's back. They ran across the deck of *Aelon's Triumph,* dodging bodies and debris. They met little resistance. Men were still recovering from the shock of the collision of the two vessels. The respite wouldn't last long. The archers were scrambling to fetch their bows, soldiers were going for their swords.

Skylan reached the point where he had last seen Aylaen. She had vanished beneath a mass of canvas and rope and what was left of the mast. He shouted her name and his heart soared to hear her voice answer him. Aylaen floundered beneath the sail. Her bloody hand reached out to him. He pulled her out and stared in astonishment. She was covered with blood, so much he could not see if she was hurt. She relieved his fears with a smile. And then the wreckage heaved and shuddered. Raegar flung the mast off him to emerge from the rubble, his face a mask of blood. He looked dazed and a little unsteady on his feet, but he still gripped his sword. He scowled at Skylan.

"My little cousin," he muttered.

"You are no kin to me," said Skylan. "Acronis, see to Aylaen. Take her back to the *Venjekar*."

Acronis had hold of Aylaen, who was protesting that she didn't want to leave. Skylan focused on Raegar, stood braced and ready for a fight.

"I've been looking forward to killing you for a long time," said Skylan.

Raegar sneered. He raised his sword, took a

step, and then his legs buckled. He crashed down face-first onto the deck and lay there, unmoving.

Skylan eyed him warily, thinking this might be a trick.

"Kill him!" said Aylaen thickly.

Acronis was trying to urge Aylaen to come with him. She yanked her arm from his grasp and stood staring down at Raegar. "Kill him!" she repeated.

"Get up, Raegar, you son of a bitch," said Skylan.

Raegar didn't so much as twitch.

Skylan swore and kicked him in the ribs. "Get up, cowardly cur!"

"Skylan, we need to leave now!" Acronis said quietly.

Skylan glanced over his shoulder. The archers had picked up their bows and were nocking their arrows.

"Aylaen, go with Acronis." Skylan kicked Raegar again in frustration. "You coward! Fight me!"

"Kill him," said Aylaen for the third time.

Skylan shook his head. "When I kill this bastard, I want him to watch my sword slide into his gut. My smile will be the last thing he sees."

Skylan turned to walk away. Aylaen clutched at him.

"Don't be a fool, Skylan! You can't let him live!"

"I will not slay a man who cannot defend himself," said Skylan shortly. "Torval would bar me from his Hall in disgrace."

"Then I will slay him!" Aylaen cried.

Raegar's sword lay beneath his hand. Aylaen made a grab for it. An arrow whistled past, just missing her head. Skylan grabbed hold of Aylaen and lifted her off her feet. He carried her, struggling, beating him with her fists, back to the *Venjekar*. The Dragon Kahg had worked to free the ship from the wreckage of *Aelon's Triumph*. His red eyes were bright with triumph. The eyes of the Dragon Fala were empty and wooden. Kahg edged the *Venjekar* as close as he could to the disabled *Triumph*.

Skylan set Aylaen down on her feet. Acronis was behind him, sword drawn, holding off the soldiers, many of whom had served under him and knew and respected his skill.

"You'll have to jump for it," Skylan told Aylaen.

Another arrow thudded into the wood. She glared at him, her green eyes blazing, and then climbed lightly to the rail. She waited for a wave to bring the *Venjekar* near, and then jumped. Wulfe and Farinn were both there to catch her and steady her. She looked back and shouted for Skylan and Acronis.

"You're next, sir," said Skylan.

An arrow whistled harmlessly past.

"Seems Raegar hired poor archers," Skylan added.

Acronis smiled. "He always was a cheap bastard."

Acronis waited, timed his jump perfectly and needed no help when he landed lightly on the deck.

A couple of waves, higher than the rest, drove the *Venjekar* back. Skylan had to wait for the ship to come near again. An arrow grazed his arm.

The *Venjekar* swung near. Skylan yelled a warning and flung his sword over first, then he followed. He made a clumsy landing, coming down hard on all fours.

"Are you all right?" Aylaen asked worriedly.

"I'm fine," he said, rising to his feet.

He reached for her, drew her into his arms.

"Queen Magali was right. You are arrogant and stubborn and willful," she said.

He stared at her, hurt.

Aylaen laughed and embraced him and kissed him on the mouth. "And I love you with all my heart!"

Acronis yelled. Wulfe screeched. Farinn cried out in horror.

Skylan turned his head. Raegar stood on the deck of *Aelon's Triumph*, holding a bow, the bowstring drawn back, the arrow aimed. He called upon Aelon and fired.

The arrow, sped by the hand of the god, thudded into Skylan's back.

He didn't comprehend at first what had happened. He didn't know he'd been hit until he saw Aylaen's eyes go wide with horror and he heard her scream and then the shattering pain gripped him and it was hard to breathe and blood filled his mouth. He staggered. Aylaen kept hold of him, her arms around him. She tried to keep him from falling, but he was too heavy. She eased him to the deck.

Holding him in her arms, she begged him, threatened, cajoled.

"Don't die, my love. Don't die, Skylan! Don't leave me!"

Skylan wanted to stay with her, but he couldn't breathe and the pain was unbearable. The darkness rushed on him, coming fast, very fast.

"My sword!" He gasped, choked on his blood. He couldn't see, he fumbled for the weapon.

Aylaen guided his hand to the hilt of his sword and closed his weakening fingers over it. She wrapped her hand around his to make sure he kept the sword in his grasp.

Skylan looked at her, Aylaen, his wife. He kept his gaze fixed on her, the last point of light in the hastening dark.

"Even in Torval's Hall, I will be lonely for you," Skylan told her.

Aylaen gathered him in her arms and pressed her lips to his as he gave her his last breath.

CHAPTER 41

Aylaen crouched on the deck, holding Skylan's body in her arms. She did not move. She made no sound. She did not cry out after that last terrible scream when she had seen the arrow coming and felt him shudder in her arms as the shaft pierced through flesh and bone and muscle.

Farinn stared down at her, at Skylan. Disaster had fallen so swiftly, he couldn't believe it was true. The song must not end like this. The hero could not die and go to Torval's Hall and leave his friends behind, his quest unfulfilled. Evil should not triumph. Songs didn't end like this.

Because such songs were never sung. The knowledge pierced Farinn, bringing nearly as much pain as the arrow that had struck down Skylan. In life, heroes died untimely deaths. Quests went unfulfilled. Wives mourned their dead. Bards did not sing such songs, for they stirred no hearts. They brought no light to the long, dark winter.

Farinn heard a low growl, vicious and savage, and he saw a wolf standing near Aylaen. The wolf's teeth were bared in a hideous snarl, its ears were back, its tail low and motionless. Yellow eyes burned. Farinn could not speak.

"Aylaen," Acronis said softly, his voice deliberately calm, quiet, but filled with urgency.

Aylaen raised her head. Her face was as pale as the face of the dead and just as cold. The blood had drained from her cheeks and perhaps her heart. She saw the wolf and then she let go of Skylan's body, laying him gently to rest on the deck. The wolf watched every move, menacingly growling. Aylaen reached out, her hand stained with Skylan's blood.

"He's gone, Wulfe," she said quietly. "We loved him, you and I, but we must live without him."

The wolf lowered its head and the beast disappeared, leaving a grubby little boy, who collapsed, sobbing, in Aylaen's arms. She held Wulfe until his sobs quieted and he fell asleep. Aylaen looked at Farinn. Her own eyes were dry.

"Take Wulfe below," she said. "Watch over him."

Farinn was glad to obey her. His own eyes burned and blurred, and he didn't want to cry where anyone would see him, especially Skylan's spirit, who would be lingering, watching. Farinn picked up Wulfe and carried the sleeping boy with the tear-ravaged face down into the hold. There, unseen, Farinn let the tears stream down his face.

He was crying for Skylan and he was crying for the death of the song.

Aylaen sat back on her knees. She gazed out over the sea and at last rose, stiffly, to her feet. Her leather tunic was soaked with blood, her blood, the blood of her foes, the blood of her husband. The light had gone from her eyes. Acronis had never seen the ghost the Vindrasi called a "draugr" but he had heard the tales and he guessed that the dead who left their graves to roam the earth must look very much like Aylaen.

"You should go below yourself," he said to her. "Try to sleep. I will do what is needful here."

"A wife tends to her husband," said Aylaen in a monotone. "That is my privilege and my honor."

She pushed Acronis's hand gently aside.

"But there is something I must do first."

Aylaen walked over to the dragonhead prow. Acronis had forgotten about Kahg. Acronis looked up to see the eyes gleam a lurid, hideous red. The *Venjekar* was adrift, floating on the waves that had gone dreadfully still. No wind blew. The water was dead, flat, calm. The clouds vanished. The sun beat down, hot and fierce. The gods themselves mourned.

Not far from them, soldiers and sailors aboard *Aelon's Triumph* were working to repair the mast and patch the gaping hole in the hull.

Raegar stood on the deck, grimly smiling.

"I warned you, Aylaen!" he called out over the leaden sea. "I gave you the choice. If you had come with me, Skylan would be alive right now."

Aylaen paid no heed to him. She lifted the spiritbone of the Dragon Kahg from the nail on which it hung and pressed the bone to her lips. Softly, quietly, she began to chant the ritual to summon the dragon.

Raegar realized what she was doing. He was still holding the bow and he bellowed at someone to fetch him an arrow. He had to kill Aylaen before she succeeded or they were all dead men.

The shot would be a long one, for the two ships had drifted farther apart. Aylaen ignored him. She had no water to use to form the dragon. She had no earth to scatter over the spiritbone. Taking the spiritbone to Skylan, she dipped the bone in his blood.

Aylaen threw the spiritbone in the air.

The bone hung for a moment and vanished. Just as Raegar fit the arrow to his bow, the Dragon Kahg came to life. His scales were as red as blood. Blood drooled from his jaws and stained his fangs. He spread his red wings and the sun, shining through them, was blood-red. The Dragon Kahg made no sound. He dove, claws extended.

Raegar had no spiritbone. He could not summon his dragon and it was doubtful if Fala would have stayed around to fight the enraged Kahg. Raegar knew he was a dead man anyway. He had nothing to lose. He stood his ground, lifted the bow, aimed at the dragon, and fired.

The arrow burst into flame and fell into the sea.

Kahg flew over *Aelon's Triumph*. Drops of blood rained down from the dragon's wings, burning anything they touched. The droplets ate like acid into men's flesh. They screamed in pain and jumped into the sea. The water boiled around them and they were never seen again. At last, the only two left on board were Raegar and Captain Anker.

The deck smoldered in a hundred places and soon caught fire. Raegar and the captain tried desperately to put the fires out, but they spread too rapidly. Captain Anker urged Raegar to abandon ship. Raegar paid no heed, kept fighting the flames. Captain Anker shook his head and leaped into the water.

Abandoned by its crew, *Aelon's Triumph* sank, hissing, into the blood-red sea. Raegar stood on the deck gazing on the *Venjekar* with hatred until the waves washed over him.

All that was left of *Aelon's Triumph* were a few bits of charred wood and the dragonhead prow which had broken off and lay floating in the water, its empty eyes gazing up at heaven as if asking Aelon what had gone wrong.

Pleased at his work, the Dragon Kahg saluted Aylaen gravely and then disappeared, flowing back into the ship. His spiritbone fell from the skies, landing on the deck at Aylaen's feet. The bone was covered with blood and from that day forward, the spiritbone of the Dragon Kahg would always be stained red. Aylaen picked up the bone. She thanked the dragon and hung the spiritbone on the leather thong from the nail on the dragonhead prow.

She went down into the hold and Acronis thought she had at last gone to rest and grieve in private. He stood gazing out at the red blotch upon the water.

"I have seen too much death, Chloe," he said. "I have watched too many men, young men, good men like Skylan, die. I have given orders that sent men to their deaths. I have killed men myself. For what? Some cause or other. Some country or other. Some god or other. And in the end, who wins? For everyone is dead . . ."

He remained there a long time, staring out to sea.

Aylaen washed off the blood. She combed her red hair and changed her clothes, putting on a sodden chemise that she had pulled from one of the sea chests. The sun still shone brightly, as though reluctant to set on this day.

She went back up on deck.

"I need to speak to you, sir," Aylaen said to Acronis. Her voice was calm and did not waver. "Can you and Farinn and Wulfe and the Dragon Kahg and I sail this ship?"

"We can, my dear," said Acronis. "At least as far as the nearest land. I have no idea where we are, but once I see the stars tonight, I can find a safe landfall—"

"You misunderstand me, sir," said Aylaen. "I do not seek a safe landfall. We must sail to the land of the Stormlords. Do you know it?"

"I know *of* it," said Acronis, astonished. "Why do you want go there?"

"These Stormlords have in their keeping the fourth Vektia spiritbone."

"I don't . . . I'm not sure . . ."

Aylaen turned from him before he could say anything more. She lowered a bucket into the sea and drew it back, filled with water. She set the bucket on the deck beside Skylan's body and with gentle, loving hands, closed the staring blue eyes. She dipped a cloth in the water and began wiping away the blood.

Farinn brought up Skylan's shirt and breeches and the armor that he had worn in Sinaria. He and Aylaen dressed Skylan and put on his armor, for he would need it when he stood with Torval in the god's shield wall. Aylaen combed Skylan's hair. Farinn laced on Skylan's boots. Last, Aylaen gave Skylan his sword, placing it on his breast and clasping his hands over the hilt.

Acronis watched, torn between admiration and pain. He could tell her what he knew about the Stormlords, that they were reputed to be powerful and dangerous wizards, who used terrible magicks to keep people away from their land. He could tell her, but it wouldn't matter. She would not be deterred.

At last, as though exhausted, the sun slipped beyond the horizon. Those left on the *Venjekar* kept vigil throughout the night. The Dragon Kahg carried the body of Skylan Ivorson, Chief of Chiefs of the Vindrasi, across the dark and silent sea.

Farinn sang his song.

EPILOGUE

The Norn were three sisters who lived at the foot of the World Tree. The Norn were ancient. Their backs were bent, their bodies twisted, their feet halt and lame. They held the wyrds of gods and men in their hands. One of the Norn spun the thread of life. One wove the thread into life's great and never-ending tapestry. One of them held the shears that snipped each thread when a man's life came to an end.

The Norn had little care for the wyrds in their hands. They cackled and gossiped and spun and wove and cut. Some wyrds were short. A young mother died in childbirth, an infant died of fever, a young man was cut down in the shield wall. Some wyrds played out long. An old woman lay on her deathbed, smiling to see her children and grandchildren and great-grandchildren gathered around her.

The Norn prattled away. The Norn who did the spinning saw her sister ready to shear through yet another thread.

"And whose is that?" the Norn asked.

"Skylan Ivorson," said her sister who did the weaving.

"Past time for that rascal," said the Norn with the shears.

She held the sharp blades over the thread and began to cut. The wyrd was thick and stubborn and the shears were dull from much use, or at least that's what the Norn would later claim. She hacked at the thread and cut apart strand after strand and still it would not break. Finally there remained only a single thread. Her old, palsied hand jerked. The shears slipped from her gnarled fingers and fell to the ground.

The Norn stopped spinning. The Norn stopped weaving. The gods in the heavens and below the seas stopped warring. They stared in shock at the shears, lying on the roots of the World Tree.

"What do we do?" asked one of the Norn, trembling.

The Norn gazed with her shrewd watery eyes at the wyrd of Skylan Ivorson—a single strand finer than a spider's silk.

"Apparently, it's not his day to die," said the Norn.

The three Norns cackled gleefully and, leaving the strand quivering in the sunlight, went back to work.

Skylan Ivorson strode up to Torval's Hall of Heroes, his sword in his hand. He stood for long moments outside the Hall, gazing up at it. The Hall was an immense structure, for it had been built by giants, who had labored on it for many long centuries. They had ripped enormous oak trees from the ground by the roots to use to form the walls. The shields of brave warriors decorated the walls. Skylan would soon see his shield hanging among them.

He could see through the windows the orange glow of a roaring fire. He longed for its warmth, to ease the chill of death, and he walked toward the door. Made of oak, banded by iron, the door was closed. He thought that odd. Certainly Torval must be expecting him. Skylan was surprised and somewhat offended that the god was not there to greet him.

He could hear the riotous sounds of song and music, jests and laughter. He could see the warriors inside, carousing, dancing with their womenfolk, fighting mock battles. He paused to look inside a window and he was pleased beyond measure to see Keeper, seated at a table, devouring a leg of venison. Skylan waved and called, but Keeper did not appear to see or hear him.

And there was Chloe, watching the dancers, clapping her hands with joy. Skylan had promised the dying girl that he would dance with her in Torval's Hall. He looked forward to taking her by the hands, leading her in the dance. He shouted her name, but she didn't hear him.

He searched and finally found Garn, laughing

with a man that Skylan couldn't see until he turned around.

The man was Norgaard, his father.

Skylan was shocked. He had no idea his father had died. Skylan had so much to tell his father. He had so much to make right.

"Father! It is me, Skylan!" he called.

Norgaard turned away, returning to his conversation with Garn.

Skylan left the window and ran to the door. He pounded with his fist and shouted, trying to make himself heard above the noise inside. His voice sounded very small and his cries seemed to float off into eternity.

Skylan kept pounding until his fist was bloody. Suddenly, the door flew open.

"Thank Torval!" Skylan gasped.

He tried to enter.

The god blocked his way.

Torval stood in the door. The god wore his armor made of the finest steel, with a steel breastplate embossed with a dragon's head. He wore furs around his shoulders and a helm of steel decorated with silver and gold.

His armor was fine, but it was dented, bloody, showing signs of a recent battle. By the sounds of the celebration, Torval and his heroes had been victorious. But they had not won the war. That much was evident by the stern, severe expression on Torval's face.

"What are you doing here, Fish Knife?" Torval demanded.

Skylan was angered. "Let me in. I belong in the Hall with my comrades!"

"When you are dead, come back. We will discuss it," said Torval.

The god slammed the door in Skylan's face.